The Uses of Illicit Art

Published by Winterbourne Publishing, Western Australia.

ISBN: 978-0-9874511-2-5 (ebook) / 978-0-9874511-8-7 (print).

The Uses of Illicit Art

Wendy Palmer

Winterbourne
Publishing

1

A S HAD BECOME HIS MORNING ROUTINE on the day the London papers arrived in the seaside village of Lovelly-on-Sea, Kit Whitely came into the bakery to collect a tray of tea and treats and take it across to share with Miss Edith Knight.

Today, he found three mugs and four pastries waiting on the tray.

Kit disliked breaks with routine. They never boded well for him. He looked to the baker, Edith's sister, for explanation.

'We've a visiting scholar,' Margaret told him, hand on white-aproned hip, a taller, broader version of her younger sister. ''E came in on the train this morning. 'E asked for a cup'o'tea, but we don't know if he likes sticky buns or cream puffs. So I thought we'd giv'e both, and see which one 'e chooses.'

Kit looked at the tray. One plate held his favourite, a sticky bun. The other held Edith's favourite, a cream puff. The third plate, indeed, held one of each. Margaret McDonnell, nee Knight, smiled at him in perfect innocence.

The Knights were an understanding family, to the point, Kit sometimes thought, of negligence of their sunny-tempered youngest daughter—though he had no experience of families to judge. They also owned half the village and kept the other half under their collective and extended thumb. They were some of the reason he had stayed here so long. The rest was down to a most particular Knight.

Shaking his head, Kit took the tray and used it to push the door back open to the high street. The sound of the sea was loud this morning; he'd been here long enough to know that meant the wind was picking up and there might be a storm later. Newly laid granite setts were underfoot. The summer visitors had asked for paving, as if country mud wasn't far cleaner than city mud, which wasn't mud.

He paused there for a moment of satisfied observation of small village life.

There went old Mr Gantry, on his way to the pier to see in the returning fishing vessels, to the slight annoyance of young Mr Gantry. Here came Mrs Nowell, for her own bakery visit, and she'd take a paper bag of scones over to Mrs Houghton who was, as ever, poorly. A milliner Knight was exiting the haberdashery with a parcel of lace, having swapped it for three bonnets. The cooper Knights and their children were out for their morning stroll; Little Tommy, thumb in mouth, waved to Kit. A couple of farmers loaded their carts with supplies from the grocer and the ironmonger, their horses standing patient. The clang from the smithy drowned out the tap from the cobbler's. Mrs Galloway clicked her tongue as she shooed her geese out towards the commons, and her sisters gossiped outside the post office with big bundles of laundry by their sides.

Some might call it monotonous. Kit called it soothing to the highest degree.

He crossed the high street, nodding greetings as he went. Edith's bronze bell gave its tinkling chime as he carefully balanced the tray and opened the door. He pushed it the rest of the way open with his hip and went on in, already looking about for the supposed scholar among the front room's shelves of new and used books, stationery, almanacks, periodicals and art supplies set in arched alcoves along the walls.

He was more wary than curious. He did not like strangers, especially not strangers who came in on the train that connected from Bristol and from whence London, especially at the time of year when strangers did not come to Lovelly.

Edith Knight, small and blond and always more curious than wary, beckoned him over to her counter, where she sat on a stool in a patch of winter sunlight streaming through the plate glass window. Her dog, Minnie, slept at her feet and barely flicked an ear towards Kit.

Edith's brushes were scattered about; she had been illustrating one of her delicate handmade greeting cards, that she would post off to London to sell in a bigger shop than hers.

'Mornin', Kit,' Edith said in her mild lilt. 'How be on, m'luv?'

'Morning, Edie,' Kit said. His own accent was nondescript and inoffensive, owing to an upbringing in an orphanage training as an upper house servant.

Edith silently turned the subscription book for her lending library, an immensely popular service when the tourists, the emmets, were here in summer, less so for the villagers themselves. The name neatly inscribed in the book was Alexander Locke, his day-rate shilling marked as paid.

It meant nothing to Kit, but of course, it could well be an alias.

'He's in back,' she told Kit. 'Looking at our collection about Knight-stone. Research, apparently.'

Lovelly's claim to fame was a derelict set of standing stones on its outskirts, called the Knightstone Circle; it was in conspicuous disrepair but sported carvings not seen anywhere else in this part of the world. Some distance inland beyond them, and popular for day-trips, was a labyrinth of tunnels and caves that was actually a Roman-era chalk mine.

Kit relaxed a little. Scholars did make their way here to research those carvings or explore the Latin graffiti left in the mines. That was why Edith's library had a substantial set of literature devoted to both topics, encom-passing the full range from local legends to scholarly discourses.

He put the tray down and Edith took up her mug of tea. She curled both hands around it and smiled, eyes closed, her face tilted towards the sunshine falling through the window. 'Papers are in back, too. Our Mr Locke was kind enough to bring them from the train for Young Tom.'

'Shall I take him a sticky bun?' said Kit dryly. Edith did not normally relegate him to the back room when he came to read the London newspapers.

'Yes, m'luv,' Edith said. Her eyes were still closed but her smile was widening. 'Do.'

That was most monosyllabic she had ever been. Kit shook his head again. He set her plate with its cream puff on the counter beside her elbow, dropped in his weekly sixpence for the papers with a clink, and carried the tray to the back, grandly styled the reading room.

Curiosity was finally outweighing caution now. The stranger, Alexander Locke, had made an impression on the Knight women, it seemed.

And, Kit reflected when he laid eyes on Locke, no sodding wonder.

The man was, as the locals would say, gurt 'uge. He looked like he belonged on the deck of a longship with battle-axe awhirl. He was almost comically squeezed into the hardbacked wooden chair at the little desk in the corner of the reading room, a mixture of unbound papers and heavy tomes stacked in front of him. He appeared to be organising the pile into an idiosyncratic sort of order. Sitting, he was probably as tall as Edith standing; his shoulders were half again as broad as Kit's, and Kit, despite having a somewhat fey cast to his features, was sturdily built, at least now Mrs Knight was willing to feed him and he was willing to be fed.

The sheer scale of the Viking before him gave Kit pause, and the rest of him was nothing like the eccentric and impoverished scholars he had become used to in the village over the summer, either. He was young, for starters, at most five or six years older than Kit's near-twenty-five years. Though he did not sport the mutton-chops and moustache dictated by latest fashion, his thick sandy hair was almost certainly cut in some new London style and impeccably neat in its arrayed waves.

In fact, he was turned out impeccably all over, from the expensive and well-blacked boots to his fine buckskins showing mighty thighs to good effect to his rather splendid waistcoat, his complicated necktie and the expertly tailored brown frock coat over those wide shoulders. Hat, gloves, fashionable cane, and woollen overcoat were laid by. It made Kit with his worn and faded coat, scuffed boots, and messy curls feel decidedly shabby.

His face, though broad like the rest of him, was fine-boned and andro-gynous with a disconcertingly sensual mouth and an aquiline nose. It had likely taken him most of his life to grow into that nose. He was not handsome, per se, but he was rather intriguing.

And Kit, despite himself, was rather intrigued.

It was the improbable pair of wire spectacles perched on the end of the dramatic nose that convinced him he was not dealing with a bounty hunter.

Locke glanced up from running a finger over the spine of one of the books on the now-orderly pile—perhaps Edith had overwhelmed the man when she had dumped every authority on Knightstone on the desk at once—and caught Kit measuring him, hands tight around the handles of the tray.

'Good morning.' His voice was low and pleasant, with an expensively educated accent overlaying a very slight burr which Kit wouldn't have even noticed six months ago. His eyes, behind the round lenses of the spectacles, were woodland hazel, warm and bright in his tanned face. 'Is that my tea?'

Kit glided forwards and, with frowning care born of habitual clumsi-ness, set the mug, still steaming, and the plate on the desk. Edith must be very taken, if she wasn't banning him from eating near her books. Alexander Locke looked preternaturally neat, though—and indeed, even as Kit had the thought, Locke pushed back from the desk, moving his plate and mug away from the tomes, and turning his chair and whole body towards Kit.

'Alexander Locke,' he said. He didn't offer his hand, but kept watching Kit as he took a sip of tea.

'Kit Whitely. Charmed. I'm just going to—'

As he spoke, Kit was edging over to the table by the tall terrestrial globe to collect the pile of London newspapers, putting them on the tray next to his own mug and plate. He was as sure as he could be that Locke was not a threat of the kind he'd been braced for, but he was assuredly a threat to Kit's peace of mind, so Kit was going to take his newspapers and retreat to Edith.

Except he heard the tinkle of the bell and Meredith's bright, false tones. She and Edith had been great friends when Kit had first arrived in the village. Then they had had a falling-out and Meredith had quite abruptly engaged herself to Young Tom, who attended the station when the trains came in.

She would have been one of the first to hear of a stranger off the train and had indubitably showed up to eye him off. Edith would keep her out, and everyone else who would start trickling in to do the same, but Meredith was the wilfully oblivious sort who would linger in hope. And Kit didn't want to have to make polite conversation with her, or conversation of any sort.

He paused in his shuffle backwards. '—read the papers in the armchair here,' he finished. 'I won't disturb you.'

Eyes on Kit's face, Locke said, 'I wouldn't mind being disturbed,' indeed imperturbably.

He smiled, and there was something feral in it.

Kit was striking in an elfin sort of way, with arrestingly pale green eyes, curly black hair, high cheekbones and delicately pointed chin. He had been told that he looked far too innocent for his own good. He'd been told he had the face of an angel but the devil in his eyes.

He therefore attracted a certain type of attention from a certain type of man.

He held Locke's direct gaze for a thoughtful moment. He did not return the smile; Kit did not much smile at anyone, and never at strangers. Instead, he gave an awkward half-bow and carried his laden tray over to the overstuffed armchair in the other corner of the reading room, near the window. He liked having the window within arm's reach.

Normally he'd take off his coat and roll up his sleeves; like most Artisans, he ran hot. But with Locke here, he stayed appropriate. It was bad enough he wasn't wearing a waistcoat in company.

He took the topmost broadsheet, and settled in to scan it for news of Artisans and Art. Or wizards and magic, in more old-fashioned parlance.

The Myriad, the most famous group of independent Artisans, had their usual mention, but he paged quickly past that, looking for the smaller articles that might hint that the Agency for the Benefit of Registered Artisans had worked out where he was.

He was keeping a little of his attention on Locke, part habit and part interest. The big man finished his tea and both pastries, fastidiously wiped his fingers on a snowy handkerchief from a coat pocket, and dragged his chair back to the desk.

But instead of bending to his research, he leaned an elbow on the desk. 'You don't seem like you're from around here, Mr Whitely.'

Now there was a line of enquiry guaranteed to make Kit tense. It read as an idle comment rather than a barbed reference to Kit's olive skin and dark hair, his general foreignness, but it still pointed out that he didn't belong here in this seaside village of flaxen-haired delicate roses with their vowel-heavy inflections. And that led the merry way to the question he didn't want asked—why he was here, then?

He made a noise of acknowledgement, hopefully on the right side of polite, and meaningfully turned another page.

It appeared the Viking did not know how to take a sodding hint. 'Are you here for Knightstone too?'

Kit, in a way, was indeed here for the Knightstone Circle. His Art was thresholds, and standing stones offered thresholds aplenty, and power too, even when much of the circle here had tumbled sometime last century. Within its remnants, his Art was strong enough to let him cross a threshold all the way to the caves, those chalk mines, nothing but thresholds that he could lose pursuers in for days, with a few careful caches of preserved or canned food, too.

That was what had made Lovelly-on-Sea so attractive to take refuge in, even before he'd met the very understanding Knights.

He raised his eyes from the broadsheet and looked at the scholar. The question could be innocent small talk, like Locke's mild tone made it seem. The question could be the opening salvo in strongarming a conversation that would eventually lead to an invitation to bed, like Locke's secretive and yet deliciously inviting smile made it seem.

Or the question could be very, very pointed. It was common knowledge that relics like standing stones powered Art.

Locke took off his spectacles and turned them in strong-looking fingers. 'I didn't expect to meet any other visitors here, in such an out-of-the-way place, out of season,' he casually explained. 'And then you're here and three more visitors got off the train with me.'

'Three more— Please excuse me, Mr Locke.'

Kit rose to his feet, bringing every inch of his immense self-control to bear to make it a slow, unconcerned movement when his body was screaming at him to run, heart thrumming, skin twitching, spine crawling.

Alexander Locke watched him, still smiling, lips parted slightly as if about to say something.

He heard a suddenly raised voice that sent his heart beating even harder. It was Edith. 'Oh God, why didn't you tell me that straight away!' She ran in from the front room and said urgently, 'Kit, Meredith just said lots of strangers got off that bloody train!'

And Kit Whitely, the Artisan darling of every London master criminal, bolted.

2

$\mathcal{E}$DITH WAS SMART ENOUGH TO RACE after him, so he could slam the door to the reading room and lock it with a flick of his Art. Meredith was just running outside, sending a sharp look back at him. He was certain she had deliberately withheld the gossip for as long as she could; how else otherwise had the news of so many strangers not raced twice around the village within minutes of them disembarking?

She must have had the news from Young Tom and sat on it, while three of the four strangers chose to not walk straight to the village and into the rumour mill. They must even now be circling in through the woods.

He heard Locke try the door. 'Is there a reason you've locked me in, Mr Whitely?' he called through the door, still mild.

He was the only one of the four strangers on the train who had come on to the village along the main path from the station. He must have exchanged words with Young Tom; he'd taken on the errand of bringing the London papers to Edith, after all. Perhaps that meant he was innocent. Perhaps not.

'Get down behind the counter,' Kit told Edith.

He flung open the shop door, almost running into a large figure on the other side. That made sense; Meredith wouldn't have spilled the gossip to Edith until she'd seen one of the strangers finally in the village.

This one was a woman, tall and rangy with thick ash-blond hair in a plait down her back. Eye-catching, and not dressed like a typical lady; she was wearing the controversial bloomers beneath her deep green and big-buttoned cape-jacket and full-skirted but only knee-length dress. She wore no bonnet, which might have marked her as an Artisan or an unfortunate, except Kit didn't think so for either case. She wore long sleeves and heavy gloves and a velvet choker above her high neckline; not an inch of skin aside from her powered face was visible.

The word that sprung to mind from this glancing assessment was Valkyrie, perhaps because the Viking locked in Edith's reading room had put him in mind of Norse legends, and perhaps that was no coincidence.

Kit hadn't escaped capture some seventeen times by failing to overreact to anything it seemed politic to overreact to. He recoiled dramatically from the new stranger, leaping well out of her reach.

'Christopher Whitebrickleyhurst?' Her voice was low and husky but she might as well have screamed her providence to the rooftops.

As she lunged at him, Kit blocked the threshold with a sudden surge of his Art. This was the equivalent of slamming a physical door, except it was invisible and fuelled by all the vigour of his fear, so it hit her smack in the face—Kit heard the satisfying crunch of it—and tossed her backwards into the street.

Edith, who had not got down behind the counter, cried out in surprise. He hadn't revealed the full extent of his powers even to her. She thought it was just doors and locks, like everyone else.

The air grunted out of the stranger as her back slammed to the ground, and her hands came up to where her nose was gushing blood. He hadn't meant to do that. Meredith, who had been standing nearby, presumably to watch what her meddling had wrought, screamed and ran off down the street. That began to call spectators.

Kit leaned forwards, hands braced on knees. It had been a violent outrush of his Art and it left him a little breathless, a little dizzy. Edith put her hand on his back. Behind them, a heavy thud preceded a splintering noise. He turned to see the locked door to the reading room shivering under an assault from Alexander Locke.

'Don't break my door,' shouted Edith.

Another splintering crash sounded out, and the lock fell out of the door. Locke pushed the door open and stepped through, tossing down the heavy lamp he'd used to crack it open. 'Don't lock me in, then, Miss Knight.'

Despite Edith's indignant placing of hands on hips, his logic was as impeccable as the rest of him. Kit, reluctant to leave his friend, skipped out of the way as the big man strode to the front door, folding his spectacles away into a case.

For a moment Kit feared Locke might close and lock the door, trapping Kit in the shop—though he could never be held by a mere locked door—but he saw the woman on the ground and went to crouch by her side.

'I think her nose is broken,' Locke said. 'Can you fetch a physician, Miss Knight?

It was such an impersonal examination that Kit was convinced he couldn't know the woman; the Viking and the Valkyrie were a coincidence, after all. Kit slipped out the door, careful to stay out of reach of Locke and the woman. Minnie, woken by the commotion, padded out after him and trotted off down the street with purpose.

Kit pushed Edith back inside and locked her own door against her. She said some nasty words through the glass at him.

'Language,' he tsked at her.

He looked down the street, where Knights and other shopkeepers were coming to the doors of their establishments to see what Meredith had been screaming about. With another burst of Art, Kit slammed every threshold and locked every door along the street. He'd trapped some people outside, but most had been still inside or lingering on their thresholds, shoved backwards when the doors slammed.

Again, he hunched forwards, breathing hard. He was using his Art up at a phenomenal rate, but it wouldn't matter, once he got out to the stones.

Alexander Locke straightened up and looked along the street and then at Kit. He stared openly, unmoving.

Oh, balls, thought Kit.

'You broke my fucking nose,' said the woman on the ground in tones thick with blood. The swearing, more even than the bloomers, even more than the use of his registered name, cemented who she was—bounty hunter.

Kit said, 'Come after me and I'll break more than that,' and started running.

Despite the urgency of the situation, he was hard-pressed not to laugh at himself for that stupid threat. He had never yet fought his way out of one of these situations; he either escaped or he was captured and forced to open the doors that needed opening.

He was an accessory to enough robberies, and at least one assassination, that he'd never get out of gaol, if the Agency enforcers ever managed to catch him in between the forced commissions from the country's master criminals and organised gangs.

He wanted, desperately, the Knightstone Circle. He wanted time to concentrate; he could go in a doorway at this end of the village and out through the doors of the summer pavilion most of the way to the standing stones if he had enough time to focus what was left of his Art after the show back at Edith's shop. Then, once he was there, his power would be replenished and he'd be able to cross all the way to the chalk mines.

He just had to get to the stones.

He was running full tilt when a knife buried itself into the shopfront brickwork an inch from his head. He spun and saw Alexander Locke charging at him.

Kit yanked out the knife and flicked it straight back at him, an instinctive reaction he immediately regretted. The Viking ducked it with a curse and barrelled into Kit, scooping him aside just as a couple more knives sang through the air, curving impossibly to thud into the wall right where Kit had been standing.

'I'm not the one trying to kill you, Mr Whitely,' Locke informed him. 'I'm trying to help you.'

Kit looked at the shiny knives stuck hilt-deep in the wall and looked up at the man comfortably holding him. Then he sunk his heel into Locke's leg and whipped out of his grip, dashing for the doorway of the greengrocer. Another spray of knives diverted him. He zagged as Locke made a grab for his collar and got to the doorway of the dressmaker's, and out the doorway of the bakery, back up the street, in a little flurry of Art. He didn't actually have to pass through the doors, still locked; the doorway itself was enough of a threshold for his Art to work on.

He sprinted across the street and into the sweetshop, unlocking the door with a touch of his hand. He ran straight through the shop, to an alarmed shout from Mrs Mason, and out the back door, through the workroom where Mr Mason and the three Mason children were boiling sugar, and into the back yard, where the gate to the common was.

He was about halfway to the gate when a swarm of rats came at him. Kit reversed in dismayed disgust and smacked into Locke, who was miraculously right behind him. The man picked him up out of the way and put him behind the bulwark of his back with one hand as he shot a pistol into the wave of chittering rodents, scattering them. Mr Mason had just come out to remonstrate, and leapt back inside with a shout of alarm, slamming and locking the door.

'Got a metalworker and a pied piper after you,' Locke commented. The feral smile was definitely in the ascendance now. 'What did you do?'

'Doors,' said Kit numbly. Locke smelled lightly of sandalwood, warm and spicy, underlying the acrid smell of the gunshot. 'I'm good at doors. Criminals love that I'm good at doors.'

He'd foolishly registered himself at the Agency, when the push to organise Artisans had started and he'd been convinced of the talk of a new age of cooperation and opportunity and protection. The only self-preserving thing he'd done was to list his specialty as doors rather than thresholds, a far broader category.

Doors had been enough to make him very much in demand, once the registry had been leaked. He'd been running ever since.

'These criminals don't,' Locke said.

He did something with his gun, which was one of the modern French sort Kit had seen at the Great Exhibition. Then he dusted off Kit's shoulders in an absent-minded sort of way. Only then did Kit regain the presence of mind to register how easily Locke had been manhandling him.

He looked up at the man as he adjusted the worn collar of his coat like a valet. 'You're very strong.'

Locke stopped fidgeting with Kit's coat. 'You're just small.' He took Kit's elbow and dragged him towards the gate he'd been running for in the first place.

'I am not!' said Kit, nettled from both the words and the way he was being so easily shifted about in apparent proof of them. 'I only seem that way because of how I look.'

Locke looked him up and down, head cocked. It took Kit a moment to realise the man was puzzled.

He waved a hand at his own face. 'Pretty. Fey. Makes people think I'm a lot more delicate than I am.'

'That must help you along.' Locke opened the gate and glanced left and right.

'What does that mean?'

'It makes people underestimate you, doesn't it?' He tugged Kit through the gate. 'Come along, Mr Whitely.'

Kit tried to free himself from Locke's strong grip. 'You don't have to get involved in this. I don't need anyone's help. I take care of myself.'

Locke's fingers tightened on him. 'It wasn't what I thought, when I first saw you.'

'What did you think?' Kit said. When Locke shrugged, he added, 'You can't say that and then not tell me.'

'I thought you looked like a wanton little bit.'

'Oh,' said Kit, unsurprised and disappointed anyway. 'Yes. A certain type of man thinks that, yes.'

Locke dropped his arm and turned to face him, the smile winking out from his face. Kit had the feeling the man had been trying to provoke him and had been unexpectedly provoked himself. 'And what do *you* mean by a certain type of man there, Mr Whitely? The certain type of man who is helping you out of trouble?'

Kit took great delight in offering him up the same shrug he'd given him. 'Let me handle my own business, Mr Locke.'

'You're being pursued by at least two assassins. You need me, my lad.'

Kit, in the middle of rolling his eyes at this bit of patronage, saw movement on the common. A couple of dogs were tearing across the common at them, snarling. One of them was Minnie, Edith's gentle wolfhound, last seen running out of the shop. Minnie didn't look so gentle now. The pied piper Artisan at work again.

'Don't shoot!' he shouted, as Locke twitched his pistol. Edith would be devastated if Minnie got hurt.

Locke growled like the dogs but yanked him around and through the gate into the yard beside the sweetshop. They were behind the haberdashery now, kept by another Knight cousin. A skittering noise came overhead and Locke pushed Kit out of the way just before more knives thudded down, lodging solidly in the packed dirt of the bare backyard. Locke grunted, brushing a hand over his arm, where his tailored coat now had a rent in it, the material rapidly reddening.

'Oh, no,' Kit breathed.

'Come on,' said Locke, shaking off his attempt to see the wound, and they ran across and through the unlocked back door into the main shop.

Kit was now hugging close to Locke's side. The sight of blood had shaken him more than anything else this morning; he was well-used to this kind of dogged pursuit, but the bounty hunters weren't usually attempting murder. Their clients wanted him alive, so he could open the doors of safes, vaults, treasure rooms and palaces for them.

He'd even warded off several determined attempts to get him to Egypt to break into a pharaoh's tomb; that had been especially annoying because he wouldn't actually have minded visiting the pyramids for their own sake.

The haberdashery was empty. If the Knight cousin who ran it had been here, she had gone out the back door after Kit had sealed the front door. They hurried across the room. Kit, stumbling, knocked a display table, sending baskets of lace and ribbons scattering everywhere.

'Damn it,' they said together.

Locke started picking up the mess while Kit wasted a few moments getting the front door unlocked; his Art was running dry enough now that he had to focus hard for that most basic of tasks. He even put his hand on the lock, which he didn't usually have to do anymore.

Even once he'd unlocked it, he paused to watch Locke as he gathered the spilled ribbons and started putting them back into baskets, sorting them into like colours as he went. The former tidiness of the man's hair and clothes, his casual tidying of Kit's coat, was beginning to make sense.

As soon as Kit opened the door, though, Locke snapped out of his fixation and took his hand again, his thumb tracing along Kit's skin in a way that made Kit forget to wonder why the man was insisting on holding on to him. Or, at least, to assume he knew why.

Most of the people who had been locked out of their premises when Kit had closed the doors had fled. There was nothing much to see for the last few hardy spectators; the knife-throwing metalworking Artisan and the pied piper animal-controller Artisan were not making themselves apparent, sticking to the rooftops, Kit supposed. He was miffed that being in a public place hadn't helped keep him safe like it normally did when bounty hunters came for him.

Locke finally let go of his hand. Kit bolted from his side, to an exasperated shout from the man. He got across the street—the Valkyrie was gone—slammed into Edith's and stood gasping.

'Kit, thank God!' Edith was by the front window, where she must have been trying to see what was happening. 'Come out the back way, we'll—'

Locke barged through the door after him; that moved Kit from miffed to moderately annoyed. Who did the interfering fellow think he was, anyway? Couldn't he take a sodding hint? He dodged the man's snatch at collaring him again, dancing backwards towards the broken door to the reading room, very much hoping not to trip.

'Leave him alone!' Edith shouted at Locke and came at him like a train under full steam, except tiny. 'I don't know who you are or what you think you're doing, but this is not appropriate behaviour for a gentleman.'

And that was just her getting started.

'Get off me, Miss Knight,' said Locke, while Kit concentrated and stepped backwards through the broken door and out the front door again in a small burst of Art. God, he needed to eat.

He looked through the glass to see Edith blocking Locke's way to the door to give him a substantial piece of her broad mind, magnificently delaying him. He fled off towards the standing stones, snickering. He would have locked the door behind him, but he didn't want another of Edith's locks broken. He heard the jangle of the shop bell as Locke came slamming out a few moments later, but he had a hell of a lead now and he wasn't giving it up to risk a look behind him.

Then someone leapt off the roof of the haberdashery and landed right in front of him.

The last few spectators screamed in a terror that had quite a bit of excited delight in it. The assassins were at least taking care to not to hurt innocent bystanders, except for the helpful Locke who only had himself to blame for playing the hero.

Kit barely evaded the cloaked figure's grab for his arm. The figure whirled and plunged a knife at his heart; in trying to dodge, Kit fell over, rolled and came up running, without looking back to see what Locke was making of the metalworker who was blocking the street. The narrow passage through to the commons loomed on his left, just before the long wall of the unoccupied and almost-derelict Grange, the old manor house.

Kit's dart towards the passageway was quite spoiled when more rats came boiling out.

A shot rang out behind him; Locke had brought a pistol to a knife fight, of course. Kit ran straight through the swarm of rodents, kicking his legs and cursing fit to pitch as he felt their claws scrabbling at him, trying to climb his legs, while others squirmed disgustingly under his boots. He ran along the passageway to the commons, crushing rat skulls under his boots with a sickening staccato crunch. It was a threshold, so he could have used Art to make it into a portal and whip through it in an instant, but it wasn't a door or doorway and he didn't want to give away that his Art was more than it seemed. He wasn't desperate yet.

He burst out the other end, shaking off the last few rats and launching into an all-out sprint across the commons towards the oak trees on the other side. The forest was not good for his Art, since he needed manmade thresholds, but he could get out of sight and circle about to the stones.

Except the sodding dogs were still patrolling the commons, and came racing towards him, too fast to evade. Swearing, he doubled back just in time for Locke to intercept him. The man was fast. Longer legs than him, Kit supposed, disgruntled.

'I am trying to help you, Mr Whitely.' He sounded out of breath, at least. 'Would you let me?'

'Don't need help.'

Kit pushed open the gate into the inn's back yard and tried to slam it in Locke's face, but the big man shoved it open again and came through, slamming it in the faces of the dogs instead. They howled and scrabbled at the wood, before he heard Minnie let out a puzzled whine and snuffle at the gap at the bottom of the gate. After a moment, both dogs wandered off.

The pied piper Artisan had let them go, or, more likely, run out of Art and lost control of them.

Kit slumped against the yard wall. He was winded from all the running, and really on his last legs with Art now too—he needed the sticky bun he'd left at Edith's or maybe a big glass of gin, since alcohol powered Art more than almost anything else—but he probably had a few more short traverses in him, given space to breathe.

Locke rested an arm against the wall next to him, also catching his breath. 'Took care of the metalworker for you,' he said, and gave Kit his feral smile.

That answered the question of why he was so determined to help; he was obviously a man who enjoyed wading into a fight, even one that was not of his own making.

'Right,' Kit said slowly.

Locke had said there were three other strangers off the train; if the pied piper was exhausted, the metalworker down, and the Valkyrie nursing a broken nose, he was safe. For now.

He glanced around. Mrs Knight was an inveterate gardener, and had turned the large back yard of the inn, which should have been bare and practical and used solely to store barrels, into a rather lovely kitchen garden. He sighed out, head tipped back so he could look up at the bright October sky. Grey clouds were gusting in from the channel, moving fast.

His blood was singing from the chase and the exhilaration of getting away again, and the sheer relief of it. It was a feeling he had only ever experienced alone, hunched in some grotty alley or other after shaking off pursuers. He had never had help to escape before.

He added, 'You have my thanks, Mr Locke. Please take off your coat.'

Locke's fair eyebrows quirked, his gaze intent. 'I appreciate the gratitude, Mr Whitely, but I don't expect a practical demonstration of it.'

Didn't expect it; the admiring look told Kit he wouldn't refuse it, should Kit desire to insist. Kit's elation turned abruptly in a more licentious direction at this blatant signalling from Locke with his stupid intriguing face and stupid wolfish smile and stupid warm hazel eyes.

But Kit was far too self-controlled for any action in that regard, no matter he had a flash of lips and tongue and hands fruitfully employed. Pointedly not meeting the man's eyes, he said, 'To look at your wound, sir.'

He touched the tips of his fingers to the ragged hole in Locke's expensive coat where the knife had winged his arm. The fabric there was darkened and damp to the touch; the cut had bled freely.

'Ah. Understood. No need, Mr Whitely. And no offence intended.'

That was just exasperating. Kit had plainly refused the signal, plainly corrected the supposed misunderstanding, plainly taken no offence. It was just Locke needling him now, prodding to get a reaction from behind Kit's cold and highly effective veneer.

He looked up into Locke's bright eyes, wearing his blankest expression. 'I shall endeavour to take none, then, Mr Locke.'

Locke's smile broadened; he looked just as amused by Kit's refusal to engage in flirtation as he might have been if Kit had responded in kind. He swung his weight and put his other arm up on the other side of Kit, and his casual lean became a prison made of muscled arms and tall, broad body. He crowded in closer, pushing Kit against the wall.

It seemed he was just as aware of Kit's tamped-down arousal as Kit was. But he stopped there, leaning slightly over Kit, waiting.

Kit could rock back onto his heels. He recognised that Locke would be polite enough to pull away if he did. He could rock forwards onto his toes and raise himself up enough to taste the mouth that hovered just above his, as he'd thought to a moment before. He was hard-pressed to hold himself still.

He managed, 'I don't believe I have indicated any sort of interest.' He had meant to sound waspish and only achieved breathy.

'You think you haven't,' said Locke pleasantly, and maddeningly. As Kit frowned—he knew his façade was bloody well-nigh impossible to penetrate so *how dare* this stranger make a damned good attempt at it?—the big man leaned in even closer, his mouth now against Kit's ear so that his words came in a warm gust over his skin. 'Go ahead and say no, then.'

Kit closed his eyes, breathing in sandalwood. He hadn't been with a man in an awfully long time, since well before he'd got out of London and away to Somerset. It was hard to trust anyone, when he'd been brought up in an orphanage where no touch ever meant uncomplicated affection. It was hard to trust anyone, when anyone could be a bounty hunter or an informer for one. It was hard to trust anyone, when anyone could be a provocateur for the police. It was hard to make the effort, for frankly poor reward. He'd long since given up.

Locke's feral smile called to the Kit who had walked out of the front doors of the Orphanage on his sixteenth birthday, shedding all that had come before like a cast-off coat, the Kit who hadn't had to be careful and wary all the time, who had thrived on risk and adventure and loved his Art instead of cursing it for a burden.

The Kit who had known how to take advantage of intriguing Viking-shaped opportunities.

He missed that version of himself, lost as soon as his powers had become public knowledge.

Wanton little bit, indeed. Kit really hated to prove the man right.

He turned his head and murmured, 'Yes.'

Locke's hands were on his hips, thumbs circling. He rocked into it, letting his head tip back against the wall as Locke's mouth moved down his neck from the sensitive point below his ear. He heard and felt the bigger man sigh against his skin where his neck and shoulder joined.

Kit sunk his hands into the thick blond hair, taking great pleasure in dishevelling it as Locke had dishevelled his entire self. He tugged Locke's head back and destroyed the necktie to lick the hollow at the base of his throat. He mouthed his way along his collarbone, nuzzling fabric aside to taste the bare smooth skin.

'You have a warm mouth for a man who acts cold,' Locke said into his hair as his hands got under Kit's coat.

'Wait till it's wrapped around your prick, baby,' Kit purred, and, to his enormous satisfaction, heard Locke whisper, 'Oh, *Jesus*.'

But as he started to sink lower, Locke pulled him back up and kissed him, his mouth covering Kit's. Kit opened to Locke, feeling his tongue lazily probing, his slight stubble rubbing against his skin, the sensation almost unbearable. His big hands cupped Kit's arse, pulling him up onto his toes and almost entirely off his feet. Kit moaned and gave up on any thought of dignity, hooking a leg about Locke's waist to climb him higher.

He heard Locke make an answering noise deep in his throat, his hips giving a pulse against Kit's own, his mouth moving on him with ferocious need. There was not an inch of air between their bodies.

Kit was, all at once, wild and frantic for release and yet wanting more than a quick fuck in the back yard of the inn—thankfully still closed till midday. The Knights were understanding indeed but he'd already tested those limits today.

'Come back to my room,' he murmured against the other man's mouth, hands sliding over Locke's shoulders. He had private lodgings in a widow's house off a small alley near the parish church. They wouldn't be seen, and it would give him a chance to grab banknotes and his single change of clothes before he went for the mines or the train. 'I'll make it good for you. I'll make it *so* good for you, baby.'

Locke cursed again, quietly, and pressed yet harder against Kit, grinding against him. He took Kit's hands and pushed them up above his head, pressing one large and capable hand against Kit's overlaid palms. Kit might have tensed if the man had tried to hold his wrists but as it was, he interlaced the fingers of his uppermost hand into Locke's and felt Locke respond with a squeeze and a bit more of his delicious weight. God, he wanted to be under that.

Locke's other hand went to his own waistband. He wasn't going to wait to get to the room, it seemed. Oh, well. Locke's hand came back up and his kiss deepened again. Kit arched against him and made a hum of pleasure into his mouth.

Which almost, but not quite, drowned out the click of handcuffs closing about his wrists.

3

'WHAT?' Kit said.

Alexander Locke had stepped back, letting Kit back down to the ground. Kit lowered his hands and looked at the cuffs in stunned disbelief and a confused sort of aggravation. He looked up at Locke.

'*What?*' he said again.

'You're right, that *was* so good,' Locke said, smiling. 'Don't know why everyone thinks you're hard to catch.'

Oh, you'll find out, you wanker. Rather than give any kind of forewarning—catching Kit was by no means keeping a-hold of him—Kit restrained himself to a fervent, 'You *shit.*'

'Yeah, I know,' said Locke comfortably. He snagged the short chain between the two cuffs. 'These are iron and silver, so don't bother with the Art. If you've got any left.' He paused, then added, less nonchalantly, 'If it burns too much, I'll pad them.'

Iron barely burnt Kit at all anymore, or if it did, he didn't need to feel it. He shook his hands so the cuffs jingled, and shrugged. Locke towed Kit across the yard, giving the chain a yank when he tried to drag his feet. The back door of the inn was locked, but the big man merely hammered at the lock until the wood around it splintered and it fell off. Edith's father, the innkeeper, was going to like that about as much as Edith had liked him breaking the lock in her paper shop.

Locke kicked open the door. It led to a storage room, filled with kegs and the scent of beer. The door to the taproom was unlocked. He pulled Kit through.

'So. The famously uncatchable Christopher Whitebrickleyhurst, and what a mouthful you are,' he said, as he glanced around the empty public room. 'You're also a bit of an idiot. Who did you think I was?'

A wealthy scholar with a feral streak. Yes, Kit was a bit dim indeed. 'You're the idiot,' he said petulantly. 'If you'd waited, I would've let you fuck me for hours.'

Locke glanced back at him, and Kit braced himself; he'd just practically incited his own molestation out of petty spite. *What makes you think he won't fuck you for hours anyway?* But Locke's over-the-shoulder look was merely deeply, warmly amused.

Kit would have smacked his own forehead if Locke didn't have his cuffs on a short leash. The whole light flirtation, right from that first appraising eye contact in Edith's reading room, had been one long act to lull him into letting his prick think for him. At least amusement was better than disgust.

He sighed. 'You don't even like men, do you?'

'I like men plenty,' Locke said, leaving unsaid the *Just not men like you* that his half-lidded eyes expressed for him.

Kit was unaccountably disappointed and then irritated with himself for it. He jerked hard on the cuffs.

Locke tutted mockingly. 'Now, now, my lad. Don't make me punish you.'

Kit knew Locke was teasing him; he knew the sort of cruel captor who revelled in keeping prisoners under the lash, and warm-eyed Alexander Locke was not one of them.

But the words struck the tender spot at the core of his being and he went wild.

He flung himself away from Locke and hit the extent of the chain so sharply that it wrenched him around and dropped him to his knees. He launched off again immediately, ramming into Locke's stomach with the top of his head hard enough to make the big man go *oof* but not enough to knock him even slightly off balance. Locke caught Kit by the shoulders and hauled him up into a bearhug.

Kit let out a wail that he cut off. Part of him knew that if he screamed for help, the Knights would come, but most of him knew silence was the only safety when a tormentor had him helpless. Crying out never helped. Instead, he began to thrash and kick with everything he had.

'Calm down, I'm not going to touch you,' Locke shouted in his ear, which was enough to remind Kit that he wasn't fifteen anymore, that he wasn't inside the Orphanage, that this wasn't then.

He found his voice. 'You're touching me right now.'

His thrashing legs tangled with Locke's and unbalanced the big man enough that he had to take a stumbling step which ended with Kit against the bar's long counter, its edge painful in the small of his back, and Locke half-fallen on top of him.

'Ow,' Kit said. 'Bloody *ow*, you arse.'

Locke pushed off him. 'You brought it on yourself, Mr Whitely.'

Kit made a spirited attempt to headbutt the sod, which Locke readily anticipated, giving him a hard shove sideways. 'Little wildcat,' he said, almost fondly. 'Look at the mess you've made of me.'

He straightened his coat, redid his necktie and finger-combed his hair back off his face, still watching Kit with that calm amusement that had him sucking in air in a valiant attempt to get his own calm back.

Kit had cultivated caution and self-control for many years. He was ashamed that he'd given in to long-buried impulses in the inn's yard, and that he'd lost his composure so dramatically in here. He reminded himself he had never yet wriggled out of one of these situations by fighting. He was certainly not going to fight off a man the size of the Viking.

Flight was his only option, and that meant soothing Alexander Locke into thinking he had accepted his fate. He sighed, straightening and relaxing his shoulders. 'I won't give you any more trouble, Mr Locke.'

Locke snorted, hands twitching quickly over his clothes as he set himself to rights. 'As if a pissant little thief like you could give me trouble.'

'I'm not a thief.'

If he was being completely honest, he would tack on a judicious *anymore*, but he wasn't, so he didn't.

'I stand corrected, Mr Whitely. Accessory to theft. Many, many times over.'

'I didn't have a choice,' Kit said bitterly. 'When one of the gangs puts out a price on my head and their bounty hunter brings me in, I don't have a choice but to take the job. If the Agency had protected its registry, things would be different.'

'Pretty speech,' said Locke. 'May I ask how you afford to lodge and eat in this village?'

Kit internally winced but did not so much as show a trace of a blush on his face. He busied himself with odd jobs about the village when he could compete with the surfeit of strapping Knight cousins; the old ladies in particular liked to engage his polite and pretty self in fetch and carry. But he had often, though not always, been compensated for opening doors and he took his cut—he even negotiated for a better cut—because it was another thing he didn't feel he had a choice about. It had made him secure, if he husbanded his savings well.

It also made his moral standing a good deal shakier.

But he shrugged it off. 'If I'm going to be fucked anyway, I might as well get paid.'

'Hmm, and does your logic extend from the figurative to the literal?'

'A pissant thief and a whore in the same conversation, well done, Mr Locke.'

Locke flicked his hands to fists and released them, lips pressed into a thin line. 'Sorry, Mr Whitely.' He sounded alarmingly sincere. 'I did not intend for that out there'—he waved towards the garden—'to go as far as it did. I got carried away. You were so...eager.' He said the last word with something like wonder in his tone.

Kit expressed his exasperation to the ceiling.

'Yeah, all right, that didn't come out how I meant.'

'At least you didn't let me get to my knees,' Kit said. 'A silver lining, to be sure.'

The Viking dipped his knees so that his whole body nodded in acknowledgement of the blandly presented barb. 'I'm not quite that awful, Mr Whitely.' And then: 'If looks could kill! I do seem that awful, do I?'

Kit shut his eyes and got his temper under control. Emotions tended to feed Art, but anger did nothing for Kit's and so he generally didn't bother with it, beyond mild exasperation. Fear, on the other hand, powered his Art to a disturbingly fine degree, but Kit didn't like to let himself feel fear. He could, though, when necessary.

Locke stymied any thought of that by adding, 'I'm trying to tell you you're safe from me, Mr Whitely.'

Kit, attention snagged, met Locke's eyes. The big man went on. 'I didn't mean to scare you just then. And I didn't mean to take advantage of you. I am not the, ah, the *certain type of man* you think I am.'

'The type of man who'll have me up against a wall whether I like it or not.'

'You were liking it.' Locke hesitated before his wolfish smile began to slyly creep across his face. 'You were very, *very* liking—'

'Till the cuffs came out.'

Locke had the good grace to look shamefaced. 'I just need you to understand you're safe from me. And you are safe with me.'

'Safe with you,' Kit repeated stupidly.

'I'll keep you safe, Mr Whitely. The way these Artisans are behaving, there must be an assassination commission out on you. I will keep you safe.'

It had the weight of a solemn promise. Kit had not felt safe for a very long time. He was not sure he had ever truly felt safe, not even here, among the first friends he'd ever had.

He must have looked wide-eyed, because Locke smiled again and said,

'You're so safe from me, I'm not kissing you even when you're looking at me like that.'

Kit dragged his gaze away. 'We should get going to the station if you don't want to miss the train back.'

Locke stared at him silently. 'What?' Kit snapped. 'I don't want to bring more trouble on this village than I already have. They've been kind to me.'

The Viking nodded. 'I saw you lock them in to keep them out of harm's way. Impressive.'

The compliment sounded genuine and he had certainly worked hard to teach himself how to lock or unlock a door without having to touch it. He refrained from ducking his head in abashed pleasure to have the technical skill acknowledged; he was as bland as ever as he said, 'Well. Good at doors, good at locks.'

'I meant the decision to use your Art to keep people safe rather than only to escape.'

Kit, even more embarrassed now—skill was one thing, soft feelings another—rattled his chain, looking at the cuffs so he didn't have to keep watching those hazel eyes watching him so knowingly.

'Iron and silver,' Locke repeated.

Indeed, the cuffs were wrought of heavy, dark iron overlaid with bright gleaming silver in a surprisingly delicate filigree. Both could dampen Art, in their different ways. Kit's own Art was immune to silver, but iron slowed him down; even now, it stung a little where it sat about his wrists. He would certainly not be able to portal through a threshold wearing iron.

It didn't completely disable him, though—after all, many locks were made of iron so it was something he'd had to fight already—but as much as he wanted to smile smugly back at Locke, he didn't give that away. It was a rare Artisan who could use their Art while wearing iron and Kit was a bloody rare Artisan indeed.

Locke, having groomed himself to his satisfaction, moved to the front door of the locked-up inn. 'Want to get this door open for me?' he asked, with a wiggle of his fingers to indicate he meant using Art.

'Certainly, Mr Locke,' Kit said, in his politest tones. 'Take the cuffs off and stand at the back of the room, I'll gladly open it for you.'

'Funny boy.'

Locke picked up the iron doorstop; he was going to open the door with his usual expedience. Suddenly he stiffened and spun on his heel, throwing the doorstop in a hard and fast overhand pass at Kit, who yelped and ducked.

An abortive answering yelp rang out as the doorstop thumped into the assassin who had been standing right behind him, knife bared. The cloaked woman went reeling backwards, clutching her chest where the doorstop had clocked her a good one.

Kit flung himself forwards at the same moment that Locke did; they passed each other. Kit got to the door while Locke tackled the assassin. He'd either lost his pistol or hadn't had time to prepare its next shot, because he went in wrestling.

'You said you took care of the metalworker,' Kit said accusingly. Locke's promise to keep him safe was ringing loud right now.

'I did,' said Locke through gritted teeth, hand locked around the woman's wrist, twisting it in the effort to make her drop her knife even as he batted another, Art-driven, out of the air. 'This must be his partner, and she is *not happy*.'

'You said there were only three other visitors on the train!'

'Lied.'

'Christ,' Kit muttered with feeling.

He put one of his cuffed hands over the lock of the front door. The iron in the cuffs would make the Art slow to gather, but he'd get there if he was patient and calm. He hoped it would take a while for the pair to finish each other off.

No. He hoped Locke would win. But the man's promise to keep him safe came with the unspoken caveat—Kit would be his prisoner, a hefty price for safety. He couldn't stay with him. He would keep himself safe, as he always had.

He watched the fight reflected in the large mirror over the bar. As the two danced around each other, the woman brought up her other hand, another knife gleaming, and tried to stab Locke in the back, which Kit watched with bright-eyed interest as his fingers began to feel warm, a tiny spark of Art tingling through their tips, fighting the iron.

Locke spun out from under the strike before it could land. 'Thanks for the warning,' he called.

'You're managing well enough.'

And he was. The assassin was becoming more energetic now she was recovering from the iron blow to her chest, but Locke anticipated every move she made, dodging and blocking her easily. She was obviously short on Art, since she was sticking mostly to hand-to-hand. She was also obviously used to fights not taking so long. She hissed in frustration.

So did Kit. This was taking too long for him too. His Art had been almost exhausted anyway, and the cuffs were muffling what was left. Then he heard a quiet tap, almost inaudible under the thumps and grunts of the knife fight, and looked up to see Edith crouched down and peering at him from around the far end of the bar. She must have come in the side door from the Knights' attached residence by the inn's stables.

She pushed three shot glasses full of amber liquid into view along the floor. She was serving him whisky from the bar. Kit scurried over to her, squeezing her hand in thanks as he threw back the contents of each glass in turn. The alcohol burned his throat and warmed his stomach.

And ignited his Art.

Edith tried to draw him with her, towards the side door, but there was no way he was leading two bounty hunters, or whichever one of them survived the fight, into her family's home. He shook his head, pushing her away, and went to the door.

He was reeling already, head spinning. He'd been hungry and exhausted, and was too cautious to drink heavily as a habit; the whisky had hit him fast.

He bent over the door's lock again. It occurred to him Edith could have unlocked it for him, if she'd thought to bring her father's keys. He looked about for her, but she was gone. Locke dodged a particularly close knife thrust and kicked the metalworker in the leg as she lunged at him again.

Kit hummed in pleasure. His fingers were hot. He was warm all through. He smiled dreamily.

'Get away from that door, Mr Whitely.'

Locke disentangled from the assassin and darted across at him but whipped back around just in time to deflect the flying knife that would have got him in the kidneys.

The lock clicked under Kit's hand. 'Good at doors,' he said, unable to resist a taunt. '*Spectacular* at locks.'

He winked and slipped out, relocking the door and leaving the two bounty hunters to it.

Alexander Locke was busy. The knife wielders were likewise occupied or already down. The pied piper Artisan was exhausted. The Valkyrie was nowhere in sight. He had a free path to the standing stones now.

Since the free entertainment had been off the street for a while, the spectators had mostly dispersed. The ones who remained stared accusingly at Kit and he twiddled his fingers at them, showing off his damningly cuffed wrists. Their expressions made him want to laugh, even in the harsh light of how he'd let the Knights down with this fuss.

Three whisky shots downed in as many seconds; he wanted to laugh at everything.

Rolling his shoulders, he started walking briskly northwards towards the stone circle. There was only the slightest of staggers in it. He mostly wanted to curl up and sleep. Maybe also to feel Alexander Locke's mouth on him again, the bastard.

That was definitely the alcohol making itself known.

Kit turned his attention to the locks of the cuffs. He had to focus hard against the iron and the fuzzing effects of the alcohol, but he wasn't completely unaware of his surroundings, so he wasn't taken by surprise when Locke appeared at his side and snatched the chain of the cuffs again.

Locke was taken by surprise, however, when his tug on the chain did not pull Kit to him, but pulled the cuffs off him; Kit'd got the locks undone at the exact right time. He ran, shot through the doorway of the milliner's, out the doorway of the barber three shops further up, did a quick hop-skip to the butcher and used that to get another quick four premises down. He lurched a bit as he came out of that doorway, head spinning. Art powered by alcohol flared bright but never lasted long.

Though he was slightly slowed in his frenetic pace by having to gauge which way he was facing each time he emerged—Kit had a shockingly poor sense of direction—he now felt he had enough distance to check where Locke was. Insultingly, the bounty hunter was strolling along with his hands in his coat pocket. His blond hair was messy again, falling rakishly across his forehead, and he had a few more rents in the coat. A few more bloodstains too. Kit guessed the second metalworker was out of the game.

He walked backwards, watching Locke. He was impressed at his own agility, even more so when he wobbled and recovered himself with a great deal more grace than he had when sober. He hummed, smiling at Locke and thinking about his mouth.

'You are very drunk,' the bounty hunter told him conversationally.

'You,' said Kit, 'are an Artisan who can either read minds or see five seconds into the future.'

Locke's smile lit up his face. 'How do you figure, Mr Whitely?'

'You knew exactly where the metalworker was going to put her knives, every time. You dodged the— You knew I—' He was losing the threads of his thoughts. He shook his head to try to clear it. *You knew I wanted your mouth.* 'What am I thinking?'

'You're thinking how tired you are,' said Locke. 'You want to let me put you to bed, sweetheart.'

Kit tittered. 'Oh, honey. Not mindreading, then.'

Locke smiled and kept stalking him in that slow and confident swagger. Kit shoved his hands into his snarled hair to push it off his face, walking backwards, hips swinging, lips parted, watching Locke.

Locke, smiling. 'Definitely some thoughts floating around about bed, Mr Whitely.'

Kit was still laughing at him when he suddenly wobbled again. When he glanced down to get his footing, he was looking down at Locke and his feet were balanced precariously on setts that were rising from the ground. Others were bobbing up around him too, so he leapt nimbly to a higher perch with far more confidence than if he'd been sober, in case Locke had the idea of hauling him back down by his ankles.

The wind swirled around him, making him sway. Clouds were still scudding over, ever-thickening, threatening rain. He turned his eyes away from them before they made him dizzy.

'Are you doing that?' Locke asked. 'If it's not you, you're walking into another assassin's trap.'

Kit, taking this under advisement, looked around until he saw a thin older woman in a dark dress and cape, kneeling on the rooftop nearby, her eyes squinting intently as she floated the setts towards her. A stoneworker Artisan.

'How many strangers *were* on that train, you most gurt 'uge liar?' he shouted at Locke. Sometimes only the local language would do.

'Might want to jump down to me, sweetheart,' Locke called. 'At least you know I don't want to kill you.'

Kit waited until the new Artisan had floated his chunk of granite to near the roof, then rolled in through the open window under the eaves and out through the doorway of the bakery below. He had meant to come out of the roll, back on to his feet, and into a sprint in one smooth, fast motion, but that last threshold had been an Artwork too far. He flopped flat on his back and lay dazed before flipping to hands and knees and pushing himself up.

Then Locke's hand closed about his wrist, hard. Kit looked up at him with wide eyes before hauling back and kicking him. Locke sighed. The setts started pelting them; Locke sighed again, extravagantly, and swung Kit around so he was sheltered from the worst of the granite attack by the Viking's bulk.

I will keep you safe, Kit heard again. Three whiskies meant he rested his head on Locke's chest out of sheer gratitude while the man's back was pelted hard.

'Yeah, all right, my lad,' said Locke, before catching one of the setts in mid-air and hurling it like a rocket back at the stoneworker Artisan. It struck her in the temple and knocked her backwards off the roof and out of sight.

Locke turned to Kit, looking inordinately pleased with that bit of physical prowess. 'Let's get to the train. You've got far too many friends here.'

Kit for a moment thought he was being sarcastic; by friends, he assumed, the man meant people who wanted to kill him and claim the bounty on his head. But then he saw Edith peeping around the corner, obviously gearing herself up to take action on his behalf.

He shook his head at her. She shook her head back at him, fiercely. Kit laughed and wobbled, and Locke took him by the elbow to steady him.

Edith popped out from hiding. 'Leave him be!' She took his other arm. 'If you think you can just walk into our village and take one of our people—'

'Would you go away, Miss Knight,' Locke said. 'This is an official arrest.'

'What for?'

'Use of illicit Art,' Locke said.

'That's entrapment,' Kit said. 'I had to use Art in self-defence just then.'

Locke raised an eyebrow at him; they both knew the crime entrapment was usually aimed at. 'In the pursuit of aiding and abetting, Mr Whitely.'

Kit flushed. 'You know that was self-defence as well.'

Edith Knight didn't intimidate easily. 'I don't believe you for a second, Mr Alexander Locke, if that's even your name. If you're an enforcer, show me your badge this instant.'

'I'll show you my badge and the warrant as soon as you let him go.'

'*You* let him go!' She kicked him in the shins, where Kit had gotten him when he'd grabbed his wrist. Kit hoped for bruises on bruises.

'You're like a pair of unruly children,' Locke said, without rancour. 'Miss Knight, I am arresting your lover. I'll arrest you too if you keep annoying me. I'll give you a chance to say goodbye to him if you'll be reasonable.'

'He's not my lover. You are insulting both of us for even thinking it.'

'It's not an insult to me, Miss Knight,' Kit said gallantly.

'Kit! It is: he's implying you're the low sort to ravish a young maiden!'

Kit held off on a snigger. Though, if being ravished required the assistance of the opposite sex, then he supposed both he and Edith still counted as young maidens in the technical sense.

Edith let go of his arm to facilitate stepping into Locke's way. 'Where are you taking him?'

33

'Thank you.' Holding Kit very firmly, Locke took a badge and paper out of a coat pocket and waved them at Edith. 'See? Now I'm escorting Mr Whitely to the train back to London via Bristol.'

She looked like she was going to argue but instead she snapped, 'Fine, but I'm walking with you to make sure you don't hurt him. You've given me no reason whatsoever to think you can be trusted so—'

'Fine,' put in Locke, mockingly and with some asperity; he did, after all, have a couple of knife wounds and, surely, a whole lot of bruises from protecting Kit.

'Stop interrupting me!'

'Stop talking so much,' said Locke with that impeccable logic of his. 'Walk quietly to the station if you must. Though what your family will think after you've walked out with two men and no chaperone...'

If Locke had thought that was a threat, he didn't know Edith, or the Knights. She snorted indelicately and took Kit's other elbow. They began to walk through town towards the station. There were figures in many of the shops, peering through the windows, all locked in.

'You can unlock the doors now, Mr Whitely,' said Locke.

'Oh, you don't want me to do that,' said Kit. 'Oh, I should do that!'

He started to gather the power to cast an Artwork, before Locke jostled him and put the silver-inlaid iron cuffs back around his wrists, muffling his Art. 'You're right, I don't want you to do that. Far, far, too many friends here, Mr Whitely.'

'Aww,' said Kit, swaying over to rest his head on Edith's shoulder. 'You like me, Edie.'

'We do like you, Kit,' she said, patting him on the head. 'What's wrong with him?'

She must have been looking past him at Locke, for the big man said, 'He's foxed. *Someone* got him drunk. Don't glare at me, Miss Knight, I'm doing my job.'

'Kidnapping innocent men!'

'Arresting guilty ones.'

Kit, lost in his whisky haze, looked up at the sky as a cool breeze touched his cheeks; the heavy clouds were fully overhead now and soon it would rain. Then he finally caught up.

He straightened, yanking against Locke's hold on his elbow. 'You're not a bounty hunter? You're police?'

'Enforcer,' said Locke. 'For the Agency.'

'Oh my God, that's even worse,' said Kit, laughing. 'Looking forwards to seeing the look on your face when I escape off the train. Hah! To imagining the look on your face because I won't be there to see it.'

'I like drunk Kit,' said Locke placidly, squeezing Kit's elbow a little tighter. 'He tells me all his plans.'

'Yes, Kit, you should probably be quiet now, luv,' said Edith.

'I'm tired of being quiet,' said Kit loudly, trying to fling up his arms to emphasise his point, forgetting he was cuffed at the wrists and held by the elbows. 'Where did it get me? Six months I've hidden here and they found me anyway.' He leaned over towards Locke now. 'How did the Agency find me?'

'I found you,' said Locke, smiling down at him. 'I followed up your last known location and tracked your movements from there. You eventually fetched up in Bristol and went west. Just had to check the villages most likely to attract Artisans after that. Finally spotted you a couple of weeks ago, headed back to London and enlisted in the Agency. You're my first catch.'

'And you what now?' Kit said. 'Why would you do that? The enforcer bonus is pitiful compared to a private bounty.'

'Salaried, all expenses paid, forage allowance, the bonus on you is rather high, it works out not so badly.'

'Makes no sense,' Kit said obstinately. '*And* look at all the bounty hunters who showed up. The Agency still hasn't fixed its security issues. They leaked your find and you led assassins right to me.'

No wonder the man had promised to keep him safe—it was guilt. Even dulled by alcohol, Kit felt unreasonably disappointed by that. He supposed he might have been moved to anger, if there were any point to it.

'All right,' said Locke. 'Fought them off for you, too, my lad.'

'I shan't hurry to thank you.'

Locke's mouth curled wolfishly but he held his tongue. They had passed out of the village now, past the summer pavilion, used as the village's assembly room, where evening concerts were a popular diversion for visitors in the warmer months. They were approaching the path to the standing stones, a little overgrown at this time of year. The wind had dropped, and the light had taken on the eerie glow of a storm about to break.

Kit glanced over at Edith. She was watching him from the corner of her eye.

'You pair might as well hold up a sign,' said Locke, pulling Kit to a stop. 'I'm not going to let you get to the stone circle, Kit. No biting!'

Kit had only just started to yank up the arm that was tightly held by Locke so he could bite the fingers clenched about his elbow. Locke twisted his arm hard while dodging a solid kick from Edith, who was aiming a good deal higher than his shins this time.

Locke dragged Kit away from her. 'You pull that knife out, I will have to disarm you, lady or not.'

'What knife?' both Edith and Kit said, one of them more convincingly than the other.

Locke rubbed his temple briefly. 'I don't know. Whichever knife you were intending to stab me with.'

'Oh, intentions,' said Kit. 'Not thoughts. He can read our intentions, Edie.'

'No wonder he knew what we were going to do,' said Edith, sounding more delighted than she had any right to. 'I took a few of the knives that other assassin was throwing around.'

'I could also read your faces,' said Locke. 'Didn't need Art for that one, innocent babies. Take the knives out and put them on the ground and I'll know if you're going to try anything.'

'Oh my God, Edith, were you going to *stab* him for me?'

'I wanted to,' she agreed. 'I'm not sure if I would have actually been able to do it, though.'

Locke made a small shrug of agreement. 'Intentions aren't actions.'

'So you're another Artisan, then?' asked Edith as she obeyed Locke, dropping two knives into the grass at her feet. She added one more when Locke raised an eyebrow at her. Kit laughed at her cheerfully chastened expression. She put on archness. 'What a cracking treat for our little village!'

Kit said, 'You're hurting me, Mr Locke.'

Locke loosened his hold gratifyingly quickly. 'I'm not an Artisan, no,' he told Edith as he stooped and collected her arsenal. 'It's a useful talent in my line of work but too weak to qualify me.'

That was likely true, since Locke handled the cuffs with no sign of discomfort. Sensitivity to iron was practically a diagnostic tool differentiating true Art from weaker talents and inclinations.

The train's whistle sounded, blasting into the still air, loud even over the peals of the midday bells from the church at the far end of Lovelly, opposite the grand town hall on the tiny square with its ridiculously ornate fountain.

'We missed the train,' Kit said. He went off into a true fit of giggles at the look on Locke's face.

'Oh!' Edith started off back to the village. 'I'll have to help Da at the inn. Everyone'll be in for nuncheon today! See you there, boys.'

She lifted the long skirts of her simple dress and ran. The wind picked up again and the first few spots of rain hit.

'Why,' said Locke slowly, 'does she think I'm taking you to the inn?'

'No more trains till tomorrow,' Kit explained. 'No carts for hire in this season. You'll need a room. All the seaside lodgings close up for winter, so there's only the rooms at the inn.'

Locke looked at him with half-lidded eyes. 'You have a room, Kit.'

Kit kept his face blank in lieu of blushing. He had, of course, invited Locke back there before he'd even had the whisky as his excuse, a fact Locke had apparently decided to remind him of.

Of all the bloody moments to be the wanton little bit Locke had decided he was. Years, *years*, of caution, thrown away for a beautiful mouth and warm hazel eyes.

Years of loneliness, driving him to it.

'I haven't given you permission to use my name,' he said crossly.

'Kit,' said Locke, smiling, making his name sound like the click of a key in a lock. 'It's far too odd to keep calling you Mr Whitely after you put your tongue in my mouth and wrapped me in your thighs.'

'Your manners are appalling, Mr Locke.'

'Let's go to your room, *Kit*.'

'Yes, certainly,' said Kit, 'please do take me back to my *own room*, Mr Locke.'

The thresholds in his lodgings were sparse; it was a small house. He had a far better chance of escaping from the inn, with its multitudes of doorways and very many windows. It didn't even matter that his intention, which must have been ringing loud and clear to Locke, was to escape. It only made it more likely he'd get his desired result, which he did:

'We'll go to the inn.'

Locke, still smiling to himself, began to stroll back towards the village, giving a single tug on the chain between Kit's cuffed hands to get him moving before, insultingly, letting it drop and not even taking Kit's arm to draw him along.

'You didn't care to swing by your room?' he asked as he ambled along.

'I don't think I've ever been propositioned quite so casually, Mr Locke.'

'To retrieve your belongings, Mr Whitely,' Locke said, chuckling.

'No.'

Locke flicked a look his way. 'You have nothing you don't mind leaving behind? No mementos, no letters, no daguerreotypes, no lock of hair tied up in a pretty ribbon? Nothing precious at all?'

Kit considered this. He had made a home here for six months. And he had nothing he would not walk away from without a backwards look. That was the way it had to be.

'No,' he said again.

He bowed his head to avoid Locke's frown and walked along through drizzle thickening steadily to rain, working hard against the fog of the whisky. After a moment, the locks clicked in unison. Kit slid the open cuffs off and put them into his pocket.

He stopped walking. Locke immediately turned and levelled a look at him.

'I'm getting wet. I want to take shelter in the pavilion,' Kit said, pointing to the structure just off the path.

'The rain will sober you up, Mr Whitely,' Locke said, unmoved.

Kit breathed out, a long sigh as he nerved himself. Then he said, 'You don't want me sober, Alex.'

Locke's unruffled expression flickered.

Hah, thought Kit. *Doesn't fuck men like me, my pretty little arse.*

The big man took a half-step towards him, and then the skies opened and the rain became a downpour. In unspoken accord, they ran for the pavilion, Kit unlocking the double entrance doors with a practised flick of his Art.

Inside, it was dark and musty. The shutters were all closed, the gaslights covered for winter, and the small amount of daylight that invaded through the cracks grey with the rain. The cushions had been put away in storage, so that only dusty wooden benches stood in tiered rows around the small circular stage. The rain was deafening on the roof, an orchestra made solely of percussion.

'Go stand in the middle of the stage,' Locke ordered Kit, raising his voice to be heard over the rain. 'Don't move from there.'

Kit did so, glancing around. His coat was steaming slightly, his Artisan body heat drying his clothes from the inside out. The double doors were the only threshold within easy reach. Locke grabbed the nearest bench and dragged it until it was at the very bottom of the steps to the stage. He dusted off a patch with a handkerchief before sitting, facing Kit. He slowly began to put himself back into order.

He took off his rent and bloodied coat and eyed it as if it had personally disappointed him before shaking the rain beads off its quality wool and laying it on the bench beside him. He started on the buttons of his pretty apricot and cream striped waistcoat.

'What a splendid waistcoat,' Kit said. 'Yes, baby, take it off for me, do.'

Locke paused in unbuttoning it, shot a wry glance at Kit, and then calmly resumed, laying it on top of the coat.

'That shirt's not nearly wet enough,' Kit said, shifting his weight slowly from side to side.

Again Locke paused and smiled before stripping off his necktie and rolling his sleeves up over his forearms, showing smooth, tanned skin packed with sleek muscles and marred with injury.

He had a deep slice across his bicep and a few more shallow cuts across his wrists and forearms from the later fight, plus what looked like a rat bite on his ankle when he pulled his trouser leg up to examine it. He wiped these wounds down with another clean handkerchief, binding the deeper cut with the necktie. Then he neatened his shirt and disconsolately put the waistcoat and ruined coat back on, ignoring Kit's ostentatiously disappointed sigh. Then he carefully put his hair to rights with a comb from a pocket.

Kit watched him until he was done. His desire for Locke had been doused when the cuffs had gone on him, but it was still there, percolating under Kit's controlled exterior. He let it rise.

He went partway down the steps to stand between the man's thighs, which Locke obligingly parted to let him in closer. Kit was on the last step, giving him some much-needed height over the sitting Viking. Locke tilted his head back and looked at Kit's mouth.

Kit slid his hands in Locke's hair, lowered his mouth towards Locke's...and then ruffled the smooth locks dramatically.

'Petty creature,' said Locke mildly, picking up his comb again.

It had been in the way of a test. Intentions aren't actions, Locke had said. Kit, who had had to be disciplined in both thought and action for many years, had been intending, hard, to kiss Locke. The man had readily picked up on that intention; the simultaneous intention to despoil his hair had been masked.

But now, of course, Kit had to disguise that it had been a test, there was simply no help for that. So he leaned down again and made good on the original intention. Locke had been caught with his hands up, fixing his hair; he dropped the comb and wrapped both arms around Kit, pulling him close. Their mouths were urgent against each other. Kit began to hum.

Locke took him by the hips and gently pushed him so that he stumbled backwards up the stairs. 'I *really* like drunk Kit,' he said. 'I think drunk Kit needs to go back to the middle of the stage and stay there so I don't feel more like a cad than I already do.'

'I think honourable Alex needs to get on the goddamned floor,' said Kit, and yanked him forwards off the bench.

Locke had been at least half-prepared for it; Kit had acted on the

39

intention very quickly but it was enough warning for Locke to catch himself on his knees and one hand. Kit straddled his thighs and kissed him all the way to the ground, letting him twist so that he was lying on the shallow stairs with his head towards the stage, his foot kicking the bench out of the way.

Kit was humming again, and Locke twisted his hands into his damp curls and held him even tighter against his hot and insistent mouth.

Kit suspected Alexander Locke had completely forgotten that Kit was his less-than-sober prisoner.

'Kit,' Locke broke the kiss to say. 'Come up here and fuck my mouth for me.'

At this point, Kit Whitely also completely forgot that he was Locke's less-than-sober prisoner.

He was too disciplined to let the thought of his prick in Locke's gorgeous mouth distract him for long, though. He crawled up the length of Locke's body in obedience to the summons. Here he had choices, but Kit, for all the caution and control he had had to learn as the darling of the criminals of London, was, at heart, a risk-taker, and so he took the riskier option.

He held up the cuffs from his own pocket and said, 'May I, Mr Locke?'

It might very well have recalled Locke to his original purpose here. But Kit was straddling his chest with his arousal tenting his trousers right there in Locke's face and his only intention, true and bright, was to chain the man up so they could play.

That was, very firmly, Kit's *only* intention. That would make Locke feel very safe.

Locke hesitated infinitesimally, glancing over Kit's head, before saying, 'By all means, please do, Mr Whitely.'

Very safe, indeed.

The big man obligingly raised his wrists above his head so that Kit could cuff one wrist, loop the chain through the railing of the stairs, and cuff the other. He slid the key from Locke's coat and set it aside, quite deliberately, an inch out of Locke's shackled reach.

Then he rose, standing with his feet on either side of Locke's chest. 'So good, baby,' he mocked.

'Oh, *come on*,' said Locke, with just the slightest touch of irritation. He'd figured it out.

Kit smirked. 'I do not believe you lay there and let me do that. Not bad for a pissant little thief.'

'It was not your thieving skills that got me on my back, my lad. Where are you going?' He hooked his leg up, shoving his knee into the back of

Kit's leg, knocking him forwards so he fell onto Locke, catching himself with his hands on either side of Locke's face.

'Mr Whitely,' Locke said. 'I do not have any objections to fucking my captor.'

'What?'

'Finish what you started, lover. Your cock, my mouth. I won't bite.'

Kit laughed, breathless. Locke had infected him with enough recklessness that he leaned in for one last kiss, only breaking it when Locke rattled the cuffs as he shifted his arms. The Viking might very well be capable of breaking either the chain or the railing if he strained those big arm muscles hard enough, so Kit slid off him, backing away.

Locke sighed out, with a drawn-out and heartfelt *fuuuuck* mixed into the exhalation. 'At least move the key a little closer,' he said, smiling his feral smile.

Kit tapped the side of his own head. 'I think you can intuit that I have no intention of doing that, Alex. Enjoy the rest of your day, though.'

'Oh, you are *such fun*, Whitely. See you very soon.'

Kit, still hazy with alcohol, couldn't stop an answering smile, just as wild and wanton as Locke wanted it to be. He had been nothing but caution and control for *years*; Alexander Locke and his spicy sandalwood smell and his warm hazel eyes and his wolfish smile—and three whisky shots on an empty stomach—had put paid to that.

He was still smiling and backing away to the doors, the threshold, when he heard a change in the song of the rain at the door and felt a presence at his back.

'Duck,' Locke advised.

Kit did, dropping into a fast half-crouch and darting forwards before spinning around to see who his new assailant was. It was the Valkyrie, soaking wet, hair plastered to her head, face powder and eye paint running….and black eyes and an ugly swollen nose extremely apparent. *Oh, balls.*

She was at least directing her killer glare past him, to where Locke was sprawled full length on the stairs, messy hair, dishevelled clothing, shackled wrists, comfortable smile.

'*Really?*' she said. 'Are you fucking kidding me, Lexi?'

Kit, by this time, was kneeling beside Locke, hand over the keyholes on the cuffs—no need to mess around with the fiddly little key—quite ready to set his own personal Viking on the Valkyrie. At her exclamation, irritated and undeniably on familiar terms with her audience, he froze and lifted his gaze to Locke's.

Locke smiled at him.

'Were you delaying me till she got here?' Kit hissed.

'Wasn't sure she *would* get here,' Locke said, and shrugged. 'You've got a choice, my lad. Who's bringing you in, the charming man who promised to keep you safe or the infuriated woman whose *nose you broke*?'

The man truly had a line in impeccable logic. Kit unlocked the cuffs.

Locke flicked them off quickly enough that Kit, with a frisson, suspected he was well used to wearing them in bed play. He rose, cuffs loose in one hand, and put Kit behind him with a sweep of the other hand, facing the looming Valkyrie with his easy confidence.

'*Mine*, Lulu,' he said.

Kit snorted at that. 'Lulu? Really?'

She glared. Locke turned around and Kit was subject to glares from both of them.

'Yes. Really,' said Locke, suddenly sounding very cold, every inch the Agency enforcer his ready smile made it easy to forget he was.

Kit shuffled backwards, put out and confused. 'If she's going to have a nickname, it quite plainly should be Brynhildr or Herja, or bloody Boadicea if you want to keep it local. Lulu sounds like she should be pouring the tea at a little girl's tea party, for God's sake.'

Locke turned around again to face Lulu—no, *really?*—whose expression was at war with itself. Kit took the opportunity to glide back another step.

Locke's hand shot back to close hard on his wrist. 'Don't even think about it, Mr Whitely.'

'I wasn't thinking about it in the slightest,' said Kit, thinking, *Balls, I was, in the fullest*; he'd been about to sidle backwards and off to the doors, leaving the two of them to fight it out. He was going to have work awfully hard to keep his intentions masked around this one.

Locke cast an amused look over his shoulder, hand tightening around his wrist. *Can you read my actual thoughts?* Kit asked him. As he sobered up, he was doubting his own guess that it was only intentions. Locke showed no change of expression. It didn't mean much; the man had already proven he was a dab hand at deception.

'Must say I'm pleased to see you here, Lulu,' Locke said.

'Yes, I could tell,' she said acidly, 'from how helpful you were when this little fucker knocked me on my arse and broke my nose.'

'Yeah, he did, didn't he?' Locke said, with a rather gratifying *Isn't he marvellous?* tone to it. 'I couldn't give away that I knew you. I needed him to let his guard down.'

Kit thought, *I will bite you.* Locke's attention didn't waver from the new bounty hunter.

Kit started to raise his captured wrist towards his mouth, fully intending, *intending*, to sink his teeth into Locke's hand. Locke yanked him, wrenching him hard enough to make his arm and shoulder throb. Kit bit off a yelp.

'No *biting*.' He didn't even bother to look at Kit this time, which annoyed Kit more than the painful correction had.

'You've got him now, quite apparently.' Lulu's gaze was cold and predatory on Kit like she wanted to eat his face.

Despite himself, he shifted closer into the shelter of Locke's bulk. No wonder the man hadn't taken his eyes off her to look at Kit. She might have gone him if he had.

'I have.' Locke clicked his fingers twice and Lulu's eyes snapped away from Kit and onto him. His smile was gone. 'For the plan we both agreed on, right?'

'Mmm. About that, Lexi.'

'No.' Locke sounded more alarmed than resolute, and Kit casually began to assess the pavilion again for escape routes. It still didn't look good. 'We agreed. Agency headquarters. All Saints' Day.'

The Valkyrie pushed her hair from her eyes. Her braid had mostly come undone and her hair was a sodden tangle about her face. '*You* agreed with your own self. I had no way to pursue my plan at the time. Now I do.'

Kit heard Locke inhale. Tension went right up his spine. He was suddenly standing like a soldier. 'You found it.'

'I know where they hid it. I know how to get to it. And I need him to open the way.' She pointed at Kit, who, partly consciously, partly instinctively, shuffled in even closer to Locke so that he was brushing against that rigid spine.

That meant he felt Locke's determined effort to relax. His voice was light when he next spoke. 'Of course. Disappointing, Lucinda, if logical. Feeling a little betrayed, I have to say.'

Hands on hips, she said, 'I don't want the discussion again. We've gone in circles about it enough.'

'Yeah, all right,' Locke said. 'Not happy. My fault for sharing the whole plan with you, I suppose. Telling you about Whitely and his unique skillset. *Trusting* you.'

'Exactly,' said the big woman, eyes frosty. She showed no overt sign of distress at Locke's hurt disapproval, except that her fingers dug hard into her hips.

'Can't help but feel that my easy-going nature is being somewhat taken advantage of.' Locke's fingers squeezed Kit's wrist. 'By everyone here.'

'I want the thief, Alexander. I *need* the thief.'

'Not a thief,' Kit said—to empty air, for all the attention either of them paid.

'He is the only one, the *only one*, who can open the door I need opening. It's why they want him dead.'

'Ah,' said Locke. 'I understand the assassination bounty now. I should have checked for new commissions before I moved on him.'

'Who's they?' Kit asked.

'Never you mind,' Lulu snapped. 'Alexander, you said you'd help me.'

'I promised I'd help you get justice. Not this.'

'The help was contingent on your plan being the only choice, then? Sounds familiar.'

Locke's body tightened. That last remark had been an arrow and it had hit its target true. 'I want to do right by you, Lulu. But what you want… It's an appalling thing, you know it is.'

Lulu rolled her shoulders, letting her hands drop, deliberately shifting to a more relaxed stance, conciliatory. 'I saw off the pied piper. Village is clear.'

Locke shrugged, unimpressed. 'We can't be partners in this, Lulu. I hope we're not going to have a problem?'

His bluntness was damnably dangerous in Kit's opinion, given her size and air of repressed rage and violence.

'We won't.' She rolled her shoulders again, then squared them. 'We can come to a deal, though, can't we, Lexi?'

The Viking held up a firm hand. 'I do not support your plan.'

She made a quacking duck sort of gesture with her own hand. 'Yap, yap, and around the circle we go again. I know you don't. You've told me. I get it. But we can make a fucking deal here, Lexi. You'll do that for me. Let me have the thief, he'll do the job, then you can hand him over to the Agency for All Saints', and then maybe we'll get both our plans to fruition, right? I get my vengeance and you get your justice.'

Kit sucked in a breath, pulling back on Locke's hold on him. He reminded himself again that he had never yet escaped custody by fighting. Locke glanced at him, face unreadable. He smiled and turned back to Lulu.

'Lovely thought. Not up to me.' He jerked his thumb backwards at Kit. 'I've taken him prisoner, not made him my slave. Ask him. If he wants to do it, I'll go along with it.'

Kit had slackened his resistance to Locke's hold in surprise.

'And there's those big eyes again.' Locke watched him over his shoulder. 'Where have you been, my lad, that a bit of common decency makes you look at me like that?'

Where had Locke been, Kit wondered, that he thought decency was common.

The tension in the air had dissipated now Locke had been Lulu's definition of reasonable, but she still sounded testy as she said, 'You're giving him more choices than me, you realise, Lexi?'

Locke shrugged. Lulu raised her eyes to the sky before addressing Kit.

'Mr Whitebrickleyhurst. My name is Lucinda Llewellyn, Mrs Peter Llewellyn.'

'That's a Welsh name,' Kit said. Locke had let go of his wrist. He shifted backwards again. His only intention was to keep distance from Lulu, whose underpinning rage was terrifying. That was his only intention. 'You can't be Welsh, you're a giant Valkyrie.'

'My husband was Welsh,' she said, glaring again. 'You only think I'm giant because you're little.'

'That's what I said,' said Locke.

Kit looked between these two big people and said, 'I'm really not.'

'You only think that because you've been living in a village of truly tiny people for months,' Locke told him.

Mrs Llewellyn, Lulu, said, 'Mr Whitebrickleyhurst, I'm offering you a job.'

'Just Whitely,' he said. 'Kit Whitely, and I'm not a thief.'

'A lot of people in London would beg to differ.'

'I'm not a thief,' Kit said.

Looking at his feet as if embarrassed, thinking only of the rain, he drifted away across the stage, as aimless as he knew how to be. The only place to go was off the stage, an easy jump, and either or both of the two giants would easily stop him before he got to the door.

'Let me tell you about the job, Mr Whitely,' Lulu said.

Kit paused at the edge of the stage. 'I don't care about the job, Mrs Llewellyn,' he said over his shoulder absently.

An edge was, he thought, a type of threshold. It was not a type of threshold he'd ever tried to use. He would need a matching edge for the other end and that was frightening to contemplate. Here, surely, the only edge he could cross to would be the eaves of the roof of the pavilion, with the rain pouring down and the tiles slippery and treacherous.

Still. He began to gather the last remnants of his Art to twist it into an Artwork.

'Your kitten's up to something,' he heard Lulu say.

'Tell me about it,' said Locke.

Kit heard Locke coming up behind him; he stepped off the edge, pushing his Art out to find the other side of the threshold. He grasped nothing, and the power fizzled, wasted. He landed on the wooden floor of the pavilion with a thump and made a small huff of annoyance.

Locke looked down at Kit. Kit looked back up at Locke. 'I have a headache,' he said. 'Take me to bed.'

'Demanding, isn't he?' said Lulu. She hadn't moved. 'Oh dear, he'll have you wrapped around his little finger in no time, Lexi.'

The Viking turned back to her. 'Care to stand watch with me, Lulu?' he asked mildly. 'Can't leave this one unwatched or he'll be out a bloody window.'

'No, I don't think I will,' she said. 'When you fall asleep and he escapes, he's fair game again. And if I catch you, Mr Whitely, I won't be nearly as scrupulous as Alexander here.'

Locke glanced down at Kit with an amused expression meant to remind Kit where his bread was buttered. Kit shrugged and went to wait on a bench until the rain stopped.

After a while, he lay down. Sobering up during the day was no fun at all.

4

$\mathcal{E}$VERY TABLE WAS FULL IN KNIGHTSTONE Inn and every table went silent when Locke escorted Kit in through the broken front door, the eyes of what looked like the population of the whole village avid upon them. Locke gave a little shake of his head, touching his temple briefly. There were a lot of people, and therefore, surely, a lot of intentions.

Having rested enough for his Art to be strengthening again, Kit had unlocked the village as they'd come back into it, but most people had already exited by their back doors by then. And gone straight to the taproom at the inn to spectate the next act of the show that was Kit's so-entertaining arrest.

Lulu, on the other hand, had waited till the rain eased the merest fraction before disappearing as abruptly as she'd arrived. Kit supposed she'd end up at the inn eventually, but for now she was about her own business.

Mr Davey Knight, Edith's father, came to greet them, giving Kit a cautious nod before turning to Locke. 'Can I 'elp 'ee, sir?'

'I need a room, and a meal,' said Locke shortly.

'I would like a bath, please, Mr Knight,' Kit said. He nodded to the room, full of people mostly friendly towards him.

'I need the room with the smallest window, which you'll need to board up,' went on Locke. 'I'll need a pallet or truckle to fit in front of the door. If there's a wardrobe or anything else with any sort of door, it needs to go out.'

Mr Knight's face had gone blank, and his soft voice shifted to a more formal register, the same one Edith used with strangers. 'Aye, sir, we can arrange that,' he said. 'Would you like to sit and take your meal while we sort it for you? My wife'll bring 'ee a plate dreckly.'

Locke looked sharply around the room. His hand touched his temple again. 'Take us to the room and send a tray up. I'll pay extra for a fire, too.'

'And the bath, please,' said Kit, catching hold of Locke's sleeve.

'No baths, no meal for the prisoner.'

Kit, who was ravenous, may have let out a whimper at that.

'Oh, no, sir, that a'en proper.' Mr Knight sounded both nervous and indignant in a flustered sort of way.

'Food powers Art.' Locke raised his voice. 'You've been harbouring a notorious thief. He's aided and abetted at least one assassination, too. Don't compound things by making trouble for an Agency enforcer.'

The room, whose buzz had been, now Kit thought about it from Locke's point of view, on the threatening side, quietened. Mr Knight took a step back and looked uncertainly at Kit.

'It's not how it sounds,' Kit said softly. 'Ask Edith, please.'

Locke took his arm and moved him briskly up the stairs. At the top, he paused only for Mr Knight to open a door for him before pushing Kit in and closing the door behind them. He slumped into the room's only chair, rubbing his temples, while Kit sat cross-legged on the bed.

'I never wanted to help kill anyone,' Kit said, looking down at his hands in his lap.

Locke ignored him. Kit looked about. He'd not had cause to be in the inn's lodgings before. The room was simple but cosy. It held the big comfortable bed, Locke's plain wooden chair next to a toiletry table set with an ewer and bowl and a pretty vase of fresh flowers from Mrs Knight's garden, a small fireplace in one corner, a full-length cheval mirror on a stand in the other, and in between them, a small window overlooking the stables.

Locke sighed and straightened. He began to groom his clothes, compulsively arranging his coat to make the rents from the knife less visible, before taking out his comb. He was visibly relaxing as he returned himself to as close to impeccable as he could get without a bath and a full change of clothes.

'Is it messy in your head?' Kit asked him. 'Is that why you have to be neat all the time?'

Locke kept right on ignoring him. Kit got off the bed and went over to the vase, drew a damask rose from the bouquet and began to pluck the petals, dropping them one by one to the rug. Locke sat through five petals before he stood and snatched the rose from Kit's hand, jammed it back into the vase, and picked up the scattered petals. He stacked them beside the vase. Neatly.

Kit hummed and retreated to the bed. 'Let me have a bath, Locke. I'm so very filthy.'

Locke might have been gritting his teeth; he kept running the comb through his perfectly groomed hair. Kit snarled his fingers into his own wild curls, now tangled beyond hope from his exertions and the rain. Locke watched his fingers.

'Let me have a bath and I'll let you comb my hair,' Kit murmured. 'You can make me just as neat as you like, Mr Locke.'

Locke leaned back, his smile at last returning. The people downstairs, their multitude of intentions, had truly disconcerted him, it seemed. No wonder he'd been so abrupt with Mr Knight.

A brisk knock sounded then, and Mr Knight himself came in, with a Knight cousin carrying boards, hammer and nails, to block off the window. More Knight cousins came in with a truckle bed, another to light the fire, and Mrs Knight herself carried up the lunch tray.

She gave Locke a challenging look as she plopped it down on the table. It held two plates of roasted chicken, creamy potatoes and fresh green beans from her garden, and two cups of ale.

Locke had begun to look tense again with the influx of people but he still managed a charmingly rueful nod of concession to the lady of the house.

'And the lad's bath an'all?' she demanded.

'He may have his bath, yes,' said Locke.

It took a while to set that up. Knightstone Inn was too old to have a modern bathroom. They had to wheel the truckle bed out again, and drag in the big tin hip tub, and then bring large brass cans of hot water from the kitchen to fill it.

Kit regretted the trouble, but it was absolutely necessary, and so was the food. He applied himself to cleaning his plate, mopping the gravy up with bread just as the two Knight cousins ferrying the buckets gave a final nod to Locke and departed for the last time. Locke had drunk both cups of ale, mainly, Kit suspected, to stop him getting hold of his share.

Kit eyed off the bath, steaming and fragrant with lavender oil that Mrs Knight made herself with help from her daughters. He didn't move yet, though. He watched Locke.

Stripping off his coat and waistcoat and hanging them neatly on pegs by the table, Locke scooped the ewer full of clean, hot bath water. He filled the bowl, and used a few of his endless array of clean handkerchiefs and the fresh cake of citrus soap delivered by Mrs Knight to wash himself down, paying attention to the wounds he hadn't been able to clean properly earlier. He wiped over his cuffs and collar with the same devotion, careful not to rinse the starch out of them, and draped them over a chair back. He put his boots outside the door for oiling and polishing.

Then, in shirttails and bare feet, he dragged his chair in front of the door, and sat, rocking it back until his head was leaning against the smooth wood of the door. 'Take your bath then, Mr Whitely.'

'Are you going to sit there and watch?' Kit asked, somewhat aghast. Only somewhat.

Locke tapped a finger to his temple again. 'You are *very purely* intending to have a bath. I've never met someone so very intent on completing such a simple task. I think it's an escape attempt. So, yes, I'm going to watch you.'

'You've boarded up the window and are in front of the only door. How do you think I can escape?'

'I'm going to watch you and find out.'

'If you think it's an escape attempt, why are you letting me do it at all?'

'So I can watch you, Kit,' Locke said, his wolfish smile suddenly very apparent.

'Oh, well, that's not—'

Kit cut himself off, inwardly sighing. It would've been too much to expect for Locke to leave the room while he bathed, but he'd hoped the man would at least be polite enough to turn his back. He took off his coat and threw it on to the bed, noting Locke's twitch; the man, without a doubt, wanted to pick it up and hang it neatly, as he'd done with his own coat. He took off his boots and stockings, deliberating kicking them aside for maximum disarray, again noting Locke's eyes drawn to the mess.

Kit surveyed the clutter with satisfaction; no one would ever guess he'd been trained to be a manservant in the Orphanage.

He started to unbutton his shirt under Locke's unwavering regard. 'It's not as if I haven't been forced to undress in front of men like you before.'

'Oh, *low*,' said Locke. 'I'm not bloody men like me.' He raised his gaze so that he was maintaining steady eye contact with Kit.

That was even more confronting than having the man blatantly watch him undress. 'Am I still safe from you?' Kit asked abruptly.

'Yes,' said Locke. 'You're safe from me. Unless you'd like to invite me to fuck you?' Kit made a scoffing noise and Locke added, 'On that note, stop bloody inviting me when you have no intention of follow-through.'

At which, Kit lowered his eyelashes and *intended* to go over there and suck Locke's prick. He saw Locke blink and rock his chair forwards so all four legs were on the ground.

Kit hummed a negatory trill of notes. 'Intention isn't action,' he said. 'Thoughts aren't permission.'

'That's just rude, Mr Whitely,' Locke said, subsiding. 'Quite the vivid imagination you have, though. Go on. Get your trousers off, my lad. All the way.'

Kit did so, and his drawers, not without feeling like blushing. But he stubbornly maintained his composure under Locke's steady gaze, which was entirely on his face and still heating him to an unwarranted degree. Naked, he climbed into the bath.

As he stepped into the water, he gathered his Art, replenished by the meal exactly as Locke had feared. The liminal nature of the surface of water made it a threshold, as long as its containment was manmade. It was not as easy as the type of threshold that people regularly crossed, but it could be wrestled into service. Kit suspected he could make just about anything into a threshold, if his own mind could be made to believe it.

He, therefore, had the unusual experience of stepping through hot water to stand in freezing cold water, the water of the fountain in the village square.

He breathed. The fountain was wide and shallow, and therefore he was going to have to submerse himself to cross the threshold all the way. Then he would be naked, drenched in icy water, and on the far side of the village from the standing stones.

It was not the most sensible escape plan he'd ever had. It was, currently, the only escape plan he had, and he'd quickly learnt to take any opportunity, once a bounty hunter caught him. His lodging room was only a few streets from the square. He would have to risk going there to dry off and dress before running for the stones. He wouldn't feel cold for long.

He took one more breath, deep.

'Ah, Kit?' said Locke, and then said, 'Jesus fuck, it's not doors!' and sprang across the room at him.

Kit dropped into the water, through the threshold. He almost made it, but Locke got a hand in his hair and hauled him back across the threshold from the fountain into the bath. The open threshold snapped shut and Kit wailed in agony, lightning bursts erupting all over his body, too fast for the part of him that swallowed pain to protect him.

There was a thump, the door of the chamber flinging open. 'What are you doing to him?' Edith shouted.

'Nothing!' said Locke, who still had one hand buried in Kit's hair, the other arm wrapped around his shoulders as he dragged him out of the bath, scraping the skin of the backs of his legs on the tin edge.

Kit had cut off his outcry, containing it to a single whimper as Locke threw him on the bed and then, belatedly, covered him with his coat. Kit turned on his side and curled into a ball. He felt the mattress compress as Locke knelt beside him, his hands on his back, stroking.

'Is this how enforcers of the Agency carry on, molesting their prisoners? I am going to put in a complaint about you, you horrible man, you—'

'I'm all right,' Kit managed to say. 'Edith, it's all right, I'm all right.' He opened his eyes. Locke was leaning over him, Edith hovering in front of them. They both looked horrified. 'It turns out it hurts to get dragged back across a threshold.'

Edith took his hand and rubbed his knuckles, glaring at Locke. He shrugged helplessly. 'He was trying to escape, Miss Knight.' He was still gently stroking Kit's back.

Kit sat up, hugging the coat to him so his naked skin wasn't visible. The Knights were understanding, but there had to be limits. At the movement, Alex looked down at his own wet shirt, clinging to him so that his nipples and well-defined chest muscles were visible through the soaked material. He looked like he wanted his own coat.

Edith wasn't one to notice the form of the opposite sex; she was fixed on Kit and his distress. 'I brought you a change of clothes.' She still looked fierce, with a layer of uncertainty over it.

'Thank you, Miss Knight,' said Kit, huddling under his coat, not looking at her. *I don't need your help.*

Edith huffed. 'Fine! I'll go. But I'm coming back to make sure he's truly all right, and you can't stop me, Mr Locke. Is there anything else you want from your room, m'luv?'

Kit shook his head, and Edith dropped fresh clothes beside him. 'He's freezing, Mr Locke, he'll catch cold,' she said accusingly as she left, closing the door behind her.

Kit was, indeed, shivering violently, with the aftermath of the pain and the ice-cold fountain water settling deep into his bones and his Art running low. He didn't often feel the cold like this, and he didn't much like it.

Locke picked him up bodily and lowered him into the warm water of the bath before he could even struggle against it. The big man took the cloth left by Mrs Knight with the soap, soaked it in the water and began to run it over Kit's cold shoulders.

'You're not lovers but she has access to your lodgings,' he said.

'One of her many aunts runs it. Any Knight could get into my room.' Kit winced away as the cloth came firmly over his shoulder blade.

'Hmm, I was yanking you around, wasn't I? You *were* trying to bite me.'

He stood and went out; either he'd forgotten how easily Kit could have ducked under the water and vanished or he knew he was far too exhausted to try his Art again yet; Kit's lack of any intentions at all would have told him that.

Kit lay in the warmth, his limbs languorous, dozing. He heard Locke return, and scented the warm, earthy smell of Mrs Knight's lanolin salve with its mix of healing herbs. Locke's fingers rubbed over his shoulder blade, easing the ache there, not helping the ache elsewhere. It felt too good in the aftermath of the pain, a familiar sensation.

'Your Art's not doors, is it, Kit? What did you say? Thresholds?'

Kit kept his eyes closed.

'Thresholds,' repeated Locke. 'You can cross any threshold to any other threshold?'

'No,' said Kit reluctantly. He looked at himself in the mirror across the room. His olive skin looked sallow and there were dark smudges under his eyes. Locke loomed behind him, large fingers moving over his shoulder as he rubbed in the salve. 'They have to match.'

'In a window and out a locked door,' Locke pointed out.

'They're close enough.' He paused. 'I think because they're both in the same building. But I couldn't go from a window to a garden gate, for example.'

'Water of the bath to...?'

Kit went mutinously silent, closing his eyes again.

Locke chuckled. 'Thresholds,' he said for the third time. 'Jesus, Kit, I don't know how you've ever been brought in.'

'I appreciate the vote of confidence, Mr Locke,' Kit said in his most politely acerbic tones, opening his eyes so he could give Locke a pointed look via the mirror.

Locke smiled back at him and Kit had to look away.

'What's this scar here along your back and shoulder?' Locke asked. 'Looks like a burn?'

'There was a fire,' Kit said. 'Mrs Knight gave me that same salve for it. Most of it healed well. That was the bit I couldn't reach by myself.'

Locke waited but Kit did not feel obliged to be further forthcoming. 'You couldn't ask Mrs Knight to salve the part you couldn't reach?' he asked eventually. 'She's a grandmother and a healer, she's surely seen plenty of skin in her time.'

Kit met Locke's eyes in the mirror. It had not occurred to him to ask Mrs Knight, or anyone, for help. Even now, he frowned at the idea.

The big man shook his head and applied a thick layer of salve over the scarred skin. Kit stepped out of the bath, ignoring the proffered hand. Locke took him to the fire, dropping the small jar of salve into his coat's pocket as he passed its peg. He picked up the towel that he'd draped over the chair by the fire to warm.

'I'll take care of myself,' said Kit, trying to take the towel from him. 'I don't need help.'

'You made me a promise, Mr Whitely, in exchange for that bath. As neat as I like, you said.'

Kit paused, surprised. He had considered it more a jest than a promise. But he was not a man who lightly broke a promise if he had had to make one, so he held his arms out from his sides and said, 'Well, then, best of luck to you, Mr Locke.'

Locke set to his task with the same meditative leisureliness with which he had tended to his own grooming. He stroked the towel gently over Kit's arms, shoulders and back, down over his arse and between his legs without any reluctance or special attention, and along both legs, bending to dry his toes thoroughly, Kit twitching at the tickle.

Last, he wrapped the towel around Kit's hair to stop it dripping on his clothes while he dressed him. He knelt to help Kit into his trousers, drawing them up his legs and fastening them with steadfast neutrality. He ran his hands over the cloth, tweaking it here and there, making it sit to his exacting requirements, his palms warm and firm through the fabric as he smoothed them down Kit's legs.

Kit lifted his eyes to the ceiling and reminded himself of the little-known fact that unfulfilled desire was even better than alcohol for powering Art. He had no idea where his intentions should be right now. His prick had its own ideas, but they both ignored that.

Standing, Locke guided Kit's shirt up his arms and over his shoulders, before kneeling again. He did the buttons up one by one, all slow focus that really should be turned to better application. His breath was hot on Kit's belly, his fingertips brushing against his skin as he fastened each button.

'This is the oddest seduction I have ever been subject to,' Kit murmured.

'Not trying to seduce you,' Locke said serenely, before glancing up with a half-smothered grin. 'Is it working?'

Kit bit the inside of his cheek so he wouldn't smile back. Locke returned his attention to his work, still looking amused at his own self. Kit's eyes began to droop again under the gentle ministrations of the big man's fingers, as he adjusted the sit of the shirt. It gave him more trouble than the trousers; he was frowning as he fiddled with the sleeves.

Then he draped the towel over Kit's shoulders, guiding him to sit on the edge of the bed. He settled behind him with the comb in his hand. It was this Kit had had in mind when he had wished Locke luck, more than his worn and cheaply made clothes, a valet's curse. But Locke worked with methodical patience, using fingers and comb to tame Kit's damp curls without causing him a moment of pain.

By the time he was done, Kit was relaxed against his chest, ensconced between his strong thighs. Kit turned his head a little towards Locke's neck, scenting the fresh citrus overlaying the spicy sandalwood. Eyelids were as heavy as his limbs, he luxuriated in the feel of Locke's fingers tingling over his scalp and along his nape. He was given all over to lassitude. He let his hands relax onto Locke's thighs, high.

'Sweetheart?' Locke murmured into his ear, one hand spread broad over Kit's stomach, warm through the cloth of his shirt.

'Sod it, I'm pathetic,' Kit sighed. He heard Locke's hesitation in the silence that followed; he imagined him tilting his head, as he did when he was puzzled. 'Take that as your invitation, Alex.'

Locke shifted to let Kit lie out on the bed, lowering to lie on his side next to him, propped on an elbow. To his credit, there was no triumph or smugness on his face, just a slow delight, just that delicious smile. He nestled into Kit, leaning over him to kiss the corner of his mouth.

Kit hummed sleepily. He started to put his hand to Locke's face, and it fell back to the bed, too heavy to lift.

'Damn it,' Locke said, very quietly. 'Stay awake a little longer, Kit, can you?'

He couldn't.

Kit woke for supper.

He'd been lying in Alex's arms, half-aware of the big man's hand making long strokes along his side and his breath warm against Kit's nape, his lips brushing the bare skin there. Kit had been beginning to rouse properly, had let his own hand slide back to rest on Locke's hip and subtly pull him closer.

Then Locke was up, moving swiftly, just before the diffident knock came. Kit, still dopey from the heavy sleep, watched as the Knights swarmed them again, removing the bath and bringing back the truckle bed. Mrs Knight brought the supper tray, savoury with two hearty serves of aromatic stew, bread, fruit, and ale on the side.

Behind Mrs Knight came one of the young Knight cousins, carrying a tray of tea things. She was shaking so hard the cups and saucers rattled as she crossed the room. Locke smoothly took the tray from her, smiling gently and taking a moment to murmur something soothing to her and to give sincere thanks to Mrs Knight, who harrumphed but looked reluctantly appeased.

He didn't like that the girl feared him. He didn't like that Mrs Knight disliked him. Interesting.

Kit could feel Locke's hesitancy when Kit took one of the bowls of stew. He had slept now, and was about to eat again. His Art would be back in full force, though the full force of Kit's Art was featherweight compared to some other Artisans'.

'Did I fall asleep?' he said. 'What a shame. I'm sure I'll be very energetic after some food.'

Locke, narrowed-eyed but smiling at Kit's barefaced audacity, let him eat. He claimed both ales again, drinking them off quickly while Kit bitched the teapot for his own thirst. It was oddly companionable to pour out tea for his captor. He kept his eyes lowered as he pushed Locke's teacup towards him.

The Viking slid the truckle bed across the doorway and sat there with his cup. Edith came back to check on Kit and was not complimentary when Locke couldn't open the door wide because of the truckle in the way. Kit spoke to her through the door to reassure her and take possession of a handful of books she had brought for him, including Dickens's latest.

He put his empty bowl back on the tray and spread out on the big bed with the Dickens book. Edith had already cut the pages for him. Locke lay comfortably on the truckle with a few of the others. He had put his spectacles back on as he leafed desultorily through the pages.

'Oh, are those real?' Kit asked, glancing up from his page. He was very taken with Locke in his spectacles, exactly as he had been when he'd first laid eyes on him. 'I thought they were part of your trickery.'

'I wear them for reading.' Locke wrinkled his nose endearingly. 'Not that they help.'

Kit thought of how he'd tidied the research books Edith had given him, rather than opening any of them. 'You...don't read well?'

Locke waved a hand at the page. 'I read too slowly. I have a sort of blindness, when it comes to the written word.' He gave a short laugh. 'Believe it or not, I did dream of being a naturalist, growing up. I'm a younger son. I wanted to travel the world, discovering new species. My father wanted me to be called to the bar, like him and my older brother, or at least go into the church. All options were moot when I turned out stupid.'

'You're not stupid,' said Kit, startled.

Locke tapped the cover of one book and raised an eyebrow, his smile in place.

'You wouldn't call a blind person stupid for not being able to see.' Kit paused. The adults in the Orphanage had said that sort of thing and worse. 'Not if you're a decent person, anyway. But, Mr Locke, you tracked me here through steadfast perseverance and impeccable logical reasoning. That is not, by any stretch, stupidity.'

The Viking adjusted his spectacles, shrugging, perhaps a little mollified.

'Do you think it's got to do with your Art?' Kit asked.

'Talent,' corrected Locke.

'It makes your mind messy, could that cause it? Can't you block it? I don't have to cross a threshold every time I walk through a door, couldn't you just *not* read intentions?'

'You've solved it,' Locke said gravely. 'Why did I not think of doing that at some point in the fifteen years since my talent manifested?'

Kit huffed in reluctant amusement. It was on the very tip of his tongue to offer to teach the man how to do it; Kit had, after all, wrestled his own Art into utility with no guidance, just bloody-mindedness.

But for all the man's easy-going kindness, for all Kit's irritatingly uncontrollable attraction to him, he was still an Agency enforcer. So he bit the tip of his tongue.

'Would you like me to read to you?' he asked instead. He held up *Little Dorrit*. 'Mr Dickens, unless you already followed the serial?'

Locke's smile became more real. Kit did not smile back, because he wasn't drunk or half-asleep and his defences were firmly in place. He turned back to the first chapter and began to read aloud.

When, late in the evening, he stopped reading, throat hoarse, he tucked the book under his pillow so it would make him a little uncomfortable while he slept, in the hopes of waking early. He had seen Locke glance his way as he stripped to his drawers for sleep, perhaps hoping for a repeat of his invitation or perhaps merely, generally, suspicious.

Kit turned his back and, determinedly, *intended* only to sleep, which made Locke laugh to himself, a low and knowing chuckle that made Kit's stomach flip over. Then Kit heard him get up and rolled over to check what he was doing.

The Viking padded over to his coat and took cord from a pocket, a thin white rope, tightly coiled. He looked at Kit thoughtfully.

Kit swallowed hard. If Locke tied him to the bed, he was done. Rope didn't have locks. Kit couldn't get out of a binding that didn't have locks. Every bounty hunter who'd successfully brought him in figured that one out, most sooner rather than later.

'Please don't,' he said.

'I have to, Kit,' Locke said gently.

He sat on the bed, taking Kit's arm as Kit tried to pull away and starting to tie the cord around his wrist. One glance told Kit that Locke was as perfectly competent at knots as he was at other physical skills.

He took a shallow breath. His dislike of restraint about his wrists went far deeper than the inconvenience of it. He was going to have to use that.

'Please, Locke, don't,' he whispered, deliberately allowing his genuine fear to show in his eyes and voice. 'Please.'

Kit could just about live with cold and impersonal metal cuffs about his wrists. Hands holding his wrists imprisoned were less tolerable, but he had learnt to tolerate an awful lot.

Rope on his wrists made him sick to his stomach. Ropes on his wrist woke up Christopher Whitebrickleyhurst.

Letting his very real fear show meant that his very real fear quickly overwhelmed him. Kit was not in control anymore; Christopher, fifteen, terrified, helpless, perpetually lost, had the reins. He was shaking by the time Locke knotted his first wrist to the bed and leant over him to grab his other one. Kit flailed away from him, pivoting painfully about the wrist already tied down.

Locke pressed a hand down on his chest and caught his free arm. 'Kit, I have to sleep. I can only do that if I know you can't escape.'

'Please, Alex, don't,' Kit said, begging now and not caring. He twisted his wrist in Locke's grip, the skin reddening. The room was flickering in and out of darkness. He could smell something piney and sickly-sweet, a mix of frankincense and poppy syrup. 'Please, I can't. I'll be good, please, I'll be good.'

'Jesus *fuck*,' Locke said.

He let go of Kit's arm but stayed kneeling over him with his hand pressed hard against his chest, eyes blank and fixed above Kit's head. Kit went still, a rabbit in a trap. If Locke was trying to read his intentions, he'd be getting nothing but a snowstorm; the fear had wiped every last thought from Kit's head.

He sucked in air. *Christopher*, he thought. *Five seconds. Five. Four. Three. Two. One. Stop.*

His breathing slowed. He looked up at Locke, mute and glassy-eyed and utterly at his mercy.

Locke sighed and undid Kit's other wrist with rough jerks on the knots. 'Jesus fuck, Kit, you better be here in the morning.'

Kit, intentions shielded under the blankness that was Christopher, certainly did not plan to be.

5

KIT WOKE IN DARKNESS WHEN THE fire died and a chill invaded the room just before dawn. *Little Dorrit* was digging into his ear painfully from under the edge of the pillow. He looked over at Locke. The Viking was asleep on the truckle bed right up against the door.

There was no way to step over him and use that threshold. Kit couldn't open a threshold another human was touching.

He rose from the bed, gathering his Art as he moved about the room, dressing, easing the handcuffs and a few other things from Locke's coat. Next was the riskiest bit, and he almost didn't do it, but he could see that Locke was beginning to turn in his sleep, restless. As quietly as Kit could move, he could not completely silence his intentions yet, and Locke was gradually being roused by them from his heavy sleep.

He knelt beside Locke. The man's face was gentle in sleep. Last night, once he'd untied Kit, he'd sat beside him, wordlessly stroking his hair, calming him, and probably himself. Kit assumed he would avail himself of the offer inherent in Kit's—Christopher's—panicked words. *I'll be good*, and Kit could be very good indeed.

But eventually he'd retreated, face sombre and thoughtful as he climbed into his own bed. Kit supposed he'd roused the man's protective instinct instead of his prick; either was fine if it helped him escape. Kit could not afford to be precious about his methods.

Sighing, he slowly, carefully, cuffed Locke to the truckle bed. It was well accepted that iron burnt all Artisans but was more likely to dampen active Arts like all the varieties of telekinesis, while silver worked on the more passive sorts like the telepathy variants. The silver in the cuffs might muffle Alex's talent, not as much as an Art but enough to mute Kit's conscious presence a little. And Kit was fairly sure Locke had forgotten to retrieve the key in the pavilion, so that would slow him substantially once he woke up, too.

Then he went to the mirror.

He stood before it. Like the surface of water, a mirror was something he suspected could be forced to be a threshold. Like edges, it was something he had not yet tried.

When he'd attempted to use the edge of the stage as a threshold, he'd been tired and in a hurry. He couldn't be sure it hadn't worked because it couldn't, or because that particular effort had been doomed from the start.

Now, though, facing the mirror, he was calm, fed, rested and, within limits, at his leisure. He put his hand on the frame and began to form the Artwork in his mind. He sensed the possibility immediately, and the resistance. Mirrors were not true thresholds—except in human imaginings and human stories, and human minds made thresholds. *Kit's* mind made thresholds. It would take work, but it could be done, he thought.

Fear would power his Art, but he'd already had his fill of that, when he'd let Christopher out of the dark.

And it wasn't fear that Alexander Locke inspired.

He began to think about Locke's mouth, Locke's fingers stroking over his back, through his hair, Locke's thighs hard against his, Locke's damnably warm, kind eyes. The desire he'd been ruthlessly suppressing rose, swelling his Art even as it swelled his prick.

Holy hellfire, he wanted the big man in the bed behind him so much.

He briefly wondered if this way of bolstering Art was so much less known than alcohol because there were as many female Artisans as male. The conversations that would have to happen between the sexes would be shocking. He imagined it was something that most Artisans knew privately, and never shared publicly.

Or maybe not. His Art was strange and weak, and a hard one to pin down; the closest analogy he'd ever managed was that the Artwork was a kind of key that he was forcing to the shape of the threshold's lock. He'd had to work hard to learn how to wring every last drop from it to make his threshold Artworks. Maybe other Artisans didn't have to resort to the tricks he had learnt to use.

He put the distraction aside and focussed every inch of his formidable discipline on the mirror, staring into his own eyes. He'd never had occasion to look at himself as he worked Artistry; he noted with a mix of detached interest and old dismay that his pale green eyes fairly glowed as he drew deep to make the new Artwork.

You've got the devil in you, Crispin, he heard Brother Fairweather whisper in his ear. He shook his head.

Behind him, Locke rolled over, hit the limit of the cuff and made a sleepy noise of surprise.

Kit stepped into the mirror.

And fell out of the mirror above the bar in the taproom.

Between the thump as he hit the ground and Locke's shout from upstairs, it wouldn't be long before he'd have Knights coming to investigate. Still, he could not resist an exceedingly small whoop of triumph, not for the escape, but for the new threshold he had conquered. It had been, honestly, unpleasant, cold and stifling in the instant of crossing. But he'd done it. He was glad the other mirror had been so close, making it a short traverse.

Loud scrapes followed by a thud rang out from upstairs. Locke had probably dragged the truckle bed over to his coat and discovered he didn't have the key. It sounded like he was going to smash the bed apart to get free rather than wait for assistance.

Kit shot out the hastily repaired door and down the street, running for the standing stones in the glimmer before dawn, free and clear.

He'd forgotten about the Valkyrie.

He woke up in the summer pavilion, arms very firmly bound behind his back—rope, no locks—and head throbbing. The lump on the back of his head gave a starlight burst of pain when he tried to sit up.

Lulu stood over him, hands on hips. 'Good morning, Mr Whitely.'

'Good morning, Mrs Llewellyn,' said Kit.

He got himself onto his knees and sat back on his heels, watching her. She looked much the same as yesterday, though she had tried to hide the swollen nose and bruising about her eyes under a heavy dusting of pearl powder and more eye paint than was strictly acceptable among respectable ladies. She wasn't wearing her gloves this morning. She wore rings on her right hand, one inset with diamonds, one with a sapphire, in addition to a wedding ring set with rubies on her left.

She looked surprised behind her powder. 'You're politer than I thought you'd be.'

'Courtesy costs nothing.' It cost pride, actually, but it gained laxness. 'Did you hit me?'

'I threw one of those loose setts from the road. Pegged you a bit harder than I meant to.' She neither looked nor sounded sorry about it.

He got a foot under him, and pushed up to standing on the second try. 'Are we for the station?'

'Yes.'

Her cold hazel eyes appraised him as she shouldered her pack; she, unlike Locke, had anticipated that Kit's retrieval would take longer than a single long day out from London.

She'd bound his forearms together, hands to elbows. It wasn't comfortable, especially in the shoulders, but he preferred it to the wrists.

'You can untie me,' Kit suggested. She laughed. 'Worth a try,' he said with a shrug.

He walked out of the pavilion ahead of her. The morning had dawned cool and fine. The smell of salt was in the air. In the distance, a dog barked, and the rest of the village's dogs answered in howls.

His head had almost stopped aching already—another bonus of Artistry. Although he was feeling more alert, he kept his pace slow, a little meandering. He even came to a stop once, and looked at Lulu confusedly when she prompted him onwards again. Let her think the blow to his head had left his thoughts in commotion, his reactions slow. Let her relax, strolling along behind him, much as Locke had the day before. He was going to make a dash for the Knightstone Circle when they passed the side path that went that way. It was his final play, until the train.

The dog barked again, closer.

'What the f—' Lulu said, and Kit felt fast movement behind him, and heard the thump of large bodies crashing to the earth.

Kit assumed Locke was forcefully reasserting his rights to his prisoner. He didn't look back, sprinting off for the standing stones, concentrating on his feet so as not to stumble. If he fell now, with his arms bound, he would hit the ground hard and struggle to get back up.

He reached the intact trilithon, two menhirs with a lintel, that greeted visitors to the circle beyond. He leaned a shoulder on one of the menhirs. The power of the standing stones was surging into him, as it had the one time he had come out here to reconnoitre. He'd already been dizzy from the feat of running without tripping over his own clumsiness, but the roar of power through his blood just about felled him. He was so hot he wanted to tear his coat off.

His Art was a curious, limited thing. Some other Artisans, like those in the obnoxiously famous Myriad team, could do things like flinging fireballs and ice bolts, without ever seeming to lack the Art for their flamboyant Artworks. He wondered if this was how they got to feel all the time, power theirs for the taking, boundless Artistry at their fingertips.

He risked a glance behind him as he formed the Artwork to cross the threshold to the mines. The power was there, just there, as easy as breathing. He didn't have to concentrate to gather it up and shape it; the Artwork practically formed itself as soon as he had the desire to create it.

A figure was running up the path towards him. It wasn't Lulu. It wasn't Locke. It was Edith. She had braided her golden hair into a thick plait. Her boots and the skirts of her simple day dress were soaked in morning dew. She must have cut through the woods.

'Edith!' Kit burst out. 'My God, go home!'

She drew up in front of him. 'I just helped you get away from that bounty hunter, Kit Whitely. Say thank you or keep running, but don't tell me to go home. I can hold my own.'

'She's twice your size, Edith.'

'It's not like you're that much taller than me,' Edith said huffily.

'That wasn't quite the point I was trying to make.' Then he made an awkward bow. 'Thank you, Miss Knight.'

She smiled, looking annoyingly pleased with herself, her grey-blue eyes shining, her dimples on full display. He nudged her with a shoulder and led her into the Knightstone Circle, a collection of monoliths, some linked with lintels, others standing solo. Any space between any two of the menhirs still upright would have served as a threshold. About half of the single menhirs and trilithons had fallen, but with the power of the rest of them surging through him, he could bridge the gaps. In this place, any width threshold would serve his Art.

They were now in a circle of thresholds, all of them easily in Kit's line of sight as he slowly rotated in the centre. Kit closed them all, a ripple of Artwork around the circle that barely cost him a thing. He hummed to himself on a surge of pleasure. They were safe and his Art was singing to him.

'How did you knock Mrs Llewellyn down?' he asked Edith.

'Minnie, of course,' she said cheerfully. 'A great big wolfhound leaping out of the bushes, no one's keeping their feet.' Kit must have looked alarmed—he was fairly sure Lulu would be even better armed than Locke—because she added, 'I sent her on home. She's probably run off to chase rabbits, to be honest.'

'Where you should be,' Kit said severely. 'Home. Not chasing rabbits.'

Edith pulled out another of the engraved knives of the metalworkers and turned Kit so she could saw at his bonds.

'I thought Locke took those off you.'

'These are all over the village,' she said. 'They're very pretty. The kiddies keep finding them. Ever had to disarm a teeny babbie?'

Kit was struck by this. 'Uh,' he said. 'Are there dead bodies all over the village?'

Edith laughed. 'None of us have been hurt. Well, Mr O'Hare fell over his cat and bruised his arm but that wasn't any fault of the knife fighters. Mr Locke didn't even kill any of the Artisans. He just dropped them. The Knight cousins gathered them up and put them on the train out yesterday with a flea in their ear and instructions for the conductor to hand them over to the Bristol enforcers. We'll be telling this story for years, Kit, everyone has had a lovely time.'

He wondered if they'd found the pied piper Artisan too, that Lulu had taken care of. He suspected her assistance would have been more permanent than Locke's.

His arms came loose from the ropes and he hunched forwards, the pain in his shoulders acute in the release of tension. Edith rubbed at his arms and shoulders behind him.

He turned and hugged her.

'Oh!' she said, startled.

The sprawling clan of the Knights were tolerant and openly affectionate, but Kit didn't much touch people. He'd never hugged Edith, and she in turn had quickly learned that, as odd as he was, he was particularly odd when it came to accepting affection, whether it be words or touch.

'Thank you, Miss Knight,' he said as he released her and took a few distancing steps.

'Shall we get to the caves now?' she asked, smiling at him.

'I do think you should go home, Edith.' He added, 'G'woam, m'luv,' in case plain English wasn't clear enough for her.

'Don't you Zummerzet at me, emmet!'

Kit was looking past her, along the path back to the main route to the station. Lulu was coming up it. He wasn't alarmed. The thresholds of the standing circle were closed for as long as he was standing here. They were caged, but safe.

'Too late now,' said Edith, rubbing her hands in satisfaction.

'There's really no call to sound so happy about it,' Kit said. 'All right, Edith. We're going to cross to the caves. I've not taken someone through a threshold before, but with as much power as this henge is feeding my Art, I don't think we'll have too much trouble.'

'How exciting!'

Edith bounced a little, about to say more, when Lulu strolled through the trilithon—not superstitious then—and poked at the gap between two of the menhirs of the stone circle. Her experience yesterday had taught her caution. She found the way blocked, of course, by Kit's invisible barrier. She glared at the two of them as she walked all the way around the circle, testing every gap.

There had once been three other trilithons outside the circle, positioned at the cardinal points, but all but the southernmost had fallen. Lulu stepped over the fallen masonry in her slow traverse and came back to her starting point between the intact south trilithon and the monoliths of the stone circle.

She looked them both over. 'Too much trouble,' she said, echoing Kit's last words. 'Indeed.'

Kit was very, very tempted to gloat. But that kind of thing had recoiled on him before so he held his tongue. He moved Edith to stand with him before the threshold formed by two monoliths and a lintel almost directly across the circle from where Lulu was standing.

He put his arms around her from behind, drawing her close. 'Sorry, Miss Knight. This is inappropriate.'

So had hugging her been, truly, no matter how freely the Knight cousins expressed their affections among their family. No matter how tolerant, to the point of lax, her parents were.

'Yes,' said Edith, dryly. 'My father will be sure to make you marry me, dearest.'

Kit glanced over his shoulder and saw that Lulu hadn't moved. She knew what he was doing, no doubt, and therefore knew there was no point trying to get closer. She could stand right on the other side of the menhirs he was going to use, she could rest her hands on their granite surfaces from that side, and it would still be the other side. He was going to use *this* side as his threshold and there was nothing she could do to stop him.

He formed the Artwork in his head; the two stone posts and lintel before him, the two stone posts and lintel that reinforced the entry to the Roman chalk mine northwards. It was quite the distance, but his Art was roaring through his blood like the whisky had, like the desire for Locke's mouth had.

He walked forwards, Edith shuffling with him in his close embrace, and they crossed the threshold.

And fell onto the grass on the other side of the monoliths.

By the time Kit, dazed by pain, worked out the crossing hadn't worked, Lulu was halfway around the circle and it was Edith who had to thrash out from under him, grab him, and drag him back under the lintel into the stone circle. He, pushing the pain off onto Christopher with barely a thought, collected himself enough to block up the threshold they'd tried just as Lulu got there.

She muttered a curse under her breath and sauntered back to her southern position.

Kit sat up. It had hurt in the same way as when Locke had pulled him out of the bath, but much worse, probably directly relative to the strength of the Art he had percolating through him. But it was as if the pain had been behind a plate of glass. He knew he had experienced it and that it had been bad, but he hadn't had to feel it most of it, because Christopher had taken the brunt of it instead.

'What happened?' Edith asked. 'I didn't feel anything, but you did. That looked painful, Kit. More painful than when Mrs Hanks burnt her fingers at the bonfire last year and she made that sound *really* painful. Mum said she complained so much her flowers died. That sounds like nonsense, I'm sure, but the point is, have you ever noticed that Mrs Taylor's garden is dismal and she's the biggest moaner in the village?'

The whole time she kept up her chatter, her hand was making soothing circles on Kit's back. Kit breathed. Touch always felt good after pain. It was what brought him out from behind his shield.

'Does she ever shut up?' Lulu shouted.

'Come in here and make me,' said Edith, without looking away from Kit. Her hand on his back clenched to a fist. 'Oh, that's right, you can't.'

'No gloating,' Kit said. 'Tempts the gods.'

'What did happen, though, Kit?'

'I think,' he said slowly, 'I can't take another person across a threshold. It didn't feel like I'd tried to go too far. It flat-out tossed us out.'

Kit had done endless experiments with his Art to turn a weak and chancy power into something actually helpful. He'd known from the start that objects could cross with him; otherwise, he would have had to strip naked every time he wanted to cross. Before coming to Lovelly, he'd never tried with a living creature. It had never occurred to him that one day he would want to take a friend across a threshold, because he'd never had friends before the Knights.

He'd had an off-the-cuff attempt at it, a few months ago, but his ears had been full of screams and his lungs had been full of hot smoke and his shoulders had taken the brunt of a falling burning strut, and it had failed, just as trying to use an edge as a threshold had failed when he hadn't had time and space to prepare. He had thought it would be different, within the standing stones, and he had been wrong.

'Ah,' said Lulu smugly, tapping on a monolith. 'Coming out, lad?'

Edith stiffened. Her lovely blue-grey eyes were wide and clear as she rose. She faced Lulu. 'Off you go, then, Kit,' she said, staring at the bounty hunter. 'You get to the caves.'

'I can't,' said Kit. 'The thresholds here would open.'

'And what would happen then, I wonder?' Lulu mused, staring right back at Edith, those strong fingers tap-tapping on the monolith.

Kit shuddered. He heard, *Oh Crispin, what shall I do with you, I wonder?* and fought down nausea.

Edith folded her arms. 'We can wait. My family will come looking for me soon enough.'

'Oh, yes?' The bounty hunter kicked lightly at the stone. 'And what do we think Mr Alexander Locke is about, back in the village, if not taking care of your family?'

Edith jerked as if she'd been punched. Kit said, 'He wouldn't, Edith.'

'So very sure of him, are we?'

His friend faltered at Lulu's scornful tone. She turned her worried gaze to him, and Kit knew she wouldn't be able to bring herself to wait. She hadn't seen how kind Locke's eyes were, when no one else was looking.

He moved close so he could speak in a murmur. 'Give me the knife, Edith. Get ready to run out of the circle. You'll know when.'

Kit stalked across the circle, twirling the knife. He'd grown up in an orphanage, the Orphanage, and on the streets, alone. He knew some tricks. Lulu watched the twirling knife cautiously, so he guessed he looked convincing. She didn't know if physical objects could pass through the invisible barrier that blocked the thresholds. Kit didn't know either, actually; he'd successfully thrown objects through an open threshold, a portal, but had never tried it through one he was holding closed like this. So many more experiments to do.

He abruptly launched into a run at her, holding the knife as if he would throw it. She jerked backwards. Kit opened all the thresholds and crossed to the trilithon behind her, coming out still running. Holding the knife out of the way—he never wanted to hurt anyone—he rammed his shoulder into her broad back.

He was far more solidly built than his face suggested, far more than the Valkyrie expected from her derogatory comments on his size. Out of balance from leaping backwards away from the direction she thought he, or his knife, was coming from, Lulu stumbled forwards from his hard shove from behind.

She fell into the stone circle. Edith came out of the stone circle. Kit closed the thresholds again, trapping Lucy Llewellyn inside.

Kit looked across the circle at Edith on the far side, smiling a very small smile. Edith raised her hands over her head in an unwary gesture of triumph and did a mad little dance. She looked delighted.

Then she looked alarmed.

Someone grabbed Kit from behind. He instinctively jerked the knife down, and it thunked into flesh. Kit, horrified, let go of the knife.

'Shitfuck,' Locke swore, and released him.

'Sorry, Alex!'

The apology burst out of Kit as he spun to face him, both hands clapped over his mouth. Locke pulled the knife out of his leg and looked at Kit. He took a lurching step towards him, knife in hand. Kit noted, in air that seemed sharpened suddenly, that one of the iron cuffs still dangled from his wrist, the other cuff hanging loose and locked at the end of the chain. It looked scratched up and dented.

He took off around the circle. 'Run, Edith!' he shouted. 'I made the Viking really cross.'

But when he risked a glance over his shoulder, he saw that Locke hadn't come after him. Instead, he'd stepped up to the monoliths, standing just on the other side of one of the threshold barriers from Lulu.

He rested a hand against the invisible barrier, looking for all the world like a mummer. 'He hit an artery, Lulu,' he told her, voice tight. 'I'm going to bleed out and die.'

Lulu shrieked, 'Let me out of here, I have to save my brother.'

Kit had already unblocked the thresholds, had already reversed direction to run back to them. 'How do I help?'

He noticed, too late, that Lulu hadn't moved to save her brother *at all.*

'You already helped,' she said complacently and Locke twisted his arm up his back and slammed him to the ground.

All the air went out of him in a compulsive cough. Locke put his knee in the small of Kit's back and swiftly arranged his arms so that his palms were flat into the earth, held there by Locke's firm hold, one large hand over both of Kit's.

For all the good it would do. Kit was not one of the Artisans whose Artistry emitted from hands or fingers. Locke must have realised that before; Kit would bet the move had been habit.

'Hoi, you bastards!' shouted Edith, and Kit lifted his head enough to see her running towards them and Lulu starting off to intercept her.

'Circle, Edith,' Kit cried.

Edith, faced with the Valkyrie bearing down on her, had a rare crisis of nerves and dodged into the circle. Kit blocked the thresholds for the third time. The easy pleasure of the Art buzzed through him again, despite his dire situation, and he hummed.

Locke pressed down with his knee, shoving him further into the dirt and cutting off the humming. 'Artery's closer to the inner thigh,' he said conversationally. 'Go for the groin and slash down.'

He traced a line down the back of Kit's thigh, illustrating the lesson. Kit jerked and Locke whipped his hand away.

'I shall bear it in mind, Mr Locke,' Kit said to the grass.

'That was such a mean trick,' Edith shouted at them from the safety of the circle. 'He was very quick to come back and help you.'

'He was pretty damned quick to stab me too, Miss Knight.'

'I didn't know it was you,' Kit said quietly. He rubbed his forehead against the grass, forcing the sensation of soft spikiness to take his attention off the hostile weight on his back.

'Would you have hesitated if you did know?' Locke countered as he pulled him brusquely to his feet.

Kit looked up at him, letting silence be his answer, since he didn't know the answer.

'Yeah, all right,' said Locke, shaking his head.

'More honest than you are,' Kit muttered.

'*Please, Alex,*' Locke mocked, voice lowered so the two women wouldn't hear. '*I'll be good.* Truly, you are very honest.'

Kit suspected Locke was more annoyed about that than the knife wound, which was bleeding quite dramatically. He couldn't admit how honest he had really been.

'I was good,' he said instead. 'For a given value of good. I'll wager you don't even know what threshold I used.'

Locke paused. 'Come on, then, boast to me. You know you want to.'

Kit tried not to look too smug. He turned his attention to the locks of the handcuffs and they sprang open and fell to the ground. Locke pushed him off into Lulu's hold and scooped them into his pocket. Then he sat and used a few of his ubiquitous handkerchiefs to pad and bind his new wound.

Kit watched that, rather than watching Lulu getting out more rope from her pack without ever relinquishing her grip on his collar. He was relieved to see that the cut, though very bloody, was a slice along the edge of Locke's thigh rather than a deep hole in his leg.

By the time Locke glanced up, Lulu was figure-eighting a length of rope around an uncomplaining Kit's wrists, binding him with his hands in front of him.

Kit was biting his lip in the effort not to complain. He kept his gaze down. In the circle, standing as close to the threshold as she could, Edith was doing enough complaining for the both of them. Locke took Kit's chin and lifted his face so he could see his expression, which Kit was doing his damnedest to keep neutral. He was usually very good at that.

'Ah, Lulu?' said Locke, slowly, staring at Kit.

'No, Alex.'

'At least tie his arms, not his wrists.'

Kit's shoulders twanged at the thought. He shook himself out of Locke's gentle hold and looked down again.

'No, Alex.'

'There's no harm in it.'

'Did he escape you?'

'Lulu.'

'No, Alex. Did he escape you? Did he escape you several times?' She finished tying her knots and wrapped the end of the rope around her own wrist.

Locke sighed. 'You know he did.'

'Whose prisoner is he now?'

'I did trick him into coming back,' Locke said, knocking one boot against the ground.

'He's mine, Alex, so you can— Oh, would you *be quiet*! You're such a church-bell.'

This last was shouted at the endlessly monologuing Edith, who glared back. '*Make me*,' she shouted, and then heaved a solid chunk of fallen monolith at Lulu.

It shot straight through the closed threshold and hit Lulu right in the centre of the forehead. She took two steps back and sat down abruptly. Edith's mouth opened in surprise.

'Oh!' said Kit, who could never not be pleased by learning new things about his Art.

'Are you kidding me? Goddamned bitch!' Lulu shouted at Edith, hand pressed to her forehead.

'Language, Mrs Llewellyn!' Kit said. Notwithstanding, he handed her his handkerchief.

'I'm a lady, you mustn't talk to me like that,' Edith informed Lulu severely.

'Come out here and *make me*,' Lulu snarled, throwing Edith's taunt right back at her while she blotted at her head with the handkerchief. 'Oh, that's right, you're too scared.'

Edith made a growly *ooooh* noise of fury, echoed by the muted roar of the train arriving in the distance, dead on time with the first church bells of the morning. She paced the boundaries of her cage while Lulu smirked at her.

Lulu hadn't noticed that the end of the rope around her wrist had come loose. Kit made a dash for the blocked thresholds, to escape into the cage with Edith, only to be brought up short by Locke's tug on the back of his coat.

'Oh, look,' said Locke cheerfully. 'Mine again.'

With a reassuring smile at Edith, Kit let himself be dragged away from the stones, let himself stumble back into Locke so his body rubbed against his muscled length.

Lulu made a disgusted noise. 'Your kitten is manipulating you, Lexi.'

'I know,' said Locke, without a change in tone. His big hands came to Kit's waist, steadying him, pushing him away.

'He'll escape you again.'

'I know he'll try.'

He undid the ropes around Kit's wrists. Kit sagged in relief, resting his forehead against Locke's arm briefly to show his gratitude.

'*Manipulating you*,' Lulu repeated through gritted teeth.

'*I know*,' snapped back Locke.

Despite Lulu's annoying astuteness, Kit sniggered at the sniping. He'd heard it enough among the Knight cousins. 'When you called him your brother,' he said to Lulu, 'you didn't mean fellow bounty hunter, did you?'

'Actual brother,' Lulu confirmed.

Kit looked between them. Sandy-coloured hair, hazel eyes, tanned, tall and broad, the Viking and the Valkyrie. He would have twigged a lot sooner if he hadn't smacked a threshold closed in Lulu's face and given her a broken nose and two black eyes. The swelling spot in the middle of her forehead from Edith's superlative aim wasn't helping either.

'If you two hadn't fucked up her face, you'd see we're twins,' confirmed Locke.

'Language,' said Edith from the circle. 'I'm a lady.'

Lulu ignored her. 'Used to be identical,' she said, 'but life got in the way.'

And the pair of them chortled and bumped knuckles with, indeed, identical slyly amused smiles.

Kit turned around and took a step towards the circle where Edith waited, hands pressing together her only sign of anxiety. Her face was set in fierce warrior lines. He felt Locke catch the back of his coat again, but the man didn't try to pull him away. Kit was telegraphing his intention very clearly.

He'd lied to himself when he'd thought he had nothing in this village he would not walk away from without a backwards look.

'Bye, Edie,' he said. 'Thank you for trying to help me. Thank you for— Well. Thank you for all that you and your family have been to me in the last six months. You are the first home I've ever had, and I'll never forget it.'

Edith Knight burst into tears. Kit looked at her and looked over his shoulder at Locke, bewildered. He did not usually get this sort of reaction when he decided to be frank. He supposed he was not usually being kind when he decided to be frank.

Locke grinned while Lulu scoffed, 'Girls.'

At that, Edith scowled and got herself under control. Sniffling, she said, 'Oh, Kit, you were a lost little waif when you fetched up here and it's been my privilege to be your friend and I can't bear the thought of what these horrible people are doing to you.'

'Standing *right* here,' Locke said.

Edith shouted, 'Horrible fucking people.'

'Language,' Lulu recited. 'I'm a lady.'

'Let me out, Kit, I'm going to punch that horrid witch in the face! And don't you laugh at me, I grew up wrestling brothers and boy cousins. If you think I can't take you on just because you're bigger than me, you're in for a surprise, you horrible woman.'

Lulu's face had hardened throughout this speech but at this last, she relaxed and turned to Locke, smiling strangely. Her brother squeezed her shoulder.

Edith, under Kit's carefully amused look, dropped her fists and laughed a little. 'Oh, Kitty.' Her eyes shone bright with the tears she'd stopped herself from shedding.

'Now, we have talked about this nickname, Eddie.'

'You can call me Eddie if I can call you Kitty!' she said, picking up their long-term summertime argument. But it wasn't enough to divert her. 'Kit, it's all right to be angry that they're doing this to you, you know. You should be outraged.'

He looked at the twins, a pointed look upwards between the pair of them that emphasised their size and strength and that there were, undeniably, two of the fuckers. 'What good will outrage do me?'

'It will at the very least relieve your feelings.'

Kit let his face assume his blankest expression. 'What feelings?'

Then he laughed, and then so did Edith, properly. That would be their other long-term summertime argument, more real than the flippancy about nicknames. The Knights were all about relieving feelings by airing them extensively. Kit was all about not feeling them.

Almost one whole year ago, he'd unquestioningly opened a door for the Yellington gang, and he hadn't known it wasn't a theft until the supposed thief walked back out with a bloody knife and the murdered man's wife had started screaming. His first assassination had been the last straw.

He'd run from London before, but this time he'd bounced around the train lines up and down England and hadn't stopped until he'd circled down to Bristol, paused long enough to visit the second-hand clothing market, and noticed the tourist posters for Knightstone Circle and its chalk mines.

He'd fetched up in Lovelly, cold to his core, emotionless façade in place, determined to feel nothing ever again. And he hadn't, he truly hadn't, until Edith had patiently, cheerfully, obliviously, broken down some of his walls. It was entirely down to her he'd found he could laugh again.

He glanced at the twins again and saw them exchanging some sort of meaningful look, fraught with the sort of silent communication Edith managed with her sister, except magnified exponentially, presumably due to the twinness.

He sighed, his amusement fading away. 'The barrier will vanish after I get out of range,' he told Edith. 'Not sure how long it'll take. But, Edith, m'luv, listen. This is important. I know what you'll want to do. So listen. *Do not follow us.*'

Edith dropped her gaze to the grass.

'No, Edith,' Kit said. 'This is over. Do not follow.' When she still refused to answer, he said, 'I shall try an experiment, then, Miss Knight.'

He strolled around the boundary of the stones. Locke walked with him, apparently still suspecting him of wanting to join Edith in the safety of the circle despite Kit making no attempt to hide his intentions.

Locke wasn't trusting that he was seeing true intentions; he couldn't tell when Kit was concealing true intentions behind other true intentions. Kit, self-satisfied, tucked that information away. He hummed in pleasure as the Art rose up in him. Normally, it was like drawing from a well, slow and deep. This felt like a geyser gushing through him. He cast a new Artwork as he walked the circle three times, Locke pacing with him the whole while, hand on his back.

'I think the boundary will hold for a few hours now,' he told them all when he was done. 'The train will be gone before Miss Knight gets out.'

'Kit!' Edith said heatedly. 'What about my family? I have to go make sure this bastard didn't hurt them.'

'Me?' Locke pointed at his own chest, looking wounded. 'I would never.'

'What took you so long to come after Kit, then?'

'Getting a bollocking from your mother,' Locke said irritably. 'Because I broke her truckle bed. And then when I offered to pay for the damages, my wallet was gone. All my money, as well as my proof that I'm an Agency enforcer. So I got shouted at some more, and then I had to give her the direction of Sir Kingsford Locke of Northfield for reparations, so there's another bollocking in my near future.'

'Oh, did we get the big bad bounty hunter in trouble with Daddy?' Edith asked, greatly pleased.

'*Enforcer*, and yes, but with my brother, thanks for that.' He turned to Kit. 'How did you make these people like you so much?'

'My natural charm,' said Kit flatly, as he took Locke's wallet out of his pocket.

He held it up just long enough for Locke to see what he was holding, then tossed it through to Edith. She caught it and burst out laughing. She put her hands behind her back, making it clear Locke wasn't getting it back.

'Pissant little thief,' Locke said, shaking his head. 'Both of you, Miss Knight.'

'Train, please, Mr Locke,' Kit said, and strolled off, with one last little wave at Edith.

'He is chaos on legs,' he heard Locke say to his sister as the pair followed.

'You love it,' said Lulu. 'Don't even try to pretend you don't, you bet-waddled fool.'

'Yeah,' Locke said on a chuckle. 'Yeah, I do and yeah, I am.'

6

They were halfway to the station when Locke made an annoyed grumble with a curse in it. 'Lucy, my darling little sister,' he started.

'Yes, but then he's my prisoner again.'

Locke hissed through his teeth. 'Kit, do you have money?'

'Why?' Kit asked. His stockpile was hidden in his lodging; he trusted Edith would uncover it and use it to settle his outstanding bills and pay for the damage he'd caused in the village. He'd liberated the banknotes and Agency identification from Locke's wallet before giving it to Edith but he was hardly going to admit that. 'Oh, the train tickets.'

'If only I had my wallet,' Locke said, holding his hands up in astonishment at the mystery of it all.

'I'll pay for all three of us,' Lulu said, 'but I get custody of the kitten.'

'Let me see if Young Tom will let me defer payment to Miss Knight,' Kit told Locke, and he looked smugly at his sister over Kit's head.

But Meredith was standing with Tom in the ticket office when they got to the station. Kit made a sceptical noise in the back of his throat, but he went and tried anyway.

'Really?' said Meredith, when Young Tom, looking very uncomfortable, seemed to be considering it. 'He's been arrested for *thievery* and you want to let him dun Miss Knight for train tickets all the way to London?'

'*First class* tickets to London,' Kit elaborated. That was quite the expense.

'Sorry an'all, our Kit,' said Tom.

He turned to sell tickets to Lulu instead. Kit made a polite bow to Meredith. 'Miss Taunston, all best wishes for your marriage to Will next spring.'

'I be marrying Tom,' she said sharply.

'My apologies! I got mixed up because you spend so much time with—

I'll be quiet now.'

He wandered off towards the train, the engine already spitting hot droplets and ash, while behind him, Tom said, 'Will? That be William Knight?'

Locke strolled beside him in a heavy silence. 'You are so petty,' he said finally.

'I'm hungry,' Kit informed him. 'Feed me.'

Lulu re-joined them, holding tickets that were not for London, merely to Bristol. Kit saw Locke clock this and then decide not to say anything.

'Stop trying it on with my brother. You're my prisoner again. You only get food for good behaviour.'

Kit gave her a perfectly compliant bow, face impassive, and she scowled.

The train along this spur line was small; there was a first-class car holding six carriages, and a third-class car, and that was all. As they made their way into the third carriage along, the Viking sighed. 'I suppose I should warn you, Lulu. Drunk Kit thinks it'll be easy to escape off the train.'

'Drunk Kit talks a lot of tosh,' sober Kit pointed out placidly, though he privately had strong words for drunk Kit. 'And you're not doing your plan any favours by warning her, Mr Locke. Or is that an end to my choices? I'm helping Mrs Llewellyn whether I like it or not?'

'You are now her prisoner thanks to your own choices, my lad.'

This was a fair enough point, within the constraints of the limited choices the Locke twins had left to him, that Kit merely nodded to it. Lulu bound his wrists again. Kit shut his eyes but composed himself enough to open them again before she was done. Locke looked like he was biting his tongue.

Lulu looped the end of the rope around her own wrist again, then sat down by the far door of the carriage. She stretched her legs out across to the other bench, blocking the door.

'He's tethered, Alexander. He can't escape. See how it's done?'

'Thank you, Lucinda, I do so love to be patronised.'

'Hallmark, Lexi.'

This cryptic comment was evidently a sibling in-joke like Edith and Margaret enjoyed, for Locke, still smiling, made a cheerfully rude gesture at his sister as he took the opposite corner. He stretched his long legs across the door onto the station to block that exit point too.

Kit sat beside Locke, next to Lulu's feet. His tether ran across the carriage to Lulu's wrist. She had a small pouch out and was using a hand mirror to touch up her face powder.

'Do you want to hear about the job now, Mr Whitely?' she asked as she worked.

'No,' he said. 'If you take me to your door, I'll open it. Spare me the details.'

She lowered her mirror so she could stare at him over it. He'd thought she'd be satisfied, but she was frowning. 'How very compliant of you.'

'It doesn't save you, you know,' Locke said quietly. 'Not knowing what's going to happen. It doesn't absolve you of your responsibility for the outcome.' Lulu looked at him sharply.

'I see,' Kit said. The screams of the murdered man's wife echoed in his head. 'And so if I hear the details of Mrs Llewellyn's job and register my strong moral objection to providing my assistance, she will, of course, immediately release me?' Silence. The twins stared at each other. 'Then please do allow me to maintain my blissful ignorance.'

He folded his hands into his lap and sat with head bowed, intending only to get through the job, as he had got through jobs a dozen times before. Despite bodily blocking the doors, neither twin was actually touching the doors. That was helpful. But all he intended to do was get through the job.

Locke smiled mockingly, thoroughly onto him. This intention wasn't true enough to fully mask his real intention.

Kit decided a distraction was in order. 'If your older brother is a baronet, how is it you're an enforcer? Or is he a knight?'

'Baronet.'

A baronet. No wonder this pair moved through the world so openly, Locke with his easy confidence, Lulu with her defiant challenge. They were shielded by more than just their size.

'So how exactly does the family of a baronet get into occupations as dirty as bounty hunting and law enforcement?'

Lulu, in the middle of applying lip salve, hoisted her foot over to Locke to give him a nudge that was more of a kick. 'No talking to the prisoner. This is how he got you in the first place, Lexi.'

'Give me a little credit, Lulu,' Locke said. He flashed a grin. 'It took more than talking.'

Kit hummed to himself and looked out the carriage window.

'Remember I said I wanted to be a naturalist?' Locke said. 'I'd go out to the pond and launch my model ship on its voyage of scientific discovery and then this little privateer'—he waved at Lulu—'would come along with her pirate ship and sink me every time. And then when we got older...' Locke bit his lip, looking over at Lulu, plainly seeking something from her. Words? Permission?

'And then I grew up and found it was too much hard work to be a pirate,' Lulu obligingly interrupted. 'I left to live with a cousin who was invited to join an exclusive mercenary squad, and she brought me along too, but it turned out they only wanted Artisans. So I set up as competition out of sheer spite, and when our father died, Lexi joined me. And that's about it, kitten. A partnership forged in the womb.'

Locke glanced at her, a weighted look. The silence that followed was uncomfortable and Kit rather suspected there was a saga contained in the words I left. Perhaps Lulu had left her family home the same way Kit had left his orphanage: hastily, in fear, and without hope.

He cleared his throat. 'But now you're an enforcer, Mr Locke?'

'Yep,' Locke said and shut his eyes.

Conversation closed.

Lulu sniffed. 'I'm going to sleep. I waited up all night for Whitely to make his escape and he did it at dawn. Very practical of you, kitten.'

'I am exceedingly practical,' Kit agreed.

She yawned widely before wrapping a shawl from her pack over her head. She was heavily asleep very soon after that, undisturbed by the sounds of a few other passengers boarding and the rail staff going about their duties.

Locke didn't relax until the whistle sounded and the train started moving. It was a little on late side; the midday church bells had sounded already by the time they finally set off.

Young Tom wouldn't be happy about that. He was having a bad day all round.

Locke raided Lulu's pack and gave Kit an apple. Kit crunched it down with enthusiasm, Locke leaning back in his corner, watching him, inscrutable.

Then he took a book out of one of the pockets of his coat. 'Read to me?'

Kit took the book. It was *Little Dorrit*, with all its unsubtle prison references, that they'd got partway through last night. The thought of Locke, beset, taking a moment to pocket it gave him an odd sensation he didn't examine overly closely. He opened to the right page and started reading aloud. Locke combed his hair and tidied his clothing, relaxing into his corner.

The train ran its rails. It was noisy and jarring. Kit shifted closer to Locke so he didn't have to strain his voice by raising it against the noise.

After a while, he leaned against Locke, half-lying on him as he read.

After a while, Locke began to comb his fingers through Kit's hair, gently pulling his curls straight and releasing them to lightly spring back.

Kit hummed and kept reading, smooth and steady.

He risked a glance. Locke had shut his eyes, absently twisting Kit's curls around his fingers with little tugs, not unpleasant at all. They pulled into a station, Bishop's Beard, and he opened his eyes as Kit sat away, in case of new passengers looking through the glass. Once they'd set off again, Kit curled back into him. There was a long run now, before they would arrive in Bristol. He kept reading.

Locke's hand stilled, fingers lightly cupping Kit's scalp. His breathing had deepened. He'd had more sleep than his sister, but it had still been an early start after a restless night, and it would have been an earlier start the day before, to make the connector train from London.

Kit eased up away from him, and he didn't move. Both Locke twins were heavy sleepers, it seemed.

Locke had left Lulu's pack open when he'd got the apple. Kit had a quiet fossick, delving past her shaving kit and cosmetics pouch. Then he stretched his hand over Lulu's legs and put his fingers to the door on her side of the carriage. He drew up his Art; he still felt full from his time at the Knightstone Circle, and the Artwork came easily.

He crossed the threshold, shifting through the closed door—the doorway—of their carriage and coming out the one next door. The tether between him and Lulu, taut, snapped as soon as he closed the portal on it, the rope-end as neat as if it had been sliced with a sharp blade. There were some benefits to rope, after all.

He crossed again, further this time, to the end of the car, with no way to walk through to the third-class car. The carriage was empty; the whole first-class car was empty of other passengers. He opened the door and leaned out. Soot-filled smoke hit his face as he looked forwards. He looked back and saw Locke leaning out of the original carriage, watching him with the patience of a predator on a stalk.

Kit closed his door. He'd gotten turned around and gone the wrong sodding way, up towards the engine rather than back towards the third-class car. God damn his appalling sense of direction. Now Locke and Lulu's carriage was between him and there. He shook his head, touched the doorway and started crossing thresholds back the other way. The important thing was to not misjudge again and end up back in the Locke twins' carriage. They were stuck in there until the train pulled in at Bristol.

He stepped through the threshold to the carriage beyond theirs, only to be immediately caught in a bearhug by Locke.

'The fuck?' he said concisely.

'It's possible to swing from one carriage door to the next,' Locke explained mellowly. 'The gap's not that big.'

'That sounds remarkably dangerous,' Kit said.

Locke shook his head. Hand firm around Kit's arm, he leaned out to communicate with Lulu, who had apparently gone ahead to the next carriage along to wait in ambush in case Kit ended up there.

'All right, we're all just going to stay where we are and behave ourselves till the station,' Locke told him.

Kit sat in the centre of the forwards-facing bench and demurely folded his hands on his lap. 'Am I your prisoner again?' he asked. 'Rather than Mrs Llewellyn's?'

Locke sat heavily opposite him. The carriages were small and he was big; their knees brushed. 'Just call her Lulu,' he said. 'It hurts her to be called Mrs Llewellyn and she hardly cares for pointless proprieties.'

'Oh.' Kit remembered, now, Lulu saying, *My husband was Welsh*. Was. 'My apologies.' He caught himself, and added, sincerely, 'I am sorry.'

He assessed Locke for signs of anger, a familiar calculation. He was glad he hadn't been caught by Lulu, who appeared to be on a perpetual simmer and was probably in full seethe in her carriage right now. Locke, on the other hand, was still calm and warm-eyed, though eyeing Kit unusually seriously.

Kit relaxed, then stiffened as Locke abruptly leant forwards, grabbed him by the arms, and yanked him onto his lap. He wrapped his arms tight around Kit's back, so that Kit's knees perforce parted and he slid torso to torso with the bigger man, straddling his hard thighs. Kit breathed out the tension that the unexpected move had jerked into him, and then leaned forwards and breathed in so he could give himself a dose of Locke's sandalwood and citrus scent.

'I woke up and you were falling out of the carriage door, Kit,' Locke said into his hair.

'Is that how it looked?' Kit asked, surprised. He kept his head nestled into Locke's neck. 'I was crossing a threshold. The door wasn't even open.'

'I know you were crossing a threshold, you damnable creature. But it looked like you were falling off a moving train.' His arms tightened. 'Jesus, sweetheart.'

That was...nice. 'If it's any consolation, you near gave me an attack of the nerves when you told me you changed carriages on a moving train, so...'

'Did I? Your face didn't show that.'

'I don't show a lot of emotion,' Kit explained. 'I don't feel it.'

'Kit,' Locke said, 'you are a little ball of rage behind a façade of blank politeness.'

Kit thought about this. He didn't think he *was*, actually. Eventually, he said, 'I don't like having my choices taken away from me and it's been happening for an awfully long time now.'

Locke sighed, a gust of air warm over Kit's hair. He let his arms fall. 'Go back to your seat, Mr Whitely, before I do something stupid.'

Kit half-rose onto his knees and kissed Locke in the soft spot where his ear met his jaw. 'Do something stupid, Alex,' he whispered, and bit his earlobe. Hard.

Which is how he ended up flat on his back across the carriage bench with Locke's delicious weight on top of him, Locke kissing him with slow-building intensity. That was a revelation. The man had plainly been holding back yesterday, given his deception in the inn yard and Kit's drunkenness in the pavilion. His mouth on Kit's now, moving slow and firm and deep, was setting him on fire.

To his frustration, Locke wasn't going anywhere with his hands, content to stroke over Kit's hair and face, as chaste as his tongue was not. It was left to Kit to send his own hands roaming, delving under Locke's shirt to explore the silk over steel of his skin and muscles, and to embarrassingly whimper and gasp against Locke's mouth and to squirm and rock his hips under him, demanding more and tighter and harder. He could feel Locke chuckling as his mouth ravished him.

The steam whistle blasted and the train gave a lurch and slowed. Locke raised his head. 'Train's pulling into the station, sweetheart.'

'Oh, baby, won't it be better with oil?' said Kit dreamily. After a moment of complete stillness from Locke, Kit opened his eyes. Locke was looking down at him, eyes bright, head cocked. 'Oh. Oh! The *train* is pulling into the *station*.'

'Yeah,' said Locke, his feral smile growing on his face. 'That's what I said, Mr Whitely.'

He helped Kit sit up and set his clothes to rights, adjusting his coat to hide the erection he hadn't been able to make go away yet. Then he got out his comb and set to work on himself, smiling. He was relaxed against the bench.

Kit's intentions were all over the place; the thought of escape was still in there, but so was the kissing and the hope for a private room soon, or a sodding private alley would do, and all sorts of other things that circled around and around the feel of Locke's mouth and Locke's body over his. Locke's eyes were half-closed under the onslaught of those milling intentions but he was still smiling.

The train settled at the station. Kit stepped out on to the platform. It was busy, with a train for London about to leave on the other side from their little local train. He stood still, waiting. Locke had only just stood up to follow him out. Lulu had come out of her carriage and, not without a glare his way, gone into their original carriage, to get her pack.

They had both let him get thresholds between them and him.

Kit locked every door on the train.

Lulu howled, 'Are you fucking *kidding* me right now?' from her carriage, but it was the soft thud from behind Kit that caught his attention.

Locke had his forehead resting on the glass on the top half of the carriage door; he'd evidently slumped hard into it when he'd realised Kit had locked him in. He didn't look angry. He looked ashamed.

'Sorry, Alex,' said Kit. 'I didn't plan that.'

Locke wouldn't look at him.

Kit bit his lip. He turned to Lulu. She had a pistol out. It was old-fashioned, a single-shot pistol, one of a pair if Kit was any judge. Which, of weapons, he probably wasn't.

'Don't break the glass, Miss Lucinda,' he warned her. 'You've got no way to pay for damages and no proof you're chasing a criminal.' He held up her wallet, that he had taken from her pack. She gave another great howl of rage. 'I've left you enough money for tickets to London.'

He glanced again into the carriage he had shared with Locke. Locke had slouched down onto the bench, staring at the opposite wall. As if he felt Kit's gaze, he shook his head very slowly, still staring straight ahead.

'Stop, thief!' shouted Lulu, which was quite the admirable move, and frankly, and for all Kit's objections, not wrong.

The shrill whistles of the station guards immediately started up. Kit knew better than to draw attention by running. He turned and casually strolled into the crowd of passengers and farewellers on the platform, letting it wash him out into the city. He looked about for anyone following him and saw only a rainbow reflecting in a puddle after last night's rain, which he took as a good omen.

He found himself a hot-coffee stall first, and had coffee and bread, and then splurged on a pie and a sticky bun from a bakery, eating them while walking himself well away from the station. He assumed the Locke twins would come after him, and there could very well be more bounty hunters in Bristol, either on their way to Lovelly or strategic enough to know he'd have to come this way if he escaped by train. He kept on the move, kept watching for followers, kept his Art to hand.

Towards the end of the day, exhausted by the constant state of watch-fulness, he found himself lodgings in a nondescript hotel in the unfashion-able part of town. He'd lay low overnight and get a train away tomorrow. He wished he could go back to the Knights, but he wasn't that foolish. He could never go back to the village, would never see Edith Knight again.

That struck him at full force, lying alone in the dark. He'd never see his friend again.

He was not sure what disturbed him towards dawn, but he rolled out of the narrow bed just as lightning shattered through the window, struck all four tall brass bed knobs at once, and set the bedding on fire.

That certainly woke him up the rest of the way.

Wary, he had slept in his trousers, but was without his shirt or boots. He snatched his coat, fell back against the door and crossed the threshold to the room on the other side of the hall. There was someone in the bed there but his quiet ingress hadn't woken them.

He soft-footed to the window. Out that, in through a window on the ground floor, and then out the front door.

He was muttering to himself as he strolled off down the street, shrugging into his coat and watching where he was setting his bare feet, since there wasn't much filthier than a city street. 'Lightning. This Artisan gets lightning and I get *doors?*'

There was more in that vein until he chaffed himself out of his mild attack of irritation and smiled at the sky in amusement at his own self. Then he finally remembered he was trying hard to not be a bad person, and doubled back to ring the fire bell, which was on the street corner. Lightning struck that too, hard enough to knock the bell from its post. It ripped a line through the dawn mist and, oddly, left behind a smell like spring.

'Oh, we want to play, do we?' Kit asked the dawn sky.

Men in their nightclothes were rushing out of the nearby premises, holding tin buckets, ready to fill at the pump and daisy-chain until the brigade could drag in the engine. Volunteers stood by, to hook up the pipes and start pumping water in strenuous five-minute shifts once the engine arrived. They'd earn a shilling or two for their efforts.

Kit looked down at himself. He was in his trousers and coat, bare-chested and barefoot in the misty dawn, practically naked and in no fit state to be seen by people or to approach the station, even if he could guarantee it wasn't being watched by more Artisans.

By God, how much was the assassination bounty worth, anyway? And why, sodding *why*, was he the target of it?

He was in a bad way. He'd used up the power he'd gathered from the Knightstone Circle, and any sort of Art gathered from unfulfilled desire had dissipated with the look on Locke's face when he'd decided Kit had tricked him on purpose. Meanwhile, Kit had either been followed to the hotel despite his precautions, or the lightning Artisan was teamed with some sort of tracker Artisan. Either way, they were going to be hard to shake.

Kit breathed, just breathed, calling on every scrap of knowledge he had about Bristol, calling on every scrap of Art left at his disposal, calling on every scrap of mental discipline he'd trained himself into.

Plan made, he turned himself to implementing it.

He couldn't remember if lightning was attracted to metal or not; even if natural lightning wasn't, this Artisan had so far struck the brass on the bed and on the bell, which was probably not a coincidence. He made a quick check of the buttons of his coat and trousers. They didn't feel like brass; he guessed they were fabric-covered lead, given the cheapness of his clothes. They were also small and on a moving target so he decided to take the chance rather than stripping down to his drawers. He did take a moment to discard Locke's enforcer badge and coins, keeping the banknotes plus *Little Dorrit*, since they were just paper.

Satisfied that he was as safe as he could be, he resumed his conversation with the unseen lightning Artisan. 'Come play where you can do some real damage, my friend.'

Then he stretched out a hand to touch the nearest doorway and started to bounce himself down the thresholds along the street, fast enough to stay ahead of the lightning Artisan, but slow enough that he wouldn't lose them and so he could still protect his bare feet.

It also had the benefit of conserving the Art he had available to him. He wished he'd thought to go by the kitchen of the hotel and take some sherry.

He went to the river harbour, a mess of shipyards and wharves and quays and warehouses, where the mist thickened into fog, where there was a lot of damp wood and tall masts and cranes to tangle up the lightning, where warehouses of sugar and oil and tallow and saltpetre meant that any hint of fire would get a fast reaction, where stevedores and navvies would not be polite if they found the Artisan throwing lightning about and causing sparks.

He stole a thin linen shirt off a line at the back of a doss, and ate a legitimately-acquired pastry while he waited by the side of a warehouse that smelt of warm spices, near the mob of men hoping for labouring work for the day.

The wall above his head was struck by lightning and burst into flames with a roar and a wave of heat that drove him backwards.

'Bold,' he said, as dockworkers swarmed up gantries, scaffolds and ladders to put it out; even the jobbing labourers joined in, because that was how dangerous fire was here.

Kit stood well out of the way of the fuss. He was being glared at, a stranger who happened to be there when a mysterious fire broke out, but he couldn't help that, and he had his pretty, saintly face to make him look delicate and innocent indeed.

And the stevedores did catch the lightning Artisan, when they—closer this time, running out of Art—aimed lightning at the metal rails of the wooden scaffolding Kit was blatantly standing under. The labourers rushed the Artisan, sitting on their back and making sure their palms were pressed into the dirt, unable to push out lightning. From their bellows, the burly men had been all set to be much unkinder than Locke had been to Artisans back in the village, but when they pulled off the cloak and saw a feminine-looking face, they sent a runner for the local enforcers instead.

Bristol had to be short-staffed, if Bristol enforcers were escorting the Artisans from Lovelly onward to London, but two appeared in short order to take the lightning Artisan into custody. Unlike Locke, or any London enforcer Kit had ever seen, the Bristol enforcers wore a uniform, all in black. Also unlike him, they carried more than just silvered iron cuffs; they carried thick sticks, truncheons, that glowed and sparked and which took the last of the fight out of the Artisan when they saw them.

That took care of the lightning Artisan. It left the tracker Artisan, if there was one, but there wasn't much Kit could do about that, so he went to the station, taking the long way around in case he was still being followed. He was here much later in the day than he had intended to be. He stood on the far side of the forecourt for some time, under a rainbow, watching the traffic. He saw nothing suspicious, so went through to the station's arrival hall.

He checked the timetables and chose a train going north in only a few minutes. Three breaths, and he went to the ticket office to buy his ticket.

From there, he moved with the crowd, slipping from group to group of travellers until he was on the right platform. Then he waited in a corner well back from train, subtly watching in every direction and keeping his hand lightly on the bricks of the archway beside him.

Only when the first whistle went did he get on the train, targeting the least crowded third-class carriage. The train lurched and started off scant seconds after he had closed the carriage door and locked it for good measure.

He turned around to evaluate the other passengers in the carriage.

Kit put his hands on his hips and said, 'All right, which of you has the tracker Art?'

'Me,' said Lulu. 'But it's a talent, not an Art.'

He tsked. 'Did you lead the lightning Artisan to me?'

'Perhaps, but not on purpose,' Locke said. He was looking past Kit's ear.

'Story of your sodding life,' grumbled Kit. He pointed at the last passenger. 'And didn't I tell you to go home?'

Edith Knight smiled.

Alex

THIS IS HOW IT HAPPENED.

By the time the Locke twins had got the attention of a conductor and escaped both from their locked carriages and from the effusive apologies, they had to make a fast choice. The London train was about to pull out; they were either on it, to regroup and return later to track Kit down, or they had to go on, short of funds and identification, and trust they could bring him down within their now scant means.

Lulu showed Alex the money she'd had stowed in a secret pocket of her pack. 'We'll get by, for a day or two,' she said. 'We can call on Kings for help, if we need to. Or, hell, we could go to him at Northfield, we're close enough.'

Alex wrinkled his nose at the idea of visiting their older brother but shrugged his agreement. 'Let's stay on the board, Lulu, play the game till the end.'

'That's what I love you about you, Lexi,' she said, before thumping him across the back of the head.

'Ow!' He had, of course, read her intention to do it well in advance, but she had to get her feelings out somehow.

'What is the point of your talent if Whitely can run rings around you?'

'He's either a very disciplined thinker or he has a secondary Art,' Alex said reasonably, rubbing his head. 'Either way, he's very good at hiding what he actually intends to do.'

His chagrined look gave him away. Lulu huffed. 'I know exactly how he's hiding what he actually intends to do. He's got a secondary Art, sure, it's in his pants.'

'Yeah, all right,' he said, sighing.

'Embarrassing for you,' said Lulu.

'You let him do it too, Lucinda.'

'I expected you to be reading his intentions, Alexander. He was standing completely still, looking innocent, for Christ's sake.'

'Standing still looking innocent is the very moment he's least trustworthy. Do you know where he's gone, or not?'

Lulu led him out of the station and eastwards. She was holding Kit's handkerchief, that he had so politely handed to her after Miss Knight had clipped her with a piece of masonry. Alex noted that, for all Lulu's complaining about Alex's incapacity with Kit, *he* hadn't complained that the exceedingly competent Lulu had been taken out by a slip of a girl with good aim and a rock.

He noted this *to himself* because Lulu could kill him with her little finger.

'Will he know I'm tracking him?' she asked.

'I told him I was the one who tracked him to Lovelly-on-Sea and he seemed to think you found us in the pavilion by arrangement. I didn't mention your talent.' He gave the village its local pronunciation, Luvleeoncy, without conscious thought.

'A hint of sense from the lovestruck fool, I may die of shock.'

'Let's not take it too far,' Alex said.

'Please,' she snorted. 'I saw how fast the kitten got his claws in.'

'Not too far, Lulu,' Alex repeated.

Lulu never really knew when to back down, but she did hesitate before saying, 'Lexi, I recognise the stupid look on your face when you look at him because I saw it often enough in the mirror when I first met Peter.'

Alex was cheered by her almost-casual mention of her husband. That had been impossible even a few months ago and was still rare now. 'You did walk around looking poleaxed in those days.'

'Just— Fuck him if you must, Lexi, but I need him, and I won't let him go for any amount of pity or affection. If you can take him to bed under those conditions, then go ahead. And remember, he's a thief and we're on the side of the angels. Your little infatuation doesn't change that.'

Alex thought of Kit Whitely, his wide, innocent eyes as he insisted he wasn't a thief. Well, he wasn't, of course. He was merely an accessory to theft, and so he could say it with that look of studied innocence intact.

I don't like having my choices taken away from me, he had said, *and it's been happening for an awfully long time now.*

And then he had cold-bloodedly seduced Alex.

Except. He'd been so damned hot under Alex, burning like a furnace, writhing and gasping and hissing, 'Alex, if you don't get your sodding hands all over me, I will sodding *die*.'

It hadn't felt cold-blooded. It hadn't felt false. But, Alex supposed, if it had felt false, he wouldn't have gone along with it. No, been swept away by it, swept away by Kit and his cold veneer and his hidden self as hot as Mount Etna. He wouldn't have been relaxed and happy and thinking, again, about taking his prisoner to bed at the first opportunity instead of keeping a hand, or a bloody rope, on the most notorious escape artist the Agency had ever seen, whose reputation had already been proven to him firsthand.

Damn, he was stupid sometimes.

And he still found himself saying, 'Could we maybe—'

'You want to let him go, don't you?' she asked.

'No,' Alex said firmly. 'I'm just as committed as you are, Lulu. But we have our opposing plans. And I came up with my plan before you decided to steal Kit off me for yours. Can't we give him the choice of which plan?'

'Absolutely not,' she said. 'He might choose yours.'

And she grinned at him, and Alex smiled back and knew the topic was closed for now. 'How did you find out where the knife is hidden?' he asked instead.

'I didn't,' she said. 'Someone put out a commission to steal it, and its location was named. So, you'd think bounty hunters would be converging on our kitten to kidnap him—'

'Like you,' Alex said innocently.

'—but instead, we're getting Artisan assassins. Which means the original commission to steal the knife is worth a hell of a lot less than the retaliatory commission to kill the one Artisan who could do the job solo. Both are worth more than the Agency bounty to arrest him, but that's not saying much.'

Alex frowned. 'Does it feel like the person who commissioned the theft was looking to get Whitely murdered without going to the expense or risk of contracting an assassination commission themselves?'

'That's not for us to wonder at,' Lulu said severely. 'Whoever it was gave away the location of the knife, and that's all that matters.'

'Aside from now needing to keep him alive as well as...' He sought and found a suitable word. 'Contained.'

'It's in Wales,' she said abruptly.

Alex was silent. *Didn't go far, then*, would be a fucking awful thing to say, even for twins who commonly said fucking awful things to each other.

'Didn't go far, did it?' Lulu added and Alex snorted and whacked her on the shoulder.

They walked on, up the streets and back down. After a time, Lulu said what had become obvious: 'He's weaving, making sure he's not followed.'

Alex was rubbing two fingers at the spot between his eyes that seemed to help the headache. The intentions of the people they were passing on the streets had weighed on him from the start, but he was getting towards the end of his limits in coping with it.

He felt Lulu take his elbow, felt her calm intention wash over him. 'You pushed a bit too long, Lexi? Let's sit somewhere quiet and eat something until he picks a direction.'

'Thanks, Lulu,' he murmured as she helped him to a tavern down a side street.

They sat and had ales, sharing an outside table where they could flag down street sellers peddling baked potatoes and paper packets of roasted chestnuts. Lulu watched the faces of the people walking by, while Alex admired their shoes; it was easier to tamp down the intentions swamping him if he didn't look at people. Both faces and shoes were reminders that Bristol was a port city, if the smell and noise wasn't enough.

Alex tended to avoid cities and even large towns. Stupidly enough, London itself was tolerable in short doses because the sheer seething mass of humanity overwhelmed his talent so much he went numb, just as the cesspool of the Thames, or the concentrated slaughterhouses and piggeries, or the whole damned city really, extinguished one's sense of smell. He still only lasted a few weeks at a time.

They had a fair few ales while they were waiting. That led Alex to once again raise the debate about vengeance versus justice.

'No,' Lulu said. Her intention shone strongly; she didn't need to keep talking. 'I don't want to see my husband's murderer escape the noose, Alexander. I don't even want to watch him hang. I want to sink the same knife he used to murder Peter into his cold heart and twist it.'

'Fair play,' Alex said mildly. He leaned back and raised his face to the autumn sunlight, closing his eyes. The headache had faded with food and rest; the intentions around them were background murmurs like voices in the distance. 'What happens after, though, Lulu?'

'I'm not planning on frying it up and eating it, if that's what you're asking.'

Alex touched her hand, trying to make her look at him. 'I'm worried that if you succeed on this awful quest of yours, it'll leave you hollow.'

She swallowed the rest of her glass of ale in one long gulp and wiped her mouth. 'I'm already hollow.'

He heaved a breath but Lulu cut him off before he could find words to even approach what he needed to say to her. 'Don't mind me, Lexi, I've got the morbs. I don't know what I'll do after. More of this, I suppose.' She made an eloquent gesture. 'All the mercenary doings. Will you join me again, once you've done what you need to do as an enforcer?'

'Would you like that?' he asked, scratching at the back of his neck.

He and Lulu had worked together now for more than a decade, turning their backs on the society their brother's baronetcy might have opened to them. They'd started as mercenary guards, which had mostly been boring but they'd seen much of Europe. Gradually they'd moved to taking private commissions, bringing in thieves and other criminals who'd escaped custody and whose re-capture was being funded by interested parties.

But the Artisan catches had always been the most enjoyable. They'd learned how to ambush all sorts of different types. Varieties of telepaths and telekinetics were the most common. The offensive weapons sort, like their cousin, were rarer and more dangerous, though their Art tended to run out fast, and they were easily disabled once you got iron on them. Shapeshifting Artisans were the rarest of all and if transmutation or timeslip Artisans even existed, they were keeping bloody quiet about it.

The twins approached their Artisan prey the same way they'd approached Kit. Alex first, with his affable confidence, reading intentions, reading body language, poking a bit, seeing where the pressure points were, what might provoke the Artisan into a flashpoint that would both display and waste their Art. Their intentions always warned him in time for him to dodge if he needed to.

Then Lulu would appear, in the pincer movement that would get their quarry on the floor, hands pressed to the ground so they couldn't fight back, iron smartly around the wrists, blindfolds for the really stroppy ones, and the job was done.

Artisans tended to be an impulsive and ill-trained lot; the Locke twins had never come up against an Artisan they couldn't handle and they had a reputation that said so. They'd even been dispatched to the Crimean to quietly remove Russia's Artisans, and a few French ones, given the international treaties that forbade Artisans directly engaging each other in open warfare.

They'd achieved their task in such a way that they might not have shortened the war, but they certainly didn't lengthen it. It had been a diplomatically flawless performance, despite their personal travails at the time, Lulu's grief and the overwhelming intentions of armies on the march for Alex.

Unsaid between them was the conviction that they could take down their own cousin and her unpleasant husband, if they had to.

And then there was Kit.

Kit Whitely, with the cleanest, most disciplined intentions Alex had ever felt and the most control over Art he'd ever encountered.

Lulu spun her empty glass, watching him. 'Of course, my darling brother.'

'Then, of course, I shall,' Alex said, very deliberately not letting himself hesitate.

She smiled at him, the edges of her smile only a little pained.

'You remember how you could pick him up with one hand?' he asked, and held his breath.

Lulu's smile teetered between pain and fondness and decided on the latter. 'Oh, yeah, he loved that.'

The twins chuckled complicitly. Little Peter Llewellyn most certainly had not loved that. Black eyes flashing in outrage, he would wriggle and complain about what she thought she was doing do a respectable and respected professional man, and then theatrically resign himself to the indignity, and then finally laugh and throw his arms around her neck, and then she would take him off to bed.

What went on behind their closed door had never been Alex's business, but he assumed it was the same process as when he took someone to bed—forthright questions, honest answers. If you couldn't manage that, you had no right to be bedding someone anyway.

Which brought his thoughts right back around to Kit Whitely.

As if she'd read his mind, or at least his expression, Lulu said, 'Look, fine. I'll give your poor little blackguard boy the choice, as long as he'll definitely choose my plan.'

'That's not really a choice, then, Lulu.'

'But, Lexi, will it comfort your conscience on cold nights?'

Alex shrugged; he was far enough down a morally compromised path that it probably would.

'We should get on,' his sister said. 'Your kitten's come to rest.'

They pegged the cheap and ramshacklum hotel where Kit had holed up. Since capturing him now would lead to another long sleepless night, they took an even cheaper room nearby. They both slept until the moon rose, then took turns to rest while the other watched Kit's hotel from the alley. Alex took the second shift so Lulu would have a chance to refresh her public face for the coming day as late as possible.

He only became aware they weren't the only ones after Kit when Lulu rejoined him near dawn.

They were standing looking up at the window Lulu had identified when Locke caught the furtive movement and muttered a few choice words. It was a shadowy figure, a woman or a slender man, climbing to the roof of the building opposite Kit's window. He could feel the flutter of the intention there, weak at this distance.

He consulted with Lulu, who said, 'Let the new Artisan drive him out, then we'll catch him.'

The Artisan created lightning between their hands.

Alex, swearing, scooped up a handful of stones and threw them at Kit's window just before a bolt of lightning smashed through it. The lightning played in the room; the smell of hot metal and smoke wafted over them as the hellish red glow of flames flickered beyond the shattered window.

Both Alex and Lulu were running for the front door of the hotel when Kit came out of it, unscathed.

He was as cool-eyed and self-contained as ever; if he hadn't been in just his trousers and clutching his coat with white knuckles, Alex would have guessed him entirely unaffected by his narrow escape. Alex was quite annoyed with him and was still about to run up and hug him in relief when Lulu yanked him sideways into the alley beside the hotel.

'Oh my, he is solidly built under his scruffy clothes, isn't he?' she said as he flitted past the alley mouth, only just beginning to get his coat on.

Her admiring tone at least distracted Alex from trying to pull away from her and turned him to glaring at her instead. She smirked.

Kit was scowling and talking to himself. 'Lightning. This Artisan gets lightning and I get *doors*? If I had lightning, I'd sodding well have some fun. Well, I probably would've committed murder. Probably good for my eternal soul that I've only got doors.'

And he sent one of his wicked smiles up at the red-streaked dawn sky, the smile that Alex had never gotten from sober Kit, but that bloody Edith Knight received all the time.

'Oh, sure, smile at the fucking clouds,' Alex muttered, before Lulu had to pull him further back down the alley because Kit had abruptly come back their way.

'You remember you're the enforcer who's trying to arrest him, right?' she said in his ear. 'He has no reason to smile at you.'

Luckily, Kit rang the fire bell then, the clamour startling Lulu enough that she didn't catch Alex's guilty wince. He'd been working up to giving

Kit plenty of reason to smile on the train, before they'd arrived far too soon at the station and the sneaky little bastard had locked them both in their carriages. The memory of Kit squirming and gasping under him, even knowing he'd been playing him, still had him adjusting his clothes while Lulu wasn't looking.

'At the risk of impugning my own attractiveness,' his twin went on relentlessly, 'you do understand that when he makes eyes at you, it's only in aid of his own escape, right? You do understand he could feel only anger towards the man who ripped him out of his safe haven?'

Alex rubbed his hands over his face. He did understand that, didn't he?

Then lightning struck the fire bell, and Lulu restrained him for a third time.

'I think the lightning Artisan can only target metal,' she whispered. 'We're covered in it, buttons and buckles and the pistols. Unless you want to strip down to your drawers and dump our pistols, we can't make ourselves targets.'

'Oh, we want to play, do we?' Kit said to empty air, face alight. Alex watched him take a few deep breaths and felt his scattered intentions resolve. He appeared to come to same realisation about metal as Lulu; he checked his buttons and emptied his pockets of metal—including Locke's shiny new enforcer badge. 'Come play where you can do some real damage, my friend.'

And then he was off, trailing his intention like a beacon in his wake.

'Harbour,' Alex said succinctly, and they followed as best they could, Alex picking up his badge as he went.

Alex was exceedingly ready to rush in to rescue Kit, metal on his person or not, but the angelic-looking lad had his own affairs well in hand. He led the lightning Artisan to the busy wharves on the Avon, made himself a target in exactly the right place, and got them safely arrested.

He turned from that rather impressive piece of engineering with no more than a faint flicker of pleasure on his face. Alex guessed Kit didn't know he was giving himself away like that. It was the same tiny smile he'd worn when he'd closed and locked all the doors in Lovelly.

That small smile had been the moment Alex had flipped from assuming it'd be easy enough to hand over a cold-hearted and suspiciously cagey, if rather pretty, criminal to the Agency, to thinking, eloquently, *Oh, shit.*

And then there'd been the crack in the cold façade in the inn's back garden. He'd already caught Kit's flash of interest when he'd walked into the reading room and openly eyed him up, thinking himself unobserved.

Alex had been amused by Kit's lofty refusal to acknowledge his own interest; he'd half-wondered if Kit was even acknowledging it to himself.

But then Kit's full-fledged desire for Alex's mouth had slid briefly into his clear, bright intentions in the garden, the first indication Alex had had that Kit was noticing the attraction too. Ever practical and increasingly fascinated, Alex rolled with it, decided to out-and-out use it.

Because, after all, what harm could it do?

And the crack had turned into a mile-wide chasm and Alex had bloody well fallen into it, crashing from, *Oh, shit,* to *Oh, holy fuck, not now, not this one.*

He'd had Kit's lithe body pressed against the garden wall, all the lad's ostentatious ice melting under his mouth, willing himself to stop and get the cuffs out before this went too far, thinking, *Too late,* thinking, *Oh, Jesus, lad, how do you feel so good,* and, *Please, let it not be this one.*

Alex watched Kit stroll off into the mist and thought the same damned thing again.

'Station,' he said to Lulu.

Kit was far more open with his intentions when he didn't know they were being read. Alex wondered briefly how he was achieving the feat of muting them or masking them. Excuses to Lulu aside, he really did have the sense that Kit had a secondary Art that was a sort of anti-telepathy, except he'd never heard of such a thing.

But then, the whole shape of Kit's Art was outlandish. Some Arts— transmutation, shapeshifting, time manipulation—were rare to the point of mythical, but Kit took some perfectly commonplace Arts and twisted them into bizarreness. Why not add anti-telepathy to that?

He and Lulu got the train station well ahead of their quarry; Kit was still weaving, it seemed.

'Are you kidding me?' Lulu said under her breath, and nudged Alex's attention to the forecourt of the station.

He turned to see a country horse and cart pulled up, with Edith Knight sitting beside the driver, who was also small and blond and therefore had to be of the inexhaustible supply of Knight cousins. Alex hadn't seen a lot of the men, back in the village. They'd be out on the farms, and the fishing boats, and, Alex strongly suspected, out on smuggling runs too. This one had a black eye and swollen jaw that put Lulu's damage to shame.

The young lad leaned over as Edith climbed down without waiting for him to get out and offer a hand. She was holding a single carpetbag and was looking far more proper than she had in the stone circle, dressed as the educated daughter of the prosperous country innkeeper that she, on paper, was. Her deep bonnet was particularly fetching, with an awful lot of lace. It even looked like she'd put on a touch of powder and rouge, though that could have been her natural complexion.

Her driver smoothed his jacket. 'Well now, our Edie, sure your parents giv'ee permission t'go t'London?'

'Yes, they surely did,' Miss Knight replied, her accent less strong than her cousin's but still very different to the more refined tones she had wielded at the Locke twins yesterday.

'It a'en jonnick if they find out I wenty and left 'ee alone in t'city when twernt z'pposed to.'

'I'm meeting our Kit here,' she said. 'It's all fine, Will. He's going to play my brother and we're going to see Obaysch at London Zoo.'

'Wazzat when it be a'ome, Edith Mary Rose?'

'It's a hippopotamus, William Thomas.'

'Well, wazza 'ippopotamus, then, Edie?'

'A strange grey creature.' Miss Knight added a rapid run of syllables, which even Alex, born and bred in the West Country, took a moment to parse. 'Damvinouno.' *Damned if I know, you know.*

Alex exchanged a fond smile with Lulu at that.

'Language, young 'un,' Will said, putting his hands on his hips and trying to look stern.

'I'm older than you, kiddie! And that be a right shambolic, with the language you used with Young Tom at the station yesterday.'

''E wouldn't 'old the train for 'ee, the right gumpy pillock!' He added, 'And then 'e 'it me in ta'face,' with slightly less indignation than he'd shown about Young Tom refusing to mess with the God-given British rail timetable.

'I know! I arrived in time for that bit, didn't I, and me in my best clothes having to deal with all that blood. That was tosh, wasn't it?' She glanced around, seeming to only now become aware of carriages trying to make their way past the cart. 'But get on now, Will.'

'That's fine thanks for bringing you all ta'way, and me up well before dawn to do it.'

'Thank you, William, my favourite cousin. Get on, you're blocking the way.'

Will Knight turned in his seat and gave a rustle look to the carriages coming in behind his cart. He turned back to his cousin. 'Now, Edie, luv, I know 'ee a'en going to London an'all with our Kit. They'm a bad lot, those gurt big people what've a-taken 'im. Why don't I get some of the lads together and we'll 'elp 'ee out?' It was his turn to run his syllables together in a bright waterfall of vowels drowning the soft consonants. 'Gohnosweoee.'

God knows we owe him, Alex translated. *Oh, yes? For what*, he wondered.

'Ah, you know our Kit,' Miss Knight said. 'He won't take nought'a'elp from anybody, the stubborn idjit. Remember when you offered to give him your spare coat?'

They both laughed. Will sobered and said, 'But then, Edie—'

'Get on, William.'

'I be a bit joppety leaving 'ee, luv.'

'Get on, William, or I'll tell tales on you to our Young Tom, I will.'

Will made the sort of dissatisfied noise Alex bet Miss Knight inspired in a lot of people, but he clicked to the carthorse and it ambled forwards. Miss Knight waved as the cart rattled off, then examined the façade of the train station before turning to stride off across the square towards the town proper, unwittingly heading the Lockes' way.

'It sounds like she almost made the train,' Alex said. 'Whitely's experiment must have failed.'

'She wouldn't have had a hope of making it. She'd have had to go home and get done up into appropriate travelling clothes,' Lulu explained, with the voice of hard-gained authority. 'Especially if she's travelling without an escort, she has to look faultless. She's fair determined, isn't she? Or the kitten inspires remarkable loyalty.'

'Apparently they're not lovers,' Alex said, and, at Lulu's raised eyebrow, added, 'All right, yeah, I asked.' She rolled her eyes.

'You again,' Miss Knight said in disgust when they politely accosted her. She was back to the crisper tones she used with strangers.

'Us again, Miss Knight.' Alex smiled in his most agreeable way. 'May we invite you to take tea?'

She narrowed her eyes at him. Etiquette demanded she concede, since it was a polite invitation from a gentleman of her acquaintance, chaperoned by his sister. But then, there was no one to hear her refuse, and she surely hadn't sworn like a rum smuggler in the standing circle because she was overly compliant with etiquette. She brushed past them and kept walking.

'If you're looking for Mr Whitely, don't bother,' Lulu told her. 'We know where he is, Miss Knight.'

'If you knew where he is, you'd have him already.'

'Biding our time, Miss Knight, biding our time.'

Miss Knight turned on them. 'I can only imagine you think you can use me to catch him, and I won't have it,' she said. 'I didn't put on a bloody travelling corset and this stupid bonnet and my best damned dress and send Will to make Tom hold the train for me, and poor Will got punched for his trouble, *I don't even know why*, and I didn't bloody get up in the middle of the night and make Will come all this way and back again just to help you set another trap for my good friend.'

'I like your quiz of a bonnet,' Lulu said, when Miss Knight drew breath. 'It's awful, I love it.'

Miss Knight looked indignant on behalf of her much-maligned bonnet. '*You're* awful. And where's *your* bonnet?'

'I don't wear bonnets,' Lulu said. 'I need my peripheral vision unobscured.'

This was true as far as it went, though actually Lulu thought her hair was her crowning glory and, since she was going to be stared at either way, preferred to pretend it was for her bare head, just as much as she preferred to cover all the bits of herself she wasn't comfortable showing to the world. Alex himself went without fashionable facial hair and forgot his own hat more often than not so they could both pretend some of the stares were for him.

Miss Knight looked taken aback, and then painfully curious about the sorts of things Lulu needed her peripheral vision unobscured for.

'Kit locked you in the stone circle, though,' said Alex, with a question in his tone. 'Did his walls not hold?'

'They did. No roof,' Miss Knight said. 'I climbed out.' They must have looked sceptical. 'Lots of brothers and boy cousins, remember? Good day to you both.' She tried to step past, and Lulu blocked her.

'Are you planning to, what, canvass hotels?' Alex asked. She was; he could read the intention. 'You'll run into trouble, doing that alone.'

Lulu stepped briskly to her side and looped her arm around hers. 'So you'll come take tea with us.'

She was tired and surrounded by familiar Bristol accents. The burr that lived below her educated tones slipped out a little more than usual.

'Are you making fun of my accent?' Miss Knight asked, sounding baffled by the very notion. 'That's not very good, is it?'

'Our mother was a lovely Somerset lass like you,' Alex said, taking her arm from the other side.

'No,' she said, drawing out the word in disbelief. 'Somerset people are *nice*.'

'Our father's people are Gloucestershire,' Lulu added, an honest-to-God smile on her face as she looked down at the smaller woman.

'Oh, that explains it,' Miss Knight said, predictably.

Alex gently tugged her arm. 'Come along, Miss Knight.'

'I'm entirely confused,' Miss Knight said as they walked her back towards the station, which had a teashop by it. 'Are you horrible people kidnapping me or just being obnoxiously hospitable?'

'We're being nice,' Alex explained. 'Like the nice people we are. Intending to go in and out of hotels looking for a man… Aren't you even slightly aware of the impression that gives?'

'What do I care?' she said, indeed carelessly. 'I live in a little village where no one gives two hoots for my reputation. I'm not looking to make a good marriage and I'm not interesting enough to gossip about.'

'You're plenty interesting,' said Lulu. 'Where'd you learn to swear like you do, Miss Knight?'

'Boy cousins,' Miss Knight repeated with theatrical patience. 'And you, Miss Lulu?'

'Boy twin,' Lulu said, equanimity itself.

Alex smiled to himself. His sister stopped. She fidgeted with Kit's handkerchief, gaze abstracted. Then she nodded to him.

Kit was approaching the station.

Locke had already eased the handcuffs from his coat pocket. He passed them to Lulu, who snapped one around Edith's wrist before fastening the other to her own wrist.

'I lost the key to those,' Alex told Miss Knight as she looked at her cuff blankly. 'You're not getting out of them unless Mr Whitely unlocks them for you.'

Both women had strong and inappropriate things to say about that; Lulu added, 'Alexander, you might have warned me.'

'Might've, my dearest Lucinda, and did not.'

'Is your name Lucinda?' Edith asked. 'You realise you've never properly introduced yourself to me, which is rather rude given you've abducted me off the streets and appear to be going to force me onto a train like a pair of white slavers.'

'Don't exaggerate,' Lulu said grumpily. 'We were going to treat you to tea and scones. Mrs Lucinda Llewellyn. Lulu is fine.'

'Pleased to meet you, Miss Lulu. Miss Edith Mary Rose Knight, of the innkeeper Knights of Lovelly-on-Sea,' Edith said brightly.

'*I know.*'

Alex rubbed at his forehead. 'Too late for scones.'

Miss Knight's hands went to her hips, yanking on Lulu's cuffed wrist without a care. 'But I'm famished!'

'He's here.'

Alex could taste Kit's intentions, that eerily cold discipline piercing the buzz of everyone else's looser intentions. His head was beginning to throb already, straining to keep hold of the bright threads in the messy morass. The more he focussed in on Kit, though, the less he noticed of the other humming intentions in the air. That was pleasant.

'He's wanting a train only minutes from leaving. He's going to wait on the platform till the last moment. He wants as empty a carriage as possible. We're going to have time this right, Lulu.'

Lulu guided their little group to the side, moving ahead of Kit on the cord of his intentions. Alex glanced over to see that Lulu, her face grim, had her arm around Miss Knight and her hand over her mouth; they must have seen Kit in the crowd, and Miss Knight had tried to warn him.

'Let's get on,' Lulu said, and all her warmth was gone.

7

'**R**IGHT,' SAID KIT, ONCE LOCKE had explained and Edith had chimed in with every last one of all the extra details she thought it essential for him to know. He was rather horrified at how clear his intentions were, when he wasn't concentrating. 'Give me back my sodding handkerchief.'

Lulu folded her arms 'No.'

Kit held up her wallet. 'I propose,' he said, as if he were playing a game of ècartè and wanted to exchange his cards.

Lulu looked like she might argue, but Locke nudged her and murmured, 'Unless you want to grovel to Kingsford, we need the money back.'

Looking thunderous, she reluctantly handed it over, snatching her wallet from him in return.

Kit balled the handkerchief in his hand, swaying with the movement of the train. Too late, he'd had a thought. 'Now give me back the other thing.'

'What other thing?' Locke asked.

'You didn't track me to Lovelly, she did,' he said, pointing to Lulu. 'So, what the hell did you use? No one has anything of mine.'

'I do have something of yours, and I'm not giving it back.' Lulu scowled at Locke as he fidgeted. 'No, Alex. It's my damned insurance for when he runs again.'

'Language,' said Edith.

'You didn't complain when Kit said "sodding".'

'And "hell",' added Locke.

'*Language*, the pair'a'ee.'

'You are so annoying,' Lulu said huffily. Edith smiled at her. 'And you have dimples.' She did not sound pleased about it.

'A'en fair, innit snugh?' Edith said smugly. She beamed at Kit in complicit satisfaction.

Kit, however, was noticing the glint of metal at her wrist. 'Get those handcuffs off her this instant.'

'She is our hostage to your good behaviour,' Lulu said coldly.

'I told'ee I'll not be,' Edith shouted, but when she tried to rise, Lulu held her down.

Kit, meanwhile, had immediately looked to Locke, who was studiously directing his gaze out the window. Kit interpreted this as indicating that the man could not bluff to save his life and was therefore trying to avoid the eye contact that would give the lie to Lulu's empty threat.

He unlocked Edith's cuff from where he sat, the click muted under Edith's complaints to Lulu, who had not let her go yet. The train rocked, Edith jerked, the cuff fell loose, and Lulu muttered but did not resist as Kit took Edith's hand and drew her to the bench on the other side of the carriage to sit beside him.

She squeezed his hand before, apparently unable to contain herself, hugging him. He stiffened reflexively at the unexpected contact. He heard Locke make a noise and glanced over Edith's shoulder in time to see him turn back to the window, frowning.

Kit breathed out and made himself melt into the hug until Edith let him go.

'Now me,' said Lulu.

'I don't think I feel brave enough to hug you, though,' Kit said.

Locke, still apparently absorbed by the view, snorted and Lulu rolled her eyes and held up her own wrist. The cuff that had come off Edith swung loose at the end of the chain linked to Lulu's cuff.

'Certainly, Miss Lucinda.' Kit bowed from where he sat. 'When you give me back whatever it is you have of mine.'

Lulu's eyes gleamed. 'If you think I can't live with a pretty bracelet or two, kitten, I'm pleased to enlighten you.' She slipped the free cuff onto her wrist, where it clinked against the locked one.

Kit folded his hands together. 'However so you wish.'

'You've got a fine line in pretending compliance, don't you?'

'It's actual compliance, Miss Lucinda.'

'You said you'd open my door for me and then you locked us onto the train and ran away!'

Edith giggled. Kit shot a look at Locke but he was still refusing to turn his face away from the window.

Kit sighed. 'Yes,' he said. 'If you take me to your door, I'll open it. *If.* It *is* actual compliance, Miss Lucinda, it's just not willing compliance. So, yes, get me to the door and I'll open it. But you have to get me there first. And best of luck to you because you've seen for yourself how easy it will be.'

Locke cleared his throat and sent a meaningful look at his twin, who scowled back at him. Kit drew his legs up so he could sit cross-legged and watched their faces as they conducted their silent twin-speak conversation.

'Whose prisoner am I now? The bounty hunter or the enforcer?'

Locke glanced one last time at Lulu, who rolled her eyes again. 'Fine.'

Her brother turned back to Kit. 'We'll offer you the choice, Mr Whitely.'

'I choose being set free,' said Kit promptly.

'Funny boy.' Locke leaned towards him. 'Come with me, I take you to the Agency headquarters in London. They'll almost certainly consign you to gaol.'

'You certainly know how to sell yourself, Mr Locke.'

'Come with me,' Lulu said, 'you'll help me steal something.'

'A knife,' Locke said. 'Lulu, be honest.'

'A knife?' repeated Kit. And she had said something about vengeance. 'For what reason?'

'None of your business. What? Alexander, that *is* honest. It's none of anyone's business but my own.'

Kit thought. 'And then? After?'

'And then I hand you back to my brother and he takes you to the Agency, I suppose,' she said, plainly reluctant to admit this, even though she'd perfectly openly suggested her twin do exactly that in the summer pavilion.

'Then that's not a choice, is it?' Kit said. 'It's just extra work.'

Lulu growled and spoke like the words were being pried out of her. 'Would it help if I told you I'm justified?'

He started to ask why. But she didn't want to tell him; he didn't want to know. He shook his head. 'Not a thief. Not an assassin. Not interested.'

'I'm not asking you to steal anything or kill anyone, kitten. Just open one door for me. I'll do the rest.'

'Mr Locke, tell me again the offence for which I have been arrested by an Agency enforcer.'

'Use of illicit Art for the purposes of accessory to theft,' Locke said resignedly.

'And tell me what your sister is asking me to do.'

'Use of illicit Art for the purposes of accessory to theft.'

'So I think we're done here,' Kit said.

Lulu glared daggers at both him and Locke before suddenly leaning forwards to put her face in her hands. Kit was outwardly unmoved but somewhat disconcerted by Lulu's sudden overt despair, that he supposed the anger was meant to hide.

Locke's fingers drummed restlessly on his knee as he looked at his sister, and looked at Kit. Kit waited, eyebrows raised, for him to go back on his noble intention to give him the choices he so sorely lacked.

Not that the choices they were offering were in any way true choices.

Locke tapped his boot on the floor of the carriage. He had the same look on his face that he'd had when he'd realised Kit had locked him onto the train. Kit thought it was shame.

'If you help Lulu, I'll give you an hour's head start after,' Locke said finally, as reluctantly as his sister.

Kit paused. He hadn't heard that phrase before. 'Like in a horse race? The horse that gets its head forwards wins?' he asked. Alex nodded. 'That's my bribe?'

'It's your reward.'

Kit glanced idly at Edith. 'This is not a real choice,' he told the twins. Alex's reluctance made it plain it wasn't a real offer, either; they'd betray him and send him to the Agency for sure. 'I'll give it due consideration.'

Then, since he really was quite petty and really was quite irritated, he turned to Edith. 'Edie, what happened with our Aunt Agnes who had that strange pain in her leg?'

'Well, you will *never* guess, luv!' said Edith, and she was off on one of her more rambling stories, her accent strengthening as she dived into it.

Kit, satisfied with Lulu's expression of dawning horror, turned his attention to the mildly amused Locke, who obviously had no idea that he was also about to get what was coming to him.

The man had every right to be angry at him for the trick he'd played on yesterday's train, and he was about to add insult to injury with this next game, but *really*. Kit had had quite enough.

He looked Locke in the eye and intended to get him alone and straddle him so he could feel those big thighs under his own.

Locke looked back at him, or perhaps just slightly over his head, own head slightly cocked, a small frown forming between his eyes.

Kit intended to unbutton Locke's shirt, button by button and spread the cloth wide so he could put his mouth on one of Locke's nipples and get his fingers on the other.

Locke flicked an eyebrow and leaned back into his corner, with an expression that plainly said he knew Kit's game now and was inviting him to do his worst.

Just watch me, baby, Kit thought, and intended to kiss and suck Locke's nipples till they were tight and rigid under his tongue, and then use his teeth.

Locke's breathing changed. He shifted his position, carefully adjusting his coat. He shook his head at Kit.

'Hmm, that's interesting,' Kit said as Edith paused. 'And then what happened?'

And he intended to rake his nails down the sensitive skin along Locke's stomach, discovering the ridges of muscles where his tongue would follow.

Both Vikings had to swallow a groan, for almost diametrically opposed reasons. Kit allowed himself a tiny smile. It was really a race as to which twin would break first at this point.

He was intending to slide his fingers into Locke's unfastened trousers when both twins said, 'God, stop!' at the same time.

'You made your point,' Locke added, with more adjusting of his coat.

'Didn't quite get there, no,' Kit murmured, blinking sleepily across at him. Meanwhile, Edith said, 'Did I an'all? Not sure what my point was, but all right.'

'I think your aunt was misdiagnosed,' Kit told her. 'She should go on over to Bristol and get a proper physician to look at it.'

Edith snapped her fingers. 'That was my point, yes, thank you, Kit.'

'Is the physician in your village not a proper physician?' asked Lulu. 'He set my nose.'

'I'd get it re-done, if you want to stay pretty,' Kit said, while Edith said much the same thing except with a lot more words and more justification for the physician's drinking problem than strictly necessary, since he was yet another Knight.

'What are you smirking about, Mr Locke?' Kit eventually gently interrupted to ask.

Locke smiled back at him. 'You called me pretty.'

Kit swallowed. He'd been courting the man's anger and so had no right to be relieved he hadn't received it. 'I did not, I called Lulu pretty.'

'Twins. If she's a pretty 'un, I'm a pretty 'un.'

'Lulu puts the effort in, so Lulu get the compliment. You're just… whatever it is you are.' Kit waved a hand in a circle at the level of Alex's face to convoy his general inexpressible attractiveness.

'Since I am an English gentleman of means, I will naturally take the credit due to the actual person doing all the work. So: pretty.'

Lulu shook her head. She had a worn and stained rail guide in her lap, which she lifted towards her brother. 'Did you notice the line the kitten picked, Lexi? We're coming into Upper Morton.'

'Are we?' Locke said, all amusement dropped so quickly that Kit queasily realised it had to be an act. Oh. He was probably very angry with him, then.

'Seems a shame not to visit, when we're so close.'

'No time.'

Lulu heaved a sigh. 'God help me, Alexander. Fine. Let's just disembark and catch a train back to Bristol to change lines, then. Newport or London, which is it to be, kitten?'

'Toss a shilling,' Kit said carelessly.

Locke tsked and Lulu made an agonised growling noise in the back of her throat.

Kit maintained his cold composure. Her pain was not his pain. 'It's not a real choice,' he told them. 'So I won't absolve your consciences by making it.'

'But you're not wanting the head start at the horse race, Kitty?' Edith asked him, an odd note in her voice.

Kit lifted his chin and looked defiantly at Locke. 'Won't need it, Eddie.'

Locke's wolfish smile made its slow appearance—oh, the man liked a challenge, indeed. Kit, face carefully blank, swore at himself. He knew better than to gloat or boast or do anything that gave forewarning, especially to someone who could read his bloody intentions anyway.

And, of course, Lulu, with her tracking talent, was apparently holding something of his, that would lead her straight to him no matter where he hid.

Then he blinked, because he had just twigged to the undertone of anxiety that had been darkening Edith's sunshiny tones. She had, after all, effectively been kidnapped this morning.

'You'll escort Edith home,' he told the twins.

'I want *you* to escort me home,' she said, before Locke and Lulu could spit out assurances or threats according to their own lights.

Her fingers were worrying at the stitching on her dress. He took her hand, lifting it away. 'I can't go back to Lovelly, Edith.' He spoke to Lulu. 'So you'll take her home, and you'll give me whatever banknotes you have left, and you'll give me anything you hold of mine that you could use to track me and you'll wait an hour before you come after me. All those, and I'll open your bloody door.'

Lulu sat up straight.

'As many doors as you like, Miss Lucinda,' Kit added with a nod, and she lit up into an unexpectedly magnificent smile that he fought hard not to answer.

'If she can get you there,' Locke said quietly. 'Right? This is still unwilling compliance.'

Lulu's smile vanished.

Kit retaliated with no thought but one highly specific intention, because he was petty as hell. 'It's willing compliance if you want it to be, baby,' he added on top.

'Mr Whitely,' Locke said sternly. 'It bloody is not.'

Kit folded his hands into his lap and would not answer. Tension thickened in the carriage until Edith could not take the heavy silence anymore.

'Are we getting off at Upper Morton?' she asked brightly. 'I am truly famished. Let's have a thing or two to eat and be feeling the better for it.'

The steam whistle signalling the imminent station blasted out, bringing Kit back to his senses before he could tell her she sounded exactly like her mother.

Her cheer, Locke's amusement, Lulu's anger, all hiding their real feelings. So much easier to just not have them.

8

*W*HEN THEY STEPPED OFF THE TRAIN onto the station, the repercussions of Kit's petty revenge immediately came clear; Locke grunted from deep in his gut and almost doubled over.

'Jesus fuck,' he muttered. 'Hasn't come on like this for years.'

Lulu got her hand under his elbow, helping him stand up straight and move to a less crowded area, Edith fluttering on his other side in noisy concern.

Locke, grimacing, said, 'Lulu, what's Kit doing?'

She glanced over her shoulder. 'Standing still, looking innocent,' she reported.

'Grab him.'

'Slander,' Kit said, as Lulu got him by the coat sleeve, dragging him with them.

Kit considered slipping out of the coat while the Locke twins were occupied, but until he got his mystery item back from Lulu, he'd always have to worry about her tracking him down.

Besides, he didn't want to leave Edith. He didn't think the twins would hurt her, as such, and Locke would take her home if Lulu wouldn't, for all the good that would do to her much-disparaged reputation, but he felt responsible for her in a way she would no doubt excoriate him for if she knew.

And then there was Locke; Kit was feeling just a teensy bit responsible about that too. That string of intentions on the train; the desire had ratcheted his own Art up and he'd completely failed to consider it would ratchet up Locke's talent, too, possibly all the way into the realm of a proper Art, and one he couldn't control.

'Are you being swamped?' Locke's sister asked him. 'Deep breaths, Lexi.'

'Everyone's intentions are so strong here,' he said, sounding bewildered.

'God.' He squeezed his eyes shut and pressed two fingers between his eyes, shoulder hunched. 'Give me a minute.'

The boost should fade, and fast. If Locke could hold on to raging desire in the face of an Art-driven megrim, he had the sort of stamina Kit would definitely like to exploit in bed. But the megrim itself was going to linger.

'Would putting the cuffs on help?' Kit politely suggested. 'Silver?'

Lulu still wore the cuffs. Locke clasped his bare hand around them. His wrinkled nose told Kit the silver wasn't doing much. He let go, wriggling his fingers. Kit would have bet currency the iron in it had tingled him.

'Damn it,' Lulu said. 'Lexi, you're in a bad way. I know you're going to hate it, but let's go to Northfield.'

'No.' Locke pressed between his eyes harder. 'Just give me a minute.'

'You can rest, we can change into fresh clothes, Kingsford might not even be there.'

Both twins paused and then snickered. 'He's a recluse,' Locke explained to Kit and Edith. 'He'll be there.'

'He'll give us money—'

'He'll call you by your old name and then apologise and then do it again. Such shiny good intentions.'

'He has his odd younger siblings, he's trying, you know he is because you can see those shining intentions.'

'He's trying, all right,' Locke muttered.

'We can catch the earliest train back to Bristol tomorrow morning, before it gets too crowded here for your head. Hell, Kings'll give us the carriage if that's what we want. But right now, I think we have to get out of here before you completely collapse.'

'I am *not* going to collapse,' Locke snapped, apparently highly offended at the very thought of it. He hunched forwards, sinking both hands into his hair. 'Fucking Jesus fuck, all right, take us to the coaching inn.'

Once they were settled into the hired carriage, a corner each, Kit took *Little Dorrit* from his inside coat pocket. 'Shall I read to you?' he asked Locke, since the man was plainly in need of distraction and Kit felt ever so slightly responsible for his current state of distress.

'No.'

'All right,' Kit said warily.

The megrim that Kit had caused, or the visit to the older brother, or both, had either put Locke in a filthy mood, or left him unable to hide the filthy mood he'd already been in—that Kit had also caused, by taking advantage of him on the train into Bristol.

Silently, he flipped to the start of the chapter they had reached when Kit had read Locke to sleep and then escaped. It probably had not been wise, to bring out the book and remind Locke of that little escapade.

And the second, successful, escape that had happened afterwards.

'What the blazes are you doing?' Locke demanded.

'Reading to myself,' Kit said.

'No reading ahead,' Locke said.

Kit was leaning towards the filthy mood being entirely down to himself.

'You utter monster,' Edith said, probably not joking in the slightest. 'That's a serialised novel. Every chapter ends by making you want to read the next one.'

Locke took the book out of Kit's hands. 'He's not allowed to read on without me.' He slammed it shut and slid into his own coat.

'Well, I mean, *really*,' Edith said, which about summed it up. She snapped open her bag, yanked out *Villette* and shoved it at Kit.

But Kit handed it back, saying nothing, because he knew to take punishment without overt defiance. He settled his back into the corner and drew his knees up so he could fold his arms around them and rest his cheek atop them.

Locke began to fidget with his sleeves, folding the cuffs of his shirt over his coat, and then unfolding them and painstakingly straightening them. He took out his comb and ran it through his own hair. Slowly the movements of his hands smoothed out from the frantic twitch of a hummingbird to long, calm strokes as he settled into his habitual placidity.

His detached gaze slowly, inevitably, settled onto Kit, or, more accurately, Kit's wild curls.

Kit began, 'You can co—'

'No.' Locke's hand clenched around the comb. 'No, thank you, Mr Whitely.'

Well. Kit had used that avenue as a precursor to escape, too, after all. He turned his face into his knees and forced himself to take a slow breath. He had been bad and now the weight of a powerful man's disapproval was upon him. Over to Christopher with that nonsense, of course. His breathing steadied, his queasiness vanished. *Good boy, Christopher.*

'Christ knows what Kingsford will say about this one,' Locke said suddenly.

Kit lifted his head to see the twins looking him over with identically unreadable expressions. 'What?'

Lulu shrugged. 'You look like you'll steal the silverware and impregnate half the maids on your way out the door.'

Kit weighed this up before saying, 'Half?'

'Half,' agreed Lulu, 'because you'll be too busy seducing the footmen to have time for the other half.'

Kit made a *can't argue* shrug. He glanced at Edith for her opinion; she was smiling fondly. 'You just have a suspiciously innocent air about you, Kit. It makes people wonder what you're up to.'

'Edith should impress the shit out of him, though,' Lulu said, and then both twins groaned.

'Now what?' Edith asked, looking a little flushed with pleasure.

'We'll have to stop swearing in front of you or Kings will have conniptions.'

'You know he's going to anyway,' Locke said gloomily. He wiped at his eyes and rubbed the furrow between his brows.

'You've got the patience of a saint, Lexi. I don't know why you have such a hard time with your own brother.'

'Says the pot to *her* own brother.'

'Saints aren't patient,' Kit said to the ceiling of the cab.

He felt all three stare at him.

''Tis the very definition, kitten,' Lulu said.

'Saint Jerome,' Kit countered. He was well known enough that he didn't feel the need to elaborate. 'Saint Basil was notoriously short-tempered. Saint Apollonia jumped into a fire rather than wait for the Romans to burn her. Saint Albinus destroyed a tower with prayer. Then there's Saint Quiteria and her eight sisters. Not renowned for their patience.'

'Fine, I accept the rebuttal,' Lulu said irritably when he drew breath to go on. 'How do you know so many obscure stories about saints?'

'Heard them growing up,' Kit said vaguely.

'Oh! Do you know, Saint Crispin's Day has just gone?' Edith said. Kit's stomach lurched. 'Patron saint of shoemakers, leatherworkers, saddles, gloves, anything to do with leather, really, so book covers, of course, *and* lacemaking and weaving. The patron saint of booksellers is Saint John of God, but he's also hospitals, so I don't really see the connection unless you want something to read when you're convalescing. But the point is, Crispin can be a diminutive of Christopher *and* it famously means "curly-haired" so that's apt!'

'Is Crispin the one with the millstone and the three cauldrons?' Locke idly asked.

'Him and his brother both,' Edith agreed. 'But in the English version, Crispin is the prince in disguise who seduces the emperor's d— Oh, Kitty, you're looking very ashy.'

Kit's stomach had invaded his mouth, no space left to breathe. Without the time to count Christopher back into his cage, he slapped himself hard across the face. When he lifted the other hand to deliver the matching slap to the other cheek, Locke caught it.

'No,' he said simply.

He slipped his fingers through Kit's and lowered both their hands to rest between them.

Trembling, Kit said, 'I was going to, ah, to flay the fox. It's under control.'

Locke flexed his fingers against his. Lulu looked out the window. Edith stared ahead, occasionally brushing her gloved knuckles across her flushed cheek, in the same spot that Kit had slapped himself.

Northfield was apparently a way out of town and Kit would not tolerate this awkwardness the entire way. He loosened his hand from Locke's, leaving his fingers cold for a moment. 'I think you need a framework to hang your Ar—*talent* on, so you can control it.'

'Don't know what you mean,' Locke said.

He squinted at Kit and then shut his eyes, most likely trying to block out Kit's intentions to protect his head. As far as Kit had observed, shutting his eyes didn't help him much.

'For example,' he went on, undeterred. 'I don't really have a threshold Art, that's unheard of and just plain ludicrous. I believe I have very specific teleport and metalworking Arts, and my mind set them around doors and locks because when they manifested, I happened to be desperate to escape and so that's the shape they took.'

Locke opened his eyes. His gaze was warm and sympathetic, any annoyance with Kit gone or hidden again. 'What were you desperate to escape from, Mr Whitely?'

'You are distracting yourself, Mr Locke,' Kit said, ignoring looks of varying degrees of pity and curiosity from all three of them, the spectre of his recent bizarre behaviour in the air again. 'I'm suggesting that if you were to conceptualise your talent in a different way, you could get better control over it.'

'It is what it is,' Locke said softly. 'I can't see it differently.'

'Would you tell me what you do see, please?' Kit watched as Locke rubbed two fingers between his eyes again. 'Perhaps another time, Mr Locke.'

'I'm fine. I see—' He stared at Kit, who politely presented to him the very clear intention to help him. Locke gave a reluctant smile. 'A picture, but it moves. There's no sound, but it's noisy. It's faint but there's too much light. It's a mess, Mr Whitely.'

'When you look straight at me, can you see Miss Lulu's and Miss Knight's?'

'No,' said Locke, and then, with frustration running rampant in his voice, 'but also yes, because intentions are *noisy* whether I can see them or not. That's why crowds do what they do to me. Closing my eyes helps a tiny bit but not really.'

'Where is it?' Kit held a hand at the level of his forehead. 'Here? Higher?'

'Higher. Above your head.'

That made sense; it was where Locke had fixated when Kit had been entertaining him on the train this morning. It was where he looked when he was actively trying to read intentions rather than passively letting them wash over him.

'Hmm.' Kit dropped his hand. 'Did you visit the Great Exhibition a few years back?'

'Did *you*?'

'Yes,' Kit said. 'The Blackwell gang kidnapped me so I could help them steal that big diamond from the India exhibit. That was the first time I got caught, actually. I was not quite anticipating the consequences of registering with the Agency.'

He was pleased to watch Locke pull a guilty face.

'Oh my goodness,' Edith said breathlessly. 'And what happened?'

'Was the diamond stolen?'

'Not that we've ever heard,' Lulu said.

'Then I escaped in time,' Kit said, 'because *I'm not a thief.* And then I had a lovely day out at the Crystal Palace. Including Alfred Charles Hobbs's enlightening demonstration on locks.'

'Fucking hell,' said Lulu, a slightly off-topic realisation dawning with the burning intensity of the summer sun. 'You could walk into the Tower and steal the crown jewels whenever you wanted, couldn't you, kitten?'

'Several London gangs have had that bright idea,' Kit agreed. 'Luckily for me, the brighter the idea, the stupider the execution. No one ever seems to realise that I'm perfectly capable of opening anything they need me to, but I can't deal with guards because I am not, in any way, a violent person.'

Locke, without blinking, tapped his leg where Kit had stabbed him.

'I will do without your commentary, Mr Locke. The most successful thefts I've been involved in are where they make me open the locks and then send in the real thief.'

'Hence the *accessory* charges, Mr Whitely.'

'Understood, Mr Locke,' said Kit, in very much the same tone that he'd just politely told him to shut up. 'If I may return to my original point, do you happen to remember the stereoscope cards they sold for souvenirs at the Exhibition?'

Edith clapped her hands. 'I still have mine! We had such a wonderful visit. Did you know there was a flushing toilet in one of the women's restrooms and it had a *mahogany seat*? Did you try it out, Lulu, because I did! And I saw a stuffed platypus and false teeth made of hippopotamus ivory, but I did not get to go to the zoo to see the real—'

Lulu grabbed the sensible option and interrupted. 'We didn't get the souvenir, but we did see stereoscopy in action.'

'Rude,' muttered Edith.

'Is the picture of the intention anything like that? Even a little?'

'Like one that moves and has sound,' Locke said. 'Though, not sound. It's not sound. It's—' He twisted a clawed hand by his temple. 'It's intention. It's bloody noisy but it's not sound.'

Kit nodded, more in acceptance than understanding. 'Would seeing the intentions be easier if you could turn the noise off?'

'Yes. And turn down the brightness.'

Kit, nodding again, settled back. 'Well?' Locke demanded, when he didn't say anything.

'I have to think,' Kit said. 'But does your brother have a stereoscopic viewer at home? For erotic daguerreotypes and such.'

'No, my brother most certainly does not own a stereoscope for the purposes of viewing pornography,' Locke said, straight-faced but with hazel eyes gleaming in amusement. 'But he does have one for looking at wildlife daguerreotypes and other scenes of life he will never see for himself, what with being a hermit.'

'Show it to me, when we get there.'

Locke nodded. He leaned back and shut his eyes, falling quickly into a doze that smoothed out the lines between his eyes and relaxed the tension across his shoulders. Lulu stretched her legs out so the tip of one of her boots was touching Kit's calf, the slightest contact to let him know she was keeping her deeply suspicious eyes on him while Locke slept his headache off.

They arrived at Northfield an hour or so later, pausing at an ornate gate for a gatekeeper to let them in upon the newly-awakened Locke's hail, and rattling in through parklands to a stately home with many windows and beautiful gardens. Kit was no judge, but it seemed to him that the Locke baronetcy was a profitable one.

'Miss Lucinda,' he said, as he and Edith both craned to look out the window. Edith was looking intimidated for the first time he'd ever seen. 'Remember how I asked for whatever banknotes you had left?'

Lulu looked up, resigned. 'Yes, kitten?'

'You best be stocking up here,' he said pleasantly. 'I don't come cheap.'

He leaned forwards and pulled her handcuffs free, giving them over to Locke and then holding out his own wrists to him to be cuffed in slightly provocative submission.

'There's that suspicious compliance again.' Locke slipped the cuffs into his coat pocket. 'I'm not planning to let my brother know I've brought a dangerous criminal into his home, Mr Whitely.'

Kit was unreasonably offended. 'I'm not dangerous.'

'Stabbed me in the leg,' Locke said with really quite inappropriate amusement.

'Not on purpose!'

Locke smiled at him. 'You do a lot of things not on purpose, don't you?'

'When pushed, yes,' Kit admitted, and Locke shrugged.

The big man made no move to get out of the carriage when it pulled up before the manse. Kit thought for a moment he was waiting to be ushered out by a servant, but he was gazing out the carriage window looking up at the façade, face set.

'I can feel it from here,' he sighed. 'The intention to respect our choices. The intention to not mention our lifestyle.' He put a sarcastic edge on that last word.

'What, fucking men?' Kit said.

Both Lockes looked at Edith.

'What?' she said.

'Language?' Lulu said. 'For *starters*, my God, kitten, her tender innocence.'

Kit sniggered while Edith said, 'Kit can say whatever he wants, because *he* is not a horrible person.'

'Sometimes,' Kit said, avoiding everybody's eye.

Locke snorted. 'No, not fucking men.'

Edith theatrically gasped. 'Oh, my tender innocence!'

He sighed, but he also smiled fondly at her. 'Kingsford would not have a single thought about any of that.'

'Wouldn't even cross his mind,' Lulu confirmed. 'Between the three of us, our father was certainly disappointed by his heirs.'

'He hates the bounty hunting,' Locke explained.

'Not suitable for a gentleman's children?' Kit asked.

'Don't think that's his logic,' Lulu said. 'I think it just makes him worry about us. He doesn't like having to be worried. He doesn't like having to deal with much of that sort of thing at all.'

'A man after my own heart,' Kit said. 'We'll get along famously, I'm sure.'

'Holy fuck,' the twins whispered in unison and Kit put his hands over his mouth so they wouldn't see him laughing. He caught Edith's eye instead, and sent her off into giggles.

An older man in livery and an old-fashioned powdered wig opened the carriage door. Locke started and then said, 'Morning, Wetherby,' and climbed out.

'Master Alexander,' Wetherby said. He bowed, and then again to Lulu as she got out. 'Miss Lucinda.'

Lulu turned back and offered her hand to Edith, an ingrained gesture. Then she flinched and dropped her hand. Locke smoothly stepped forwards to offer his instead.

'Kit,' he said, leaning back into the carriage. 'Really, do try not to make trouble, all right?'

'As your prisoner, I believe I am morally obliged to make as much trouble as possible, am I not?' Kit politely enquired.

'Nope,' Locke said. 'No, that is definitely not a thing that prisoners are supposed to do. But if it is, remember you're Lulu's prisoner now.' He flashed his wolfish grin.

Kit hopped out. He was looking up the steps to the front doors when one door came ajar and the older Locke brother made his appearance. Sir Kingsford Locke was a small man, only a little taller than Kit but, unlike Kit, slender to the point of scrawniness with it. He was dark of hair and eye, with lines about his eyes that suggested pain. He leaned, heavily but expertly, on a well-worn cane, which suggested to Kit the pain was chronic. He was very much nothing at all like his younger siblings.

Kit saw Locke stiffen, and he turned and looked up at his brother. Sir Kingsford's look of polite greeting dissolved almost immediately into horror as soon as Lulu also turned around. Both twins were standing taller under their brother's scrutiny.

'Alist— Lucinda, your face!'

He had no trace of the West Country lilt that still lay under Locke and Lulu's educated accents. Leaning heavily on the cane but ignoring the arm offered by another liveried servant, he hurried down the steps and seized his sister's hand, staring at her intently. The bruises and swelling had gone down, and she had found time this morning to apply her cosmetics, but the damage was still visible.

'I knew this sort of thing would happen!'

'Less than three minutes between making the intention and breaking the intention,' Locke said, grimly satisfied. 'That's a record.'

'It was my fault, Sir Kingsford,' Kit said, assuming his most innocent face and his politest tones. 'I hit her in the face with a door.'

'By accident,' Lulu added, narrowing her eyes at him.

'Unavoidable accident,' agreed Kit, smiling sweetly at Sir Kingsford. 'Deepest apologies.'

Sir Kingsford blinked at him slowly, like a lizard, before turning to Locke. 'Where's your hat, Alexander? Practically naked.'

'Where's Lulu's bonnet?' Locke said, jerking a thumb at Lulu.

Lulu glared at him. 'Alexander, you rat.'

Sir Kingsford did not dignify this blatant dodge with any indication that he had heard it. 'And I've had an angry letter from an innkeeper demanding reparations on your behalf.'

'Also my fault,' said Kit. 'I handcuffed him to a bed and lost the key.'

He intensified his false smile, which he knew would flip his visage from angelic to wicked. Wanton, if you were so inclined to label him so.

To his great disappointment, Sir Kingsford didn't even show a flicker of shock, though the footmen went a bit wide-eyed. He merely looked at Kit, waiting.

Locke cleared his throat. 'Sir Kingsford Locke. Mr Kit Whitely.'

Kit, who had been trained in niceties only so far as one destined to be a servant would be, and patchily at that, and who had not met a titled gentleman socially before, took a guess and bowed. Sir Kingsford nodded to him before shooting an unreadable look at Locke.

Locke ignored it. 'And Miss Edith Knight.'

Here, Edith put out her hand and Sir Kingsford took it. Politely but without sign of pleasure, he raised it to his lips to kiss her knuckles lightly.

'No hat, gloves *or* shoes,' he commented. 'A pair of strays you've brought home.'

Kit was still as barefoot as when he'd rolled out of bed and fled the lightning Artisan, and never wore hat or gloves, an Artisan's privilege. Edith showed no such sartorial sins.

'Not me,' said Edith, showing her dimples. 'I'm the daughter of a gentleman.'

'Are you indeed?' Sir Kingsford asked. 'Do I detect a Somerset lady here?'

'Like your lovely mother, yes,' Edith said.

'No!' the twins said in unified horror.

'Like my siblings' mother, yes,' Sir Kingsford corrected without overt offence or even a blink of reaction. 'But you have had some sort of education, I think I hear?'

'Oh, yes, a governess and a finishing school,' Edith said brightly, perfectly content to be interrogated. She shot a look at Kit, her dimples making a mischievous appearance. 'I have a thorough knowledge of music, singing, drawing, dancing, and all the modern languages.'

From Caroline Bingley's lips to Edith's ear. 'Don't forget improving your mind through extensive reading,' Kit added.

'Indeed,' she said. 'That too.'

Sir Kingsford nodded gravely. Edith was lucky he hadn't read *Pride and Prejudice*. He didn't seem the type to enjoy novels, to be fair.

He started in on another question, but Lulu said, 'Kingsford, let's allow our guests inside and feed them before you keep indulging your curiosity, can we?'

That made him turn to the twins. 'I suppose you're visiting because you need money and supplies. Your rooms are, as always, ready for you. I will have two guestrooms made up.' He hesitated. 'Yes?'

'Yes,' said Locke, with the slightest flicker of surprise.

'You may call for a luncheon whenever you're ready. I will be in my study, Alexander. I will see the rest of you at dinner.'

He nodded once more, glanced at Kit expressionlessly, squeezed Lulu's hand, and limped away.

'Luncheon,' Locke repeated, as soon as he was out of earshot, smirking at Lulu. 'We dainty flowers need our sustenance, I suppose.'

'Well, he seems nice!' Edith said. 'Though anyone who offered me food right now would earn my undying devotion. May we please call for that lunch, luvs?'

Locke rubbed his hands over his face and huffed out a long breath. He nodded to the other footman. 'Manage that, would you, Wellerman?' The servant bowed and hurried off. Locke rolled his shoulders. 'I'll suppose I'll get the lecture out the way now before we eat.'

Lulu tapped her fingers against her leg. 'You don't think that maybe some food first will help it not turn into a shouting match, Lexi?'

'How remarkably reasonable of you, dear sister. No, I'll take the lumps with consummate good grace. Do you want to take our sprites for a walk around the gardens? Don't let Kit near any gates.'

'I *beg* your pardon?' Kit said.

'Compliant right up until you're not, Mr Whitely.'

'Ooh, you hold a grudge.'

'Can I see the library?' Edith blurted. 'I bet it's ever so spectacular.'

'Gardens first, poppet,' Lulu said, holding her hand out to Edith, who took it with only a small hesitation. 'Library after lunch. Come along with us, kitten.'

'I need to see your brother's stereoscopic viewer,' Kit said.

Locke sighed. 'You might as well come with me to his study, then,' he said. 'God forbid we disturb him twice.' He took Kit's elbow.

Kit looked down at the hand. 'Where would I escape to?' he grumbled. 'We're miles out of town.'

'Far be it from me to predict how your twisty little Art works, Mr Whitely.'

'And Lulu can track me regardless.'

Locke made a noncommittal noise and tightened his grip, walking Kit up the stairs and into the grand house. Kit had the impression of a high-ceilinged entry hall with chandeliers and parquetry flooring before he was hurried into Sir Kingsford's study.

It was well-appointed, with a large desk and lots of shelving. Heavy curtains blocked the windows. Two comfortable wingback chairs sat by the fire, but the rest of the room was not remotely welcoming. On one of the few spaces on the wall not covered by shelves sat a portrait of a man who looked like the Locke twins, with a dark-haired wife and babe in arms. The same man was depicted again in a second family portrait, older and now with a small flaxen-haired woman with two babes in arms. A narrow-faced boy stood beside the family grouping in this second portrait, face serious.

The baronet gave his brother a curt nod. He was wearing half-moon glasses now, which made him look older. Alex nudged Kit towards one of the chairs by the fire.

'Do not move,' he told him *sotto voce*. 'I'll be watching.'

Kit hummed, not his usual tuneless hum of pleasure but a pointed rendition of Burns's *Whistle and I'll Come to You, My Lad*. Alex huffed out in impotent, and amused, annoyance and faced his brother across the desk.

'I've called on Nurse to attend to Lucinda's injuries. Are you in need of her services?'

Why not a local physician, Kit wondered, before understanding: Lulu wouldn't like that. A provincial village physician probably wouldn't like that either. Nurse was likely literally the nurse for the Locke twins as they grew up.

'I'm well enough,' Locke said easily, hand brushing his thigh. Well. He could hardly strip off his trousers for a nurse, old retainer of the family or no, could he?

'Ah, well. And your guests?'

'Well enough,' Locke repeated, glancing at Kit, who gave one of his *I'm fine* shrugs before deliberately getting up to wander about the room, revelling in the narrow-eyed look he got from Locke.

'To business then,' Kingsford said crisply, and Locke's attention snapped back to him.

Kit drifted to the stereoscopic viewer on a table by the window while the Viking stood tall before the desk and received the predicted bollocking from his mousy little accountant of a brother. Sir Kingsford did not at all seem put off his stride by Kit's presence, or if he was, then Kit hated to think what sort of dressing-down Locke normally endured.

This one started with the family's good name—an odd tack to take, given his obvious willingness to shield his younger siblings no matter their public behaviour—and indeed he moved on from that quickly to hit the high notes of hectoring as regarding Lulu's safety on the one hand and the current deleterious state of Locke's common sense on the other.

Locke took most of it with the good grace he had promised Lulu; at a few points, he gave a little huff and a little bounce with his knees, and once he went so far as to say, 'Unfair,' which was duly ignored by Sir Kingsford.

Kit examined the stereoscope. The apparatus itself was not much larger than the cheap and simple handheld ones at the Crystal Palace, but it was crafted of good quality wood and set on a pedestal whose height could be adjusted. The distance between the eyepiece and the stand where the stereo daguerreotype cards were held was also adjustable with a dial on the underside, and it was this that Kit had been hoping for.

He flipped through some of the daguerreotype sets Sir Kingsford had sorted and shelved beside the stereoscope. There were indeed no erotic images whatsoever. He resisted the urge to ask where the French series was hidden and loaded a card with a pair of daguerreotypes of a reclined tiger, fiddling with the pedestal and the dial until the three-dimensional effect came clear.

Meanwhile, the reprimand was edging dangerously close to crossing the murky border between questioning Locke's common sense to impugning his intelligence. Alex didn't seem to mind his sister calling him an idiot; Kit would bet good money he wouldn't pocket it from his brother.

'Sir Kingsford, may I borrow Mr Locke for a moment?' he asked.

'No,' said the baronet.

Kit glanced at him over the viewer, with all the unshakeable expectation of the most self-entitled of guests.

'Oh, very well, I've had my say.'

'Pleasure as always,' murmured Locke, strolling over to Kit.

'Sarcasm is the hallmark of a small mind, Alexander,' Sir Kingsford said, bending over to peer at some papers on the desk. He took up a pen.

Kit dramatically widened his eyes at Locke, who looked at the ceiling with a quickly smothered grin. He'd been unusually grim going in to the scolding but he appeared his usual relaxed and patient self now.

'See the dial on the viewer?' Kit said. 'Turn it one way, the image comes clear, turn it the other way, it's blurry, turn it too far, it's just two separate pictures?'

'Yes, I know how the focus on a stereoscope works, Mr Whitely.'

Maybe not quite his usual relaxed and patient self.

'Less noisy, less bright?' Kit said.

'There's no sound or light on a stereoscope,' Sir Kingsford said, as crossly as if he'd been personally affronted.

Kit looked at him again and bit his tongue damnably hard to not say, *Eavesdropping is the hallmark of a small mind, Sir Kingsford.* His politely surprised expression must have communicated something of the sort; Sir Kingsford raised a disapproving eyebrow and turned back to his work.

Locke was twiddling the dial, either oblivious to the interplay or studiously pretending to be.

'Fix that dial in your head,' Kit said, 'and we'll practise before dinner.'

9

$\mathcal{L}$ OCKE TOOK KIT UPSTAIRS, WHERE WETHERBY was fussing with the fire in what was obviously one of the guestrooms. Kit had not completed his Orphanage-gifted service training, but he had rather thought that was a job for a maid, not a footman. Wetherby bowed himself out and Kit in. Kit nodded his thanks.

It was a luxury to have a fire upstairs in a bedroom, a wealthy man's thoughtless indulgence towards a guest, perhaps. Kit vaguely wished he'd bargained better with Lulu.

He saw the exact moment Locke realised he'd misplayed his hand. It was when Kit turned at the door and said, 'Do you dress for dinner?'

Locke stood very still in the hallway, hands lightly curling in and out of fists. 'Yes,' he said slowly. 'Yes, Kingsford is formal with his dinners.'

'Very well,' Kit said. 'Mr Locke, if I could trouble to borrow some clothing before then? Sir Kingsford looks more my size than you do, if his hospitality will extend so far? Or perhaps Miss Knight will loan me a gown of some sort. Won't I look pretty?'

His intention was firm on having a wash before lunch. Locke was looking past him, at the doorway of the guestroom. At the wardrobe. At the window. All those thresholds.

With one smooth movement, he had Kit's hand and was drawing him down the corridor to his own quarters. Despite the welcoming fire and the immaculate state of the room, there was certain mustiness to the air which told Kit that Alexander Locke did not often call on Sir Kingsford.

The room was huge, and dominated by mahogany, with a large four-poster bed tucked away from view of the door, a wardrobe and chiffonier. The rug had a design of green leaves with red splotches Kit assumed were meant to be fruit. The toiletry table was beside the tiled washstand, near the fireplace where low flames already took the chill from the room. A comfortable-looking highbacked armchair was set before the fireplace. There were two large windows that had to overlook the back garden, with a pier glass worthy of Versailles in between.

He wondered if Locke had guessed yet that he had used the mirror to get out of their room in the Knightstone Inn.

'My goodness, Mr Locke, you liked the gown idea. Whatever will the servants think?' Kit asked, the very picture of moral rectitude.

'Whatever they like. Middle of the room, Mr Whitely.'

Kit obeyed, but when he turned to see Locke's suddenly severe expression as he stood before the door, he retreated as far away as he could. His hands tried to link themselves chastely in front of him. He drifted to the toiletry table, fidgeting with the candle there, rattling the box of safety matches and picking up one of the bottles precisely arranged on its surface to unstopper and sniff at it. Sandalwood.

'Is this your childhood bedroom?' he asked, forcing himself to idly trail fingers over the spines of a couple of books on a low shelf under one of the windows.

The rest of the shelf held crumbling rocks and bits of petrified wood, a mason jar or two of samples long since turned to slime, and a battered-looking model ship under full sail. Kit thought of the little boy who had just wanted to be a gentleman scientist, launching his journeys of discovery in this toy sailing ship. He wondered if Lulu's room still held her pirate ship, and if her room was full of heavy mahogany furniture too.

'It is, yes.'

'I wanted to travel,' Kit said quietly, running his fingers over the model ship. 'Not as a naturalist, of course. Just would have liked to see the world in a way that didn't involve robbing it.'

'Why didn't you? I believe you've been well-paid for your previous endeavours.'

'No papers, though,' Kit explained. 'And I don't look so very English, do I? I may very well have not been let back in.' He put the little ship down.

Locke tipped his head in a *fair play* sort of gesture. 'Go to the middle of the room, Kit.'

Kit obeyed. 'May I ask why both you and Sir Kingsford are so concerned for Miss Lucinda's wellbeing? She appears extremely capable and highly willing to take care of herself but you both fret over her quite a bit.'

Locke slowly stripped off his coat. 'Ah, well.'

Kit waited, but that was all.

'I suppose I mayn't ask, then,' he translated. 'Quite right, not my business.'

Locke gave a jerky half-nod. 'Most of it is Lulu's story to tell.' He shrugged. 'I can tell you a little.'

He yanked off more of his dirty, torn clothes, shedding waistcoat and shirt, deliberately paying more attention to the process than necessary. It was perfectly possible to wash modestly under one's clothes; he wanted to be busy for this conversation, it seemed. Or he just wanted to torment Kit.

'You know about Lulu, right?' he went on. 'She wasn't born Lucinda, you're observant enough to have realised that?'

'I have,' Kit said cautiously. 'I understand it can't be easy for her.'

'We made it much harder.' Kit watched Locke debate with himself before he couldn't bring himself to leave his clothes in a messy pile despite their reprehensible state. 'My father doesn't come off well in this story,' he added as he stooped to pick up the discarded garments. 'Well. Neither do I.'

Locke smoothed each item out and hung them carefully over the back of a chair. As he worked, he talked. 'We were sixteen, Lulu was becoming herself, and Father wasn't happy about it.' He added his ruined trousers and drawers, as well as the makeshift binding on the cut Kit had given him. 'He evicted her.'

He stood then in glorious nudity, an absolute warrior-god of a man, all broad, lean muscle with a blond fuzz of hair on his chest and in a trail down to his glorious prick, proportionate to the rest of him, long and thick, and not particularly shy under Kit's equally not-shy gaze.

Kit made a tiny humming noise and put his hand over his mouth, utterly, callously, distracted. He wanted all of that. Who the hell cared if Lulu had been thrown out of the family home at sixteen? Kit wasn't given much to pity towards vengeful Amazonians at the best of times. These were not the best of times.

'Copping an eyeful, sweetheart?' Locke said. The lines of tension in him had eased. He might have been preening a little, the bastard.

'Baby, you're a landscape,' Kit told him.

Locke, grinning, strutted over to the washbasin—Kit riveted to the long lean lines of his back and the muscled bulk of his arse the whole while—set with a neat row: soap dish, sponge dish, toothbrush dish, and nailbrush dish. Reflecting the wealth of the baronet, the basin had piped water installed. He turned the taps and began to wash. Droplets of water traced paths over his smooth skin that Kit wanted to follow with his tongue.

God, Locke must be drowning in his intentions right now. He wanted to lick all that skin. He wanted to bite the ridged mound of his mighty arse. He wanted to push his tongue between—

Locke fumbled the soap and turned around. His half-mast erection was solid iron now. 'My God, you'd think you'd be blushing.'

Kit let out all his air in one quick gust. 'I don't blush, baby,' he said, hoping that was holding true.

Get yourself under control, he told himself sternly. It had been a long time since his bodily reactions could override his mind's control, but there it was. There Locke was, a danger to all that Kit held dear, his self-control, his peace of mind.

'No private washrooms yet?' he asked weakly. *That'd be helpful.*

'Steady on,' Locke said, returning his attention to his ablutions. 'Kingsford's working on it.'

Kit nodded. 'Go on. I am listening, despite every appearance.'

Locke soaped up the cuts on his arms. 'He threw her from her home and neither Kingsford nor I acted to help her.'

'Weren't you sixteen?' Kit asked.

He had a weird doubling sensation; he was simultaneously thinking that Locke had been young, to be expected to somehow save his sister, and thinking that he himself had walked out of the Orphanage on his sixteenth birthday and been plenty old enough to survive. But either they'd been too young or they'd been old enough, they couldn't be both at once.

'I could've been as brave as Lulu and told him I like to fuck men,' Locke told him. Foot set on a stool, he was carefully washing the cut in his thigh, which looked a little red, but was scabbing over. 'I certainly knew by then. He'd have had to throw me out too, or keep both of us. We would have at least been together, either way. But I was too enamoured of my father's good opinion.' He shrugged, too offhanded. They were reaching the heart of the matter now. 'It wasn't that she was left destitute. She went to London. Kingsford could have taken her in. He didn't. Father's orders. Our cousin Ginnie gave her a roof and all the support we should have.'

Kit shifted restlessly as Locke used the dentifrice.

'Something to say, my lad?' he asked when he was done, laying the toothbrush back down and aligning it within its dish.

'Seems a lot of guilt pointlessly tossed about. You were young, Sir Kingsford was dutiful, your cousin stepped up, Lulu got through it.' *Tell me what you're not telling me.*

Locke, now drying himself with a soft towel from the rail beside the washstand, made a mild noise of disagreement. 'I let her down rather than disappoint Father. I'm still atoning for that. Kingsford carries his own weight about it. But the true problem was Father dying when he did.' He wrapped himself in a light green dressing robe. 'He would have come round. He wasn't as shabby as all this makes it seem. He would have brought her home and bought her so many damned dresses and every last damned bonnet. But he fell off his horse and died, and Lulu thinks to this day that he died hating her.' He spread his hands awkwardly. 'He did die hating her. But it wouldn't have been for much longer. And it wouldn't have taken as long as it did if he'd known both his twins were raging perverts instead of just the one. And that's on me.'

Kit stood with his hands in his coat pockets, biting his lower lip as he gazed at Locke thoughtfully. It was one of the rare times when he wished he knew what a decent person said to these sorts of heartfelt confessions.

Locke smiled ruefully and waved at the washstand. 'Wash up, if you like.'

Kit took off his coat and availed himself of the water—it was even warm, glorious—while Locke sat at his toiletry table to re-bind the deep cut on his thigh and shave and pomade himself. He was smelling of sandalwood again by the time he'd finished his toilet, and Kit, still dripping, couldn't resist tracing fingers over the back of his neck and leaning in to catch the wonderful warm and subtle scent of him. Locke swivelled on the stool towards him.

'It seems to me,' Kit said slowly, 'that it must have been a confusing time for you, if your talent took the shape of wanting to know what the people around you were planning. And Lulu's talent shaped up to let her find her way back to you whenever she wa—'

Holy sodding hellfire.

Lulu didn't have a damned thing of his. She had something of Locke's, so she could come to her brother anytime.

He saw her big hands—the wedding ring on her left hand with its ruby cluster. Rubies for passion. Her husband, Peter Llewellyn.

A subtle sapphire inset into silver on her right hand's index finger. Sapphires for the pure and remote protection of the heavens. Sir Kingsford Locke.

The plain gold band inset with diamonds on the little finger of her right hand. Diamonds for steadfast strength. Alexander sodding Locke.

Locke had spoken the truth when he'd told Kit he'd tracked him to Lovelly with mundane means, but then the twins had let him make his assumptions about how Lulu had got there once he knew about her tracker talent. Three seconds of thought would have told him it was impossible for anyone to have anything of his personal enough to use for tracking; he would've had to be recently wearing it or carrying it in his pockets, like the handkerchief. Anything else, anything he'd be happy to abandon—and that was *everything* else—wouldn't have a strong enough connection.

The only thing that saved him from giving his realisation away to Locke was that he didn't know if he intended to immediately escape or to pause long enough to slap Lulu for lying, Locke for backing the bluff, or himself for swallowing it whole.

Then, just as Locke began to frown, Kit slammed another true intention into place over those flickering intentions and instantly followed through by flinging himself into Locke's lap hard enough to almost knock him off the stool. As it was, Locke's side hit the table and he caught himself with one arm, the other coming up to catch Kit. Kit got his hands into Locke's thick hair, nails raking along his scalp as he disarranged the sleek waves.

'Always the hair with you,' Locke managed to say before Kit had his mouth on his and his hands on his shoulders, feeling his muscles flex under the silken material of his light dressing robe. He rocked his hips against Locke; the man made a distinctly tortured sound and a moment later Kit found himself bodily lifted and tossed onto the bed.

Locke came down hard on him, dressing robe falling open, the full naked length of him crushing Kit down into the mattress; so far, so good on following his masking intention. Kit lifted his chin and offered his mouth and Locke took it and then Kit dissolved into sensation and rhythm. Locke's large hands spread under Kit's thighs, helping him arch his body against him and they rocked and rutted together, fast and desperate. Kit bucked under Locke's weight and clawed against his back, cursing the soft material in the way of Locke's smooth skin.

'You really are a little wildcat, aren't you?' Locke's mouth was suddenly assaulting Kit's collarbone, teeth grazing his skin.

Kit gasped, 'Alex.'

'Love the way you say my name,' Locke murmured, and Kit threw his head back and said it several more times as Locke bit and sucked at the skin along his clavicle. 'You like that, sweetheart?'

Kit whimpered his agreement. 'More,' he demanded.

Locke shifted back to rip Kit's stolen shirt open and trail kisses and bites down to his nipples, licking and nipping and sending Kit into a writhing, gasping mess. He slid his hand between their bodies and into Kit's trousers, fingers wrapping firmly about his length and beginning to work him. Kit's moans turned into a hum of unalloyed pleasure as he helplessly thrust against the friction.

Locke used his spare hand to push Kit's hair out of his eyes and cup his face. Kit turned his head slightly and took Locke's thumb into his mouth to lick and suck at the pad and heard Locke whisper, 'Jesus, the heat of you. You want more?'

Kit whimpered a more emphatic agreement. Locke tightened his hold and moved it faster, adding a twist. Kit's humming broke into abandoned moaning and panting, and he arched and thrust hard into Locke's fist, balls tightening, close, so very close.

Locke was rutting lightly against Kit's thigh and, since he apparently got chatty in the midst of his pleasures, murmuring into his ear. 'That's good, sweetheart, that's good, you feel so good in my hand, oh and you're being so good for me, tell me what you need, sweetheart, I'll give you everything you need and what was that first intention again?'

The sod almost had him. Kit flung up *On my knees for you, baby,* blocking his own thoughts from twisting back to his realisation that he was safe to escape and the intention that went along with that.

Locke had stilled, his body and frustratingly, given how close to the edge Kit had been, his hand. 'You are irritatingly adept at that.'

'That's right, baby,' Kit purred. He pushed at Locke's shoulders, trying to make room to squirm downwards. 'I'll make good on it.'

Locke chuckled. 'Irritatingly adept at hiding true intentions. You can stop the game now, Kit.'

He rolled off Kit to lie propped on one elbow beside him, tying his dressing robe one-handed to return himself to modesty. He was smiling his predatory smile but Kit could sense a watchfulness behind it.

Kit lay panting for air, bereft without Locke's weight holding him enclosed, and doubly bereft for the loss of that strong hand around his prick.

Once he had his breathing enough under control that he could approximate his usual politely detached tones, he said, 'That was quite uncalled for, Mr Locke.'

'Ah,' Locke said. His breathing wasn't all that steady either. 'It's fair play when you fuck with me, but not fair play when I fuck with you?'

'All I want you do is fuck with me, baby.'

'Oh, Kit. You barely even want to be touched.'

Kit blinked. 'Patently not so,' he said, rolling into Locke to rub his cheek on the silken material over his chest. He could feel Locke simultaneously tensing and leaning into it. The man had decided to torture himself, apparently, as well as Kit. 'You might have at least finished me off.'

'You held out longer than I thought you would. I mistimed the bloody question.'

Kit pressed his face into Locke's chest, smiling where he couldn't see. 'Well, then. Have another try, baby, I guarantee it won't take long.' It really sodding wouldn't.

Locke caught his face and lifted it so he had to look at him. His eyes were wary. 'You're absolutely determined to turn me into your certain type of man, aren't you? I've seen you tense up when Miss Knight touches you, Kit. *Miss Knight*, of all people. But you're so very good at pretending you like it when it suits you. How far were you planning to let me get before you told me to stop?'

Kit looked at his hands, resting now on Locke's shoulders. The man was rigid under his touch, not in the good way, and his control was slipping; his voice was showing true annoyance, perhaps even anger.

Locke and Lulu were mirror images in a way. Her constant simmer of rage made her flashes of good humour more precious; his constant good humour made the possibility that he would upend into true anger more alarming.

Kit carefully removed his hands and shifted away to get some space. 'Don't insult me,' he said quietly. 'I wasn't pretending.'

Locke scoffed. 'Of course you were. You were distracting me from that intention you almost gave away. Just like you were distracting me on the train.' He made a sound that was simultaneously amused and frustrated. 'And the pavilion. And the inn.'

'Oh my God, you really do hold a grudge,' said Kit lightly.

He suspected Locke had forgotten that not only was he engaging in the same game, but that he had sodding *started* the game, in the back garden of the pub. He was probably just annoyed because Kit was, mostly by accident, winning it.

'Fool me twice, indeed.'

'The only way to mask a true intention is with another true intention. I haven't had a single thought about you I'm not happy to follow through on, Alex. *More* than happy. So, fine, yes, I'm using it. But I'm not faking it.'

That gave Locke pause. He opened his mouth, closed it, and studied Kit for a long time. He relaxed and a small smile grew on his face. 'Then I must admit to being flattered,' he said at last. 'Except...*you fucking liar.*'

Kit flashed into indignation. 'That's rich, when you— *God damn it!*'

The intention to shove the Locke twins' lies in Locke's face had been unstoppable. Locke flopped onto his back, clapping his hands and laughing.

'Arsehole,' Kit said.

Locke wiped at his eyes, still chuckling. 'That was so satisfying.'

'Sod off.'

'So. Bloody. Satisfying.'

Kit got a grip on himself—temper did not help his Art, but desire did, and Alex had certainly fed it when he'd decided to go along with Kit's seduction and turn it on him. Kit took that for a secret comfort as he rolled out of bed, façade in place.

'Nice if it had been, baby,' he purred. He slid into his coat and buttoned it up over the shirt Locke had wrecked. In his normal tones, he said, 'All you've gained is knowing I know it's safe to escape. You were already assuming I'd try to escape anyway.'

'And now I know for sure you will try. I do like to be right.' Locke moved to sit on the side of the bed.

'But was it worth throwing the trick away just to get one over on me?' Kit smiled silkily. 'It's not going to work again, you know.'

'Yep,' Locke said. 'Absolutely worth it.' He stood and stretched luxuriously, the dressing robe sliding down one shoulder. He was smirking by the time Kit tore his gaze away from tanned skin and chiselled muscles and met his eyes again. 'And are we very confident it won't work again, there, sweetheart?'

Kit answered the smirk with his own smug smile. 'Are you, baby?'

Locke, laughing, stalked towards him. Kit stood his ground but Locke merely brushed past him, with a little more contact at the hip and shoulder than strictly necessary, to his fully-stocked wardrobe. He dressed rapidly in fresh clothes and ran his fingers through his hair in lieu of combing it again, a certain casualness to it all that told Kit that Alexander Locke was in the one of the few places in the world he felt comfortable.

Then they went downstairs, Locke holding Kit's elbow again, and rubbing at the spot between his eyes with the other hand. He'd be having trouble with intentions again, Kit knew, given the little game they'd just played.

Lunch was a subdued affair of cold leftovers. Sir Kingsford was obviously not a partaker of the newfangled midday meal. Kit had been rousted out of bed by the lightning Artisan and was beginning to flag, and the twins mustn't have slept much last night either. Lulu, who had stayed awake in the carriage so Locke could sleep, practically dozed off over her cold chicken pie.

Edith was bright enough to make up for the rest of them. 'The garden's beautiful, Kit, you should definitely take a walk, especially when we're so lucky with the weather today, bright blue autumn skies. Lulu showed me some lovely late-blooming flowers, crocus and goldenrod, and there was one from *Japan* which Ma would love, and then there's a whole greenhouse growing all sorts of exotic things, and this is amazing, Kit, there was a date palm in there that was grown from a thousand-year-old Methuselahan seed! Lulu's husband planted it.' Edith trailed off there before rubbing her ear and saying quietly, 'Lulu wanted to come inside after that.'

Lulu pushed away her plate and Wellerman cleared it, and the rest of the plates at a nod from Locke, leaving them alone with a last half-bow. Kit realised he'd still only seen the two footmen. There was probably Cook in the kitchen preparing dinner, and at least one scullery maid named Mary to help. There might be a lady's maid and a valet upstairs. Otherwise, the house had the eerie feel of emptiness.

He didn't think that was usual for such a big house—there should be more footmen, and a butler and housekeeper and private secretary, and maids of various categories, and stableboys and groundskeepers too. Sir Kingsford looked like a man who did not want to much be bothered, and the easiest way for a wealthy man to not be bothered was to employ a lot of people to be bothered on his behalf.

When he asked, Lulu said, 'Most of them have today off now.'

'Is it a half-day?' asked Edith, sounding puzzled, probably because they were between saints' days at the moment.

'Kings sends them away when Lexi visits, because of the headaches.'

'How awful it must be to have a brother who thinks of you so considerately,' Kit said.

'Funny boy,' Locke said, sighing.

'Goodness,' said Edith, with some determination. 'It looks like you've got some of those wooden clubs from the Great Exhibition in your cabinet of curiosities here.'

Kit followed her line of sight to a large mahogany display cabinet. The doors of the top half were of glass, set into heavy frames. A large brass key extruded from the brass keyhole. Behind the glass were all sorts of collectibles, Locke's shelf of boyish treasures writ large and with less charm, the curse of maturity upon childhood pleasures.

There were gemstones, corals and bones, a whole row of preserved bright blue butterflies and one translucent one in the middle, the deformed foetus of some animal in a specimen jar, amber and green apothecary bottles, a creepy wax doll tucked into a bottom corner, and a mix of curios and priceless artefacts from all corners of the world, some, indeed, looking like they'd come directly from the Crystal Palace.

'Oh, yes,' Lulu said. She looked at Locke, a meaningful smile curving her generous mouth. 'Kings collected those, for Lexi.'

'How *awful* it must be to have a *wealthy* and *generous* brother who thinks of you so considerately,' Kit said.

'I don't like a single thing in that cabinet,' Locke said. He scowled at the cabinet, fingers twitching.

Kit had the sudden suspicion he rearranged the contents on every single visit trying to find the configuration that didn't offend his very particular sense of harmony.

'Ungrateful sod,' he said, greatly amused and not bothering overly to hide it.

'So I have been informed on many an occasion. It's practically a hobby.'

'At least your brother cares about you,' Edith pointed out. 'I mean, it's good my family is so understanding but I literally stuck my head in the door of the inn and told them I was going to London to see Obaysch with Kit *who had just been arrested*, and they had nothing to say. It's nice how much they trust Kit an'all, and, of course, Kit, luv, we all love you very much even if you are a hardened criminal, but I mean, they do care but it'd also be nice if they cared enough to be a teensy bit joppety. The point is, I know there's a surfeit of Knights in the village but still, it'd be nice to be as precious to my parents as you two plainly are to your brother.'

Alex snorted gracelessly. 'Don't think precious is the word, Miss Knight.'

'Pray tell me the word, then, Mr Locke?'

The Lockes had one of their twin moments of silent communion. Lulu said, 'Look, Kings is a lot older than us. His mother died when he was young, and he was at boarding school by the time our father remarried and had us. And then we were at school. We saw him once a year, at best.'

'He came down from Oxford for our mother's funeral. We saw him twice that year.'

'And then our father died.' Lulu closed her eyes. A flash of something that was deeper than grief crossed her face. 'Kings had a promising career at Artisan's Inn and he had to give it up and come be Sir Kingsford and run the estate and raise two bratty adolescents. One of whom wasn't very gracious about it.'

'Yeah, all right,' Locke said. 'Neither was he. No, Lulu. My powers were coming on. I knew exactly what his intentions were.'

'Bad?' Kit asked.

'Stupidly, no. Good. So very earnest in his good intentions towards his younger siblings.'

Kit looked at Edith, who was returning him the same puzzled look. 'Is that terrible?'

'Imagine if every time you walked into the room, you were assailed with a guardian who was absolutely determined to do the right thing by you.'

'Oh, I see,' Edith said.

'Since I have no family of my own, I will bow to the expertise of the lady with the village full of cousins, but I ask again—is that terrible?' Kit said.

Edith nodded. 'Not from love, right? From duty.'

'Duty,' confirmed Locke. 'He does his duty by us. And he has to steel himself to do it every time we come home. There's not one iota of love here. Not towards me, anyway. Kingsford and Lucinda get along wonderfully.'

'I suppose because I don't know what he intends. I just know how hard he tries.' Lulu shifted, clearly dropping the subject. 'Kit, did you just say you have no family?'

'Did I?' Kit said innocently.

'Kitten,' she said. 'You did.'

He shrugged. 'None that cared to keep me, anyway.'

'You have us now, Kit, luv,' Edith, who had already known this about Kit, said stoutly. 'The Knights, I mean.'

'Thank you, Edie,' Kit said, smiling at her.

Locke said something under his breath and glared at the creepy blue-eyed wax doll in the cabinet.

'Were you raised in an orphanage, then?' Lulu asked, with an odd note in her voice.

Alex's head whipped around. The attention of both twins was now razor-edged on Kit.

'Yes,' he said cautiously. 'I mean, isn't that in my Agency records? Oh, no, it wouldn't be.' He'd escaped the Orphanage the day he'd turned sixteen; the Agency had been established a few years later.

'Which one?'

'*The* one,' Kit knew he had lost all expression from his face and voice. 'The United Benevolent Orphanage System for the Welfare of the Innocent in the Hallowed Name of the Holy Mysteries, Essex branch.'

Lulu shoved back from the table. She paced up and down along its length, prowling, tapping her fingers on her leg, scowling, the rubies on her ring glinting in the light. She looked at Locke.

'I agree it's worth a try,' he said with a shrug, 'if you can bring yourself to talk about it.'

'Let's go to the parlour,' she said abruptly.

'Oh, is there no pudding?' Kit asked, just to be difficult.

Lulu practically dragged him across the hall and over to the parlour, where tea things were already waiting, with teacakes and scones, so he was mollified. Locke served him a plate of little cakes and watchfully planted himself on the settee next to him. Edith perched on the armchair nearby, wearing a small frown.

'We want to get you to agree not to escape,' Locke explained. He sounded either insultingly or realistically sceptical about their prospects. 'Lulu's going to tell you her story.'

Lulu was markedly reluctant to start. While Kit slowly ate a cake, she sighed, she stood and paced, she sat and heaved a few deep breaths.

Then she rattled out, 'I need to murder a high-ranking member of the church and I need a certain knife to do it.'

Unlike Edith, she apparently didn't think a story needed too many antecedents.

Locke winced. 'Not where I would have started the narrative, Lulu.'

Kit had already jerked to his feet. He could hear an echo in his ears, the screams of a murdered man's wife. He looked between the twins' faces, Lulu's set, Locke's rueful. He was bewildered more than anything; she'd have been better off not saying a word than laying this on him. He raised his hands in silent approbation and turned to walk out.

'I'm after Varley, Mr Whitely,' Lulu called after him. 'I'm going to steal his own knife from the Orphanage vaults and cut out his heart with it.'

Kit stopped dead with his hand on the threshold of the parlour. 'You're going to rob the Orphanage and kill Bishop Varley?'

'Yes.'

He turned. He came back. He sat down.

'You could have saved yourself a boatload of trouble if you'd just told me that in the first place, Miss Lucinda,' he said. 'Count me in.'

10

'**W**HAT THE BLOODY BLAZES?**' Locke said, with some indignation.

Fair enough. 'My reasons are my own,' Kit said, 'just as Miss Lucinda's are her own. I don't even need to hear the rest of the story. We are united in our target, so our purposes don't matter.'

Edith stood up, the abrupt motion drawing all their eyes to her. Aside from a small gasp when Lulu had laid out her cards, she had been silent. Kit saw now that she was ashen.

'That's not good enough,' she said. 'Aiding and abetting murder? That is not you, Kit.'

Kit wrapped ice around himself. 'And how would you know, Miss Knight?'

If he'd thought to make Edith Knight quail, he'd misplayed his own cards just as badly as Locke had earlier. 'Don't you pull that bullshit on me, matey,' she said. 'You are not a murderer. If the man needs killing, the man needs killing, but you better be prepared to prove to me why.'

'I owe you nothing.'

Her hands went to her hips and she stared him down with her storm-blue eyes until he said, 'Uh. I'm sorry, Miss Knight?'

'You bloody better be, Kit Whitely.'

Kit rose to face her. 'Here is my justification, Edith. Bishop Varley is an unidentified Artisan.'

'We know,' Lulu interrupted.

'He's unregistered, but not unidentified,' Locke said firmly. 'The Agency keeps a file on him.'

Kit accepted this with an indifferent shrug. 'He's a telepath sort who can see the true shape of the Art rising in others. But he thinks it's devilry. And when he sees the devil rising in the orphans under his care, it's not just a beating in the ordinary manner. He has them tied to a wooden whipping frame' —here, Kit mimed wrapping rope around his wrists and raised them like they were being lashed to the top of the A-shaped frame— 'and thrashed with a tawse until they can't stand up.'

He was met by silence and looked under the window made by his crossed wrists and raised arms to see the faces of the other three, staring at him. Edith looked horrified, Lulu wore a look of expectancy and fellow feeling, and Locke was gazing at Kit's feet with a pained expression.

Kit looked down too and realised he'd shifted his legs apart so his ankles could be strapped to the struts of the whipping frame.

'Oh,' he said. He dropped his arms and stepped his feet back together. 'Oh, no, you don't, Mr Locke. I'll take your scorn but I'll have none of your sodding pity.'

Locke instantly wiped his face blank.

Kit flicked his fingers, releasing fists he hadn't know he'd made. 'And,' he went on coldly, 'once an orphan's powers fully manifested, they were chained up in silver and iron and vanished overnight. Unless they were like me, and their Art came on quietly enough that they could get away before Varley spotted them.'

He would be forever grateful that nine years ago his Art had risen on the morning of All Saints' Day, when Varley and the other high-ranking Orphanage staff had been in London for the annual ceremonies. He had felt an irresistible pull towards the locked wooden door of his confinement cell, where he had been left to recover from his latest visit to the whipping frame. He had put his hand to the door and passed through his first threshold. He had just kept walking, trying not to think, until he was out the front doors of the bleak Orphanage building and into the back streets of Colchester. He'd washed up in London a few weeks later.

'Vanished?' Lulu seemed the only one capable of speech.

'Sent to the mountain,' Kit said. 'That's what we used to tell each other. I don't know what we thought that meant. Hell, probably.'

'The mountain.' Lulu's shoulders straightened. 'That's where the knife is, kitten. The orphanage vaults, under the mountain. Officially it's Old Aneirin, the original Orphanage headquarters, by the Cambrian Mountains, north of Cardiff. But all my sources call it the mountain.'

Kit lowered his head and turned this over in his mind. 'The mountain's a real place. Well, then. Varley either genuinely doesn't know he has an Art, genuinely thinks the Art he sees in others is a sign of the devil and sends Artisan orphans to the mountain to be executed to save their souls. Or he knows it's Art, he has us beaten to deliberately bring it on stronger, and sends us to the mountain to break in a private army of Artisan slaves.' He glanced up at Lulu. 'Either way, the man's top of my very short list.'

Locke cleared his throat. 'Who else is on it?'

'Worried you are?' Kit asked cheerfully.

Locke shook his head at him, smiling, and then asked, 'Am I?'

Edith sat down. 'I think torturing and murdering orphans probably counts as justification,' she said huskily. 'Kit—'

'Will not take your pity, Miss Knight,' Kit singsonged.

'A'en pity,' she said fiercely. 'It's sympathy. And concern. And—'

'And well and truly outside of enough. I will not have it.'

Edith lifted her chin, mutinous. She eyed Lulu narrowly. 'Your turn.'

'What?' Lulu said sharply. 'No.'

'If you want me to go along with this, you need to justify yourself just as much as Kit had to. You were about to tell Kit anyway.'

'I don't care if you go along with it or not,' Lulu snapped. 'I would've told Kit because I need Kit. You're an obstacle, if anything.'

'I certainly am,' Edith said, sounding quite pleased about it. 'So give me one damned good reason why I should go along with letting you murder someone.'

Lulu looked genuinely taken aback. 'You can't stop me, Miss Knight.'

'I'll wager Sir Kingsford can,' Edith said. The twins exchanged a fast look. 'Shall I share your plan with him? Shall I tell him you've kidnapped me from the very bosom of my family to play hostage?'

Locke snorted. 'Hostage? We all know you'd merrily wave Kit goodbye as he abandoned you to our tender mercies.'

Kit did not bother to defend himself. 'But they would be tender, wouldn't they?' he pointed out instead.

'Mine are,' Locke said. 'Lucy's, not so much.'

'Varley murdered my husband,' Lulu shouted, so suddenly they all jumped. She slammed her fists down hard, her face flushed and twisted. Locke leapt to her side. He took her by the arms and rested his forehead against hers. 'All right, Lulu,' he murmured. He began to stroke her back. 'All right, little sister. All right. Shall I…'

Lulu, spinning away from him, made a gesture which was apparently permission. She stalked to the corner of the room and stood with her back to them, the set of her shoulders clearly showing she was fuming.

Locke sighed and turned his gaze from his sister to address Kit and Edith. 'When we were first working together, we took quite a few commissions to guard archaeology expeditions organised by a church group. Which we now know was the Orphanage. Or, really, it was—'

'Varley,' Lulu gritted out, talking to the wall.

'—financed and led by Bishop Varley. He liked that we were a matched pair—we looked even more similar back then—so he kept hiring us on for all his expeditions. He was looking for a certain artefact that showed up in myths and old stories and we went all over Europe and into Egypt and North Africa looking for it. The chief archaeologist was Peter Llewellyn. Those were good times.' Locke turned, but Lulu remained rigidly locked into her corner. He went on, voice still matter-of-fact. Kit could hear the effort it took him to keep it matter-of-fact. 'He was a lovely little Welshman, he and Lucy were smitten with each other, things gradually took their course over many expeditions, and they eventually married.'

'And we lived happily ever after,' Lulu said, so bitterly that Edith took a couple of steps towards her, face crumpled.

Locke stopped her with one hand and a slow shake of his head. 'Peter had moved away from working with Varley by then. The Llewellyns were based out of Cardiff, I was lending Lulu a hand with commissions, Peter was doing some local work, and then about two years ago, Varley contacted him for an excavation right there in the Vale of Usk.'

'He said I didn't need to come.' Lulu's voice was hollow. 'That a local expedition wouldn't need guards. We think Varley told him to come alone. We think it was just him and Peter.'

'We think Peter finally uncovered the artefact Varley had been searching for all those years,' Locke said. 'Near Caerleon, the seat of Brenin Arthur.'

'We think it was a knife and we think—' Lulu rubbed at the rubies on her wedding ring.

'Varley killed Peter to keep it a secret.'

'He killed him with the cursed knife he'd just dug out of the ground,' Lulu said harshly. 'It was a fucking pagan sacrifice, Alexander.'

Locke looked at her for a long moment before saying, 'Yes, that too.'

Kit fidgeted, then said, 'How do you know he used the knife if it was just him and Peter?' He was trying not to be brutal and thought he was being so anyway.

Lulu's fingers were wrapped tight around her wedding ring. 'I felt it.'

Kit took a breath and Edith made a small sound of appalled shock.

Locke put a careful hand on Lulu's shoulder. 'It was—' Kit saw the stark look of remembered grief in his eyes. 'It was a hard time. We had to get away. We took work in the Crimean.'

The big woman straightened, shaking off her brother. She swore under her breath, and went on, deadly calm. 'When the war ended, we came home. And I had a certain level of *clarity*. I've been hunting Varley since. He got paranoid and dropped out of sight, months ago. That's why I need the knife. It will let me track him down. If ever he had a personal item…'

Kit eyed her and then Locke. He rather suspected that wasn't the only reason she wanted the knife. 'If it means that much to him, why doesn't he keep it on him?'

'Too dangerous, we think,' Locke said succinctly. 'He's locked it up where only an Artisan like Kit could reach it, to protect himself from it. As well as protect it from others who might want it.'

'Who's trying to steal it?' Kit shook his head. 'Aside from us? Who put the commission out, that made Varley put an assassination bounty on me?' When the twins stared at him, he added, 'You think I couldn't work that one out, Vikings?'

'We don't know. He's kept the secret closely, so only a few people within the Orphanage hierarchy would know about it. One of his rivals, perhaps, who wants the knife for themself or wants to make sure Varley doesn't have it.' Locke hesitated. 'Or someone who knew you'd be the obvious thief and knew Varley would have you killed for it.'

Kit considered this. Someone within the Orphanage complex wanted him dead.

Or, perhaps, merely retrieved.

He shuddered, hard, and shook it off.

He turned to Edith, who was pale and whose hands were wringing together without her seeming to notice. 'I believe Miss Lucinda is justified,' he told her.

Edith nodded slowly. 'Yes,' she said. 'You are both justified. But. Does it have to be murder? Can the police not take action?'

Locke rubbed at his eyes, and Kit remembered the discussion he and Lulu had had in the summer pavilion. Locke and his plan for justice; Lulu and her plan for vengeance.

'No evidence,' Lulu said. 'No proof. No—no *body*.'

'Oh, I'm so sorry,' Edith burst out.

'You cannot demand the story and then turn about and be sorry to hear it!' Lulu snarled at her.

'No, I mean…'

Locke patted Edith gently on the shoulder, and Kit experienced a stabbing moment of jealousy as hard and bright as diamonds, not so much because of the touch, but because Locke had an ally in the room who wasn't Kit. He slammed down on that; it really wasn't the time, even if he had any claim on the man.

His sudden cold blankness, the masking of his inappropriate intentions, drew a narrow-eyed look from Locke, which Kit did not pay enough attention to.

Lulu scowled. 'Even if we had every scrap of evidence we needed, he's far too wealthy to face the courts. You know it, Lexi. Your plan is a poor cousin at best.'

'I'm with you, Miss Lucinda,' Kit said. 'Justice is just another luxury meant only for the rich. I'm all in on the vengeance plan, honey. I'll open anything you need opened.' He paused and then deliberately added, to the baronet's daughter, 'My word on it.'

Lulu smiled, hard and gleaming, and Kit smiled back.

Locke gave a sigh. He said, reluctantly, 'Lucinda.' That got Lulu's attention immediately. 'I'm sorry, little sister, he's lying to you.'

'What?' the other three said with various tones and motives of indignation.

'I'm not,' Kit tacked on.

'He still intends to escape.' Locke wasn't looking at any of them.

Lulu's shoulders sagged and she glared at Kit with impotent fury. It was the phrasing, of course, the specific reference to Kit's intentions. Except, there was simply no way Locke could be reading that intention in Kit. He did not hold it.

'But I don't intend it,' Kit said. 'And you know I don't intend it.' He tapped his temple. 'So why say it like that?'

'He's proven he can hide his true intentions from me,' Locke said, still avoiding Kit's eye. 'He's shielding them right now.'

'That's—'

'And he's telling you what you want to hear so you relax your guard.'

'I'm not going to escape. I promised Miss Lucinda I would help her. I gave my word.'

Locke finally looked at him, his hazel eyes as cold as Lulu's. 'You're giving her what you know she wants, to lull her,' he said flatly. 'Just like you gave me what you knew I wanted, to lull me. Repeatedly.'

Kit, riled, said, 'How's the view from your high moral ground over there, Mr Locke?'

'Spectacular, Mr Whitely.'

'I take it I have to remind you how you first got those cuffs on me,' Kit said. 'And our game upstairs just now, too. How's that moral ground now?'

There came a long pause while Locke closed his eyes and Edith looked between the two of them with some interest before exchanging a complicit look with Lulu.

Locke cleared his throat and rolled his shoulders. His expression was grim and set. 'Yeah, all right, a little shaky.'

Kit hummed a satisfied agreement to that, which made Locke look gratifyingly exasperated.

'Goodness, what did he—'

'That is off the topic, Mr Whitely.' Locke turned back to his sister. 'Lulu, he'll say whatever he has to, to escape you. He has no real intention of helping you. If he were actually invested in your plan, wouldn't he show a bit more glee at the prospect of getting revenge?'

'He doesn't do that,' Edith said. 'Show emotion. He hardly ever does.' Locke made a sceptical face. Kit remembered the man had said he was a ball of rage behind his façade. Edith, ignoring Locke's expression, went on with gratifying faith. 'But you have his promise and that is enough.'

'Are you just saying this because you like your plan more than mine?' Lulu asked.

'No,' Locke said. 'Though I do, of course. But Kit's an out-and-out liar—'

'Again with that?' Kit said.

'He promised me, too, Lulu. He promised not to escape. And yet.'

Fidgeting, Kit tried hard to stay quiet; it was apparent he wouldn't achieve anything by arguing. Eventually, he couldn't hold it in. 'I didn't, though. I didn't promise you anything.'

'Yes, you did,' Locke said. 'You said—' He sat back, eyeing the women. *I'll be good, please, I'll be good.* The words hung there, deafening for all they went unsaid.

Kit felt his face cloud over. 'The fact that you won't say it aloud tells me you understand what it really was, Alex.'

'You can shut up, Mr Whitely.'

'Rude,' said Edith.

Kit could tell Locke came within a smidgeon of telling Edith to shut up too.

'The patience of saints after all,' he said lightly. 'I think I shall retreat before my reputation is further slandered.'

Locke rose, moving to stand in front of the door out of the sitting room. He stared Kit down, unsmiling.

'I could have escaped five times already,' Kit told him.

'Still lying,' Locke said flatly.

Kit looked at him. Then he darted left, touched the mirror on the wall, and came out through the large mirror in the hall. He glanced up at the portrait opposite, of the blond wife, the twins' mother. He opened the door back to the parlour; he'd been so fast that none of them had even moved and had only just begun to vocalise their varied reactions.

'*At least* five times, Mr Locke,' he said to Locke's back and the Viking turned around, glaring like his sister.

'The mirror?' he said. 'Is that how you got out of the room in Lovelly? The bloody mirror? I thought it was the fireplace.'

'The fireplace?' Kit repeated, surprised out of his smugness. 'How could I possibly use a fireplace as a threshold? It has to be a path human minds use.'

'Says the man who walked out through the *mirror*.'

'Hell Mary,' Kit said. 'And innumerable oral stories about using mirrors to go to other worlds.'

'Witches, elves, fairies, brownies,' countered Edith, who apparently thought showing off her encyclopaedic knowledge of a heretofore-unsuspected trove of stories involving fireplaces was more important than supporting her *best friend*.

'Santa Claus,' Locke added.

'Who?'

As was becoming annoyingly frequent, all three stared at him.

'He comes down the chimney at Christmas to give children presents,' Edith said, in an Of course you've heard of this very weird *tradition* sort of voice.

'Like a more generous version of Old Father Christmas?' Kit asked. 'A winter spirit?'

'He's the American Saint Nicholas,' Lulu said.

'Kingsford hates him, of course,' Locke felt obliged to add.

Kit shook his head. 'Henry VIII murdered Saint Nicholas three hundred years ago.'

'Oh, my innocent young ears,' said Edith, clapping her hands over her ears theatrically.

'Have you really never heard of Santa Claus?' Lulu wanted to know. 'Jolly fat man, fills stockings and shoes with presents, comes down chimneys.'

'If he's fat, how does he even fit?' Kit said mutinously.

'*Says the man who walked out through a mirror,*' repeated Locke. 'Hell Mary, bloody hell.'

'Stop destroying my childhood, Kitty!' Edith said.

'It's all far too new for you to have actually been visited by Santa Claus as a child, poppet,' Lulu told her. 'You would have had visits from Old Christmas like the rest of us.'

Edith blushed prettily. 'Presents for children, *and* children-at-heart with very nice older brothers.'

'I have a very nice older brother and *I* don't get visits from Santa.' Lulu tapped her fingers; Kit suspected she'd be getting one this year.

'Right,' Kit said, frowning. 'So fireplaces are thresholds.' He let his mind touch on his Art. It didn't seem convinced yet. It looked like he'd have to read some children's stories.

'Not like you to have a failure of imagination when it comes to means of escape, Kit,' Locke said.

'The magic of Christmas must have missed the Orphanage chimneys,' Kit said. 'We were too busy getting beaten and telling each other gory ghost stories about Hell Mary hiding in the mirror, apparently.'

Satisfyingly, Locke winced. Lulu merely yawned heartily. 'I'm going for a lie-down until Nurse gets here, Lexi,' she said. Rolling her shoulders as she rose, she added, 'For all it's worth, I believe the kitten.'

She nodded to Kit and he bowed to her with a slightly sarcastic flourish for Locke's benefit. 'I would also like a lie-down,' he told the Viking.

'Allow me to show you to the library, Miss Knight. Then Mr Whitely can have his lie-down.' Kit could practically hear quote marks on the word. 'The need for which has so conveniently arisen.'

11

*L*EAVING EDITH IN RAPTURES IN THE library, Locke took Kit back to the rooms. He would not let Kit go to his assigned guestroom, guiding him back into his bedroom instead. Kit, too warm, discarded his coat immediately, leaving himself in the shreds of his shirt.

'On the bed and stay there,' Locke told him.

'Well, then,' Kit said, sitting on the edge of the perfectly-made bed and leaning back on his hands, looking at Locke through heavy-lidded eyes. 'I think I enjoyed your first few seductions more.'

'Mr Whitely. If you try to touch me, I'll assume it's an escape attempt and I'll tie you to the bed.'

Kit, taken aback by the stern words, smiled sweetly. He scooted until he could grip both hands to the top of the heavy wooden headboard. His heart was thrumming. Here was the easiest way to calm a man. It was nothing he wouldn't have chosen for himself, the very moment he'd laid eyes on Alexander Locke.

'On second thoughts,' he murmured, 'being ordered about is having its inevitable effect. As you like, baby. I promise I won't touch you.'

Locke held the glare for one more beat before he suddenly gave a bark of reluctant laughter, more disbelieving than amused. He shook his head in exasperation. 'Jesus fuck, my lad, you are incorrigible. What the blazes am I supposed to do with you?'

Kit's whole body relaxed. 'I have some thoughts on that,' he said, 'as you can tell.' He flexed his fingers on the headboard and tilted his head, the picture of expectancy.

Locke, still smiling, rubbed his eyes and then sank his whole face into his hands and scrubbed. 'You are *exhausting*. You can't be left alone for a second and I can't bring myself to tie you up, you manipulative little bugger. And I don't even know if you really are scared of ropes or if it's just another performance.' He dropped his hands and sighed. 'Another bloody convincing one.'

'"Go, set a watchman",' Kit said, in lieu of pointlessly defending himself. 'Or a footman, as the case may be.'

Locke snorted. 'Pardon me, Mr Whitely, are you quoting the bible at me when we both know Lulu wasn't kidding about you seducing the footmen? There's a couple of minor verses about that, too, you know.'

Kit laughed. 'Seduction isn't in my usual repertoire of escape techniques, Alex.'

Locke was staring at him, head on one side. He sounded distracted as he said, 'Just for me? I am truly blessed.'

'Just for you, baby,' Kit confirmed agreeably.

The smile that had blossomed when Locke had made him laugh still hovered, a real smile, one of the first real ones—not drunk, not mocking, not vulnerable and exhausted—that he'd allowed Locke to have. Kit could see it was having its effect.

And Locke could see that he could see. His own smile fading, he gave another shake of his head, a firm negation.

Kit, chastened, moved from his louche sprawl into a cross-legged watchfulness, hands linked in his lap. 'As you like, Mr Locke,' he said again, very meekly.

'What I'd like,' Locke said, 'is a little less compliance and a little more honesty, Mr Whitely.'

Kit refrained from rolling his eyes. Men never wanted either of those things.

'I've been nothing but honest.' When Locke openly laughed, Kit insisted on it. 'I've spoken not a lie to you, Mr Locke.'

'*Please, Alex, I'll be good,*' Locke recited. 'And then you bloody escaped.'

'That wasn't a promise, it was an offer,' Kit said, a touch crossly, because he did not like to be reminded that he had been reduced to pleading. 'I was offering to fuck you because I couldn't bear those ropes on me. Sorry it was too subtle for you.'

Locke's eyes flickered; Kit thought back over his own words and winced. He suspected Locke thought Kit was calling him stupid, which had not been his intention; at least Locke would see that.

'So you weren't lying. You merely thought I'd take advantage of someone who at the very least was doing a very fine impression of literally shaking in terror. So much better. You really do have me pegged as your certain type of man, don't you? And the shit of it is, I fucking *am*. As you so kindly pointed out.'

Had he? 'Oh, you're angry at yourself!' Kit said, enlightened at last.

'And you,' Locke said dangerously. He sighed and abruptly pulled out his comb. 'But mostly myself, yes.'

'Alex,' Kit began.

'Don't. You don't want to be touched, and who could blame you? And I don't touch where I'm not wanted, except you look at me with your pretty eyes and suddenly I do. Christ, I've been all over you. Repeatedly. A certain type of fucking man, indeed.'

'If I may clarify,' Kit said, speaking with precise and aching courtesy. 'I don't like unexpected affection, because it's...'

'Unexpected?'

'It takes me by surprise,' agreed Kit, 'and I'm not a great one for surprises. But I like to be touched by you, baby.' His voice was barely above a murmur. 'Did I not make that crystal clear?'

'You do not like it, Kit. You just worked out damnably fast the exact escape plan that would work on me. Probably because I put you up against a wall the first chance I got.' He jerked the comb through his hair, hands shaking.

'Did I protest overly much, against that sodding wall? Or was I the wanton little bit you knew I was the moment you saw me?'

Locke sighed and shut his eyes briefly. 'I'm sorry. I shouldn't have called you that.' He grimaced. 'And the rest of it. My behaviour was indeed appalling. I was trying to provoke you, find out the extent of your Art.'

'Consider me provoked, then, Mr Locke.' Kit held up a hand to hold Locke to silence. 'You saw it in me because I'd bend over for you at your word and we both know it.' He rose and went to stand in front of the big man. 'I will not trouble you to revise your impression of me as a pissant little thief, Alex, but I will certainly oblige you to treat me like I know my own sodding mind.'

He had managed to argue Locke to a standstill. The big man turned the comb over and over with his strong fingers, face set in an anxious frown. Kit took the comb and threw it aside, noting with some amusement Locke's twitch after it.

Kit was already pushing him towards the bed; Locke let himself be walked backwards for one step before planting his feet.

'What did I just say, you utter menace?' he said, holding his hands well away as if to illustrate his point.

'That I have pretty eyes and you can't resist me.' Kit deliberately nestled in closer to the warmth of Locke's bare neck, breathing in the warmly delicate scent of sandalwood, pushing on him hard. 'So don't.'

'*That's* what you decided to take from what I said?' Locke said, immovable.

Kit hummed in satisfied agreement, sliding his thigh between Locke's legs.

'I *said*, I know you don't want to be touched. I *said*, I don't go where I'm not wanted.' Locke tried to push Kit off him. 'You great bloody lump.'

'And what did I just say?' Kit said. When Locke went quiet, he repeated, 'I like being touched by you. And I like touching you. I want to touch you, baby. Let me.'

'Only so you can lull me into letting y— *Christ.*'

That agonised exclamation was because Kit had slid his hot hands beneath Locke's waistband. Locke caught both hands and pulled them away from his skin.

'Stop,' he said, cold and flat. 'Get away from me. I'm not fucking for ulterior motives.' He pushed, just a little.

Kit, both mortified and ashamed, obeyed, stumbling back and catching himself with a hand to the toiletry table, knocking over a bottle. 'My apologies, Mr Locke,' he managed to say. 'I quite misunderstood.'

'Jesus *fuck*,' said Locke. 'Yeah, I'd say you did.'

He rubbed his face in his hands again, swearing softly. Kit stood, eyes down, waiting. He had linked his hands in front of him, he saw; he flicked his fingers in annoyance and moved his hands to his sides.

Locke looked at him then. 'Sorry. I didn't mean to be so sharp with you.'

'No apology required, Mr Locke.' Kit carefully rescued the bottle before it could roll onto the floor.

'I don't—' Locke cut himself off before squaring his shoulders and abruptly saying, 'I don't have room for you, Kit.'

'Understood,' Kit said immediately. 'You have been clear.'

'No. You need to hear this. I don't have room for you. Lulu has to use you, Kit, we have to use you, and you're not going to get me to let you go by fucking me into fond feelings for you. I *will not* let her down again. Not even for you. You're wasting your time and your—' The word, when he found it, was bitter. '—*tolerance* if you think seducing me is going to advantage you in any way.'

'It is understood,' Kit repeated. 'I understand, Alex.'

He lay back down on the bed; he was truly tired and had genuinely wanted the lie-down. But he couldn't doze, so after a while he sat back up.

Locke was sitting in the wingback chair by the fire, flipping desultorily through what looked like correspondence or other paperwork that had been left for him. He wasn't actually reading it, though, and glanced up as soon as Kit moved.

'Do you want to practise controlling your Art now, Mr Locke?' Kit asked him.

'Talent.' Locke stared at him, head on one side. 'You'd still help with that?'

'Why wouldn't I?'

Locke raised one finger to explain himself, and then lowered it. 'Why wouldn't you, indeed,' he said, looking very much like he didn't know.

Kit shrugged. He moved close to the fire. He formed a clear intention involving Locke, the bed, and a great deal of bare skin and sweat. He figured he might as well keep his Art burning strong, fed with desire, while he helped Locke turn down his talent, via sending him an intention he'd be motivated to shut off.

Locke licked his lips slowly and shook his head, probably not appreciating the two-birds-one-stone aspect as much as Kit was. He stood and moved to the centre of the room, shaking his arms out as if he thought he was going into battle.

Then he took out his spectacles and perched them on his nose, which was just precious, damn the man.

'Let's start simple,' Kit said. 'Picture the intention sitting in the stand of a stereoscopic viewer. That's all for now. We'll worry about the dial later.'

'I can handle more than simple, Whitely.'

Tetchy. 'You can handle anything you like, Mr Locke.' Kit swayed on the balls of his feet before settling with his weight to his left leg, letting that hip cock out. 'But when you learnt to shoot a pistol, did you start with...' Kit ran out of analogy. He'd never learnt to shoot a pistol himself. 'Let me start over. When you learnt to fight...' Kit didn't know how to do that either. 'When you learnt to take a man to bed, did you—'

'Stop it, Mr Whitely.' Locke fought with himself before biting back a smile. 'I did not start simple, no. All in on that one.'

'As you will, then. Picture my intention positioned in the viewer. Picture the dial. Now turn the dial so my intention goes out of focus.'

Locke stared into space and then said, 'It's not working.'

'Patience of a saint,' Kit said pointedly. 'It'll take longer than three seconds to learn this technique, Mr Locke. That's why you should start simple.'

'It would help if you were giving me an intention I actually want to dial down, Mr Whitely.'

'What?' Kit said indignantly. 'Yes, you do, you just told me so, with some sodding vehemence.'

'I didn't say I didn't want you,' Locke said. 'I said I can't let that interfere with Lulu's plans.'

'Oh!' said Kit, and, '*Well*, then.'

'Mr Whitely. Can we please call a truce on using sex as a weapon?'

Kit offered a wicked smile. 'I will if you will, baby.'

'I mean it. It's striking me as . . .' He wrinkled his nose, almost dislodging his spectacles. 'The Greek general? Too destructive for either of us to count it as a winning strategy.'

'Pyrrhic. That's the word you're looking for. What? I had to do something with my time, and subscription libraries are cheaper than molly houses.'

Locke said something under his breath. He said aloud, 'Simple, then. Give me a very virtuous intention, please, Mr Whitely. If you can.'

Kit intended to innocuously dress for dinner. 'Put the intention on the stand of the stereoscope.'

Locke closed his eyes, and opened them again, and huffed in frustration, and closed them again and did the whole performance over again.

'Breathe, Alex,' Kit said. 'This kind of control takes time.'

'I know. It's just difficult to ignore everyone else as well as picture the viewer.'

'Ignore everyone else,' Kit repeated. 'Oh. You can feel the others in the house?' He hadn't thought Locke had anywhere near that much range.

'Yes. Everyone in the house, and Wetherby out at the stables, and I think there's someone riding by on the road right now too. That one's faint.' He frowned. 'Not well-intentioned though.' He half-turned his head as if trying to listen. 'I don't usually feel intentions so far out, it's the same as in Upper Morton. Stupidly intense.'

Kit bit his lip. What a shame Christopher didn't eat guilt as well as he did fear. He cleared his throat. 'I'm not starting you simply enough. You need to learn to narrow your focus to just one intention first.'

He stood right in front of Locke. He gave him an intention, to hold the man's hand in his own, and then made good on it. He turned Locke's palm face up and began to trace slow circles with his thumb.

'I used to use this technique when I was first teaching myself to control my Art. Focus on the touch. It's right here in front of you. I'm right in front of you. Nothing else matters, Alex. Just this.' He turned Locke's hand over and caressed his knuckles, running his thumb in firm strokes over the skin. 'You can't hear anything else, you can't see anything else, there are no other intentions but mine. Right here.' Kit looked up. Locke had shut his eyes. His face was calm and neutral. That seemed right. 'Do you just see this one intention now, Alex, the intention just to touch your hand?' Locke nodded, eyes closed. Kit kept running his thumb over his knuckles, back and forth, gradually lightening the touch. 'Put it on the viewer stand, then, Alex.'

'It's on the stand.' Locke's lips were slightly parted. Kit slid his fingers to Locke's wrist and felt his pulse thrumming; his heart was racing as much as Kit's.

'Hold it there, now. That's all you need to do.'

Locke's hands closed into fists. 'That's not all I need to do *at all*.'

Eyes still closed, he swayed towards Kit. Their lips brushed and Kit sighed into it.

Then Locke jerked back. 'No. Come on, Whitely, we called a truce.'

'I wasn't,' Kit protested with true innocence, before ruining the effect. 'It's hardly my fault you have no self-control.'

Locke's fingers twisted into Kit's shirt; Kit guessed he came within a whisker of getting shoved on to the bed and ravished for his trouble.

But Locke shook his head, stepping away and pressing his palms into his temples. 'Worse and worse. How am I supposed to help Lulu with my talent going wild like this?'

'Uh,' Kit said, the guilt moving in for the kill, closing its ghostly fingers about his throat.

The Viking flinched and recoiled, hand twitching as if he were reaching for his pistol.

Kit's intentions had gone as frantic as the rest of his thoughts, apparently. He was going to have to tell Locke the truth.

Locke was going to be so angry with him.

The bloom of fear coming low and fast like black mould overwhelmed Kit. He was rifling through intentions like a deck of cards, flicking so fast through his limited options—run, plead, comply, appease, kneel, submit— that it must have felt like an assault to Locke, who strode to him and got him by the shoulders.

Kit shuddered and Locke jerked his hands away. Kit stared up at him blankly, thinking, *Christopher, five, four, three, two, one, stop, holy hellfire, stop, stop, stop.*

He blinked. He breathed. He stepped back. 'Apologies,' he said to Locke. 'Shall we resume?'

'Ah, no.' Locke took off his spectacles to rub at his eyes. 'I don't know what that was all about, but your very first intention before you went into a white-out blizzard was to tell me the truth about something, so how about we go with that now, my lad?'

Kit froze. Locke turned slowly and put the spectacles aside and then came closer. Even more slowly, giving Kit time to back away, he put his big hands to Kit's face and lifted his gaze to meet his.

'Sweetheart,' he said. 'Tell me. You don't have to be afraid. Not of me. Never of me, Kit.'

'I'm not afraid,' Kit said, and ignored Locke's disbelieving look. He wasn't; he left that sort of thing entirely to Christopher. That was what Christopher was *for*, locked away in his dark cage. 'It's my fault, what's happening with your talent.'

Locke said nothing, just watched Kit's face, thumbs gently stroking along the tops of his cheekbones.

'It's unfulfilled desire, Alex,' Kit told him. 'It's wound up your talent so far it's probably an Art right now. An Art you can't control. An Art you can't even start to learn to control until you deal with the desire. For me. That I caused. By fucking around with my intentions. Because I was being petty and self-indulgent.' He winced. 'And manipulative.'

Locke looked at the floor. His shoulder shook. Kit swayed, still trapped in his hands and desperate to pull away, before realising the man was laughing. He made a huffy noise which he couldn't decide was relief or indignation or an exquisite mix of both.

'Oh, this explains so much about my adolescence,' Locke got out after a moment. 'Jesus.' He wiped at his eyes with one hand, keeping the other cupped on Kit's face. 'Never change, sweetheart. Now if we just put you under Lulu's supervision so I can have privacy for, my God, probably less than a minute by now, I'll take care of it.'

'Uh,' Kit said, one knee jiggling. 'I have to. Um. Take care of it.'

'I have my own good right hand.'

'I caused it,' Kit said. He pressed his forehead into Locke's shoulder, hiding his eyes. 'Has to be me, because I caused it.'

Locke gave another choked laugh and planted a kiss on the top of Kit's head. 'Of course. It just explains *so much* about my adolescence.'

Kit straightened. 'All caveats regarding truces and fond feelings accepted,' he said, 'how would you like it? Quickest would be on my knees, I should think, but I'll be pleased enough to play at all fours if you—'

'Jesus!' Locke held up both hands. 'Can we just hold up there a—'

'How would you like me?' Kit asked impatiently.

His cold façade was locking into place. Locke had just told him he didn't want to fuck for ulterior motives. Well, Kit didn't want to fuck under sufferance; the thought that Locke would take him reluctantly, because he had to, was not a pleasant one, and so he ensconced himself in his defences.

'Let me see,' Locke mused. 'Shall we say, *not* crossing off a chore from your list?'

'I've made it clear I want you. You've made it clear you won't have me. This is harder for you than for me.'

Locke stared at him. Kit waited impassively. At last, Locke said, 'Based off my many unrequited loves when I was sixteen, this must go away by itself. Keep up the cold front, it's helping. Rather quickly.'

'You're risking Lulu's plans.'

'We should dress for dinner.'

'At this point, I think I have to be insulted,' Kit said. 'Won't even fuck me when logic says he has to.'

Locke reached out and ran his thumbs lightly down Kit's torn shirt, a whisper of a touch against his skin. 'Let's dress for dinner, Mr Whitely.'

'Definitely insulted.'

'You're *relieved*,' Locke said, with a devastating accuracy that almost made Kit twitch in surprise. 'God damn your unwilling compliance, I'll have none of it.'

'It's willing,' Kit said. 'Wanton little bit, remember?'

'You're hardly letting me forget it.'

'I am very petty, Mr Locke.'

Locke poked him lightly. He was smiling when he moved away but the usual warmth was missing from his woodland eyes. He was plainly unsettled as he dressed, but he became calmer as he tweaked each piece of clothing into place—he wore a garish orange floral waistcoat tonight over a pink striped shirt, the very epitome of someone trying very hard to annoy a staid older brother—and Kit became calmer and stiller as he waited.

Then it was his turn. Locke helped him into borrowed clothes from Sir Kingsford. They were old-fashioned, and of a heavier material than Kit was used to, with more layers; he was already hot by the time he was in his tailcoat, and it had nothing to do with Locke's gentle hands helping him dress.

Or only a little, anyway.

He and Locke had overcomplicated this; Kit, for one, was not used to wrestling with this kind of emotional nonsense and who knew what the hell was going on in Locke's head. They both openly wanted each other, they had both agreed to call a truce on lust-based warfare, and they had a problem, Locke's uncontrolled talent, that would be perfectly simple and perfectly agreeable to solve if they could get over their own selves.

Therefore, Kit was quite delighted to discover that while the coat was an adequate fit, if tight across the shoulders, the trousers were outright indecent.

Locke apparently thought so, too, when he stood back and gave Kit a final once-over that turned into a double take. 'Jesus. Don't try to bend over in those.'

'Best peel them off before you bend me over,' Kit agreed.

'So funny. Such a funny, funny boy.'

'You are going to fall apart as soon as we're around crowds, Alex, and we'll just have to find an alley where I can suck you off.'

'I look forwards to the romantic interlude,' Locke said dryly.

'Or you could fuck me now so I don't ruin the knees of my new trousers,' Kit pointed out.

'And that romantic interlude sounds equally as enjoyable.'

'Oh, you want it to be romantic?' Kit asked. 'Are you sure you're not the girl twin?'

Locke shook his head, halfway to amused. He sounded friendlier even as he said, 'Kit, you're being so cold about all this. It's not doing a thing to convince me you weren't pretending before.'

'I'm cold, baby, but you know just how hot my mouth is.'

Locke went all the way to amused, then, putting a hand over his face and laughing. 'And filthy. Hot and filthy.'

'You know it, baby,' Kit purred, hand on one cocked and tightly clad hip.

He accompanied the ostentatiously brazen pose with a real smile—working to soothe Locke out of his mood had jollied Kit out of his own defences too—and saw Locke helplessly respond to it.

Then a gong rang out and he snapped out of his playfulness back into blank stillness, hands linking together in front of him.

Locke was watching him closely, expression sombre. 'It's just the dinner gong.'

'Yes,' Kit said. He flicked his fingers, forcing his hands apart, forcing himself to relax. 'Because big houses have dinner gongs.'

'Orphanages, too,' Locke said, very quietly. 'Right?'

Kit turned his back, gathering the borrowed stockings and shoes. 'I'm hungry,' he said. 'Feed me, Mr Locke.'

12

OUT IN THE HALLWAY, THEY WAITED as Lulu came striding down from her room. Her thick wavy hair had been undone from its usual fat braid and dressed into elaborate curls about her ears. She was out of her bloomers, in a wide-skirted crinoline of pale green silk taffeta, with plenty of flounces and ruffles on the skirt, though the bodice was notably simple and her arms and neck remained covered, with a diaphanous material. She had to be well-corseted under the dress. She had abandoned her practical boots for a large but dainty-looking pair of prettily-buttoned shoes that had to have been as especially tailored for her as the dress was. Her pearl powder and eye paint were a little more elaborate now, hiding most of the damage Kit had done and making her hazel eyes shine, the green flecks more prominent than usual.

Kit gave an appreciative whistle. 'Magnificent, Miss Lucinda.'

'Oh, be quiet,' she said, pleased. She stalked by him.

'Magnificent,' repeated Locke smugly. It was good to see him back to smiles, even if it was mostly for an audience.

Kit obligingly rolled his eyes. 'Your sister, not you.'

'Twins. I'm magnificent.' He took his sister's arm to escort her down the stairs. 'Miss Knight! As lovely as ever and then some. A regular stunner.'

Edith's transformation was less dramatic than Lulu's, but she had changed her dress's day bodice to an evening one, had her skirt brushed and pressed, put on prettier shoes, and evidently borrowed cosmetics and hair-styling from Lulu. She gave a curtsey at the compliment and offered her own by means of a silently approving sweep of head to toe over all of them.

Kit offered his arm with a smile. 'Bang up to the mark, my dearest.'

She gave a gracious dip of her chin and then laughed at him. The four of them went two-by-two to the dining room.

Sir Kingsford was already seated. There were stilted greetings all round. The first part of the meal was taken up with Sir Kingsford dryly updating the twins on the state of affairs of various relatives and neighbours.

'And cousin Ginnie is with child,' he finished the update, with no more inflection than he'd shown when telling them their great-aunt had died or another cousin had scandalously eloped.

Lulu sighed and Locke said, 'Shame.'

Sir Kingsford looked severe. 'That is not an appropriate response, Alexander. Especially since a son of hers is likely to be my heir.'

'We all know her husband's a nasty piece of work, Kingsford,' Locke said. 'A child just ties her in tighter.'

'It can only be of benefit, after she lost the first—'

Sir Kingsford face went blank. All three of the Locke siblings' faces went blank. It was odd, and a sure sign of some sort of embedded Art working on them, as far as Kit could tell. He exchanged raised eyebrows with Edith, but really, Locke family matters were not at all their business.

The baronet shook himself and turned an appraising eye towards Kit. 'You appear to be of Romani descent, Mr Whitely?'

'Hah!' said Edith, before wincing and turning her eyes back down to her soup.

She had been uncharacteristically quiet; perhaps she was feeling the difference in position between her father, a gentleman only in the modern sense, and Sir Kingsford, a gentleman of an entirely separate class.

Kit smiled at the top of her demurely bent head. She was no doubt remembering when Kit had first walked into her little store, looking for the London papers, his second errand after getting off the train. The first had been a visit to the bakery. Him being a stranger, Margaret had put on her thickest accent, which Kit had defeated by pointing to a sticky bun wearing his politest expression and silently holding out coins.

When he'd walked into the bookshop, Edith had burst out, 'Oh my goodness, I've been hoping you'd come in! Are you Romani? You look like Romani; I really want to meet a Romani and Young Tom said one had got off the train! Oh, no, is that rude? I mean, I know some people don't like Romani just for being travellers but it's probably still bad if you go the other way and like them just for being travellers too, but I don't mean to judge you on your appearance and actually it's none of my business, and my point is, the papers are over there and you're welcome to sit and read them here and I won't interrupt you at all.'

Kit, silent and inexpressive, had nodded once, slowly, and sat to read the papers. Edith had interrupted him twelve times. By the end of it, she'd pried from him a reluctant but true smile, his first for months.

He had been frozen inside by the time he had made it to Lovelly. Edith Knight had thawed him.

He said, 'Some people have said as such, Sir Kingsford. Others have implied I may be of southern European or Moorish heritage.' By calling him dago or filthy Yid or darkie or blackamoor or various other epithets implying the very opposite of a heritage to be proud of. 'But I don't know my family origins.'

With a hint of impatience, the baronet said, 'You must have some knowledge, surely.'

Kit, with very much an Elizabeth-Bennet-under-the-gimlet-eye-of-Lady-Catherine-de-Bourgh sort of feeling, said, evenly, 'I do not, sir.'

'Well.' Kingsford glanced down at his soup. '"Upon my word, you give your opinion very decidedly for so young a person",' he quoted.

Kit gave a startled laugh and Edith blushed to the roots of her hair.

Sir Kingsford adjusted his cutlery for the next course with a small curve at the edges of his lips but he was not diverted for long. 'Why do you not know?'

'Kingsford,' Locke said. 'Leave the lad alone.'

'I was abandoned at an orphanage by my parents when I was four,' Kit said, turning upon the pushy man his most saintly look. 'Apparently it was because I was too wicked of a child to want to keep. So they weren't inclined to leave me my family tree. That's why not. Glad you asked?'

He was sweating, overheating by the fire, in the heavy coat and the thick stockings, the unaccustomed necktie and waistcoat. He pushed his soup away.

'That's ridiculous,' Kingsford said flatly.

'I see tactfulness missed every last one of the Locke siblings,' Kit said. 'Good thing they have all been gifted with such an overdose of charisma instead.' He took a long drink of his wine.

'If parents abandoned their children for misbehaving, every child would be an orphan.'

'I would be,' Edith said helpfully. 'He's right, Kit.'

'They probably couldn't afford to keep you. Children are often left for a winter when their parents cannot feed them.'

'No,' Kit said. 'I was reliably informed that their reason for leaving me was that I was born with evil in me. That I had to have it beaten out of me. That it was God's blessing that I was brought to the care of the Orphanage, for the sake of my eternal soul.'

Lulu dropped her spoon. Locke had put his down. Edith, beside him, still had hers halfway to her mouth; she was frozen in his peripheral vision. He felt them all looking at him. 'What?' he snapped. 'I already told you this.'

'Can't say you did,' Locke said.

'Ah,' Sir Kingsford said, in the manner of a man who had solved a puzzle. '"Thou shalt beat him with the rod, and shalt deliver his soul from hell". Proverbs 22:14. Was that it?'

Kit's hands were in his lap. They were shaking. He squeezed them into fists and shook them out.

'Kingsford, for Christ's sake,' Locke said, almost snarling it. Kit's hands shook harder. 'Whitely—'

Christopher. Five, four, three, two, one. Stop. He blinked and straightened and smiled his pretty, false smile. 'Precisely, Sir Kingsford. That is, as they say in Somerset, the badger itself.'

'We do not say that,' Edith said.

'Arrant codswallop,' Sir Kingsford said, wiping his fingers in his napkin with an intense concentration that finally gave him some resemblance to his younger brother. Edith looked moderately surprised before he went on, 'Some scoundrel was having you on, probably for nefarious purposes. I have never heard such utter twaddle.'

Kit pulled at the tight necktie and drank more wine. Nefarious purposes. That was one way to put it, indeed.

'And then?' Sir Kingsford went on, unblinking. 'Your orphanage situated you as a servant somewhere?'

'Kingsford—'

'I cannot place him,' the baronet said to his brother. 'It bothers me.'

Locke rapped his fingers on the table before shooting an apologetic look across at Kit and slightly sitting back in a silent sign of resignation.

Kit was not fussed. Sir Kingsford wasn't demanding anything personal of him. 'I left the orphanage. I was trained to service, but it turns out no one brings on someone as old as I was unless they already have experience in a big house and proper references. Too old for a quite a lot of jobs, actually.'

Unable to logic out how to use his new and unreliable Art to turn a profit beyond the obvious illegalities, he'd tried all sorts of jobbing labours left to the honest poor, down to sweeping the crossings or holding the reins of horses or porting luggage off the omnibuses for tips.

He'd been driven off by gangs of younger boys who had worked their stands for too many years to let an upstart like him waltz in, and his elfin prettiness led to too many offers of tips for more strenuous work than carrying luggage, offers that quickly turned insistent. The same appearance of feyness made foremen overlook him for unskilled labouring work amid waiting crowds of burlier men.

'So?' prodded Kingsford.

'It was the workhouse or whoring and thieving for me. Guess which one I chose.'

After flicking a glance at the ladies to check their response to his language, Sir Kingsford looked him over in open and unblinking assessment before announcing, definitively, 'Workhouse.'

'That's impressive, Sir Kingsford. I'd've bet the house you'd assume the worst of me.' Kit slanted a pointed look over to Locke, who volleyed back his unperturbed wolf's smile.

The workhouse had been, without exaggeration, soul-murderingly awful, as it was meant to be. Kit was no stranger to the degradations inflicted by those with power on those without, and had tolerated the arbitrary, demeaning strictures and the grinding, pointless work as par for a very predictable course. He'd had it no worse than any other pauper there, after all, and better than some. He had certainly not been the only orphaned child in the throng of the needy.

It had been the food—terrible, and never enough of it—that broke him. He was an Artisan and a growing boy, besides. He'd stopped growing, in fact, and he'd whittled down into a waifish urchin sort that only increased the harassment from a certain type of man. At least Fairweather had made sure he'd never had to fight for rations at the Orphanage. When his thoughts turned to contemplating that advantage and the Master of the workhouse in the same breath, he'd left.

His hopeless half-starved situation was finally enough to overcome his natural and Orphanage-instilled moral objections and drive him to petty larceny. Ironically, given both his Art and his clumsiness, his best results there had come from quick hands in crowds during peasoupers. But then he'd opened the door to a rich man's house to impress a boy, and the whole blackguard gang of them had been nabbed robbing the place.

Once he'd walked himself out of that situation, he'd resigned himself to the inevitability of putting himself under the care of yet another institution supposedly dedicated to aiding unfortunates: he'd registered himself at the Agency. With a naivety even more touchingly stupid after his past experiences, he'd assumed they'd be able to help him find honest work, either using his Art or in some safe profession like clerkery. Oh, it was to laugh.

Casually deliberate cruelty was one thing. Well-meaning incompetence quite another.

'Are you well, Mr Whitely?' Sir Kingsford said. 'You appear…flushed.' He said the word with delicate distaste.

'I'm an Artisan,' Kit said. 'I run hot.'

Sir Kingsford raised an elegant eyebrow. 'You are not obliged to keep the coat on.' When Kit hesitated, he ordered, 'Remove it before you faint, for heaven's sake.'

Kit rose smoothly, putting his napkin to the side. Without a word, he stripped coat, waistcoat, and necktie, and rolled up his shirtsleeves. He expected Sir Kingsford to protest at this show of skin, for his sister's sake if not Edith's, but the man once again looked at the ladies for their reaction to Kit's nakedness. Since they did not react, he didn't.

'Why did you overdress like that when you're an Artisan?'

Kit rested his hands on the back of his chair. 'Locke said you dress for dinner.'

'I don't insist on formalwear for dinner,' Sir Kingsford told his siblings. 'That was Father, not me.'

Kit laughed, a little giddily. 'So the Lockes are all for the blunt talking, but you don't actually talk to each other? That is just *delightful*.'

'I rather thought you two liked to dress for dinner,' the elder Locke told the twins. 'Your flashy waistcoats, Alexander.'

Locke rolled his eyes while Lulu looked down at herself. 'I quite like the chance to dress up but you two don't have to.'

'Oh,' Sir Kingsford said.

He looked like he wanted to take his coat off. He looked, frankly, like he'd like to roll up his shirtsleeves too, and also take his plate to his study so the basic necessities of life and society didn't disrupt him so much. His eyes gleamed as he turned his attention back to Kit. He looked like he'd like to take him with him, to dissect in there.

'What kind of Artisan are you?' he demanded.

'Doors and locks.'

'That's *ridiculous*,' Sir Kingsford said, almost angrily. Locke groaned.

Kit laughed again, rocking lightly from side to side. 'I know, it really is, Sir Kingsford.'

He noticed Locke's gaze following the rock of his hips. The trousers really were very tight.

'You must be some sort of telekinesis Artisan.'

'How clever of you. That's what I think, too.'

'See?' Kingsford said to Locke. 'If this one can conceptualise a useful way to control his Art, so can you.'

'Oh, no,' Kit said, very quietly.

'Thanks for the encouragement, Kings,' Locke said.

'You know how I feel about sarcasm, Alexander,' Sir Kingsford said.

'Thank you *so much*, Sir Kingsford,' Locke said, with even more sarcasm.

'Show me what you can do,' Kingsford commanded Kit. 'Open a door.'

'Oh, I can't open a physical door except in the mundane way,' Kit said, holding the back of his chair, still gently rocking. Locke had straightened and was watching him with some suspicion. 'I can walk through a door to another door. There's not much to see, aside from me.'

'Do it anyway.'

Kit took a couple of steps back towards the door to the dining room. He smiled at Locke, one of his falsely sweet smiles that made him look angelic. 'Where shall I go? To the front door, perhaps? And from there to the gatehouse, perhaps?'

'And where from there, Mr Whitely?' Locke asked him. 'A long walk to the next threshold, right?'

'I can walk, Mr Locke,' Kit said. 'I did make a promise, though, as universally scorned as it is.'

He returned to his chair, sitting smilingly under Locke's distrustful gaze and reaching for his wine. Locke stretched a long arm across the table and snatched the glass before he could get it.

'Teleport Art based around thresholds,' Kingsford said with great satisfaction. 'Show me.'

'Not obliged to, Sir Kingsford,' Kit said. 'Thank you for your gracious hospitality, though.'

As he had guessed, Kingsford took the blunt refusal with a shrug. 'What about the locks, then?'

Kit bowed slightly. 'I can open any lock at a distance.'

'Oh, so it is telekinesis *as well*. Or is teleporting considered a form of self-telekinesis?'

Best to ignore that can of worms for now, as interesting as it was. 'Telekinesis, but just locks,' Kit said. 'So, formal categorisation would be a limited metalworking Art.'

'Mr Whitely,' Locke said. 'As little as I like my brother's charming habit of interrogating people for the sake of his own curiosity, I do feel the need to remind you that you blatantly closed a bunch of actual doors back in Lovelly right in front of me.'

Kit remembered locking the villagers in. 'I closed the shops' *thresholds* and locked their doors.'

'And you closed the doors themselves, where they were open.'

'You did,' Lulu agreed. She'd been on the ground clutching her nose, but she'd seen it, he supposed.

Kit thought about this, staring fixedly at the tureen of soup. He blinked back to awareness as Wetherby whisked it away and Wellerman replaced it with a platter of sliced roast beef. Roast potatoes and gravy soon joined the platter. Edith helped herself to a roast potato before Wellerman could serve her and then squirmed when the footman quickly took the tongs.

'I closed the thresholds,' Kit said slowly. 'If someone was standing on the threshold, that pushed them back inside. And then the doors naturally swung shut.'

The twins shook their heads at him in a unison that was both disconcerting and irritating.

'I wanted to lock the doors,' he said, with more of a question in his voice now despite himself. 'The doors closed so I could. I moved the locks, not the doors. Metalworking Art.'

Then he shook his head at himself, not, thank God, in synchronicity with the Locke siblings having one of their twin moments. The shape of his Art might have been telekinesis, but his Artworks were based firmly around opening and closing thresholds and locks. And maybe doors. If he accepted a diagnosis of metalworking Art, he was limiting himself when he didn't have to.

'I need more wine,' he announced, trying to hook his wineglass back from Locke.

'No,' Locke said. 'He gets very inappropriate when he's had too much to drink,' he added to his brother.

'Has he been drunk since he got here?' murmured Sir Kingsford.

The twins chortled. Even Edith gave a sharp giggle, mostly in surprise.

Locke, still helplessly laughing, hunched and bowed his head over his plate under Kit's reproving look. Sir Kingsford looked down too, examining his well-shaped fingernails, and Kit caught his slight smile, his soft-eyed pride in bringing the brother he had ripped to shreds in his study to open mirth now.

Kit would never understand families for as long as he lived.

'Fine,' he said. He raised his eyes so he could fixate his gaze on Locke. 'I can open anything,' he murmured. He thought about Locke's mouth, Locke's touch, scalding across his skin. 'I can open anything.'

'Yeah, all right,' Locke said. He was still smiling. 'Can you?'

'Yes, you can, Kit,' Edith said in her optimistic way. 'You can open anything!'

'Look at his eyes,' Lulu whispered.

'Well, this is fascinating,' Sir Kingsford said. 'Why is he staring at you, Alex?'

'Damfino,' Locke said to his brother, which was *damned if I know*, Edith's village had a version of the same thing.

Kingsford tsked. 'For what purpose did Father fund your expensive education if you're going to insist on going about speaking the language of the gutter in front of guests?'

At which, Locke, naturally, shrugged, leaned back in his chair and said, enunciating every syllable, 'Damfino.'

Kingsford rubbed his hands over his face exactly like Locke did when he was frustrated, and then inelegantly snorted with laughter.

Locke slumped forwards again, laughing too. 'Sorry, Kingsford, I'm being a pillock.'

'Never mind, Alexander, I know I'm not your favourite person.'

'Oh, no, Kings, that's not…'

Their voices were receding like tidal water. A new Artwork was shaping in him. 'I can open anything.'

He stared unblinkingly at Locke, who was turning away from Sir Kingsford, looking dismayed. The big man fisted his hands together, a new smile beginning to curve his lips as he was caught in Kit's gaze again.

He knew *exactly* why Kit was staring at him.

Kit smiled dreamily. 'I can open anything,' he told Locke again. *I want your skin under my mouth. I want your hands everywhere on me. I want your prick in me.* 'I'm not saying that aloud, am I?'

'You're just telling us you can open anything,' Locke said. 'For which I think I better thank God.'

'I *can* open anything.'

'Go ahead, then, sweetheart,' Locke said, before shooting a guilty glance his brother's way.

Kit turned his head and looked over Sir Kingsford's head, at the display cabinet with its curiosities behind the heavy glass doors. 'Open,' he said.

And the doors flung open, hard enough that the glass trembled. Edith clapped delightedly. Locke leaned back in his chair, face sober, but he gave Kit a wolfish smile when Kit looked at him, eyes intent.

'Jesus, don't wreck us,' Lulu said. 'Well done, kitten.'

Kit stood up. Elation bubbled through him. God, he loved doing new things with his tricky, contrary Art.

'I can open *anything*,' he said, and opened everything in the room, drawers, cabinets, the actual door, the serving hatch, the little hinged flaps on the many decorative items on the sideboard, everything.

'My apologies,' he said, as startled as everyone else.

He closed it all again and sat, smiling a tiny smile to himself as the only sign of the ecstasy thrumming through him. Wellerman, hands trembling a little, replaced his napkin in his lap and served him three slices of beef and five potatoes. He was going to have to double that, at the least.

Sir Kingsford had his hands pressed together as if praying, his fingertips pressed to his mouth. 'Thank you for that wonderful demonstration of your Art. Let's finish our meal.'

Sir Kingsford excused himself straight after dinner, retreating back to his study. The rest of them went to the parlour, or a parlour, anyway. Edith vanished to the library and came back triumphantly with a book of poems containing *A Visit from St. Nicholas*, which had an inscription from a great-aunt on their mother's side, who, though elderly when she started mailing presents home to her nieces and nephews, had scandalously run away to the Americas as a young woman just in time for the War of Independence.

'Her letters about what she got up to are much more interesting than this,' Lulu added, 'but Kings has got those locked up under archival conditions.'

Edith, not deterred, opened the slim volume and performed the poem for Kit, with plenty of silly voices and movement and zero self-consciousness, while Lulu watched her with an odd little smile.

Kit, curled beside Locke on the settee, applauded quietly but sincerely when Edith was done. She handed him the book. *Down the chimney St. Nicholas came with a bound*, he read, and *And giving a nod, up the chimney he rose.* He read the words, over and over again, until Locke took the book away.

'Stop researching your next escape,' he said softly. 'It's time for bed.'

'Oh, *good*,' Kit said, gifting him with a slow blink. He'd managed to snag his wineglass back when Locke was distracted, and Wellerman was a diligent sort of footman.

Locke both smiled and sighed. He took up a candle and guided Kit up the stairs. The women had gone ahead to their respective rooms.

'Tell me to get naked and on the bed, baby,' Kit said, once the door was shut behind him.

'Yeah, all right, pretty much,' Locke said, setting the candle on the table. 'Just get ready for bed, my lad. We've talked about this. Don't fuck around.'

Kit pivoted and raked Locke from head to toe, putting all his weight on to one hip, fluttering his eyelashes and purring, 'But fucking around's my favourite thing, Alex.'

Locke held up a firm hand. 'I'm still assuming all this flirting is ultimately in aid of escape, Mr Whitely.'

'I've promised I won't.'

'I don't believe your promises.'

'I gave away my mirror trick,' Kit said. 'That's not the tactic of a man planning to escape.'

'I'm sure you have plenty more tricks up your sleeve.'

'I do,' Kit said, with a lowering of eyelashes. 'Are you truly, *truly* going to make me get on my knees and beg for it, Alex?'

'Go on, then,' Locke said, sounding decidedly unimpressed.

Kit slouched out of his provocative stance. 'It's shabby to call people's bluffs unless you're on the gaming table, Mr Locke. Oh my God, you must clean up on the gaming tables.'

He watched as Locke dragged the chair in front of the door. He glanced about the room, obviously assessing other bits of furniture. Kit couldn't help a small laugh and Locke straightened and looked at him with narrowed eyes.

'If you build a barricade, you're just bringing the threshold closer to me,' Kit told him.

'Christ's sake, your ridiculous bloody Art,' Locke said in muted outrage, and then laughed ruefully. 'It's as twisty as you are, and that's saying something.'

Kit flopped back onto the bed, laughing quietly to himself. He made a weak effort to toe off the shoes that had come with his evening wear. He was still down to shirtsleeves otherwise.

He felt Locke's hand on his calf, and then the man was gently taking his shoes off. 'Am I talking to sober Kit or drunk Kit?'

'Little of the one, little of the other,' Kit said.

'More of the other, I think.'

Kit sat up and watched Locke carefully put the chair back in place and set the shoes neatly beside his own boots. He stripped off his necktie, coat and waistcoat and laid them over the back of the chair. His old clothes had already been taken, for cleaning and repair; Kit's old clothes were gone too, but a neat pile sat on a side table, dark colours that looked like more of Kingsford's dull tastes.

'I'm not really drunk, Alex, it's just euphoria,' Kit explained. 'Doing something new with my Art, especially something like the doors tonight... That's, oh, that's like nothing else, baby.'

'Yes,' Locke said quietly. 'Yes, it was quite something to watch, too.' He stood poised, looking at Kit with the same intent gaze as he had at dinner before physically giving himself a shake. 'So this is happy Kit?'

After thinking about it, Kit said, 'Yes. Happy Kit.'

'Well, isn't that just a little bit adorable?' Locke sat heavily on the bed and smiled at him.

Kit bit his lip, hesitating. 'And is it...is it a little bit irresistible, Alex?'

'Might be.' He shrugged. 'I'm not going to take you to bed for the sake of controlling my own talent, Kit. That's not fair to you, and since it gives you a bloody leg-up on your escape plan, it's not fair to me either. It's back to ulterior motives and pretence and I'm done with that.' He made a cutting off gesture with one hand. 'Do you want more of that salve on those burn scars on your back?'

Locke, the naïve fool, probably thought he'd made a change of topic. Kit never took help but he certainly knew an opportunity when he heard one.

He peeled himself out of his shirt and, sitting side by side with Locke, waited while the big man smoothed the salve over the scars on his back. The oily smell of the lanolin, mixed with Mrs Knight's herbs, rosemary and mint and lemon balm, suffused the warm air of the bedroom. Locke's strong hands moved slowly, surely over Kit's skin and he felt a shiver starting in him, down low and rising.

'You're working on my Art, too, you realise,' Kit said as he relaxed under the strong, gentle touch. 'I'm also getting the boost from unfulfilled desire.' *Right. Bloody. Now.*

'Yeah, all right, I noticed that at dinner. Everyone noticed that at dinner. Except Kingsford. He really has no clue.' Locke screwed the lid back on the glass jar of salve.

'*Therefore*, I do truly desire you. Wildly. You must believe that by now,' Kit insisted. 'And it's very strong. I feel like I'm powered by standing stones.'

He turned his head in time to catch Locke looking very amused at a private joke he was having with himself.

'You're thinking you've got a standing stone right here, aren't you?' Kit palmed the front of Locke's trousers, felt the hard length there and pressed again, firmer, rocking the heel of his palm. 'Alex, you know my intentions.'

'Which disguise your *other* intentions, Kit.' Nevertheless, Locke's hips rolled under Kit's hand and he didn't push him away.

'I want you. For your own sake, no other motives, no pretences, nothing but pure want. Your mouth on me, your hands on me, your cock in me.' And then, because Kit was pretty sure he could guess the bent of Locke's true proclivities by now, he said, 'I *need* it, Alex. I need *you*.'

Kit felt something in Locke then, a certain relaxation or shift in his weight that told Kit his mood was pliant, his resistance had crumbled, he was Kit's. He got a thigh over Locke's and kissed him; the man rocked back but didn't stop him. Kit threaded his fingers into Locke's hair, humming into his mouth.

'Touch me,' he ordered between kisses. 'Touch me everywhere.' Locke pulled back, trying for air or even self-control. Kit was not going to let that happen. 'Give me what I need, baby,' he wheedled. 'You're the only one who can.'

Locke muttered, 'Your manipulation is now so blatant, it's just open contempt for the very idea I'd say no to you.'

Kit had a fistful of his shirt. 'Are you going to complain or are you going to fuck me?'

Locke's gaze went hooded before he gave a reluctant smile. 'I'm going to do both, because I am a hypocrite of the first water and I cannot bloody resist you.'

'Oh, baby, you do know how to talk dirty after all,' Kit crooned, magnanimous in triumph.

He gave Locke a shove and followed it with his whole body; the mattress whomped as Locke fell back hard under Kit's relentless gravity. 'Jesus, Kit, don't make me break the bed.'

Kit crawled up his prone body. 'Let's break the sodding bed, Alex.'

He put his mouth, hot and insistent, over Locke's. Once Locke was relaxing helplessly into the kiss—really, he made Kit feel astonishingly powerful, the way he melted like that—Kit fitted himself closer, sliding his thighs tight on either side of Locke's waist, feeling Locke's big hands close around his hips to hold him even tighter, his fingers clenching on his arse compulsively.

Kit plundered his mouth with his tongue and rocked his hips in time to the rhythm. When he was sure Locke was well and truly converted to the merits of going along with fucking him, Kit released his mouth and licked and bit his way downwards, fingers already working at the buttons of Locke's shirt. He heard Locke groan, and felt his hands stroke over his back, leaving heat in their wake. He slid down Locke's body, kissing and licking warm skin and undoing buttons as he went.

Locke didn't manage to bestir himself to protest until Kit had his trousers open and a hand in his drawers, freeing his glorious erection, and his objection—he appeared to think it was Kit's turn first—was cut off into a gasping moan as Kit took him in his mouth, revelling in the taste.

Locke made an explosive noise through his teeth as Kit began using lips and tongue and throat; he was able to keep the man incapable of words, except a heartfelt, 'Christ Almighty, your *mouth*,' as his hands sank into Kit's hair, fingers hooking into his curls.

Kit popped up long enough to announce, 'Told you,' with no little smugness, before he swallowed him down to the root, sliding up and down in blissful rhythm, feeling the desire ricocheting ever higher.

Hips jerking, Locke gasped out, 'Stop now, sweetheart, or I'll shoot in your mouth.'

In answer, Kit hummed and sucked harder. He swallowed the hot, salty spend when it jetted into his mouth a moment later, Locke's groan sounding almost pained as he thrust convulsively down Kit's throat. Kit sat back up, swallowing his cough.

'Fucking hell, Kit.' Locke caught him under his arms and pulled him back up into a kiss, before nuzzling into his neck and murmuring, 'Fuck me now?'

'You're going to fuck me,' Kit informed him. Locke had to be seeing that intention, shining.

Locke's soft chuckle tickled his neck. 'You blew up your chances, sweetheart.'

'Nonsense,' Kit said. 'Recover yourself, Mr Locke, and then you're going to last long and hard inside me.'

'Such faith in my virility,' Locke remarked.

They coiled together, Locke's fingers absently working over Kit's skin in worshipful strokes, until Kit judged Locke had caught his breath. Then he reached a hand between them and began to work Locke's sensitive prick, Locke whimpering under him in a tormented sort of ecstasy.

'Long and hard, Alex,' Kit repeated. 'That's how I need it, and you want to give me what I need, don't you, baby?'

He leaned down to kiss him again, hand still working away. Locke's prick was obligingly responding to Kit's ministrations and Locke's own explorations as he slid his hands over the back of Kit's skin-tight trousers and squeezed hard.

Kit couldn't help a whimper of his own at the intensity of sensation, and

Locke urgently peeled them both out of the last of their clothes and pushed him flat on the bed to lie atop him and kiss him.

Adolescent Alex apparently had some foresight, or at least some chafing from overenthusiasm, for Locke had oil in the cabinet by the bed and was soon slipping oiled fingers into Kit's hole, starting gently with one, working slowly up to three. Kit mewled and scraped fingernails down Locke's back, arching and thrusting against the incursion, fucking himself.

'Need more,' he got out eventually. 'Want your cock.' He pushed at Locke and when the big man eased back, Kit got himself to hands and knees.

'No,' Locke said, and rolled him onto his back again.

'I think you don't know how to fuck, Mr Locke,' Kit said.

'I know how to fuck plenty, sweetheart,' Locke said. 'I want you under me, I want to see your face.'

'That's far too—' *Intimate.*

Locke made a small too-knowing noise. 'Finish that thought?'

'Have it your way, then,' Kit said. 'But just have your sodding way with me, would you?'

Locke gently pushed on one of his knees, guiding him to bending that leg up. Kit was glad one of them knew what he was doing in this position. He spread under him, raising and tilting his hips, and felt the burn as the big man breached him, breathing into it.

Locke took him slowly, murmuring, 'Easy, sweetheart, easy,' into his hair, one hand cupping the back of his head gently. At last his whole hot length was seated deep inside. All in on that one, indeed. 'Jesus, you feel good.'

Kit hooked both legs around him. 'Move for me, baby.'

Locke obeyed, pulling out a little and giving him a hard thrust that seemed to brush against a nub inside Kit and let loose such a rocketing pulse of sensation that he threw back his head and yowled like an alley cat.

Locke stilled, looking down at him intently. 'Did I hurt you?'

'No, keep going,' Kit gasped out. 'I wasn't expecting it to feel quite that good.'

Which meant he was going to have to be iron-clad in his self-control, if he wanted to keep his desire unfulfilled and thereby his Art running strong. Before he'd met Locke, he would have backed himself in any test of his own willpower.

'Sweetheart, have you not done this before?' Locke asked, looking almost comically dismayed at the thought.

'Sure, baby, you're my first,' Kit said with a roll of his eyes to disguise, indeed, a certain level of inexperience in the matter. 'Of course I have, it's just never felt quite so pleasant.'

'Then why were you so damned keen to— We didn't have to— I know how to do everything else!'

He patted the endearingly baffled Locke clumsily on the shoulder. 'You're so sodding competent, I knew I'd get a decent ride out of you. Now get on with it.'

Locke relaxed. 'Oh, such a sweet-talker.'

He began to move again and Kit moaned, pushing back against each thrust and digging his nails in hard. His eyes were practically rolling back in his head as wave after wave of bliss coursed through him.

Locke rested up on his forearms so he could watch Kit as he arched in his wild pleasure. 'My God, you're beautiful.'

Kit needed him to stop looking at him; it was too intense. He got his hands into his hair and tugged him to his mouth, humming. Of course Locke gamely tried to give him what he wanted but their size difference made kissing awkward, craning Locke's neck down and making him hunch, taking the power out of his thrusts.

So Kit lay back and tolerated the looking, watching the pleasure washing over Locke's face with intent interest of his own, until it was too much and he had to close his eyes against it and drag Locke's weight all the way down on to him.

He angled his hips and lifted his knees higher yet so he could squeeze Locke's ribs, urging him on. To his own mild embarrassment, he found himself whispering the man's name over and over. He'd been clutching Locke's arse, revelling in the flex of the big muscles there as Locke thrust deep into him, but he was too close to spending now. He fisted his hands into the sheets and bit his bottom lip hard to stave off the inevitable.

They moved together in frantic pleasure, thumping the headboard into the wall with abandon, until Locke gave a stifled cry that sounded pained. 'Can't hold off,' he muttered thickly.

He tried to slow down. Kit was having none of it. He writhed and swore and demanded and pleaded, locking his legs tight and rocking with his hips, and Locke, uttering curses of his own, drove into him wildly, gasping, 'Kit, oh, fuck, Kit.'

Kit fell back, floating in the remnant of warm sensation and luxuriating in the press of the big body atop him. He'd held on to his control by the merest skin of his teeth and he was fairly satisfied with himself. He stirred when Locke took hold of his still-hard prick with his big, calloused hand, pushing him away in mute refusal.

'You do not make me spend twice and then refuse to let me pleasure you in return,' Locke said, mock-severely. 'That is the height of bad manners, Mr Whitely.'

Kit shook his head.

'It's all right to let go, sweetheart,' Locke said, sounding confused.

Kit shook his head again. His instinct was to continue to refuse any sort of explanation or excuse, but he saw Locke's dawning frown and relented.

'My desire needs to stay unfulfilled,' he explained, 'so I've got as much Art as possible for Lulu's plan.'

'Sneaky little bastard. You could have said that before we got started.'

'No, I couldn't. You'd've refused to fuck me,' Kit said.

Locke made a noise of irritated agreement. 'On the other hand, that's the first thing you've said that's made me think you might truly be intending to help us.'

'I don't give up la petite mort for just anybody, baby.'

Locke laughed. 'No need, sweetheart. You said it yourself.'

He manhandled Kit until they were both sitting on the edge of the bed, Kit between Locke's thighs. They were facing the pier glass, the full length mirror, between the windows. Kit could see his own sturdy body, prick still standing proud, and Locke's muscled mass reflected dimly behind him.

'You're beautiful,' Locke said, and Kit felt himself flush. 'Take yourself in hand.'

Oh, that low voice of command went straight to Kit's groin and set his hard prick twitching. He didn't even like being ordered about; he didn't like being watched; he certainly didn't like abandoning control.

And yet he obeyed Locke, thrusting into his own fist, back arching so that his head fell back against Locke's shoulder, watching his own self in the mirror like it was someone else who writhed wantonly and gasped and moaned and spurted under Locke's steady gaze.

'Christ, if I were ten years younger, I'd take you again right now,' Locke muttered into his hair. 'So beautiful, Kit.'

He shifted till he got his head down and gave a long slow swipe of his tongue over the top of Kit's sensitive prick and across the slit, licking up his spilled seed. Kit whimpered and Locke chuckled. He laid him down and came back with a warm, wet cloth to clean him up. Then he pulled Kit into his arms, Kit's back to his chest, legs entangled.

'Staring into my eyes while we fuck and cuddling after,' Kit murmured as his eyes drifted closed. 'You're asking for trouble with the fond feelings, Mr Locke.'

'Let me worry about that and you worry about yourself.'

Kit's eyes opened. 'Oh,' he said, laughing a little. 'Oh, you think you can get *me* attached to *you*. You've got no hope, Alex, I'm heartless.'

Locke squeezed tighter. 'I just like it how I like it, sweetheart. Go to sleep.' Kit was almost asleep when he heard the sentimental fool whisper, 'You are not.'

13

KIT WOKE SOMETIME IN THE DARK hours of the morning. The fire was low. Alex's arm was still draped around his waist, a dead weight to match his heavy sleep. The blankets were a tangled mess at the foot of the bed; Kit ran hot enough to keep them both warm.

When he began to squirm away, Alex murmured and tightened his hold, pulling him till his back was again against Alex's strong, bare chest.

Kit stayed there and enjoyed that for a disturbingly long time before whispering, 'You're hurting me, Mr Locke.'

Just as he had done in Lovelly, Alex immediately released him, making a small noise Kit tried to pretend wasn't distressed. He rolled away, back into deep sleep.

Kit slid out of bed and tucked the blankets up around Alex. He put on a shirt and drawers that he pulled from the neat stack left for him. The fine material was light and soft on his skin. He went to the fireplace.

He had an itch he had to scratch.

He touched the stones of the lintel and found them still warm, though the firebox itself held barely more than embers now. He fixed in his head that iconic visit from Saint Nicholas, written more than thirty years ago in America, several generations of American children dreaming of Saint-Nick-now-Santa coming down the chimney, English children beginning to join in. Stockings by the fireplace. Reindeer on the roof.

Down the chimney he came, up the chimney he rose.

Santa across the threshold. Children believed it. Kit made himself believe it too.

He gathered his Art and pictured the fireplace in the dining room downstairs. He cast the Artwork and felt it connect, felt the threshold open before him.

Kit closed his eyes and smiled. He loved a new threshold. He stepped into the fireplace, and out of the dining room fireplace. Easy, far easier than mirrors.

'Thanks, Old Nick,' he murmured, and turned to go back, before Alex woke up and hated him again. He thought he might even wake his lover up when he got back into the room, for another round.

A shadow moved by the sideboard.

Then it had him by the wrist, fingers wrapped around bare skin, and every nerve in his body lit into scalding agony. Kit dropped, curling into the pain, but the shadow—a pain Artisan—kept hold of him.

Kit mercilessly shoved Christopher to the front of his mind to take the brunt of the pain and the fear, and so it was Christopher who whimpered and begged for it to stop while Kit coolly looked about for a means of escape.

The pain Artisan let him go. The crescendo of agony eased but his body was still afire and he couldn't move to drag himself towards a threshold. Above him, the pain Artisan pushed back the hood of his dark cloak and looked at him dispassionately. He was thin and pale-faced, the very incarnation of Medieval Death. Kit had the fleeting thought that he seemed familiar before his focus was considerably concentrated by the large knife making its appearance in the Artisan's hand.

Kit supposed it was a mercy the assassin wasn't dispatching him by holding on to him until the pain stopped his heart. He guessed he was conserving his Art, assuming the sudden and extreme pain had incapacitated his victim.

Unfortunately for the pain Artisan, Kit had learnt well enough how to endure pain during the time when Brother Fairweather had tried to rip the devil from his soul under Bishop Varley's orders.

That had been Kit's misfortune then. He was pleased to turn it into someone else's now.

The pain Artisan gripped Kit's hair, yanking his head back. The pain sparked hot again, though not at such a peak this time, perhaps because the Artisan wasn't bringing Art to bear, perhaps because Kit was safely behind the shield held over him by Christopher, lost and terrified and so very brave.

The Artisan jerked the knife towards Kit's throat. Bent over Kit as he was, the man's head was level with the bottom edge of the glass doors of the display cabinet.

Kit opened those glass doors with some prejudice, using Christopher's pain and fear as fuel for his Art. The heavy mahogany frame hit the Artisan with enough force to knock him back. He lost his balance, and tripped forwards onto his knees, hunching over. Kit slammed the doors shut, clocking him on the back of the head, and then, with a truly mammoth effort, opened them one last time so hard that when the righthand one hit the Artisan just as he lurched to his feet again, the glass shattered all over him.

He staggered but recovered dismayingly fast, shaking bits of glass from his hair, wiping at blood on his face where flying shards had struck him, he went for Kit, knife a weapon in one hand, his bare hand his other weapon.

The bottom doors of the display cabinet had flung open, shut and open again when Kit had worked on the top glass doors; Kit suspected he'd been in enough pain and enough panic to have opened every damned door in the house in exactly the same pattern. Kit rolled and scrabbled through the contents.

It was mismatched bits of crockery, mostly, and Kit, without a thought to the antique status of any of it, hurled chipped teacups and cracked plates and a teapot missing its lid at the face of the Artisan. He missed his first tries, the cups shattering on the wall behind his target, but got his eye in with the plates.

The pain Artisan ducked and cursed, the hand with the knife shielding his eyes as he forged forwards, free hand groping to try to touch Kit's bare skin anywhere. Kit slammed the glass door on the back of the assassin's head again for good measure and scrambled away.

He had not really been aware of the uproar in the rest of the house, building ever since he'd slammed every door and started smashing the valuables. Now, a huge figure rushed into the room, brandishing a pistol.

'Alex, look out!' Kit shouted.

The pain Artisan ducked, spun, and got his hand onto Kit's rescuer, who turned out be Lulu in a voluminous white nightdress, silky dressing gown flung loosely over it. She screamed and hit the floor as hard as Kit had, or harder, given the size of her. Alex was just behind her and crashed into the Artisan with an outraged bellow, knocking the knife from his hand and sending him flying.

Incognisant of the danger, Alex went after the intruder, kneeling on his chest to land a few facers. The much-abused Artisan was slow to react but he brought shaking hands up towards Alex. His head might have been aching and muzzy but his Art was obviously running strong, probably fed by fear now.

Alex, reading the intention too late in his enthusiastic defence of his sister, reared back but he couldn't get clear quickly enough.

Kit grabbed both wrists just before they would have touched Alex's bare thighs under his dressing robe. In retaliation, the Artisan twisted his hands till his long, bony fingers were pressed to the back of Kit's hands. Agony lanced through every nerve in his body, but Christopher again took the brunt. Kit, distantly hearing himself sob with the pain of it, forced their entwined hands flat to floor, well away from any bare skin of Alex's.

He managed to say, in between Christopher's whimpering, 'Knock. Him. Out.'

And then Edith dropped a vase on the Artisan's head from shoulder height, which did the trick.

It was aftermath then, so Kit decided to stay curled up behind Christopher for a while longer.

Sir Kingsford, wrapped in a silken candy-striped vintage-looking banyan, sent Wetherby for the local contingent of enforcers and delegated Wellerman to stand over the unconscious Artisan with a heavy iron rod in case he dared try to wake up.

Alex and Lulu discussed how to keep the pain Artisan contained; once they probably would have relied solely on the silvered iron handcuffs but Kit had taught them the folly of that. Or perhaps they didn't want their only pair to go walkabout to Bristol when the enforcers arrived.

When prompted, Kit advised them to wrap their prisoner's hands in whatever iron or silver they could, be that wire or jewellery. The maid acting as Lulu's lady's maid, French and unflappable, was sent to raid caches of jewellery for what she could find.

'Then put gloves on him. Strap them on so he can't strip them off with his teeth.' Kit looked down at the slumped captive. He should tell them to chop off the Artisan's hands. 'It's probably just his fingers, but tell the enforcers to be wary anyway.'

Having answered what was asked of him, he resumed his meekest pose, hands linked together in front of him, head bowed, Christopher's desperate attempt to radiate commitment to good behaviour. He could feel Alex frowning at him and lowered his head further. He wasn't sure what he was doing wrong, so it was safest to stay small.

'I'll wait here for the enforcers. You take Mr Whitely and Miss Knight upstairs,' Alex instructed his sister, who was still shaking from the aftereffect of the full dose of pain she'd been hit with.

Edith opened her mouth, presumably to argue being bundled off like a child, but Kit turned in instant obedience. Hands together in front of him. Head bowed. Compliant. The defence of the powerless. He walked up the stairs, Lulu wincing and limping behind him, hand on the banister for support.

'How are you not hobbling after that?' she said to Kit, but it didn't feel like a real question so he didn't answer. 'How in hell did you still function with his hands on you?'

That one felt like a real question. Lulu sounded annoyed about it. 'The first time he touched me, I dropped like you did,' Kit said. 'The second time, I was ready for it.'

'Holy Mother of God, *the second time?*' Lulu said. 'Fucking hell, kitten.'

'Language,' Edith whispered but it didn't sound like her heart was in it.

He went where he was directed, which was into the guestroom he hadn't yet used. He sat where he was told to sit, which was on the bed. Lulu sat on the other side, groaning as she lowered her weight down.

Edith hovered. 'Kit? Kit, can you hear me?'

'I can hear you, Miss Knight,' Kit said blankly. Hands in his lap. Eyes down. 'I'm right here.'

'Oh, Kitty,' whispered Edith.

Lulu, with an outburst of air through her nose that implied she was biting down a moan, lay back on the bed. 'Oh God, I feel like shit.'

'Rub the skin,' Kit said. 'Soothe the nerves. Give her poppy syrup.'

Edith, after a long moment in which Kit braced himself in case she tried to touch him, turned and sat beside Lulu, taking her hand. She began to move her thumb over the back of Lulu's hand and along each finger. Lulu made a small noise of pure relief. Edith continued up her arm, hands small against Lulu's broad muscle. By time she was at the Valkyrie's shoulder, Lulu was mostly asleep, limp in the beautiful rush of bliss that came when pain was gone. Edith ran gentle fingers over her face and frowned, the back of her hand stroking Lulu's cheek, before continuing to caress across the back of her neck and start down the other arm. Lulu relaxed further into the touch, the tension in her face slackening.

There were murmured voices on the stairs, the Locke brothers coming back to bed. Sir Kingsford sounded irritated. His cane was thumping hard along the rug in the corridor.

'I don't care if he followed you or if he followed Whitely. I told you not to bring your choices home with you.'

Alex's reply was quieter, a tired murmur.

'No. This has to stop. You—' A long pause, and then Sir Kingsford, his tone distraught, said, 'Alexander, I can't welcome you here if you persist in this.'

'Fine,' Locke said sharply. 'That's fine, then, Sir Kingsford. We're going in the morning. Good night.'

Kit heard Sir Kingsford's uneven footsteps, punctuated by the thud of the cane, retreating down the hallway. Alex came to the door of the guestroom, mouth set, eyes snapping, looking more like his twin than he ever had before.

'The enforcers are taking the Artisan to the Agency London office,' he said. He watched Edith for a moment before looking at Kit, where he sat stiffly still on the edge of the bed. 'And you got your comeuppance for trying to escape, you little weasel.'

'Yes, sir.' Hands in lap. Head down. Compliance, his only defence.

'If Kit were trying to escape, he would have escaped,' Edith said stoutly, from where she half-lay beside Lulu.

'Then what was he doing downstairs, Miss Knight?' Even as he bit out the words, Alex stepped to Kit, to lift his chin in one strong hand so Kit was forced to meet his eyes.

Kit lowered his gaze quickly. Alex seemed to want an answer. Kit couldn't contradict Alex by insisting he wasn't trying to escape; he would be beaten for arguing. But he couldn't agree he had been trying to escape; he would be beaten for lying.

He took refuge in silence, knowing it wouldn't work. Christopher began to shiver.

'What the blazes is wrong with him?' Alex asked Edith.

'I don't know,' she said. 'He was a little bit like this when he first came to the village. Sort of cold right down inside where you couldn't reach it. But you know what? I remember when he was most like this. You asked what he'd done to make the village like him so much? We had a fire a few months after he arrived, old Mrs Talbot left a candle burning and it set her cottage on fire and spread to the cooper Knights' house next door, and they thought Little Tommy was with the other five children when they crawled out, but he wasn't, he was trapped inside and the fire was too hot to go back in after him, and his mother was just *screaming* and trying to beat the flames down with her bare hands to get to him, and before anyone else could find a way in, Kit walked in, well, you know, he didn't *walk* in, of course, but he went in without so much as a moment of hesitation and he walked back out with Little Tommy in his arms and gave him to his mother, and he had quite bad burns on his arms and shoulders from it, and afterwards everyone was congratulating him and buying him beer and literally *patting his back*, Alex, and he didn't even flinch. He just sat very still like this and was very polite and just not really there at all, and he wasn't there for quite a few hours. It was only when Ma put him to bed that she found the burns. Luckily her salve works wonders or he'd be scarred worse than he is.

'But it was like he was hiding from the pain, and from feeling a'feared of walking into an inferno like anyone would be. Oh well, maybe you Locke twins wouldn't be afraid to do that but any reasonable person would be, and the point is, Kit isn't fearless, but he can put the fear away somewhere.' She took a shuddering breath. 'And so, I think—I think he's hiding right now, Alex.'

The words were a gentle lilt over Kit's head. Alex had stood quietly to listen, his hand still gentle on Kit's chin. 'He needs the physician?'

'I don't think so,' she said. 'There's nothing physically wrong, after all.'

Alex brought his other hand up and cupped Kit's face. 'Kit,' he said softly. 'Come back. You're safe now, my lad.' Kit didn't answer and Alex glanced at Edith. 'I feel like a bloody idiot, Miss Knight. Mr Whitely, you're safe, you can come back now.'

'It took hours after the fire,' Edith said again. 'I think this one is worse. Kitty?'

'Miss Knight?' he said.

'No,' she said. Her voice sounded peculiar. 'No, argue with me and call me Eddie, for God's sake.'

'I don't argue, Miss Knight,' Kit said. 'I'm very good.'

He frowned. He had just argued. He made a breathy, panicked little sound and clamped his mouth shut.

'Yes,' Edith said urgently. 'Yes, you are very good, Mr Whitely. You were very good when you saved Little Tommy from the fire and you're very good now.'

'Thank you, Miss Knight.'

'He should sleep. I'll put him to bed,' Alex said. Lulu muttered and pulled a pillow over her head. 'Easier to move him than her. I'll put him in mine, I'll take Lulu's, you can go back to yours.'

'Very well, Mr Locke,' said Edith. 'I'll just finish rubbing her skin, when you boys have given her her privacy.'

'Yeah, all right, there's a reason you're putting your hands all over my sister?'

'Excuse me!' Edith said. '*Rude*. Kit said it'll soothe the pain.'

Alex had taken hold of Kit's shoulders and was drawing him, unresisting, from the room. He glanced back. 'Does he need that, then?'

'Presumably,' she said. 'We all saw him take the hit from the Artisan to protect you and that was the second time he got hit, so…'

Alex, one hand still on Kit's shoulder, drew his other hand over his eyes. 'Kit,' he murmured.

'You do it, Alex,' Edith said softly. 'I know you intend him no harm. But I don't know that they need the poppy, though. Ma says not to overdo stuff like that.'

'He always gave me poppy syrup,' Kit said dreamily.

Alex took Kit down to his room. Kit stood passively as Alex built up the fire. He undressed him by its flickering light, peeling off the loose shirt and drawers, damp with the sweat of Christopher's fear. The big man fetched a clean cloth from the washbasin and wiped Kit down, washing his face and neck, running the cloth over his arms and shoulders, down his back to the curve of his arse, a mirror echo of how he had dried and dressed Kit in the Knightstone Inn.

This too was part of the ritual. After Fairweather was done trying to cast the devil out of Kit, he would purify him like this, smooth the pain away. That's how Kit had known Lulu would need it. That's how he had known how good it would feel. That was how Fairweather had made being good feel so right.

Alex moved lower, sponging down Kit's legs and then briefly washed his groin, cloth firmly between his hand and Kit's skin, a cool, impersonal nurse's touch, the water chilling his skin.

Kit put his hand in Alex's hair without looking down.

'No,' Alex said immediately. He rose and stepped away, turning his back to wring the cloth out. 'Lie down, sweetheart.'

Kit obeyed like he had been compelled, lying flat on the bed, staring at the ceiling, waiting. Compliant.

'No,' Alex said again.

He eased Kit over and pulled the blankets away before sliding Kit under them, tucking them around Kit so tight he couldn't move. That was all right. Kit lay cocooned, looking up at the ceiling, unblinking.

Alex stood beside the bed, hands over his face, murmuring something into his hands. He breathed deep once, twice, then dropped his hands and smiled down at Kit. 'Close your eyes, Kit. Go to sleep.'

'Stay with me?' Kit asked.

Alex traced his thumbs over Kit's cheekbones. 'Come back, sweetheart.

Come back to me, sweetheart, please.'

'I'm here,' Kit said. 'Right here. Stay with me?' He turned his head from his contemplation of the ceiling and met Alex's eye. 'Stay with me.'

Alex shook his head and moved towards the door, and Kit let out an inarticulate cry of anguish he hadn't been aware was building in his chest. The big man was back by his side in an instant.

'Stay with me.' Kit blinked and felt tears run down his cheeks. His arms were tucked in too tight for him to get a hand free to wipe them away. Alex obliged, thumbs smearing the wetness over his cheeks. 'Don't leave me, Alex.'

He blinked again and made a little gasp. The deadened feeling was gone. He could hear the gentle pop of the fire eating wood, smell Alex's warm sandalwood scent, feel the weight of the blankets and the prickle of heat because he was already too warm.

Alex hesitated for a long time before he finally relaxed from his position hunched over Kit and lay beside him. 'I'll go when you're asleep.'

Kit struggled until he was loose and could nestle into Alex's neck, breathing him in. 'You'll stay,' he said firmly. 'Get under the blankets, Mr Locke.'

'Oh, hello, Kit,' said Alex, voice choking a little. 'Shit. Hello, sweetheart.'

'I've been right here the whole time,' Kit said, puzzled. 'That was a thing, wasn't it? I wasn't escaping, Alex, I was practising. I need to sleep now. Get under the damned blankets and hold me so I feel safe.'

And Alex got under the damned blankets and held him, and he felt safe.

14

KIT HAD NEVER SPENT A WHOLE night with a man, and, barring the nap in Lovelly, had never woken in a man's arms before. It was an extraordinarily safe feeling, it turned out, at least when the arms belonged to Alexander Locke.

Alexander Locke, the enforcer.

Kit pushed the feeling away. He could not afford to let this man make him feel safe.

More carnally, he was interested to discover that Alex, like him, sported a morning erection, and wondered if that was a universal trait. Idle speculation aside, he did not hesitate to take merciless advantage. He had both hands sunk into Alex's hair, fingers cupping his scalp, his mouth on Alex's, and one leg locked around Alex's waist before the man was even properly awake.

Alex groaned deep in his throat, and then he was moving over Kit, rutting helplessly against him in exact accord with his blazing intentions. And then he was swearing and tearing himself away, all the way out of bed to wrap himself in his dressing robe, which was not at all the direction of Kit's intention, desire, or liking.

Kit recognised the look on his face, stern and tender and slightly anxious. Last night had apparently roused every last one of the man's protective instincts to full alert. That could not be allowed to stand.

He tsked. 'Do you have to make everything so sodding difficult?'

'Oh, pot, kettle!' Alex said, quite affronted, and that was surely very far from what he had been about to say, so Kit was satisfied.

'I have been *very clear* about the extremely simple things I want,' Kit said. *Choices, and you.*

'With words,' Alex said. 'But I've had half my life now knowing exactly what the people around me intend and, I have to say, not knowing with you is sending me up the wall.'

'And naturally,' Kit said, 'the obvious course of action is therefore to assume I'm lying about everything.'

Alex stopped dead, a startled expression on his face, before he slowly nodded. 'Yeah,' he said, sounding as surprised as he looked. 'That is what I've been doing, isn't it?'

'Possibly you shouldn't have fucked me, then.'

'I did inform you I was being a hypocrite. I just didn't realise how much of one.' Alex started. 'Stop that.'

'What?'

'Distracting me. What was going on last night, Kit?'

Kit would have given a good portion of the funds he'd abandoned back in Lovelly to avoid that question, so, smiling sweetly, he said, 'The aforementioned. It wasn't so memorable, then?'

Alex folded his arms. 'After that, Kit.'

'Cuddling,' Kit said, still smiling. 'Very sweet.'

Lifting his gaze to the ceiling, Alex breathed out very slowly. 'Where did you go, when the pain Artisan hurt you?'

'Nowhere. I took the pain. For you. You're welcome.'

Alex knelt on the bed. 'I know you did. You were brave, and kind, and— and *brilliant*. And it wasn't to throw it in my teeth like this. Please, talk to me, Kit.'

When Kit, suddenly shamed by the sheer goodhearted sincerity of the damnable man, could find no words, Alex added, 'You wanted me to stay with you for a reason.'

Oh, well, this he could do. He lazily caught the flap of Alex's dressing robe. 'You know the reason, Alex.'

'Because I make you feel safe.'

Kit twitched. He'd said that, hadn't he, last night, in the residue of his daze. Alex certainly liked to pick and choose what he'd believe from Kit, and oh, wasn't he self-righteously satisfied about this one.

He shrugged it off. 'I'll make you feel amazing, baby.'

Alex put his hand over Kit's where he still lightly tugged on the dressing robe. 'I won't be distracted, sweetheart.'

'And I won't talk about it, Mr Locke,' Kit said, abruptly dropping all pretence at coquetry and retreating behind his wall of icy courtesy. 'We are at an impasse. I'll have breakfast now, please.'

'If I make you feel safe, why won't you talk to me about it?'

'I don't need you to make me feel safe,' Kit said through gritted teeth. 'I don't need anything from you.'

Alex made a disgruntled sound. 'You needed me last night.'

'You're an enforcer,' Kit retorted. He saw a flicker in Alex's eyes that suggested he'd forgotten that. 'And you don't have room for me.' Ah, yes, definitely guilt now. 'So you have no right to demand I roll over and bare my belly for you.' Realising he was sounding quite annoyed, he controlled himself. 'Well. You could demand it, except you're apparently incapable of just enjoying a meaningless dalliance without getting sodding stupid about it all.'

The problem with sounding calm and cold when inside he was boiling with what could have been outrage or could have been panic was that when he called Alex stupid, it sounded like he'd deliberately chosen to do so. At least he'd not had any sort of intention to do so, and Alex could probably read the intention to apologise that Kit clamped down on because he was still too hot to apologise.

Alex shoved his hair back with both hands with blatant disregard. 'Don't like feeling vulnerable, do you?' His voice was tight.

'No one *likes* it.'

'Not everyone has a conniption about it.'

'I do not have conniptions,' Kit said, scandalised. 'About *anything*.'

Alex leaned over him, looking stern and tender. 'It's all right to be vulnerable, Kit.'

And Kit promptly had a conniption.

With a few choice swearwords, he put his palms to Alex's chest and shoved. 'Get *away* from me.'

Then a brisk knock came at the door, which opened immediately on the last rap. Edith came stomping in, her face a picture of distress.

Kit looked at her past Alex's shoulder, well aware of what this looked like.

Edith had stopped, her distress erased so she could glower at Alex. 'Mr Locke! You said you were going to put him to bed and sleep elsewhere and now I find you half-naked and all over him when he was so bloody vulner—'

'Jesus fuck, don't make it worse!' Alex backed off the bed and got well up on a high horse as he jerked his dressing robe tighter around him. 'I stayed because he begged me to stay,' he snapped at Edith. 'But God fucking forbid he ever admit he might have fucking needed me.'

And then he stormed out of the room and slammed the door so hard that plaster dust rained down.

"'Ark at 'im!' Edith said, looking around at the door in astonishment. 'I suppose there 'ad to be a temper in there somewhere, given the twin.'

Kit had taken the opportunity to hurry into the banyan he'd been left from Sir Kingsford's supply so that he was slightly more appropriately dressed to receive a visitor. He folded his arms and waited.

Edith looked him up and down slowly. 'I see your refusal to accept help is standing you in good stead.'

Kit shrugged but he fidgeted with the sash of the banyan with some discontent.

Edith sighed. 'I'm glad to see you well and I don't wish to be selfish,' she said. 'But can we address my crisis before we address yours?'

'I have addressed my crisis,' Kit said. 'I made it leave the room in a pet. I am at your disposal. What can I do for you, dear Edith?'

'So,' she said, drawing the word out into a long sighing sound. 'I fell asleep next to Lulu last night.'

Kit looked at her blankly for a moment before saying, 'Oh. Your morning has been quite interesting, then.'

Edith balled a fist in thwarted frustration. 'Might have warned me, Kit! Instead of letting me make an ass of myself.' She frowned, chewing on her lower lip. 'I kissed her.'

Kit was genuinely impressed. 'Brave girl. She's sodding terrifying.'

'She's fierce and interesting. But kissing led to—' She made her thumb and index finger hover an inch apart. '—just a few teensy questions and then I was really rather startled, and I exclaimed aloud about a part of her anatomy I had not been aware of and— well, I hurt her feelings, Kitty. Badly.'

'I'm sure you did,' Kit said bluntly. 'Once you apologise, she'll be ready to talk to you again in a few months or so.'

'But.' Edith splayed her hands in confusion. 'I mean. I like her. And I was attracted to her. But now... I'm not trying to be rude, Kit, but I think I only like cream puffs in that way.'

Kit shrugged. 'She's a cream puff.'

Edith looked doubtful. 'She's a sticky bun dressed up like a cream puff, though?'

'Let's say Margaret mixed up a batch of cream puff batter and then she got distracted and used it as a dough for sticky buns instead. Are they going to taste like sticky buns just because they were shaped like sticky buns, or are they going to taste like cream puffs?'

'This is a terrible analogy,' Edith said. 'Somewhat blasphemous, to boot.'

Kit assessed her. He wasn't sure how innocent she truly was, and therefore how much more he could say. They had their cheerfully coy euphemisms; she'd pegged Kit as preferring sticky buns when she'd noticed his quiet appreciation of the fishermen when they hauled in their catches in wet shirts. She'd also had her intense friendship with Meredith and had been mopey when they'd fought and beyond wounded when Meredith had announced her sudden engagement to Young Tom.

'I wouldn't know what to do with the, the sticky bit, Kitty!' she said all in a rush.

That answered that. 'In my experience, people with *sticky bits* are extremely good at letting you know what they'd like you to do with, to, or about their sticky bits,' Kit told her. 'And then you can tell them yea or nay as the desire takes you.'

'Your vast experience,' Edith said.

It was almost a question. Subtly ogling the fishermen aside, Kit had spent his six months in the village living like a particularly devout monk. He returned to her a look as straight-faced as her own and waited her out.

Hands on hips, she sighed out a long hiss of air. 'I need to go think for a while.'

She opened the door and went back out, almost bumping into Alex, who had been waiting outside. He was looking steadfastly neutral; either he was trying not to be angry at Kit or he'd heard something of the conversation.

He had to come in, since he was in his dressing robe and all his clothes were in his bedroom, which Kit had usurped. He slowly assembled an outfit without looking over at Kit where he was picking through the assortment of clothes from Sir Kingsford. He checked the cut on his thigh and apparently decided it had healed enough to leave the covering off. Then he started to dress.

And, of course, the process of ordering himself into layers of clothing soothed him into his usual good-natured self, so that once he was fully dressed, he said to Kit, 'I'm sorry. I shouldn't have tried to make you talk to me. It's your choice who to share it with, and when.'

Kit had elected to ignore most of the layers, sticking with trousers—snug but not indecent this time— shirt and coat as per his usual wont. There was a pair of walking boots there, too, which he left for now. He had therefore finished dressing a while before Alex, had been fidgeting about the room, and was not actually a whole lot calmer.

'There's nothing more to share,' he said, disordering the bottles on Alex's toiletry table. 'I was beaten. Lots of us were. A few of us were beaten more severely than the rest. Some of us vanished. I got out. I'm alive, and I've kept myself safe for near-enough nine years without needing help from anybody. There's nothing more to share.'

'Plainly, there is,' Alex said mellowly. 'But I won't push you again. You'll tell me in your own time.'

Patronising sodding *wanker*. 'I'm not some sort of fragile creature who needs handling with kid gloves.'

'I'm not saying you are.'

Kit turned around to scowl. 'You're thinking it, and acting like it, and I won't have it. I'm not your lover, I'm your prisoner, I might escape at any moment, so sodding well behave accordingly.'

Alex snorted. His voice was very gentle when he said, 'Oh, Kit. Sweetheart. You're not going to escape.'

Kit truly lost his temper then, and this time there was no stemming it so that the rest of the world only saw mild exasperation.

'I do not need your pity, Mr Locke,' he spat. 'I do not want your mercy. I do not require anyone's help. I save myself, always.' He stepped back smartly and slammed his hand onto the mantel of the fireplace. 'So you can take your fond sodding feelings and *shove them*.'

And he was gone, through the fireplace.

15

K IT STUMBLED OUT OF THE FIREPLACE in Sir Kingsford's study and threw himself sulkily into the nearest fireside chair.

Aside from Kit's stuttering breathing, only the light crackle of the fire, the ticking of the clock and the scritch of Sir Kingsford's elegant steel pen along paper disturbed the sepulchral quiet of the room.

'Good morning, Mr Whitely,' Sir Kingsford said eventually.

He dipped his pen and went on writing. It looked like a letter, from what Kit could make out. His desk was piled with lots of letters, with many different handwritings, but no order, apparent in the correspondence.

There was also what looked like a brochure for gas fixtures and fittings sitting on housing schematics. The man was old-fashioned in his tastes in clothes and habits, but he certainly had a liking for modern conveniences.

'Good morning, Sir Kingsford.'

'That was rather interesting to observe, thank you, Mr Whitely.'

'You're very welcome, sir.'

'My clothes look well on you.'

Kit looked down at himself. His lungs were easing now, breath coming more readily. 'Thank you for the—' He couldn't, in good conscience, call the clothes a loan. '—gift.'

'It behoves us all to practise Christian charity towards those less fortunate,' Sir Kingsford said serenely as he turned over the page and kept writing.

Kit could absolutely see why Alex struggled to maintain good relations with his brother.

As if Sir Kingsford had seen the thought—and perhaps he had; Kit had assumed the Locke twins' talents had come via their mother but it could very well be from the Locke patriarch—he asked, 'Will Alexander be looking for you?'

'No doubt.'

'Ah, well,' Sir Kingsford said. 'Let him come knocking then.'

To Kit's own amazement, he found himself saying, 'I like you, Sir Kingsford.'

Sir Kingsford remained unperturbed. 'I am neither surprised nor gratified to hear this,' he informed Kit as he wrote another thought into his correspondence.

'You're an odd duck, aren't you?' Kit said, smiling.

Sir Kingsford looked at him over his half-moon glasses. 'The duckiest.'

Alex did come knocking then, tapping briskly twice before opening the door and snapping his attention onto Kit immediately. 'Come along, Mr Whitely,' he said stiffly from the doorway.

Kit rose obediently.

Sir Kingsford put down his pen and picked up a pipe that was carved in the shape of a dragon. He began to pack it with tobacco. 'A word, Alexander.'

Alex shot an accusatory look towards Kit before presenting himself before the desk and resignedly waiting, standing ramrod-straight and obviously expecting more hectoring.

'I believe your young man is correct when he suggests we do not speak frankly enough,' Sir Kingsford told him. 'He is perhaps a good influence on this family.'

'Not my young man in particular,' Alex corrected neutrally.

'Ah,' Kingsford said. 'I have misinterpreted, as I so often do in these affairs. Then it is Lucinda with whom is he playing at St George?'

Alex now delivered a positively murderous look Kit's way. Caught between petty amusement and mild concern, Kit sat back down in his chair, as avid as if he were spectating a tennis match in which the favourite for the win was in fact receiving a thrashing and a half.

Alex managed to say, 'I would prefer you confine your more outlandish speculations towards my behaviour, sir, and not our sister's.'

The man could bluff after all, it seemed.

'Very well. I shall move on. I rescind what I said last night.' Kingsford leant back, clasping his hands over his stomach, pipe caught between his fingers. He watched his brother unblinkingly. 'You are welcome here and always will be. I will never not shield you.'

Alex twitched all over at these conciliatory words.

Kingsford tapped the pipe slowly on the desk. 'I do wish you would have a long think about what you actually want to be doing.'

'I'm doing what I actually want to be doing, sir.'

'You're doing what Lucinda wants to be doing,' Kingsford corrected him. 'What do *you* want, Alex?'

It might have been Kit's imagination, but Kingsford seem to glance at him as he asked this. Alex returned only stubborn silence, and his brother sighed, a heavy sound in the quiet study.

'I miss him, too, you know.' The baronet had stopped tapping his pipe and was staring down at it as if it had come alive in his hand to breathe fire.

Alex shifted his weight. 'Miss who?'

'Llewellyn. Lucinda lost the most, but she wasn't the only one. You lost him. And I lost him, too. He was my friend, too. And I lost you both when we all lost him.'

'Not true.'

'You ran off to the Crimean—'

'That was respectable government work.'

'Alexander, you well know it was you abetting Lucinda's attempt to outrun grief, an exercise in futility.' A small frown crossed his narrow face. 'And I've barely seen either of you since your return. I know you both have your plans. I'm not as oblivious as you think I am. I will not try to stop you. Just. If you need help. If it goes wrong. Send for me, Lexi. I'll help you. No matter what. I'm still your brother and your shield. You may count on me for any and all assistance. No matter how much you dislike me.'

'Don't dislike you,' Alex said. His tone was gruff but he looked utterly shamed.

Kingsford abruptly jerked up and took a stumbling step around the desk. He embraced Alex. He was a full head shorter, but Alex, eyes wide, looked very much the little brother in that moment. 'Promise you'll call on me if you need help.'

'We will,' Alex whispered. 'We will, Kings.' Reluctantly but inexorably, his arms lifted and he held his brother.

'I like your young man,' Kingsford added quietly. He lightly stepped away again, saying over his shoulder, 'He keeps you on your toes. You'll enjoy that.'

Kit laughed and Alex gave him yet another look. 'Yeah, all right, we're going to go now,' he said. 'Good day to you, Sir Kingsford.'

'I've had Wetherby set out a breakfast and Wellerman prepare the carriage. Lulu has your funds. Eat and be on your way. I trust I will see you again soon. Good day to you, Alexander. Mr Whitely.'

'Sir Kingsford.' Kit bowed.

Alex wrapped his large hand around him and hastened him out. He took him along the hallway into the morning room, which faced east over manicured gardens and was pleasantly lit by the rising sun glinting through the large French doors.

Only then did he pause to huff out a shocked breath. 'Well, you're an influence of some sort, aren't you?'

Kit, on the other hand, was ready to resume the argument they'd already been having. 'Point adequately demonstrated?'

Alex shook off his somewhat stunned expression. 'You didn't escape though, did you?'

Smug git. 'That's unnecessarily obstinate.'

'I don't see what the problem is. You wanted me to trust you, and lo! I trust you. Revel in it, my lad.'

'I want you to trust my word because you believe my word is honourable, not because you think I'm in thrall to your c—' Alex made a small noise just as Wetherby went soundlessly by and Kit seamlessly changed tack. '—charismatic personality.' Since that had been far too honest, he added, sparking, 'And definitely not because you pity me.'

'Yeah, all right. No pity, no mercy, et cetera, you're our prisoner and we'll use you accordingly.'

'Use me at will,' Kit murmured, lowering his eyelashes. 'I await your convenience, sir.'

Alex looked at the ceiling, smiling. 'Help yourself,' he said, waving at the chafing dishes on the side table. 'Eat well, Lulu will be in a mad rush when she gets us going.'

Kit took the lids off all the chafing dishes and eyed off crispy bacon, fluffy scrambled eggs, poached eggs beside them, smoked haddock, and thick slices of bread.

Beside him, Alex was laughing now. 'Jesus, if you looked at me like you look at food, I'd be powerless to resist you.'

Kit, halfway through piling his plate high, set it and the serving spoon for the eggs down and pivoted towards him. 'You're already powerless to resist me,' he said, making Alex laugh again. It felt warm to make Alex laugh so he added, 'Come here, then, baby, I'll eat you right up, you make my mouth water.'

He sashayed into Alex's space and Alex caught him by the shoulders. His face was still light with amusement, but he spoke seriously. 'I didn't thank you, though.'

Kit looked at him blankly.

'You've done me a good turn, Kit. It's all back to a low hum,' Alex said, tapping his head with his free hand. 'Much better. So—thank you.'

'Always pleased to be of service, Mr Locke.' Kit removed himself from Alex's hold with a bow and turned to collect his plate.

Alex went off into laughter again; the relief of his talent behaving itself, or the relief of Kit not escaping when he could have, or the relief of his brother forgiving him for the Artisan's ingression, or perhaps even the pure physical relief of bedding Kit: the man was in a cheerful mood indeed.

'Oh no,' he mocked. 'Someone's being sincere in my vicinity, it's terrifying! Better deflect.'

Making an unimpressed hum, Kit thumped his plate back down, the better to face off to the Viking with hands on hips and eyebrows raised. 'No need for discourtesy, Mr Locke.'

Alex slid closer again and took hold of his coat lapel. 'I'd like to thank you for saving me from the pain Artisan too, but Christ only knows what that will provoke.'

'Thank me and find out, baby.'

Face open and alight with amusement and rising desire, Alex tugged hard and Kit let himself be pulled close. Alex kept his fist knotted into Kit's coat; his other hand nestled into Kit's hair, tightening in a way that made Kit sigh and press against the bigger man.

For all his hold was commandingly firm, his mouth covered Kit's gently at first. As the kiss deepened into urgency, however, he got a little rougher, sucking and biting lightly on Kit's bottom lip, shoving him back against the sideboard, thigh pressing between his legs, as hard and insistent as the erection he could feel against his belly.

This was all precisely to Kit's intentions; he was beginning to see the benefit of a lover who could read his sodding mind. When the big man finally let him go, sagging slightly against him, Kit stayed very still, eyes closed, breathing out and letting his tongue slowly taste the remnant of Alex over his lips.

'Sweet Jesus,' Alex whispered, and Kit opened his eyes to discover him staring down at him, eyes hot. 'This unfulfilled desire business... What happens when I want you again? Because, holy fuck, do I want you again.'

Kit threaded his fingers into Alex's hair. 'I'll take care of you, baby. Any way you like it.'

'Mr Whitely, may I have a serious answer, please?' There was no heat to the words; Alex was still smiling, still leaning lightly on him, letting him have his warmth and his weight.

Sighing, Kit admitted, 'It won't have any effect on your talent anymore, Alex.' He tilted his head back. 'Kiss me again anyway?'

Alex brushed his cheek with his thumb. 'Planning to, yeah,' he agreed.

'Get on with it, then,' Kit ordered him. 'And I'll lock the door.'

Alex, chuckling, was leaning down to obey when Lulu stomped in with a face like thunder, banging the door Kit had regrettably failed to lock in a timely fashion.

The storm intensified when she saw them, Alex pressing Kit against the sideboard and hovering over him shamelessly. She muttered, 'Alexander, for fuck's sake,' under her breath and slammed about slapping eggs and bacon on a plate before thumping it down onto the table and refusing to eat any of it.

Kit eased away from Alex, who watched him go like a fox stalking a hen, and quietly finished filling his plate without looking at either twin. He meekly went to sit at the far end of the table. Alex poured his sister a cup of tea and brought a cup over for Kit too, giving him a light caress on the back of his neck and a reassuring smile as he did so.

Then he leaned against the sideboard, putting bacon onto a piece of bread with casual concentration while casting looks at Lulu from the corner of his eye.

Lulu drank her tea with moderate aggression, after which Alex evidently felt safe enough to say, 'Good morning, Lucy.'

'Is. It.'

Kit decided to have communion with his plate of food and keep very quiet and out of the way. Alex, on the other hand, sprawled next to Lulu and ate his laden slice with a jaunty *It's a hell of a good morning for me* sort of expression on his face. At least he wasn't incautious enough to say it aloud.

Lulu ate a few mouthfuls of food like she was swallowing ashes. Finally, she sighed heavily and turned towards Alex. 'Do you wish you had the twin you grew up with?'

'I do have the twin I grew up with,' Alex said. 'She's sitting right here with me, flagrantly disrespecting Cook's bacon.'

'Don't play silly buggers, Alexander, you know what I mean.'

Alex shifted, stretching long legs out, looking out over the gardens, which stretched down to a long pond with ducks on its shore. 'Remember when we were ten and I made the rash decision to put a frog down the back of your shirt?'

'Yes,' she said, sounding satisfied.

'And what did you do?'

'Beat the shit out of you,' she said, sounding even more satisfied.

'And if I were to do the adult equivalent?'

'You mean, block my plan to get vengeance with your stupid notions of justice?'

'Not entirely convinced that is the adult equivalent of putting a frog— Yeah, all right. If I were to do that?'

'I'd beat the shit out of you.'

Alex grinned. 'Lulu, my darling baby sister, you *are* the twin I grew up with.'

She said, 'Less than two minutes younger than you, Lexi.'

'Which, do correct me if I am wrong, makes you my darling baby sister.'

She smiled, fondly, helplessly, a smile that Kit would have happily bet that only Alex and Kingsford ever got to see, and her husband, once. He ducked his head further over his plate in case she remembered he was there.

It really was good bacon.

The door opened again with enough force that it almost hit the wall, but Edith made a graceful swipe and caught it before it could.

'Sorry,' she said, clutching the edge of the door. Her face was flushed. 'And sorry, Lulu, sorry, it just took me by surprise.'

Lulu flicked at her food and sent a piece of bacon tumbling across the table. Edith scuttled forwards, knelt by Lulu's side, and tried to take her hand. Lulu pulled away, staring at the wall.

'I am so sorry,' Edith said again, mournfully. 'Please. I would never, ever, want to hurt a friend's feelings like that.'

Lulu pointedly ignored her. 'Let's go, Lexi.'

Alex shooed Edith away in automatic defence of his sister, and Kit murmured 'A few *months*, I said,' and Edith had to be content with that.

Lulu wanted to move fast; it was a long day in the baronet's private carriage with another to come to reach the remote Cambrian Mountains. Wellerman had taken them to the first coaching inn with the Locke estate's fine carriage horses, leaving them there to employ postilions and post horses in a chain from inn to inn into Wales.

With Lulu seething with angry embarrassment and Edith writhing with guilt, added to the roughness of the speed of their travel—extra rough on Kit, given last night's activities and the discomfort of the increasingly poorly-kept roads—it had been a quiet day.

Alex was withdrawn but didn't seem out-of-sorts; he spent quite a bit of time looking over the heads of the women, his spectacles in place. Kit finally worked out he must be practising putting their intentions on his mental stereoscopic stand and twisting them out of focus. That was probably of great personal benefit in its own right, given their moods. Kit himself looked out the window, glimpsing rainbows.

They went on as far as they could until darkness and exhaustion forced Lulu to accept the stop. They took a quick meal at the inn, and then Alex rose to sort out the accommodation.

'Get three rooms,' Lulu ordered him, without looking up from her bowl of greasy stew.

'Two is fine,' Edith said.

'I could use some privacy,' Kit said. 'Get four.'

Lulu slammed her spoon down. 'Three, Lexi.'

Edith said, 'Two. It's perfectly normal—it's practically expected—for women to share—'

'Do not feel obliged to *demonstrate* your *understanding*.'

'I'm *not*.' Edith was turning red; she looked like she might cry but she rallied. 'The more of your money we save, the more Kit gets at the end of this debacle. So, two rooms.'

Alex rubbed his face in his hands. 'I am going to go see how many rooms are available,' he said, speaking very evenly. 'There's probably only two. There might only be one.'

There was two, or at least, Alex, wisely silent, slid only one key across the table towards the women before beckoning to Kit with his own key in hand. They visited the jakes and then Kit followed Locke into their room, a surprisingly clean, if simple, chamber. Alex shut and locked the door and then leaned on it, surveying the room.

He was no doubt counting the thresholds. Kit headed him off.

'Tie me up,' he said. 'Get yourself a decent night's sleep.' Alex looked at him in silence and Kit shrugged, looking away. 'I'll cope. Better that than having to keep a hand on me all night, I'm sure.'

'I'm not going to do either of those things,' Alex said quietly as he shrugged out of his coat. '*Not* out of pity, before you have conniptions again. It's because I trust you.'

'You trust me,' Kit parroted in blank astonishment.

Alex nodded.

Kit pulled himself together and tsked complacently. 'Those fond feelings, Alex, you know better. Logic dictates there is no downside to mistrusting me, and the possibility of catastrophe if you trust me and are wrong.'

'I'm not wrong,' Alex said. 'I've seen the heart of you, Kit Whitely, and I absolutely trust that you're not going anywhere until you hand Lulu that knife.'

Kit put his hand over his stomach, taken aback by the shocking flood of warmth suddenly swirling there. For a moment he couldn't say anything. He felt the impulse to repel Alex's faith with insincere courtesy or coquetry.

Instead, speaking very formally and keeping his gaze on the floor because that was the only way he could get the words out, he said, 'Perhaps I could request your assistance in applying the salve to my back, Mr Locke?'

He felt like he'd offered a stale crumb to Alex's three-tiered cake, but Alex was aglow, as if Kit had handed him a gilt-edged invitation to an entire feast. He helped Kit out of his coat and shirt and guided him to sit on the bed. Kit had assumed Alex would sit too, and have Kit between his thighs, but instead he knelt behind him and maintained a respectful distance even as his gentle hands smoothed the salve over Kit's scarred skin.

'It's less red now, I think.' Alex sniffed at the salve before putting it safely aside and going back to his ministrations. 'This is good stuff.'

Kit let his mind wander, let his intentions go where they would. After a while of that, Alex, hands slowing and pressing deeper, cleared his throat.

'If you're intending it,' he said, 'go ahead and act on it. You surely don't think I'd be anything other than eager?'

Kit didn't bother to dissemble. 'If I get my cock anywhere in you right now, unfulfilled desire will very rapidly be fulfilled, and I can't risk diminishing my Art till after we get the knife.'

Locke laughed. 'See? If anything proves your true intention to help us, it's that. But I didn't need the proof. Because I trust you.'

Again, the burst of warmth took Kit by surprise. His hands still resting against Kit's shoulders, Alex bent down and pressed an open-mouthed kiss to his shoulder blade and then rubbed his cheek against his skin, his soft stubble prickling him and waking up all his nerve endings.

Kit half-turned to lightly touch Alex's face. 'May I... I want to ride you, Alex.'

'Anything you want,' Alex said promptly. He bit lightly at Kit's shoulder.

'Do you always let your lovers act out their every intention upon you?' Kit queried him.

He tugged on one of Alex's hands, bringing it over his shoulder and pressing it over his own heart. Alex's fingers spread wide, and he applied pressure so that Kit's back was held firmly against his thick thighs and ridged stomach, the back of Kit's head against the centre of his broad chest.

'I am an uncomplicated man,' Alex said, as he began to move the palm of his hand over Kit's skin, rubbing over his nipples with scrupulous attention, 'who takes uncomplicated pleasure in uncomplicated ways.' He ran his thumbnail over Kit's puckered left nipple, making him shiver.

'You've taken a wrong turning with me, then.'

Alex's huff of laughter ghosted over his hair. 'Which is to say, if I may quote a complicated man of my acquaintance, are you going to complain or you going to fuck me?'

Kit wriggled about until he was kneeling on the bed too, his face uptilted to Alex so the man could have his mouth. They'd been fast and sloppy yesterday; Alex was slow and intent and in control tonight, gradually lowering himself backwards onto the bed so that Kit could straddle him. Their pricks rubbed together through their trousers and Kit whimpered.

Alex's hands spread wide along Kit's ribs. He gazed up at Kit, all fond smile and soft eyes.

'It's just fucking, Alex,' Kit said, not sure if he was warning the soft-hearted idiot under him or himself. 'Uncomplicated fucking.'

The stupid tender look on Alex's face didn't alter one whit. 'I know what it is, Kit.'

His warm hands slid over Kit's hot skin and Kit closed his eyes and hummed, moving his body against him until he felt obliged to pull away.

'I'll need to—' He indicated himself with a vaguely obscene gesture. '—in case of accidents.' He turned away as he stripped the rest of the way.

'Let me watch,' Alex said.

Again Kit thought, *But I don't even like being ordered about in bed*, even as his prick gave a definite twitch in response. He rolled to lie on his back, fully naked and achingly hard, while Alex lay on his side beside him, head propped on his elbow. He was still mostly clothed, which added another layer to the feeling of exposure. Kit fought through it as he wrapped his fist around his bared prick, comforted and made shameless by Alex's warmly appreciative gaze.

He urgently worked his fist, arching his spine, humming to himself in broken gasps, wishing for nothing more than to feel Alex's hands at his hips, Alex's mouth taking him. If he hadn't needed as much Art as he could get...

'That's it, sweetheart,' Alex murmured. 'You're lovely, so very beautiful.'

Kit closed his eyes again at that, hand moving faster. Locke went on, 'I'm looking forwards to being the one to make you spend. I want you utterly undone with pleasure. I want you writhing for more and crying my name and all your walls crashed down and you laid bare and open to me and— Shit, don't mind me, sweetheart, I talk all sorts of twaddle in bed.'

Kit's eyes had snapped open and he had gone very still. Something twisted dangerously in his chest, heavy and sharp. His voice was flat as he got out, 'And will all that be before or during my hour's head start, Mr Locke?'

Alex winced. 'Stop.' He pulled Kit close, back to chest so that they were spooned on the bed. 'I shouldn't have said that, I know it was too much, I'm a slow learner and I got carried away again.' His arm around Kit's chest flexed. When he spoke again, he was no longer placating. 'No, you know what? Fuck it. In for a penny, in for a pound. Kit—'

'Indeed, sir, pay your penny and take your pound,' Kit said, icy. 'Take your pleasure upon my body, enforcer. Order me to spread for you.'

As he spoke, he rocked his hips to rub his arse against Alex's prick, but the big man didn't respond; that kind of thing was apparently not even involuntarily to his liking in bed.

'Please stop, Kit. I'm trying to tell you it's safe to be vulnerable.'

Kit choked. He'd gone still again, the rabbit in its trap. Which part of his upbringing in an orphanage where he had been routinely bound and beaten and had compatriots repeatedly vanish overnight made Alexander Locke think it was safe for him to ever let himself be vulnerable?

Alex sensed something of his thoughts or read them in the rigid tension of his body. 'Safe, here, with me.'

The frustration was seething up in Kit. He struggled against Alex's hold. 'You are an enforcer,' he hissed. 'It's your job to hand me to the Agency. You make me feel safe and that's a bigger lie than anything you've ever assumed of me. *Let me go.*'

Alex did. Kit didn't think he was capable of literally holding him against his will right now, as much as he'd metaphorically done so for days. But he propped himself on his elbows over Kit before he could roll off the bed.

Kit was not pinned, and technically he wasn't trapped, but Alex had made it hard for him to get away. He had a stubborn look on his face like he was going to insist on hashing this out.

Unable to easily get distance physically, Kit aimed low psychologically instead. 'Men like you know precisely how to target the weakness in men like me. Like a sodding arrow.'

'Men like me,' Alex repeated.

Kit met his eye and doubled down. 'Certain types of men.'

Alex sucked in air and a very Lulu-like expression crossed his face. He pulled away, shifting onto his back to stare at the ceiling. 'You go for the jugular when you're cornered, don't you?'

He spat out an insincere, 'My apologies, Mr Locke.'

Alex, without quite verbalising his wish for Kit to sod the fuck off with his bullshit apologies, turned his back and made a good impression of going to sleep.

A few restless hours later, Kit rolled into him and murmured, 'Sorry, Alex.'

Alex's arms immediately came about him. He muttered, 'Me, too.'

He kissed Kit in the ticklish place where his neck became his shoulder and pulled him tight into his arms before falling into a heavy sleep.

16

THE NEXT DAY'S TRAVEL WAS SLOWER, autumn rain drumming relentlessly all morning and turning the rough roads to a muddy slog. Kit shortly grew bored of that and bored of the tension in the carriage and said to Edith, 'Edith, thinking of Young Tom, remind me about Old Tom, would you?'

'Old Tom died, didn't he?' she said in her cheerful lilt.

'So why isn't Young Tom just Tom now?'

'I think Just Tom would have a thing or two to say about that!'

Alex took the bait, knowingly or not. 'How many Toms do you have?'

'Well!' said Edith, delighted, and she was away, her accent thickening as she went. 'There's Young Tom and Just Tom and Black Tom since his surname is Black, and Red Tom Knight, we don't know why since Black Tom is the ginger one, and No-Nickname Tom, and Thomas, who obviously went about things more sensibly than No-Nickname Tom'—she got a breath in without breaking stride—'and then there's Big Tom and Little Tom, who is bigger than Big Tom now so they didn't think that one through, did they, and of course, Little Tommy but hopefully his parents learnt the lesson there, and there's Smithy Tom and Horse-Thief Tom, it was just the one time, and Clever Tom and Weaver Tom, and Tommy Boy, and our Davie.'

'Davie?' asked Lulu, sounding like she couldn't help herself.

Edith beamed at her. 'Thomas David, but of course almost all our Toms have that middle name, because of Thomas David Knight, our mutual ancestor, so that trick only works the once. Our Will was almost Thomas William but Ma had a word with his ma because he wouldn't want to go through life being Tom Will, because the question is always Tom Will What?'

'Now it's Will Tom,' Kit pointed out. 'And will he?'

'He might, if you were asking,' Edith murmured from behind her hand, eyes sparkling.

'What!' Kit said, sitting up straight. 'Six months you had to mention that, Edie!'

'Hmmm, we all had things we might have mentioned, Kitty.'

'Will Knight,' Alex said thoughtfully. 'Popular man.'

Alex had been disconcertingly thoughtful all morning. Kit didn't like it.

He'd woken literally entwined with the man. When he'd tried to disentangle himself, knowing he'd had the knives out the night before, Alex had murmured a protest in his sleep and nuzzled into him, and he hadn't had the strength to squirm away.

He'd started to trace his fingers over Alex's skin where his shirt had rucked up, taking sweet time to explore, finding scars, finding the sensitive spots that made Alex's breath hitch in his sleep and the ones that made him sigh and nestle closer.

Then he'd realised that although sleepy Alex was a habitual and accomplished cuddler, awake Alex wouldn't be all that impressed with Kit after last night. Accordingly, Kit had kept his bloody hands to himself until Lulu thumped on the door and ordered them on their way. They'd barely had time to exchange polite good mornings after that.

And now Alex was being quiet and contemplative and Kit *hated* it.

He sagged back into his slouch against the carriage seat so the jolting wouldn't go straight through his spine. 'And what about Welsh Tom?' he asked, keeping a smile off his face only by dint of years of practice.

'A'en any Welsh Tom,' said Edith sternly, since Welsh Tom led the subset of fishermen who did less fishing and more quietly travelling between an isolated Welsh cove and Lovelly as a longstanding leg of the undertaxed goods run from Ireland through to England. He was lucky he wasn't outand-out called Smuggler Tom. 'Only Fisher Tom.'

'I'm sure I heard mention of Welsh Tom about the village.'

'Ooh, you can shut up about Welsh Tom an'all, Kit Whitely,' Edith said, arms folded.

After that, things were eased enough that Alex let Kit finish reading the Dickens to him and Lulu let them pause at the next coaching inn for coffee and pastries. She exchanged a few stilted words with Edith, which, slowly but surely under Edith's ministrations, turned into a spirited discussion of the merits of fabrics and patterns for disguising broad shoulders and accentuating the slightest suggestion of a waist into actual curves.

'Though,' Edith said thoughtfully, 'there is something to be said for appearing exactly as you are.'

Lulu stiffened. 'I'm trying to appear exactly as I am.'

'No, I mean—you're a big, fierce woman and you look like a big, fierce woman. I'm big and fierce in my head and I get treated as small and uninteresting all the time and it is rather wearying.'

After a moment of considering this, Lulu said, 'You're hardly uninteresting.'

She took Edith's hand for a companionable squeeze and the smaller woman looked glowingly happy. Kit looked out the window and mouthed, 'Brave girl,' to himself.

Near the middle of the afternoon, their carriage brought them to Gallentry, a town nestled into the ridged arms of a narrow green valley. They sat at the tavern on the main square and watched the deconsecrated and heavily fortified building that had once been the town's church but was now the traditional headquarters of the United Benevolent Orphanage System for the Welfare of the Innocent in the Hallowed Name of the Holy Mysteries. The grimly imposing stone church, Old Aneirin, was built into the very ridge that sheltered the town. It had once held the very first orphanage to bear the hallowed name, a hundred or more years ago.

Arched double doors, barred and guarded, loomed at the top of wide granite stairs. Though many people came and went, no one was granted entry without first showing papers to the pair of sentries at the top of the stairs, their identification or invitation or other credentials.

'I can just about open those doors from here,' Kit said to Lulu. 'I don't think that's what's needed, is it?'

'True,' Lulu said. 'I have a contact inside. There's guards everywhere. We're not going through the front doors unless we have a fighting force to take out every guard between the front hall where the altar used to be and the vaults set into the ridge behind.'

'No offence, Lexi,' Alex said. He was eyeing off the guards out front, eyes gleaming with anticipation.

The man really did like to wade into a fight. Well. Hadn't Kit learnt that one firsthand?

'No offence, Lexi,' Lulu agreed.

'None taken, Lulu.'

'I love you, brother, but you and I do not add up to a fighting force by ourselves. We'd have to hire on the Myriad if we wanted to make a frontal.'

They both wrinkled their noses in evident disgust at this idea, as unlikely as it was.

Carriages drew up in the square, but no passengers got out. Instead, after a pause, the front doors opened wide, and a procession of Citadel hierarchy and servants made its stately way down the stairs, led by a boy in his early adolescence, swinging a gleaming thurible.

Kit could not look away from that boy.

'Ah, see,' Lulu said. 'Most of the upper echelon is headed to London for the ceremonies on All Saints' Day. That'll empty the place out some.'

'All Orphans' Day, too,' Kit murmured without looking around. It was the birthday given to any orphan whose birth date was undetermined, which was most of them.

He watched the boy, so young, so proud to lead the procession. His glossy curls and the starched ruffles at his collar and cuffs gleamed in the sunshine. It was unlikely this boy was an orphan. Though the old church was the headquarters of the Orphanage complex, no actual orphanage sullied the site anymore, according to Lulu's obliging, though perhaps not willing, source. The boy was probably the son of a local dignitary, chosen for this special duty to flatter a powerful town luminary.

He was probably safe.

The procession reached the carriages, breaking apart into milling as the personages sorted themselves into a precedence of travel. A beringed hand came down on the boy's shoulder, patting him twice in a congratulatory manner before resting casually there. Kit followed the hand up the arm of the white robe to the thin and hunched shoulders.

His skin was prickling all over. But it couldn't be. He forced himself to look at the face.

The mild, unassuming face of Brother Jerome Fairweather.

Fairweather was smiling gently down at the boy. He wore the vestments of a deacon now—he had been ambitious, when Kit had known him—but looked as kindly and meek as ever even as he moved up the hierarchy.

The twins were wolf-focus on their prey. 'Let's do it, Lulu,' Alex was saying, his smile turning feral already. 'Wind me up and point me where you want me.'

'What's the matter, Kitty?' Edith asked, her voice low and quiet under Alex's.

Kit stood up. Heat was shooting along his arms and legs from his stomach. In his head, Christopher tried to break loose. A different emotion was roiling behind the fear; he didn't know what that was, and it did not seem to him that Christopher was in control of it.

Alex had stood too. He reached for Kit's arm. Kit flinched and Alex jerked his hand back as if he'd grazed flames. He turned to follow the direction of Kit's fixed gaze.

'No,' Kit said.

He wasn't sure if he was rejecting Fairweather or turning down Edith's concern or refusing Lulu's commission or preventing Alex from seeing his shame or forcing Christopher back into the dark.

All of those, perhaps, as he took two steps backwards, touched the solid frame of the doorway into the tavern and crossed its threshold as far away as he could get, which, with Christopher's fear raging unchecked through him, was very far indeed.

And then he just kept going.

By the time he came to rest in an alley on the far side of town, he was breathing too hard to get air, too hard to pull what was left of his Art into another Artwork to get through another crossing. The sound of his harsh, panicked breathing filled the alley, blocking out the distant sounds of the folk of the town, going about their daily lives like there was any point to it at all.

'Christopher.' His voice was a rasp, barely distinguishable from his gasps for air. 'Five seconds, Christopher. Five. Four. Three. Two. One. Stop.'

He sucked one last breath in. As he let it out slowly, he slumped against the warm wall of the bakery on the southern side of the alley. His legs gave way; he slid all the way to the ground and hunched over to put his head on his knees.

And then began the long argument between the Kit who had to, absolutely had to, keep running and the Kit who'd made the naïve promise to Lulu. The Kit who owed more to Edith Knight than he could ever express. The Kit who thought maybe he and Alexander Locke could mean something to each other, if Kit could do this one little thing for Alex's beloved and hurting sister.

He was still sitting there, head down on his folded-up knees, when he heard soft footsteps at the head of the alley. They paused for a long time. He was too exhausted and heartsick to look up. In the first reckless, heedless years after walking out of the Orphanage on the strength of his fledgling Art, he'd have been content enough to get caught out in an alley, knifed for what would have no doubt been a disappointing take. Some part of him hoped for the same now.

The footsteps went away and came back a little while later. A familiar body settled beside him, shoulder close to his, but not touching. A large hand offered him a paper package, the smell enticing him to raise his head.

He would have said he was too sick to eat but that smell told him otherwise.

He silently took the pasty from Alex and pushed back the paper to bite into it. It was glorious, warm meat and spice and chunks of carrot and potato, wrapped in buttery pastry. He had to eat the whole thing before he could speak.

'I was trying to come back.' When Alex didn't say anything, Kit elaborated. 'I didn't mean to escape. I was trying to make myself come back.'

Alex slowly shifted until the warmth of his body touched against Kit. 'Was that— I saw him. Was he your certain type of man?'

Kit stared at the wall opposite. 'My very first.'

'Don't do that, Kit,' Alex said softly. 'Don't push me away. Let me touch you?'

Kit hesitated and then turned onto his side, curling into Alex. Alex's arms came around him; his face came down to rest against Kit's hair.

Kit murmured, 'Alex,' and felt Alex's strong arms tighten. Kit ran his fingers up and down Alex's forearms, feeling the tension of the muscles and tendons even under his coat. 'Alex.'

He bit his tongue before he could say more and make himself even more vulnerable than he was now.

'Lulu and I have quite the ongoing argument about vengeance verses justice,' Alex said. 'Lulu won the argument today. I would have slit that man's throat if I'd been closer.'

Kit tried to draw himself back together. 'It wasn't like that,' he said. 'It wasn't. I seduced him, Alex.' That was what Fairweather had told him; he'd been floating in poppy dreams, mostly unaware.

He heard Alex suck in air and he hunched his shoulders, but Alex held tight and all he said was a careful, 'Oh, yes?'

'Those beatings really hurt,' Kit said dispassionately. 'And he would take such *care* of me after. He would make the pain fade away. He would make me feel good. So I made him feel good.'

Alex said, 'I don't know how else to say this other than to just say it. You were young and in pain and he took advantage and some part of you knows that or you wouldn't have conniptions about being vulnerable in front of other men.'

'He told me he couldn't resist me,' Kit said. 'You couldn't resist me either.'

Rubbing at his eyes, Alex swore, long and low. 'What a damnable fool I am,' he said. 'That was an excuse to be a hypocrite, Kit. Of course I can bloody resist you. I just didn't want to.'

'I made you. I seduced you.'

'Listen to me, sweetheart. There's no such thing as not being able to resist someone. There's just pretending you're not making your own choices. He made his own choices and he put them on a scared boy. God *damn* him, I would hunt that fucker down and slit his fucking throat in a heartbeat if he hadn't already got away.'

All at once Kit was gasping, falling apart. 'He's gone? He left town? He went to London with the rest? He's gone?' He bit his lip hard to make himself stop saying it, and then burst out, 'Did the boy stay behind?'

Alex stroked his back, slow and warm. 'He's gone. All the carriages went south. And the boy went home with his mother.'

Kit let out a noise that was probably a sob, torn dry from his throat. He put both hands over his mouth. *Back into the dark, Christopher*, he thought. *Go away now. Take your fear with you, I don't want it*. Calmness—numbness—dropped over him like a cloak, coldly familiar.

'Kit, sweetheart, I'm sorry. I'm so sorry we made you come here.'

'You didn't know he was here. I didn't know he was here. He was in Essex. And now he's gone.' Kit pushed against Alex's arms and the big man let him go. Kit got to his feet and looked around, taking in the alley for the first time. It was dirty and smelly and nondescript. 'How did you find me? Lulu?'

'Luck,' Alex said. 'Also, have you noticed you're being followed by rainbows?'

Kit looked up and saw that the sky was dusky with oncoming night but that there was indeed an impossible rainbow over the alley. God, he really needed to do something about that weirdness.

'Well, then. Thank you for not assuming I'd stabbed you in the back again,' he said. 'Let's go steal a knife so Lulu can stab someone else in the back.'

'She'd never stab someone in the *back*.' Alex looked over his shoulder, a reflexive move Kit wasn't sure he knew he was making. 'Kit, I'm not going to make you do this.'

Arms folded, Kit demanded, 'What is the first rule, Mr Locke?'

Alex paused. 'I don't do well on tests. But—' And here he smiled his devil-may-care smile. '—I think it must be—keep those claws sheathed, kitten—pretend Kit has no human frailties whatsoever.'

Kit shoved him, half-playfully, but only half. '*No pity*. I'm not fragile. Don't treat me like I am. And don't let down your sister for the sake of my pretty eyes.'

Without waiting for an argument, he led the way out of the alley. He ached all over, but when he reached for his Art, he felt it there, expectant. The rest and the food and Alex's gentle arms had replenished him.

Alex seemed to want to keep talking, but Kit shook his head and walked briskly back towards the square. He was ready to go.

17

'There,' said Lulu with satisfaction. 'See up there, in the side of the mountain? That's the secret entrance. I need you to unlock that door, Kit.'

They had met up with the women back at the square, Edith miserably tracing circles on the table and Lulu looking utterly despondent until she had seen Kit coming back in with Alex. Her smile had lit up the square in the gloomy dusk.

As soon as it was dark enough that Kit's pet rainbow was no longer so visible, she took Alex and Kit straight up to the location her contact had given her. Edith had been delegated to wait in the town, to her vocal disgust. Her eventual capitulation was signalled by her handing over to Kit a full flask of brandy from her ever-helpful and apparently bottomless carpetbag.

They were in a patch of scrubby trees with a view up to the rocky crag backing the church and securing its vaults within its heart. This, then, was the so-called mountain—a weathered limestone ridge, speckled with pale grey moss and layered with bright green grass.

Kit stood very still, following Lulu's pointing finger.

There was a shadowy gap in the rock, more a slumping collapse than a cave opening. It wasn't manmade, so it was no good to him as a threshold. But within its dim recess, with Lulu's prompting, he could just about make out a suggestion of wood, of metal, a hatch-like door, blocking further progress into the mountain. Any door belonged to him.

Except one little problem.

'I can open it for you,' he agreed. 'Except, Lulu. How do I get up there?'

'What do you mean? You can open it from here, can't you?'

'I need to be closer than this. And—' He looked between the two, frowning. 'Do you truly not understand? I have to go in with you.'

'No,' said Alex.

'Don't be bloody stupid, kitten,' Lulu said.

Kit sighed theatrically. 'That door,' he said, jerking his thumb in its general direction, 'could be reached and opened by any thief with rope and lockpicks. Practically any weapons Artisan could blow it open or set fire to it or melt it. If there's a door between you and the knife that can only be opened by someone like me, and there must be or I wouldn't be under threat of assassination, it is *not that door.* I'm going in.'

The twins eyed each other and moved away for a quiet consultation while Kit rolled his eyes and cocked a hip to fold the ankle of one leg over the shin of the other in a parody of patient waiting. He straightened in expectation as they returned.

'We'll all go in,' Alex confirmed. 'But stay close to us, take no risks and keep well out of the way as soon as you've opened the right door.'

Kit patted him comfortably. 'I'll keep so far out of the way it'll be my head start, Mr Locke.'

'If that's how you want it.' Alex wore that thoughtful look again.

'Well, then.' Kit was abruptly disquieted. He turned, frowning, to Lulu. 'Are you planning to strap me to your back and climb up to it?'

'There's a goat trail, kitten,' Lulu said irritably. But when she turned to point it out, she stopped and her hand fell to her side. 'Oh.'

At first Kit couldn't see what had caused her dismay. Then he noticed the patch of lighter colour in the ridge wall, pale grey in the dim moonlight amid the weathered darkness of the rest of the ridge. It was freshly exposed rockface, with tumbled rocks fallen below to block the route she had intended to take them.

'Do you think that was an accident, Lucy?' Alex asked quietly.

'A bloody convenient one, if so,' she said. 'I suppose they took extra precautions once the bounty on the knife went out.'

Alex adjusted the cuffs of his coat, slowly and precisely making them symmetrical mirror-images of each other. 'I might go sort out that pair of sentries we saw patrolling earlier south a ways,' he said slowly.

'If there's two of them, shouldn't Lulu help?'

Kit was treated to quite the twin-look for this innocent question before Alex smiled like a predator and said, 'Not necessary.'

Lulu shook her head. 'Premature, brother. It'll give us away when they don't report back.'

Alex murmured his acquiescence to this wisdom and returned to fidgeting with his cuffs. Lulu met Kit's eyes; they'd both been watching Alex gathering up his worry, usually so well concealed, eaten by the wolf in him.

'We'll buy some rope tomorrow,' Alex said finally. 'Between the two of us, we can get Kit up there, even if we do have to strap him to our backs.'

Lulu shook her head. Kit could almost feel the tension radiating off her. All her plans, all her dreams of vengeance, had narrowed to an obsession with getting the knife that would lead her to Varley. She was as fixated on it as ever the bishop must have been when he had made her husband help him find it.

It had all come to this moment, and the thought of waiting even one more night was tearing her up.

She turned to him. 'Can't you take us up there, Mr Whitely?' she asked, very deliberately.

Us. That deceptive *us.* She had watched when he had tried and failed to bring Edith across a threshold. She knew there was no *us.* Alex looked at her, frowning. Her intentions must have been telegraphing something to him, but whatever it was, it was not her deception.

'I need a threshold down here to cross to get up there,' Kit told her.

She turned away in frustration, kicking the trunk of a tree hard. It shivered all the way along its height and gifted them a shower of leaves and the startled chirps of a few escaping birds. She put her hand over her eyes briefly and in that quickly contained gesture, Kit saw her grief and pain laid bare. He saw it echoed in Alex's face as he took her in his arms.

Kit paced about the scrubby trees until he'd found two branches straight enough and long enough for his purposes. He cracked them off with sharp jerks.

'Whittle the bark off this,' he ordered Alex as he handed him a branch.

Alex smiled like he always did when Kit got peremptory with him. He took out one of the pretty knives from the metalworker assassins and began to scrape at the bark, slow and methodical.

Oh. He thought it was a task to calm him down.

Kit gave the other one to Lulu, who attacked it with a knife of her own, paring it quickly and roughly, just enough to put a human touch on it, turning it from a branch to a manmade stake.

He took both stakes back, Alex frowning at having only half-finished the job. Kit had to give an extra tug to get the stake back from him.

'You must never tell anyone I can do this,' he told them.

He drove the two rough stakes into the ground, wider than hip width apart. The width of a doorway apart.

'What are you doing?' Alex asked. 'Kit. Your intentions aren't clear.'

Kit smiled and wrapped his hands around the top of each stake. He gathered his Art, looking at Alex as he did so, thinking about his mouth, his weight, his hands caressing over his skin, his prick thick and hot inside him.

Alex shook his head, failing to fight off his answering smile. 'Yeah, all right, *now* they are, but that's never a good sign with you.'

Kit tightened his grip on the stakes and released the desire-fuelled Art. He was lost into the Artwork, his body swaying loose between the two stakes, his gaze fixed on Alex. 'It's a gate,' he murmured. 'It's a gate.' His voice slowed, thickened. The wood was rough under the skin of his palms. He could smell the sap. 'You're a gateway. A gateway.'

He paused. He wasn't trying to reach a gate. He was trying to reach a door, a hatch. He needed the two ends of his crossing to be the same. Or similar. They just had to be similar. The wood of the stake-branches to the wood of the hatch. That was enough. He could open anything.

He took hold of Alex's coat lapels and pulled him through the two stakes. 'It's a gateway,' he told him dreamily, fingers locked into his coat, face upraised to him, eyes on his mouth. 'A wooden gateway.'

'Yeah, all right,' said Alex again, in his most patient tones.

He let Kit turn him around and pull him back through the two stakes, and then again. Lulu followed them through this time. Through the gate they went, over and over, Kit murmuring his Artwork under his breath until it became a soft hum. At last he stopped. He let go of Alex's coat and touched the two stakes again.

'Kit,' Alex said. 'Hold on.'

The Viking reached for Kit, tried to catch him about the waist, tried to wrap his arms about him so they could cross the threshold together. Kit sidestepped him without really noticing himself do it.

'Hold him,' he said to the air, and saw Lulu lock her muscular arms around her brother.

Then he let Alex have a true intention, of where Kit intended to be. *Front entrance. One hour.*

'No!' Alex howled, and made a concerted effort to fight off Lulu. 'Let me go right now, Lucinda!'

'Don't wait if I'm not there,' Kit told her. He put his hands back on the stakes. 'Gateway,' he said firmly.

The threshold flared to life between the stakes and Kit fell into it.

He stumbled out of it, landing on his knees before the door of the secret cave entrance. He'd struck stone hard enough that the right knee of his trousers and the skin underneath had torn.

He was exhausted already, but, oh God, that had felt good.

Taking the flask Edith had given him from his pocket, he took hurried sips of brandy before turning his attention to the door. As he'd guessed, it was more a hatch, low and square, solid wood crisscrossed with metal, blocking an entrance to what looked like it'd be a tunnel he'd have to crawl along. He suspected, seeing it up close, that it was not meant to be a secret entrance at all, but a secret escape route for the highest echelon of the Orphanage.

It was the work of an alcohol-driven moment to unlock the door. Only then did he look back to the copse of trees where Alex and Lulu were hidden. He could see them down there on the very edge of the trees, but Lulu was dragging Alex back out of sight. Alex would not be happy about this.

When he tried to push the unlocked door open, he found it was barred on the inside. No matter. He crossed the threshold from the outside of the doorway to the inside of the doorway, ducking as he came through so he didn't brain himself on the low ceiling beyond. Crossing the threshold took more Art than just having to unlock the door did, but another sip of brandy rectified that.

He stayed motionless on the other side, waiting for his eyes to adjust to the dark. He hoped no torches meant no guards, but he wouldn't assume. They'd destroyed the path that gave access to the door, they'd locked it and barred it, and, despite Lulu's talkative contact, it was a close secret. Surely they would think they didn't need guards. He listened, but all he could hear was the sound of his own breathing, his own heartbeat.

Eventually the pitch black resolved into a murky grey. That was from a tiny bit of light making it through the seams of the hatch behind him. Kit shuffled about to consider it. It was barred by two shafts of wood. He started to take them off, to open the door and let more light in, and to make his escape easier if things didn't go to plan.

Then he paused. He really didn't want Alex blundering in after him, and he imagined the Viking was outraged enough to scale his way up to the hatch with his teeth, beat it open with his fists, and tear his way through the tight squeeze of the tunnel with his fingernails.

Really, if things didn't go to plan, he wasn't coming out any door.

He re-locked the door and left the bars on; if Lulu couldn't keep Alex sensible, that would slow him down. He started to crawl along the tunnel, pausing every few minutes to listen. After a while, it made no difference if he had his eyes open or closed, and it took all his discipline to keep crawling. His palms and knees stung. The air tasted of stone. He wanted to cough. He wanted to push the walls away. He kept crawling.

And then, at last, there was a grey patch ahead in the blackness, and he found the end of the tunnel. It was another small door, bigger than the hatch, light filtering through around its edges. Kit leaned his forehead against it and just breathed until his breathing calmed. Then he listened, ear pressed against the wood.

He heard silence for long enough that he had his hand on the door—it was neither locked nor barred, it just needed to be opened—when distant sounds stilled him. From the muffled nature of both light and sound, he suspected the door was behind a tapestry or screen, in a room or corridor that was isolated but not, obviously, completely unused. He wished he'd given himself longer than an hour before Alex would abandon him.

He waited for as long as he could stand after the muted noises stopped before easing the door open and slipping out. Heavy black curtains, thick with dust on this side, blocked any view of his new surrounds. Kit edged along behind them until he could peek out around one end.

It was a bedroom, presumably belonging one of the highest-ranking officials of the Orphanage, with its access to a secret escape tunnel. However, his fast glance about showed it empty, though the air was warm and a dying fire in the grate bespoke recent occupancy. The room perhaps belonged to someone who had gone to London. Perhaps the noise he had heard had carried from some unknown turn in the tunnel he had crawled along; he shivered as he thought about accidentally crawling into a side tunnel in the dark and never finding his way out. Perhaps it had been a mouse, his nerves magnifying the sound. Perhaps it had been a loud sound coming from further away than he had thought.

He went to the door, resting a hand on the doorframe in relief. He could now cross further in, to any threshold he had line of sight on, or back to any door or window or the entrance to the tunnel behind the black curtain as long he held them in his mind's eye firmly enough.

Looking back, he saw the curtain on this side was an elaborately painted cloth showing a scene from the life of a saint. Kit felt his mouth downturn as he looked from the bed to the wall hanging.

Then he passed into the next room, a parlour. From there to the door out of the suite. From there to the hallway, lit by flickering torches, an odd anachronism in the modern age of gaslights; no windows in the middle of the mountain. Kit paused here, alert and still like a wild animal watching for danger, but there were no sentries, no sounds of movement. The air had the feel of midnight about it. He had to move out of the residential area, find the treasure rooms.

He saw a sprawled mess up ahead and approached cautiously. Here was a sentry at last, sprawled unconscious, at a junction of dank corridors. Kit frowned. He followed a trail of downed sentries further, he hoped, into the mountain, towards the vaults. His sense of direction was not all that it could be, but he thought he was going in the right direction because the number of unconscious sentries was increasing as he went and the hallways were getting narrower and darker, old mining tunnels chipped from solid rock.

Once, a wide and dimly lit hallway went off at right angles. Kit paused here to listen and sniff the air, but eventually chose to go straight on. He could feel a change of light and air that way. He slowed and hugged the wall, sliding around the corner into a cavern of sorts.

The start of the famous vaults of the Orphanage's treasure mountain, and the great double doors, iron bound by silver, were ajar. The locks and latches were scarred and pitted. Someone had worked hard to get them open.

Well. There had been an open bounty on the knife, hadn't there? Lulu hadn't called the commission, an enemy of Varley's had done that; she'd just taken advantage of it.

Moving faster now—his way forwards had been cleared by another thief, after all—Kit crossed the chamber, stepped over yet another pair of slumped sentries, and entered the vaults.

From there, he just had to follow the noise. The thief—the thieves—weren't bothering with quiet now, if they ever had. Kit passed rooms piled with gold and gems like a dragon hoard, rooms of shelves of artefacts that he guessed would be physical Artworks, rooms of paper and books, the first editions of the damned.

The prize was deep in the vaults, at the end of a long room lined with mirrors with torches set in between. The mirrors on each wall were offset from each other, so that each one reflected the torch opposite. It gave the hall an eerie cast, the feeling of walking through cold flames.

At the far end of the room, five people bickered in front of a shallow alcove that was blocked by a door made of iron bars, a sort of vertical grill. It was a bigger group of thieves than he'd ever seen tackle a job, but then, there had been an awful lot of sentries in their way.

'For Christ's sake, shut up, Genevieve,' one of them shouted suddenly.

Kit paused at this rather startling rudeness, then kept walking. He was about halfway along the hall before one of them finally glanced about and saw him. She was a small, brown-skinned woman, very curvy, dark hair piled on her head in an untidy bun, maybe in her late twenties. She didn't look alarmed to see him, but she did nudge the white man next to her, who wore thick black leather gloves like hers. He was very upright, with a supercilious expression, his dark hair oiled down under a very proper top hat. Artisans were the one segment of society generally excused from hatwear, so that hat said something about its wearer.

'Stop there, you,' he said when he saw Kit, and the other three turned too.

Kit did come to a stop, and stood demurely, hands linked in front of him, letting them examine him. His fingers twitched; he put his hands behind his back instead.

They were all older than him, the small woman the youngest-looking. There was a red-haired, broad-shouldered man, handsome, and a tall platinum blonde with ice-blue eyes and a dress to match. Those two had been doing most of the bickering. The man had been the one who had shouted.

The third was a giant of a man, even bigger than the Locke twins, scarred and tattooed and bald, his roughly-woven shirt tight over his shoulders. He would have been quite frightening, if Kit hadn't recognised the same slow kindness in his eyes as in Alex's.

Kit admired the tattoos he could see. He could make out abstract floral motifs in lurid colours. They matched the worst of Alex's waistcoats.

'So.' The redhead stepped forwards, palms sliding over each other. 'You'd be the door boy, right?'

Kit offered a slight flick of his eyes to the ceiling in return.

'You know what?' the man said. 'I think we'll get that assassination bounty while we're here.'

And he took a spear of ice from the air and threw it at Kit. Someone cried out, a shocked protest.

The spear's trajectory jigged and stayed on track for his heart when he danced sideways, so he stepped into the closest mirror and out the next one along on the opposite wall. The shaft of ice shattered all over the floor where he had been. He stood quietly until one of them spotted him again.

'My goodness,' he said, bouncing on his toes. 'A group of five, with an ice-wielder as their leader. Could I possibly have the privilege of meeting the Myriad, premiere Artisan bounty hunters of London?'

'That's us,' said the small woman, a hand to her hip and a flash of pride on her face. 'Crime fighters, though, not bounty hunters. Normally, anyway.'

She had a sweet smile. Kit smiled back at her.

Kit had drunk the entire flask of brandy on his way through the vault.

The redhead was rubbing his palms together again. 'Reuben, don't kill him,' said the blond woman, taking his elbow. 'If he's the door Artisan, we can use him to open this door.'

The redhead, Reuben—Reuben McAvey, captain of the Myriad—tugged sharply on his coat, pulling out of her grasp. His coat, unusually, was red; it clashed horribly with his hair.

'Fine,' he said resentfully. Kit didn't need Alex's talent to warn him he still intended to claim the assassination bounty. 'Go get him, Oliver.'

The giant gave a grunt and moved slowly down the hall, one hand lightly fisted. Kit thought Oliver didn't much like obeying Reuben, but he was obeying anyway.

He swayed lightly. 'Yes, come get me, Oliver. Remind me, what's your Art? I know the one dressed like fire is ice and the one dressed like ice is fire. So confusing! And is ice a weather Art or a projectile weapons Art? So hard to classify the hybrids, don't you agree? The other two, I'm fairly sure have to be touching me to work an Artwork on me. You, though. What do you do? Or are you just the muscle? I shouldn't say "just", should I? Nothing wrong with the somatic Arts when you end up super-strong or super-fast.'

'Motley,' the giant rumbled.

'Oh, that's a rude word, Mr Oliver,' Kit said. He was watching Oliver's feet. 'Like calling a dog a mongrel. I've always preferred "medley" for an Artisan without one true Art. The French say "melange", of course, which has a nice ring to it.'

Oliver was close enough to grab for him now; Kit danced backwards, laughing. 'Still, you must have one Art that stands a little stronger than the rest. What is it?'

The giant merely smiled at him, a smile both ugly and weirdly charming. Then, faster than Kit had expected, if not in the realm of a somatic Art, he ran at him. He was not at all light on his feet like Alex but he reached a decent speed for all his lumbering.

Kit dived into the closest mirror, out of another, and kept going, bouncing his way up the hall on the back of his alcohol-fuelled Art. He saw glimpses of the others, running hither and fro to try to catch him; another few bursts of wasted ice sprayed across the floor. Reuben was swearing with furious intensity. The dark-haired man was red-faced and sweaty, his own fault for insisting on keeping his head covered when Artisans ran hot.

Kit dodged between the members of the Myriad, back and forth through the mirrors, colder and colder each time, which would have been worrying if he hadn't been enjoying himself so much. He couldn't do it for much longer, but he would get to the door they had all abandoned and be through it into the alcove before they could find their balance and work together to stop him.

Then he was tossed out of a mirror passage with a too-fast burst of pain so severe that he thrashed where he had landed, gasping on his back like a dying tortoise and shaking with cold. A shivering sound was still lingering in the air. When he regained control and raised his head, he saw a shattered mirror, its shards littered all over the floor at Oliver's feet.

Kit had been too predictable, for fear of confusing his shaky sense of direction. Oliver had predicted his pattern and smashed the mirror he had been about to come out of, precipitating his rejection back out the one he had gone in to. He had a moment of pure gratitude that he hadn't been trapped inside instead, as impossible as that was. It felt possible, within the mirrors.

The other four were merely gaping in surprise. 'Oh, your Art is *thinking*,' he said, as Oliver strolled over and picked him up off the floor. 'Seven years' bad luck, though, friend.'

'Worth it,' Oliver growled.

'Am I being annoying?' Kit asked. 'Drunk Kit is quite annoying. So's sober Kit, to be fair.'

Oliver gently set him on his feet by the grilled door the Myriad had been trying to break through. Kit could see evidence of scorching on the bars, to no effect in melting them. No doubt Reuben had tried his ice Art on it too, but that had left no mark. He saw no sign of the quiet two's Arts— they had people-focussed Arts, he thought, and they had to be touching, bare skin to bare skin—or any clue to any of Oliver's Arts, many of which would be weaker talents or even weaker inclinations.

Reuben shoved him roughly. 'Open it.'

Kit took another long look at the door. It was of iron, which limited many Arts. It had no lock to pick, no hinges to unscrew, no latch to jiggle open, so it was impervious to traditional thievery. It wasn't really a door at all, by any definition, but solid iron bars that looked melted into the rock at top and bottom and which would be hard to dislodge or cut or melt, as the Myriad had discovered. Heavy horizontal bars, bolted into the rock on either side, reinforced the grill. He was surprised it wasn't a solid slab of metal.

Beyond in the dim alcove, he could see a pedestal. He guessed the knife had been placed on there and then sealed in, or that Varley had a pet Artisan, of the teleport or ghost Art variety, who could get the knife in and out when necessary. He could see why Varley had feared thieves catching Kit and bringing him to bear against the long trail of sentries and then this door, which was, after all, a threshold.

Finally, he looked back at Reuben. 'Can't,' he lied. 'It's iron.'

The ice Artisan made a glittering dagger appear between his hands. It was already melting, but its edge looked plenty sharp enough to slice a wide smile in Kit's throat. Kit heard someone whisper, 'Reuben,' with a good measure of unfeigned shock. Their leader wasn't usually so unsubtle, then, he guessed.

'I'll try,' said Kit, theatrically quailing back against Oliver's broadness. 'But I'm not so good at opening things without a lock. I'll need stronger Art. Can someone give me a drink, please?'

'I rather thought you were already drunk,' said the thin, supercilious man. He was still looking sweaty and flustered from chasing Kit around the hall.

'Hush, Fletcher, leave the boy be.' The small woman reached into the reticule hanging from her wrist and handed Kit a small, ladylike flask, copper with a filigree of bronze.

'Pretty,' he said, holding it up in the flickering torchlight. 'For when you just can't get through another society tea?'

'As if I get invited to society teas,' said the woman lightly.

'I'd invite you to tea,' Kit said, smiling at her but also drunkenly annoyed on her behalf. 'Though I do overall prefer sticky buns.'

He absently patted at big, silent Oliver behind him, getting him somewhere in the region of his ribs, as he took a long sip from the flask. Gin, bitter and burning. The woman giggled, a merry sound in the firelit hall. The other woman, stern and fierce, cracked a smile, warming her icy demeanour. She was looking up and over Kit's shoulder, at Oliver.

'I'm partial to a sticky bun myself,' the small woman said, still laughing.

'Cecelia!' Fletcher said disapprovingly and her laugh cut off.

'My apologies, Miss Cecelia. I didn't mean to get you in trouble,' Kit said.

'What a polite boy,' Cecelia said. 'Would you be so kind as to open the door for me, Mr…Kit, was it?'

'There's no need to bother with any of this,' the mean-mouthed Fletcher said. He tore off a glove and grabbed Kit's wrist, pressing his fingers in hard enough to bruise. 'Open the door.'

Kit turned like an automaton to obey.

'Oh, Fletch,' Cecelia said with gentle censure. 'He was about to do it anyway.'

Ah. Compulsion Art.

Even as he had the thought, his own Art, or some part of it he didn't have control over and hadn't really had cause to notice before, was frothing up and around Fletcher's invasion, tasting it, learning it, fighting it off. He would not be taken by compulsion Art again, at least not Fletcher's compulsion Art.

'He was wasting our time and being impertinent towards you,' Reuben was saying glacially, and Cecelia bowed her head, chastened.

'Sorry, Miss Cece...' Kit muttered, trailing off in the middle of her name as he took another sip from her flask, twisting up his Art as far as he could.

He had been planning to open the door and then block the threshold in time to break Reuben's nose when he tried to follow, but it wasn't going to be possible to literally open the sealed grid. Instead, he put his hand on the rock surrounding it, took a little hop forwards, and crossed the threshold into the alcove, passing through the iron with no more than the slightest of jitters.

He had worked bloody hard to teach his Art how to beat iron, and was fully self-satisfied as he turned to enjoy the show, taking celebratory sips of the gin.

'What is this?' Reuben demanded. He started to reach through the bars, and Kit blocked the threshold just because he could. Reuben shoved at the invisible barrier between the iron bars, scowling.

Kit watched him silently. He turned again and looked at the knife, which was on the pedestal behind him. He'd half-expected gold and jewels, but it was small and relatively plain antique-looking dagger, its hilt and blade all of copper. He considered it for a moment, before stepping to the side to see the effect of the torchlight reflected in the mirrors on its shining surface. The entire hall had been laid out to glorify the knife.

'What the fuck is this?' Reuben shouted.

'Language,' Kit murmured, which provoked the ice Artisan into a foot-stomping rage.

The blonde, the fire Artisan, who by a process of elimination must be the Genevieve who Reuben had told to shut up—and that would make her Genevieve McAvey, Reuben's wife—merely watched him coldly.

'Really, your powers are the wrong way round,' he informed them. 'It offends my sense of order.'

He rocked back and forth from foot to foot. He was, honestly, concerned about what might happen to him if he touched the knife. Lulu hadn't warned him of anything, but there had obviously been plenty Lulu hadn't known. He didn't have gloves. He took a handkerchief from his coat and used that to protect his bare skin as he picked the knife up by the hilt.

He turned back towards the main hall, looking and listening for any sign that lifting the knife off the pedestal had triggered a trap. But there were no new sounds, and his view was mostly blocked by the two humourless men, Reuben and Fletcher, who were standing right at the bars, glaring as if to intimidate him. Genevieve was beside them, still looking calm. Behind them loomed Oliver, the giant. And pretty Cecelia must be with him, but she was too small to see past the three in front.

'Vivi,' Reuben said as soon as Kit met his eyes. 'Let's see if a fireball can get through his barrier.'

Kit heard a gasp he thought had come from Cecelia, and a frown crossed Genevieve's face.

'Did you use up your Art?' he asked Reuben. 'Careless.'

He didn't think so. He thought Reuben liked making other people do his dirty work for him, just because he could.

Reuben pressed on Genevieve's shoulder. She raised her hands and fire formed between her palms. She spread her hands apart and the fire bloomed into a fireball.

Kit watched this with the detached calm that came from a great deal of brandy and gin and a great deal of practice burying fear. Living things could not come through a blocked threshold; Edith had proved that objects could. He didn't know where Artworks sat on that spectrum. If this wasn't a bluff, he was about to find out. He could feel the heat from here, and the other Artisans had had to shift away from Genevieve.

She herself showed no ill effects. She watched his face. The frown had implanted itself between her eyes.

The knife gave a hard twitch in his hands, and he instinctively clamped his fingers tight around it, crushing the cloth of the handkerchief around its hilt.

Oliver coughed. 'Save your Art.' He showed his empty palms. 'Doesn't pass through.'

Kit looked from the giant's scarred and blunt-fingered hands to the copper knife and guessed he'd tried and failed to hook it with some sort of telekinesis Art. He'd failed not because the Art had completely failed to pass through like he was claiming, but because it was either partly blocked by the closed threshold and the iron bars, or because Oliver's medley Art had been too weak to manage it.

He looked at Oliver but gave no sign of his appreciation for the lie. He rather thought Oliver was doing it for Genevieve, not him.

Reuben snarled, 'Maybe your teleport Art is just as useless as the rest of your motley shit.'

'Rude,' Kit said, even though he'd had pretty much the same thought. Thoughts weren't nasty words.

'Do it, Vivi,' Reuben gritted out. 'Incinerate the fucker.'

Genevieve gave a tiny shake of her head as if a mosquito were buzzing by her ear.

'It would melt the copper,' pointed out the giant. He put out his hand; Kit guessed he was calming Cecelia, who he still couldn't see but who he could hear making outraged noises, spitting like a kettle.

'Love a thinker.' Kit smiled at Oliver, even though he knew the big man was speaking for Genevieve's sake rather than his own. He awkwardly wrapped the knife fully in the handkerchief and dropped it in his pocket.

'You can't hold this barrier forever,' the ice Artisan told him.

'Oh, I've experimented,' Kit told him. 'I pretty much can. I'm very good at doors.'

Reuben smacked the invisible block and glowered, to no effect whatsoever on Kit. 'Then we'll starve you out.'

Kit smiled at him.

'Shit,' Oliver said, low and fervent, and turned and began to run down the hall, his big boots thumping across the marble.

'*Love* a thinker,' Kit repeated.

He crossed the threshold, stepping out of the little alcove and back into the hallway via its entrance at the far end, about his limit when he wasn't powered by standing stones. Oliver, who had put Kit's door Art together with his game with the mirrors and understood exactly what he could do, was bearing down at him at full speed, which was impressive given his lumbering gait. It was like a carthorse coming at him.

Kit waved farewell to him and took another sip of gin as he turned his back and strolled through the entrance, crossing from there to the furthest threshold he could reach back out of the vaults.

From there it was easy.

Some of the guards were beginning to stir. Presumably, the unpleasant Fletcher had compelled them to sleep, or Cecelia had used whatever her Art was on them. They didn't show ice or fire damage, or any bruises beyond what might have been delivered by falling asleep standing up. They were sitting up and looking at each other and around themselves in shame-faced confusion, and the ones who even noticed Kit were too slow to do much more than shout after him.

And then he had left the vault and was into the rest of the mountain, passing more stirring guards. And then he had left the mountain and reached the back corridors of the old church, strolling past a last few clerks or servants about their late evening business, who gave him odd looks but didn't try to stop him.

And then he was in the front hall, ducking his head as he mingled among members of the public who were here for the final service of the night, in the part of the church that was still consecrated as such.

And then he was at the front doors, swaying with exhaustion.

It had been longer than an hour. He swallowed the last of the gin and crossed through the front doors. He was on the top step of the steep flight of stairs down to the square, and the two guards he now stood between were looking at him in shock, and he was exhausted and completely alone.

Alex

THE TWINS AND EDITH KNIGHT SAT at the same table outside the inn with the good view of the double doors of the church. People regularly approached the guards and were admitted or turned away depending on their credentials, but no one came out.

'I love how you two can argue without saying anything,' Edith said brightly, into the deathly silence of the siblings glaring at each other over their ale glasses. 'When me and Margaret argue, it's words for days. But you two, well. You're having a raging screaming match without a single word being exchanged, and 'tis surely quite the talent. But then, Mrs Galloway and Miss Young, they're sisters, they didn't say a word to each other for forty-three years and that takes some bloody dedication in a village the size of Lovelly, and then Mrs Galloway broke wind in church and Miss Young stood up and screamed, "I a-told'ee 'ee put too much vinegar in the pickles," which was especially funny because we all thought she was angry that Mrs Galloway had married Mr Galloway but it turns out the argument was over a recipe, which—'

Lulu stirred. 'What?'

'The famous Young pickle recipe. My point is that Mrs Galloway messed it up and the sisters argued about in silence for, oh, forty-three years, 'twer.'

Lulu downed the contents of her glass in one go and looked appealingly across the table at Alex.

That was enraging. 'I can't believe you did that to me, Lucinda,' he fumed.

'Oh good, now we'll get it out in the open.' Edith sat back, satisfied.

'He chose to go,' Lulu snapped back. 'You're all about his choices, aren't you?'

'Not stupid choices.'

'Stupid choices are when you find out if you really mean it when you're offering choices!'

'Fine, then, I didn't mean it when I offered him choices! I hate that he went in there alone and I hate that you helped him do it and I hate that it's been longer than an hour and I hate how fucking chipper you are about it!'

That last was directed at Edith, who took a sip of her own drink. 'Language.'

'No, really,' Alex said, forcing his words to come out calmer. 'How are you so cheerful when your best friend went into the mountain and hasn't come back out?'

'Mr Collins,' Lulu said, thrusting her chin towards Edith's glass, which Alex supposed could indeed have a shitload of gin in it.

"Tis zider,' Edith said indignantly. 'I'm naturally a ray of sunshine, not that you pair'a 'orrible people would know anything about it.' She paused for a rare breath before adding, 'Kit's fine, Alex.'

Alex whacked his knuckles on the table like he was backhanding the certain type of man who had so scared Kit, who had hurt him in unimaginable ways that Kit wouldn't even begin to talk about.

'He is. He's fine. He's clever and he's fast and he's fine.'

'And his hour is up and we should go before we get caught too,' said Lulu, who was truly without mercy. 'Maybe he's already out. Maybe he took the knife and ran away with it, Lexi. You were the one who warned he couldn't be trusted.'

Edith slapped her lightly on the arm. 'He's fine and he's coming back to us with that knife. You'll see. Have a little faith, Locke twins.'

Alex picked up her glass and sniffed at it. 'Really. Just cider?'

'Give me that!' She snatched it back and drank the rest of it as fast as Lulu had finished hers.

'Another round, then,' Lulu said, standing up. And then, 'Alex!'

Alex followed her eyeline and saw, at the top of the steps to the old church, Kit bouncing down, being chased by one of the guards. The three of them were across the square like a shot.

Kit danced across the steps, dodging the guard. 'I don't know how you didn't notice me walk up the steps, sir,' he was saying. 'I walk quietly, maybe. I certainly was not trying to break *in*.'

Three steps from the bottom, he glanced up and saw them. His eyes widened; Alex did not miss the look of sheer relief that briefly flickered across his face.

'Mr Alexander Locke!' he said, spinning the syllables out, and jumped off the steps into Alex's arms, grinning hugely—and bringing a miasma of alcohol fumes with him, if Alex had needed the extra clue.

'Oh, hello, drunk Kit,' Alex said. He put him down, trying very hard not to feel the length of that lithe body sliding against him. Kit didn't help when he struggled and tried to get his legs around Alex's hips. He pushed him off, murmuring, 'In public, sweetheart.'

Kit rocked into him. 'We might get arrested, baby, but I'm game.'

Alex looked at the sky—Kit's rainbow was still there, faintly reflecting in the lamplight in the corner of his eyes—and patted Kit's shoulder, trying awfully hard not to smile.

Kit went off into spluttering giggles, leaning helplessly into Alex. He waved his hands, gasping. 'I'm an Agency-registered Artisan so the only person who's entitled to arrest me is an enforcer. That's you!'

'Thank you, I'd forgotten,' Alex said dryly. He tried to draw Kit away, but the merry-eyed Artisan had not finished his thought yet.

'And—' He laughed too hard to talk for a moment. '—And, Alex, the only thing you're empowered to arrest me for is use of illicit Art. I could literally rob a bank and as long as I don't use my Art, no one can touch me.'

'That's…' Alex said. He looked at Lulu. 'Does that make any sense?'

'That's a really big loophole,' Lulu said. 'If he's not so drunk off his arse that he's making it up out of whole cloth.'

'I'm not!' said Kit happily. 'I am so drunk off my very fine arse that I forgot I wasn't going to tell you people about it, but there it is. Yertiz,' he called to Edith in a travesty of a Somerset accent.

Edith had already moved to block the guard with a particularly focussed ray of sunshine likely to incinerate him if he stayed still too long.

'Sorry, sir, our friend is a little worse for wear! He wandered off, I trust he didn't cause trouble—'

'He appeared at the top of the—'

'—when we're just trying to have a nice evening walk, I wonder how he got to the top of the steps without you noticing, maybe your captain would have a few ideas about that, what do you think, maybe you could have him summoned or maybe we could just move along and you get back to your daydreaming, perhaps?'

The guard, a young man with a big, crinkled forehead, took off his cap and rubbed at his short dark hair, obviously unable to reconcile Edith's sweet tone with the threat implicit in her words.

'We're going to walk away, sir.' Alex flashed his most good-natured smile and, unpeeling Kit's arms, gently turned him around, the two women falling in on either side of them. 'Thank you for helping us find our friend.'

'Oh, did he, that was kind of him, who's your friend, would I like him?' Kit squeezed Edith's hand, smiling at her. 'You smell nice, Edith. Like lavender.'

Edith laced fingers with him. 'Thank you, Kit. Got through the whole flask of brandy, did you?'

They made it across the square, dimly lit by the widely-spaced gas lampposts, and turned down the street towards their inn.

'And this one!' Kit held up a pretty copper flask, overlaid with a bronze pattern of leaves. 'Gin.'

Alex exchanged a glance with Lulu. 'Where'd you get that, Kit?'

Kit jerked. 'Shit!' he said. He pulled out of Alex's supporting hold, lurching into Lulu, who pushed him off with an irritated shove. He suddenly sounded sober. 'I'll take my head start now, Mr Locke. Bye, Edith. These two will make sure you get home safe. Sorry I can't.'

'Hold on there, Mr Whitely,' said Alex, snagging him as he started to stroll off.

'I knew that head start wasn't a real offer,' Kit said smugly. He eased out of Alex's grip. 'So I'm off before you catch me again.'

'It was so a real offer,' Alex said, childishly provoked into arguing with a drunk man.

'Then why'd you look so ashamed when you offered it?'

'Because it's corrupt and morally reprehensible to bribe prisoners?'

Kit paused. 'Oh,' he said. 'Oh!' He favoured Alex with a crooked smile that shot straight into his heart like a pulse of lightning.

Alex coughed and regained control of himself. 'So of course you can have your hour's head start, because I promised that you could,' he said. 'But you can take it in the morning, surely.'

'That's outrageously forward of you, Mr Locke,' said Kit, from beneath lowered lashes, reminding Alex that he was indeed two full flasks to the wind.

'I *meant*—'

'I know what you meant, and I am truly shocked. Show a little decorum, Mr Locke, my goodness.'

Kit was giving him with his best wide-eyed innocent look now, encouraged no doubt by Edith's giggles. Even Lulu was sniggering. Alex put his hands on his hips, fighting laughter. Drunk Kit was a hell of an entertaining ride.

'But anyway,' Kit added, turning around again. 'Regardless. I better go before those wankers catch up with me. No need for you to be in trouble too.'

Alex, grabbing Kit by the back of his coat, exchanged another fast look with Lulu. He knew that flask looked familiar. 'Which wankers?'

'Those wankers,' Kit said, pointing back towards the square, where another commotion had broken out as five people stormed down the steps of the old church, to the great chagrin of the already-confused guards. 'Ooh, let me go, Alex.'

'Myriad,' Lulu spat.

She said it so much like a swearword that Edith murmured, 'Language,' before frowning and saying, 'What?'

Alex and Lulu drew together, pushing Kit and Edith behind them. 'We can handle the Myriad, Kit,' Alex said confidently. He trusted his confidence was warranted. It usually was.

Lulu sighed as the five Artisans stormed towards them across the square, having dismissed the gnats who were the guards. Alex knew his sister was watching Genevieve's stride in the dim lighting. When she'd first been learning to walk like a woman, it had been Genevieve's long-legged, self-assured gait she'd done her best to copy.

She still struggled with it, whereas Alex, in helping her practise, had perfected it. He'd always been the better dancer, too.

'It's in the hips, Lulu,' he whispered. She swore at him under her breath and he nudged her.

'The Locke twins,' Alex heard Fletcher say in disgust.

In unison, he and Lulu chorused, 'Hello, Ollie,' at Oliver, who immediately slowed down and turned red. Cecelia, walking beside him, grinned at them. Cecelia was lovely.

'Hey!' said Kit, poking Alex hard in the back. Lulu made a noise like Edith might have poked her too.

'What?' said Lulu. 'We don't often meet men bigger than us.'

'He blushes like a brick,' Alex explained, 'and Reuben hates it when any of the others get attention.'

He pressed the spot between his eyes that was already beginning to ache. Their intentions, mixed and messy, were rolling over him, and he had to work hard using Kit's technique to focus down to just Reuben, their foul-tempered leader. Kit stroked his hand with his thumb, rubbing hard across his knuckles, and it got easier.

'The Locke twins,' Reuben said when the Myriad were finally close enough so they could converse without shouting. 'Hello, boys.'

Edith gave an audible gasp as Alex stiffened all over. 'You want to start this with a punch in the mouth, is that it, Ruby?'

He managed to produce his smile to soften the threat into a jest, but it wasn't one of his better efforts.

Lulu squeezed Alex's arm. 'Hello, Gin,' she said. 'Still letting yourself be held back by incompetent men, I see.'

'Please don't talk about my husband like that,' Genevieve said, pushing a loose strand of her pale hair from her eyes.

'I didn't name anyone, but, sure.'

'Enough pissing around,' Reuben said. 'Hand over the little shit hiding behind you, Locke.'

'Which little shit?' Kit asked. 'This little shit?'

He pointed at himself left-handed and Alex was surprised to see that not only was Kit now cuffed, but he was cuffed to him. He'd slipped the much-abused cuffs from Alex's pocket and cuffed his own right wrist to Alex's left one.

He really would make a spectacular thief.

'He's already in our custody, Reuben,' Lulu said, also eyeing the cuffs, which Alex guessed now were stage props.

Reuben's intention swamped him. He barely heard him say, 'I don't believe you've had a chance to register the bounty.'

Alex watched the faces of the other four as the implications of their leader's flat threat to steal a catch off other registered bounty hunters sunk in. Fletcher looked nervously smug while Cecelia looked appalled. Genevieve was, as ever, unreadable. She was in a difficult position now; he'd pity her if she hadn't chosen to marry the bloody man.

Oliver slowly rubbed his tattooed hand over his big, bald head. 'Not fair play.'

'Shut your motley mouth, Oliver.'

'Rude,' said Kit and Edith together.

Reuben glared at Kit and then at Edith. He gave a dismissive sniff, returning his fiery stare to Alex. 'Hand over the knife and you can keep your little door boy.'

He got a special sneering twist on those last two words, like what he meant to say was *backdoor boy*. Alex sighed.

'This little door boy pissed all over the Myriad,' Kit informed him, from well behind Alex.

'Shut up, drunk Kit,' murmured Alex.

'I took you on with door Art,' Kit shouted. '*Doors*. If I had your Art, I'd be ruling the world and you're using it to throw *ice spears*.' The utter contempt he threw into his last two words put to shame Reuben's own try.

'Really, shut up, Kit,' Alex said, watching Reuben, reading his hardening intention. He slid his hand halfway to his revolver. He glanced to Lulu, who pulled Edith all the way back behind her again.

Reuben raised his hands, ice beginning to crystallise out of the air between his palms. The rest of the Myriad drew closer together, clustering around Genevieve, who was the only one who could talk her husband down if he really got started.

Indeed, it was brave Ginnie who stepped to his side. 'Reuben, no.'

He roughly shoved off her restraining hand and she fell a step back before Oliver steadied her, big hands briefly to her shoulders and gone again. Alex took a step forwards, bristling, and was warned off with a single shake of her head.

'Reuben, the baby,' Cecelia said reproachfully.

Reuben snarled and drew a shaft of ice from the air. 'Hand over the fucking knife.'

'What knife?' Alex said. 'All I've got is my shiny new revolver. It's French. Lefaucheux.'

The ice Artisan pointed the icy spear at him, his intention right there on the cusp of action. Alex swallowed bile and reached for the gun.

'Use of illicit Art,' Kit crowed, oblivious. 'That's what I was arrested for as well. We'll all ride to London in the same train carriage, that'll be… entertaining.'

Peeking out from behind Alex, he must have winked or made some sort of face, because Oliver blushed and Cecelia giggled and then looked guilty. The intentions flying back and forth between the two groups twisted and eased.

Alex froze. Then, diverting from his shiny new revolver, he drew out his shiny new enforcer badge and showed it to the Myriad.

'Since when are you an enforcer, Locke?' Fletcher demanded.

'Since last week,' Alex said. 'So, where are we at, Ruby? You making a scene on a public street against an Agency enforcer? That'll be an interesting addition to the newspaper clippings about the Myriad.'

Reuben flicked his fingers and the sharp shaft of ice shattered against the paving. 'Search him,' he demanded. 'He stole an artefact from the Orphanage. We're getting it back.'

'Liar,' said Kit. 'You want it for yourself.' He smirked and then transformed it into a saintly smile. 'I mean, what knife?'

'*Search him.*'

'Search me, Mr Locke,' Kit said, spreading his hands wide and accidentally jerking on the chain joining them. 'It'll make the handcuffs even more fun.'

'Drunk Kit should shut his mouth,' Alex murmured, as, without a choice that wouldn't make him look exactly as corrupt as he was, he moved to pat Kit down.

'Don't get too handsy there, sir,' Kit said as Alex slipped fingers under his coat to prove he'd checked for a hidden sheath. He was smiling at someone: Cecelia, possibly, or Oliver.

'Really, really, shut your mouth, sweetheart.' Kit hummed and Alex swallowed a laugh. 'There's no knife, Reuben,' he was able to honestly inform the Myriad leader a moment later.

He glanced aside to where Lulu was quietly keeping Edith out of the way. He saw her flash of mingled relief and disappointment, echoing his own.

'He has it,' Reuben insisted. He took an aggressive step towards Kit. 'I'll search the little fucker myself.'

'Oh, but can't Oliver do it?' Kit neatly slid back behind Alex, dancing away from Reuben's grab for him. Drunk Kit was so much more graceful than sober Kit. 'Oliver, don't you want to search me?' he called, setting Oliver off into yet another blush.

'Drunk Kit's a little too friendly,' Alex muttered.

'Drunk Kit's your special friend, baby,' Kit whispered to him. At least, he probably thought he was whispering. Alex patted him and sighed again.

He needed to extract them from this situation, but Reuben was obviously convinced Kit had gotten away with the knife. He was not the type to let it go. The tension had eased off a little, but Reuben could easily escalate them into fight territory again, and the Myriad would win that, eventually.

'Kit,' Cecelia called suddenly. 'May I have my flask back? It was a gift, you see.'

'Certainly, Miss Cecelia,' Kit said, flipping straight into his habitual blandly polite tones.

He held out the flask and Cecelia stepped to take it. Her right hand, gloved, took the flask; her left hand, ungloved, came up to take Kit's wrist where his coat sleeve had pulled back.

Alex waited in silent agony for her bare fingers to touch Kit's bare skin. He couldn't warn Kit, not without giving away his talent for reading intentions, not without giving away that he had a vested interest in helping him keep his secrets.

'That's not acceptable to do to a prisoner,' Edith suddenly shouted. 'They have rights!'

Alex jolted. He'd forgotten people could guess intentions without actively reading them with Art—with talent. He'd also forgotten it was his job to uphold Agency law in every respect, and that meant that, while Agency Artisans could tear Kit's mind apart howsoever they liked, random Artisans weren't allowed to.

Thank God for Edith Knight, taking up the slack on his stupidity.

Kit had yanked away. 'Tricky,' he said, wagging a finger. 'Was that another use of illicit Art Edith just thwarted? Oh, Miss Cecelia, will you join me in my carriage after all?'

Cecelia dimpled sweetly, not looking at all discomfited.

'What were you going to do to me, my slippery girl?'

'Read your memories,' she told him. 'See what you did with the knife before all this goes too far.'

Kit laughed, swayed, and steadied himself on Alex. 'What. Knife,' he said, speaking to Reuben, suddenly all spite and flashing challenge.

'Yeah, all right, we're walking away now,' Alex said. 'If you really think he stole some artefact, you can interview him at the Agency once you get your permits in order.'

'Make him let Cecelia touch him,' Reuben ordered.

'Use of illicit Art,' Edith said promptly. Kit laughed.

Reuben scowled at Edith. 'Who are you, anyway?'

'A witness,' she said coldly.

He turned to Alex. 'You've got no reason not to, Locke. Unless you're hiding something too.'

'No reason not to?' Alex said. 'I've been in the job a week, Ruby. I can't be flouting the rule of law, in front of a witness no less, as a favour for a—' He thought about it, because "friend" was stretching the hell out of the truth. '—acquaintance.'

'She can touch me,' Kit said, smiling and swaying.

'Subject granted permission, you all heard,' Reuben said to Alex, pushing Cecelia forwards. 'You heard, didn't you, witness?'

'That's not proper,' Fletcher said stiffly. 'He only said it to be lewd.'

'He said it because he's drunk,' Alex said, 'which isn't proper permission.'

'Oh, baby, don't be like that,' Kit purred. 'Come and touch me, Miss Cecelia. I've got a wonderful memory lined up just for you.'

Alex, reading Kit's intentions loud and clear, felt himself turn as red as Oliver. 'Cecelia, definitely don't touch him.'

'Some hints for your wedding night.'

Cecelia jerked her hand back and looked wide-eyed at Reuben.

'He can't force a memory on you,' he snapped. 'You force the memory you want to see.'

Fletcher was finally looking uncomfortable too. 'Reuben, let me use compulsion—'

'Oh, you *will not*,' said Edith fiercely.

Reuben waved Fletcher off, his gaze intense on Cecelia. 'Do it.'

'Come on, then.' Kit suddenly sounded very sober indeed, and very cold. He seemed to forgotten it was Cecelia who would bear the brunt of touching him, not Reuben. 'Find out if I can or not.'

Genevieve shook her head but Reuben pushed at Cecelia again. Alex met Oliver's eyes and stared him down with all the casual confidence at his disposal. Oliver sagged and put his meaty hand on Genevieve's shoulder. She in turn took hold of Cecelia as the smaller woman visibly tried to steel herself, her lips gone white at the edges as she pressed them hard together.

'We're done here, Reuben.' Genevieve looked impassively at her fuming husband until the ice Artisan shrugged and turned away.

'All right?' Oliver asked Cecelia in a low rumble.

'Sorry, Miss Cecelia,' Kit said, looking at his boots in what appeared to be genuine remorse. 'That was too far. I sincerely apologise.'

'I'm all right, Ollie,' she said. 'All right, Mr Kit.'

'Thanks, Gin,' Alex said, and 'Bye, Oliver,' Lulu said.

Kit waved at the Myriad as the Locke twins hooked their elbows though his and hurried him away before he could provoke them again, Edith in their wake.

It was after dark, which made travel all but impossible. They hurried away and fetched up at the inn where they'd left the carriage, on the very edge of the little town, with barely a word exchanged between them.

They collapsed at a table by the fire in the taproom. There weren't many other guests, and most were solitary, finishing up their meals and drinks and heading for the stairs, not interested in socialising.

After a while, Edith straightened. 'I'm very annoyed with you, Kit.'

'Is that at drunk Kit in general, or something in the specific?' Kit enquired owlishly.

'I know you prefer sticky buns,' she said severely. 'That's all fine. But if you'll flirt with Miss Cecelia, why don't you flirt with me?'

'Edith Knight,' he said, hand theatrically over his heart. 'You're my best friend, I would never!'

'Unfair,' she said sulkily, crossing her arms.

'I think I told you smelled nice?'

'Was that flirting, Kit?' He made a seesawing gesture with his hand and she unfolded her arms. 'All right, then.'

Lulu's face was like stone. Alex leaned over to take her hand. 'Sorry, Lulu.'

'No, I'm sorry, Alex,' she said. 'Because you know we have to do your plan now, don't you?'

'Why are you all sorry at each other?' Kit asked. He was beginning to sound sleepy.

'You didn't get the knife, Kit,' Alex reminded him.

'Oh, I got the knife.' Kit flashed his wicked smile. 'I'm not a thief, but I'd make a bloody good one.'

He reached into Lulu's coat pocket and drew out something wrapped in his own handkerchief. He gave it to Lulu. She unwrapped the bundle enough to reveal a flash of copper. She gasped and flung an arm around Kit's shoulders, holding the knife to her chest with her other hand like it was her baby.

'That's right, honey,' Kit said, eyes closing. 'Stashed it before they got to me. No one's searching Lulu, she's terrifying.'

Alex eased him out of snuggling with Lulu, eyes narrowed at his sister. Really, the cheek of her. It was outside of enough.

Lulu, smirking at him, ruffled Kit's hair. 'Thank you, kitty-cat.'

'You literally petted me like you think I'm an actual cat,' Kit said querulously.

'You literally purr when you're happy like an actual cat,' Lulu countered as she slid the knife back into her pocket.

'I do not,' said Kit, which meant Alex couldn't resist sliding his hand up Kit's shirt and stroking his back until he started dreamily humming.

Alex and Lulu exchanged a complicitly amused twin-look while Edith giggled.

Kit wriggled under Alex's touch and then abruptly turned to him, eyes burning, hands reaching very inappropriately. 'Whoops,' Alex said, fending him off. 'I better get him to bed.'

'Finally,' Kit sighed.

'Don't make this difficult, Kit.'

'I'll make everything easy, baby, I promise.'

Alex winced and looked at Edith. 'I'm not taking advantage of drunk Kit—'

'I know,' she said. 'You're a decent person, Alex, I know that.'

'Miss Edith Mary Rose Knight thinks I'm a decent person,' Alex said, with enough sarcasm to disguise that he was truly pleased. He gave Lulu her own smirk back. 'You're still a horrible person, though, Lulu.'

'Put him to bed. I'm going to stay and have a drink with this horrible person here to celebrate. Not the soft cider this time, Lulu.'

'But I want a drink to celebrate,' Kit said, even as he tried to wrap his arms and legs around Alex.

'You've done plenty of celebrating from the look of you,' Alex told him, gently disentangling him.

'Two women can't drink alone in a public-house.' Kit shuffled his feet on the spot; he probably thought he was dancing. 'I can chaperone the hell out of them, just watch me.'

'If anyone bothers us, I'll kick them in the face,' Lulu said, reclining back in her chair and laying her arm across the back of Edith's. 'Take our chaperone to bed, Lexi.'

Alex nodded to her. She was celebrating; she was also keeping watch for a few hours in case Orphanage men found them.

'Come along before you pass out,' he said to Kit, and had to half-carry him up the stairs to bed.

18

*K*IT HUMMED UNDER ALEX'S HANDS AS the Viking peeled off his coat. 'I like where this is going, Alex.'

'You're going to bed, Mr Whitely.'

Alex knelt and tugged on one of Kit's boots, sending Kit tumbling back onto the bed. He felt Alex's fingers, gentle on his calf. 'You're coming to bed, Mr Locke.'

The fingers tightened and Kit moaned. Alex turned his attention to the other boot. 'I'll lie with you, sweetheart, but that's all.'

He hung up the coat and tidied Kit's boots before sitting on the bed. Kit immediately folded himself around him but Alex soothed him down with a firm hand on his chest. Kit wrapped his hands around Alex's wrist.

'It's lovely that drunk Kit thinks he wants me,' Alex murmured.

'All over you, baby,' Kit agreed. 'In you.'

Alex's eyes fluttered closed. He breathed out and then pushed on. 'But sober Kit likely has different ideas, so—'

'Sober Kit wants you to rip all his clothes off and fuck him senseless,' Kit told him, digging his fingers into his wrist. 'Sober Kit wants you to put him in your pocket so he can curl up safe and sound like a little hedgehog. Sober Kit adores you. I think he probably loves you.'

Alex went very still.

'But—' Kit put his finger to his lips. '—Shush. Alex. Alex. Be quiet. Sober Kit likes to pretend he doesn't have any feelings, so we can't talk about it. All right, Alex?'

Alex put his hand over his face, smothering a smile. 'Sober Kit would certainly want drunk Kit to shut up, I think.'

'The only way to shut drunk Kit up is to shove your cock in his mouth,' Kit informed him with lofty authority.

'Yeah, all right,' said Alex. Now he really was laughing. 'Drunk Kit has a filthy mouth.'

Kit tried to climb onto his lap but Alex pushed him down again. Kit pointed out that he could fit in *Oliver's* lap and Alex abruptly stopped laughing and let Kit clamber on top of him. Kit held his face and kissed him, and Alex's mouth moved under his with a slow intensity that made Kit make some unashamedly desperate sounds.

But Alex kept catching Kit's hands whenever he slipped his fingers under his waistband. 'When you're sober, sweetheart.'

This was infuriating. 'Please, Alex,' Kit said, hips rocking against him. 'Please, Alex, please, I want you, please let me have you.'

'Tell me that in the morning, when you're sober,' Alex said. 'Then you can have me any way you want me and I'll make you spend so hard you see stars.'

This only served to make Kit whimper and he latched his hands around the back of Alex's neck and kissed him again. 'Please, Alex,' he whispered. 'Can't you be the certain type of man I try to pretend you are? Just for tonight?'

Alex sighed. His hands pressed over Kit's shoulder blades and Kit arched against the touch, trying to make contact with every part of his body at once. 'I can't have you hating me in the morning, Kit. I won't have that.'

'Sober Kit won't even remember anything,' Kit assured him.

'That's not selling it, beautiful,' Alex said.

Kit felt the flex of his muscles as Alex lazily shifted and peeled his hands off and he whimpered again. He was hazed with alcohol and out of control with thwarted desire. 'Please, Alex, haven't I been good, haven't I earnt it?'

'My God, Kit, you never had to earn it,' Alex said, something tight in his voice. His arms looped around Kit and pulled him in.

Kit assumed this meant his words were working, so he went on in a similar vein, murmuring against Alex's ear. 'Haven't I been so good for you, haven't I pleased you?'

'Oh, I don't like this.' Alex's hands came to Kit's hips and he lifted him aside with no sign of effort. 'Kit,' he said firmly, holding him down. 'You didn't have to perform for me to earn my affection, for Christ's sake.'

'You don't think so?' Kit asked. His drunken energy was dissipating. He fell back against the sheets, no longer fighting Alex, and went on muzzily, 'You didn't like me till I saved you from the pain Artisan. Lulu didn't like me till I got the murder knife for her. The village didn't like me till I went into the fire for Little Tommy.' He patted Alex's face and murmured, 'I'm a means to an end, baby. It's all right. I always have been.'

His eyes slipped closed then, and he dozed for a moment or two, and drifted back up with things a little clearer and Alex leaning over him, staring at him with an odd look on his face. He made a questioning noise, somewhat startled to wake up to that.

'Hey, listen, Kit,' Alex said. 'I don't like you because you got the knife and saved me. I like you because you're clever and brave and loyal and funny.'

'Are you inebriated, Mr Locke?' Kit asked bemusedly.

'This isn't a transaction,' Alex went on. 'I hope this is a friendship. I hope it can be more.'

'Oh, dear,' Kit said. 'The Viking is being sincere at me again, I have to deflect.' He wagged a somewhat wavering finger chidingly at Alex. 'You forgot to list my hot filthy mouth in your recitation of my sterling qualities.'

'I most certainly have not forgotten that,' Alex said. 'I am looking forwards to introducing you to *my* hot filthy mouth as soon as you're sober enough to appreciate it.'

Kit moaned to show his current level of appreciation but couldn't summon the energy to resume his assault on Alex's chastity. He brushed his hands over Alex's shirt and said, 'Drunk Kit just wants your magnificent arse, but sober Kit loves your kindness and your bloody stubborn sincerity and your steadiness and also your truly bizarre willingness to put up with his shit.'

Alex smiled down at him, chuckling softly. He kissed Kit chastely on the forehead and said, 'Good night, little hedgehog.'

That odd endearment was the last thing Kit remembered until his bladder and a headache insisted on waking him up a long way before dawn. He frowned in puzzlement—hedgehog? Why a hedgehog?—even as the headache faded; Artisans didn't get sick and they didn't suffer hangovers.

Then he rolled his memory back further.

He clapped his hands over his eyes. '*Oh my God!*'

Beside him in the dark, the big shape that was Alex stirred. 'Good morning, sober Kit.'

'Oh my God. Alex.' Kit slid out of bed. He was still in his street clothes, of course, and damn messy with it. He shoved his hands into his wild hair, face aflame. He'd rutted on Alex like a green boy; he'd begged Alex for it, repeatedly; he'd told Alex— 'Oh my *God.*'

'Drunk Kit was so sure you wouldn't remember anything,' Alex said, sleepily adding, 'my little hedgehog.'

'Holy. Sodding. Hellfire.' Kit pressed his hands to his stomach. 'Drunk Kit can go fuck himself!'

'Come back to bed, sweetheart.'

It was too dark to read Alex's expression, but his voice was low and warm and sparked an answering low and warm glow where Kit was pressing his hands. 'I need to— I'm going to go—'

'All right,' Alex said. It was nice to have a man who could read his intentions instead of expecting eloquence at the arse-end of the night. 'Then come back to bed. I promise I won't be sincere at you or do any of the terrifying talking. I'm hoping my mouth will be too busy for that, yes?'

Turned out Alex had quite the purr on him too.

'I'll be *right back*,' Kit blurted and bolted out of the room.

The inn was big and modern enough to have a single bathroom for its twelve rooms, which was blessedly empty at this time of the morning, and Kit availed himself lavishly. He came back out, as clean as he could get and much calmer.

He looked at the closed door of their room. Alex had been very sleepy; he had probably fallen back asleep, as deep as ever, and never mind his hopes for his hot filthy mouth. Kit himself was still worn out from the excesses of his little adventure and should go back to sleep himself.

Still.

He soft-footed down the stairs and across the taproom, heading for the kitchen to steal some oil, relaxed and anticipatory.

He should have known better.

Arms came around his neck from behind, the crook of an elbow slamming up into his throat, the other hand smacked over his mouth. Kit choked and kicked wildly, getting both hands around the forearm at his throat, tearing uselessly at coat fabric with his nails.

His fingers went red with cold, as red as the coat he was clawing at. They throbbed with a deep ache as if he'd been playing in the snow for hours. He'd not felt cold quite like it since his Artisan powers had come on.

A voice hissed, 'I'll freeze the blood in your veins.'

Kit went still, fingers resting on the forearm of the man who held him. Reuben McAvey adjusted his grip, releasing the hand clamped over Kit's mouth to lock that arm around Kit's own arms, holding him tight now by throat and torso.

'Here's what's going to happen, you darkie piece of shit,' he whispered. 'You're going to get me that fucking knife, understood?'

'I don't know what you mean,' Kit managed to say. He couldn't tell whether it was Reuben or fear that had turned him to ice inside.

'Just for that, I'm letting you lose a finger to frostbite. Try again.'

Kit whimpered and struggled and stilled again as the cold intensified around his hands and now his feet. He felt like he was trying to breath in a snowstorm. 'It's in Miss Lucinda's room.'

'You're going to go get it. If you fail to get it, I will go up there and turn Locke's heart to a block of ice. If you try to wake them up, I'll turn them all to ice sculptures and smash them to pieces.'

The cold, calm part of Kit's mind reminded him that Art was very specific. Reuben could surely not do all of what he was threatening to do. His Art sought and froze the water in the air and let him shape it. He couldn't literally freeze people. He could freeze the air surrounding them, though, and, judging by Kit's extremities, he could probably freeze whatever water was inside flesh and blood too. He could definitely freeze the air they were drawing into their lungs.

None of this detached analysis was helpful.

Reuben released Kit's arms to savagely wrench his hair, sending pain in an expanding ripple over Kit's scalp. 'Don't you ever fucking tell me I'm not using my fucking Art right again, you shit.'

Kit shut his eyes, remembering saying, *If I had your Art, I'd be ruling the world and you're using it to throw* ice spears.

Never taunt, he thought. *It always comes back. You knew that, drunk Kit, you sodding idiot.*

Aloud, he said, 'Yes. Yes, I'll get the knife. Wait here.'

'You know what will happen if you fuck with me.' Reuben shoved him away.

Kit stood shaking. *From the cold, from the cold*, he told himself. *You're not used to the cold anymore.* He slowly turned to face the redheaded ice Artisan. 'I need the use of my hands and feet.'

'Fuck off.'

'If you don't want Miss Lucinda to wake up,' Kit insisted, 'I need the use of my hands and feet to get quietly into her room and take the knife.'

Reuben sneered at him, but he made a gesture and the biting, numbing cold in Kit's extremities eased off, except for the little finger of his right hand, which stayed bright white and hard. That was the finger Reuben had designated he lose to frostbite, he supposed.

Blowing on his hands to warm them faster, Kit backed away from Reuben, towards the nearest doorway. Every instinct told him to run. He had no doubt, not a single doubt, that Reuben would make good on his threat against Locke, and probably Edith and Lulu too, if he did.

It was plain to him that without the eyes of the rest of the Myriad on him, Reuben was an out-and-out villain who too desperately wanted the pretty little copper knife.

He considered the room, thinking of closing off the thresholds, locking Reuben in, the same sort of trick he'd played on Lulu in the standing stones. But he didn't have the power of the standing stones now, nor did he have the clear line of sight needed for such a variety of different thresholds, which meant he'd struggle to close them all and keep them all closed.

Besides, he still wasn't sure if Art could cross a blocked threshold. He remembered the twitch the knife had given, when Oliver had tried to teleport it out of his hands. Had the threshold blocked Oliver's Art, or had Oliver's Art been too weak? He knew which one Reuben believed. Could the treacherous snake reach upwards and freeze Alex from here?

He racked his brains, desperately trying to find a solution that would keep both himself and everyone else safe. Here, *here*, was the problem when you gave your heart away. You couldn't protect it and yourself at the same time.

'You stop and think one more time and Locke will be breathing ice,' Reuben told him. 'Move. You have thirty seconds.'

Kit stumbled sideways and touched the newel post of the stairs, coming out up on the landing. He stole along the quiet hallway, pausing to touch the door of his and Locke's room.

Wake up. Wake up and wonder where I am, he thought, and, at exactly the same time, *Stay asleep, Alex, stay safe, don't come looking for me.*

Rather than risking Lulu or Edith waking up when their door opened, Kit crossed the threshold from the outside of their door to the inside of their door. The room was the mirror image of his and Locke's. The two women were cuddled together in bed; a small part of Kit's mind noted their intimacy even as the rest of him was pinpointed on Lulu's coat. Turned out fierce Lulu was just as inveterate a cuddler as her soft-hearted brother.

He found the knife readily enough, still in the pocket of Lulu's coat. He eased it out and checked on the women again. Lulu was still sleeping, but Edith had opened her eyes. She otherwise had not moved. Kit paused when he saw her watching him.

She shook her head at him. Kit put his finger to his lips, signalling silence. He showed her the handkerchief-wrapped knife, and then ostentatiously let the handkerchief slip from the hilt and drop to the ground. That left him touching the hilt directly for the first time, but he was neither immediately struck dead nor gifted with inhuman Art.

He backed away towards the threshold, holding the knife low in his left hand, using his right hand to again signal silence before pointing to the handkerchief. Edith gave a minuscule nod.

Kit crossed the threshold back into the hall, and then down to the doorway between the kitchen and the taproom. Reuben was facing towards the stairs as if he expected Kit to walk back down them.

A semblance of a plan presented itself. He would wait, and Reuben would start up the stairs to carry through on his threats. At that point, Kit could close the thresholds at the top and bottom of the stairs and show Reuben that he had the knife. Reuben wouldn't be able to get to the others past Kit's barrier, and Kit had to trust he wasn't close enough or precise enough to hurt them from there. By the time he'd worked out he could jump the banister back down to the taproom, Kit would have enough distance on him to lead him away without falling afoul of his vicious ice Art himself. He wasn't sure how it would play out after that; he just wanted Reuben away from Locke and Edith and Lulu.

It was risky. And there was an unfamiliar sort of heat rising in Kit.

Reuben's back made a broad and tempting target.

Kit shifted the knife from his left hand to his right, the little finger sticking out painfully. He took a soft step forwards. And another. He thought about arteries. Alex had told him where the artery in the thigh was. His hand tightened around the hilt of the copper knife.

It was burning in his hand, and that burning was in his veins, and that burning was in his head, and that burning was melting a wall of ice that Kit had not suspected he had inside him and behind that wall was dammed an ocean of rage, wide and still and fathoms deep.

He was going to kill Reuben and then he was going to find Varley and Fairweather and inflict on them every bit of torment they had ever seen fit to gift him before feeding the knife with the hot scarlet blood of their withered hearts, and then he would be safe, safe, safe.

Kit all at once understood what the power of the knife might be. It didn't change his intention one iota.

From upstairs came an inarticulate shout of alarm.

A bag went over Kit's head from behind. The knife spilled from his hand and he was dragged kicking and struggling to the ground. He didn't call for help.

Calling for help never worked.

Alex

ALEX YELPED AND ROLLED OFF THE bed before he was even fully awake, landing hard on the floor and raising his hands to fend off whoever it was with the powerful intention to slice open his femoral artery and stab him in the heart.

He lay on his back, breathing hard and fully primed for attack, before he woke up fully and understood that the room was empty.

His shout had woken Lulu and Edith, and a few other people if a couple of loud scuffling sounds from below were any indication.

Lulu hammered on the wall between their rooms. 'Knife's gone,' she shouted.

'Oh, Kit, you fucker,' Alex said, more with resignation than anger.

He met Lulu in the hallway. In unspoken accord, they moved downstairs, Alex with his revolver to hand, Lulu her fists; her single-shot pistols were more a memento of Peter, whose heirloom wedding gift they had been, than useful weapons. Despite the noises he'd heard a few minutes before, the place was empty, just an overturned chair out of place. He set it to rights. Outside, somewhere nearby, he heard a carriage start off.

Lulu came back from checking the kitchen. 'Back door's unbolted. No sign of anyone out there now, though.'

Alex nodded grimly. Kit tended to unlock doors and walk through them if he could; that took less Art than crossing a threshold did. Their duplicitous little thief was long gone.

He sank into the chair he'd just picked up. 'Lulu, I'm sorry, he got me again,' he said, resting his face in his hands. 'I'm such a fucking idiot.'

Lulu spun on her heel, picked up another chair, and hurled it across the room with enough force that it dented the wall in a shower of plaster and shattered into shards fit only for firewood.

Edith must have been delayed by feeling obliged to dress. She came down the stairs now, still doing up the last of her buttons. She froze, face pale, as the pieces of chair smattered to the floor.

'You're assuming Kit took it?' She sounded very subdued.

'He took it,' Alex said.

'But why would he?' she asked desperately.

'Because he's a fucking thief,' Lulu shouted at her.

'He's not,' Edith said. She still had that strange desperate note in her voice. 'So why else would he have taken it? Can we think about this for a moment?'

Lulu slowly turned her head and met Alex's eyes. They had one of their twin moments, and then Lulu charged across the room, seized Edith by her arms and yanked her the rest of the way down the stairs. Edith yelped in alarm and tried to twist away, but Lulu was too angry and too strong.

'What do you know?' Lulu snarled. 'You saw him, didn't you? You fucking treacherous bitch.'

'Language,' Edith whispered, gone ashen as she hung helplessly and let Lulu shake her like a dog with a bone.

Alex stood up and laid his hands over Lulu's shoulders, feeling the rigid tension there. 'Let's not murder Miss Knight, little sister,' he said. 'Miss Knight, did you see him?'

Lulu was lowering Edith down, but when the smaller woman gave a tiny nod, she snatched her back up again, pulling her face-to-face. 'When?'

'Maybe ten minutes ago,' she said. 'He was taking the knife—'

Lulu gave a disconsolate howl and shoved Edith over.

'—but I don't think he wanted to!' Edith shouted from the floor. Her face was crumpled. 'I need you both to calm down so we can talk about it rationally because right now I don't dare send you after him in case you kill him before you ask him what's going on.'

Alex knelt in front of her. 'I am perfectly calm.'

'Oh, you're certainly not,' she said, edging away from him, heedless of the dust on her skirts.

'What do you mean, send us after him?' he asked.

'He didn't steal it,' she insisted. 'Promise me you'll give him the benefit of the doubt when you catch up with him.'

'What do you mean, send us after him?' Alex repeated without a single change of expression.

Edith swallowed. Then she held up a small white handkerchief.

Lulu snatched it from her. It took only a second before she said, 'He's heading back to the mountain. He's taken the fucking knife back to get a reward.'

'I don't think he has.' Edith rose heavily to her feet and squared off to them. 'He's in trouble, Alex.'

'He surely is,' Alex said coldly.

Edith rubbed a hand along her hip. She still looked fierce but her eyes had darkened. Alex realised she was hurt, from where Lulu had flung her to the ground. He realised he'd stood aside and let Lulu do that.

The little woman stood her ground as Lulu turned back to face her. Her hands were trembling and Alex resisted the urge to step between them. He trusted his sister. She knew she'd done wrong. He waited for her to apologise to Edith.

Lulu naturally read his expectation. 'A gentleman's supposed to protect ladies,' she said, sneering at them both. 'Yet again, that's your failure, Alexander, not mine.'

The link between them tugged, tightened, frayed. Alexander put Edith behind him.

'All right,' he said, keeping his voice as steady as he could. 'Miss Knight, if you want to help Kit, get the carriage readied and wait with it. Lulu, go get your public face on, and I'll find rope. We're going in.'

19

WHEN KIT WOKE UP, THE RANKLY familiar smell and taste of the air washed over him and placed him firmly in time and space. He barely even needed the feel of rough ropes around his wrists and ankles to tell him that he was tied to the whipping frame in a dank and dismal stone cell.

He wasn't, in that moment, Kit Whitely. He was Christopher Whitebrickleyhurst, fifteen years old, terrified, and alone. His breath was coming in harsh pants, sucking in so little air that the cell was spinning in alternating flashes of light and dark. He thrashed mindlessly against the ropes, an animal in a trap. His skin was flayed by the chafe of the ropes and still he fought, until his wrists and ankles were scraped and his shoulders, held taut and twisted against the frame, were screaming.

Kit felt like he watched the wild flailing from a cold place just outside himself. *Five more seconds, Christopher*, he told the panicked, helpless boy he had left behind. *Five. Four. Three. Two. One. Now stop.*

He stilled. His breathing slowed and eased. He looked over at his right hand, which was particularly throbbing, and had a weird sense of disorientation as he counted his fingers a couple of times and finally realised his frostbitten little finger had been severed and sewn up while he had been unconscious. The stub was leaking blood after his struggles.

Kit sighed and swallowed it, for there was nothing else to be done.

He took stock. He'd been tied to face the frame, his back to the cell door, as per usual. He was not naked, not as per usual, but instead had been dressed in a clean and simple white robe, like a penitent. His feet were still bare but had been washed. In fact, he felt like he'd been washed all over, which was an odd and unpleasant sensation.

He swallowed it.

'Need a knife,' he said to the air.

He had had a knife, the copper knife, but that was gone. He didn't know if his kidnappers, Orphanage men, had been in league with Reuben, or his competitors for ownership of the bloodthirsty thing. It might be safely back in its alcove in the depths of the mountain vaults. It might be in the hands of one of Bishop Varley's rivals. It was probably miles away, the tool of the ice Artisan, for whatever reprehensible purpose Reuben had wanted it for.

Shadows danced across the wall in front of him and he heard scrapes from behind him; someone was coming down the corridor towards his cell. He heard footsteps, low voices, and the unmistakable sound of a key in the lock.

Christopher tried to panic; Kit remorselessly locked him away inside his own head, in a move that felt like it had Art behind it. He craned his neck to get a glimpse of the cell door—it was an archetypical dungeon cell door, aged wood with an inset barred window—and set his Art to it. He refused to let it be unlocked.

That bought him time. It left him tied to the sodding whipping frame.

Kit looked up at the knots holding the ropes tight on his right wrist. 'I don't have a door and lock Art,' he told the knots. 'I have a telekinesis Art that I use to open things. *Anything*. And now I am going to open you.'

Untie, said a treacherous part of his brain. *Not open.*

'Open,' insisted Kit. 'I open locks, I open doors, I open thresholds. I can open anything, and I will open these knots.'

Untie.

'Open.'

Untie.

'Would you please be quiet, Christopher?' Kit politely enquired of himself. 'I. Will. Open. These. Knots.'

His focus narrowed. For almost nine years, he had disciplined himself to milk his odd Art to its last drop of potential, and he now brought every last iron bar of that discipline to bear on the knots. He was sweating with the effort of it, penitent robes drenched, muscles quivering.

He could hear, as if in the far distance, bangs and thumps as his captors tried to break into the cell. That would have been amusing, if he'd had attention to spare. He heard a gentle tapping and a familiar voice calling his name and he twitched, warding off Christopher's panic and narrowing in even harder on the knots.

He had just felt the first knot begin to give when a change in the light and a wash of fresher air through the dank cell gave him the warning the noises should have given him, if he hadn't been blocking them so hard.

They had just taken the door off its hinges.

Kit closed the threshold and returned his attention to the knot, hoping it truly had loosened and that it wasn't just hope itself perfidiously misleading him.

'Crispin,' said a soft voice from the doorway. 'My curly-haired prince. Welcome home, sweet boy.'

He couldn't help himself. He started to glance over his shoulder. He looked straight back at the knot. It was looser, it *was*.

'You left me a boy and have returned to me a man.'

Part of him turned from ice to water to hear the crooning tones of Deacon Jeremy Fairweather, but a voice that sounded exactly like Sir Kingsford Locke said *What utter twaddle* in his head and it steadied him like only the sight of the Locke twins storming in could have.

They would not come storming in. They would know the knife was gone by now. They would think he'd stolen it. He *had* stolen it.

'I've missed you, Crispin,' Fairweather went on. 'I turned back as soon as I got the message about the theft. I knew it was you. Almost nine years to the day since we were last in this position together. The world has not been kind to you, has it, my dear boy? You look tired.'

The knot was looser, God damn it all to the darkest depths of the circle of damnation into which Fairweather would be dragged kicking and screaming by the very demons that lived in his soul. There wasn't a pit there deep enough for him.

'Crispin, my dear, why work so hard? You know I don't want to hurt you. You know I've never wanted to hurt you. I'm happy you've come back to me, sweet.'

Again, Kit flicked him a glance. Again, he made himself look away, back to the knot. In his head, something was rising like floodwater, surging further and faster every time Fairweather called him Crispin, and Christopher was screaming in his cage.

Kit never screamed. Screaming didn't help.

The knot came loose.

Kit didn't believe his own eyes. He stayed motionless, staring up at his wrist. Then he wriggled it, and the rope gave, and he slipped his hand free, accidentally banging the stub of his little finger on the wood of the whipping frame and giving himself a sickening jolt of pain that there was no time for Christopher to swallow for him.

He rolled his shoulder and then reached up again to work on the knots around his left wrist. He was sick, with fear, with the extension of his Art into uncharted territory, with the blow to his head that had brought him down, with the sound of the deacon's softly crawling voice.

'Look how far your little Art has come along. I didn't put iron on you because I thought the rope would be enough.'

Kit tore his fingernails digging into the rough knots but he got one loose and was able to wriggle his other hand free too. He rested his forehead against the frame as he rubbed at his wrists and rolled his shoulders. Then he bent and untied his ankles.

'How long can you hold this barricade in place, I wonder?'

Kit finally turned around and looked properly at Deacon Fairweather, the man who had turned Christopher into a gibbering wreck inside Kit's cold, disciplined mind. The man who had created tidal stirrings in the ocean of rage that Kit had never guessed he held until the copper knife had cracked the immense seawall holding it back.

He was closer, much closer, too much closer, than he'd been when Kit had spotted him across the square and fled in blind terror. Kit could see his face properly. He looked more aged than nine years would account for, hard lines around his full mouth, shadows under his pale eyes. He was still small, stooped, humble, harmless, wanting nothing but the best for the souls under his care.

He smiled as Kit's eyes met his own, and Kit saw not one whit of guilt or understanding in them.

'I hoped my commission on Varley's knife would draw you out,' he said. 'Well. I hoped to get the knife. But I was willing to trade one for the other. I was looking to make trouble for the bishop, and curious about this artefact he took so much trouble to secure. But *you*. It's been such a long time, Crispin. I've missed you.'

'Yes,' Kit said softly. 'So you said.'

Every inch of him wanted to recoil away, but he made himself walk forwards until he was just on the other side of his invisible barrier from the deacon.

The deacon pressed a finger to the barricade, watching him with bright butcherbird eyes. 'Does a wall made of Art keep Art out, I wonder?'

Fairweather himself was not an Artisan. No doubt the Orphanage kept Artisans on a string. They would have to wait, staring at each other, while one was summoned.

'Good question,' whispered Kit. 'Try it.'

He watched the smile curve Fairweather's dry lips.

Alcohol powered Art. Desire powered Art. And so did fear.

Kit let Christopher out to play.

His hand smacked the frame of the doorway. Terror-fuelled Art surged through him and he practically leapt through the threshold, landing in another cell somewhere else in the dungeon.

This cell was also occupied.

'Oh,' Kit said. 'Hello.'

He automatically went to straighten his coat, his hands still shaking from the fear he'd allowed loose, and discovered again that he was wearing a thin white robe, naked by any decent standard of the day, and that his little finger had recently been cut off.

Four-fifths of the Myriad, chained with silver-latticed iron manacles to the walls, looked back at him.

Well, of course. Reuben had been unencumbered when he'd come after the knife. He'd used Fairweather's men to restrain his walking consciences so he could carry out his plans unimpeded. Any Artisan could be taken down if they were surrounded in their sleep and disempowered with iron and silver. That told Kit, more than Fairweather's words, that Reuben had got away with the knife.

Cecelia was the first to recover from the surprise. 'Hello, Mr Kit. Did they get you, too?'

'Are Alex and Lulu here?' That was Genevieve. She was looking less than immaculate, her blond hair coming loose from its plait, her dress stained and torn, her icy eyes wild.

'Why didn't they put iron on you?' Fletcher demanded.

Kit smiled at him innocently and said, 'Does iron stop you? You need to work harder.'

Oliver rumbled, 'Let us out?' over Fletcher's outrage.

'I'm having a bit of a day right now, Oliver,' Kit told him. 'Maybe later.'

They were all Reuben's allies, unwitting or not. If he could have freed just Oliver and Cecelia, he might have, but he didn't put it past them not to force him to release the other two, and he didn't trust them at all, especially Fletcher.

He reached a trembling hand to the threshold of the cell door behind him.

'Wait!' Genevieve said. She sounded desperate. 'Reuben's not in here with us and he's not answering when we call. Please check the other cells, make sure he's not hurt?'

Kit stared at her. Her husband, he reminded himself. She didn't know he was a violent, treacherous snake. 'The other cells are empty,' he said. 'Sorry.'

He crossed the threshold, picturing generic egress, and this time came out through an archway into a carved-out room with shelves of stone that held dust and bones. The only light came from torches in sconces on the walls, casting a deep red on the walls, the Gothic touch they seemed to enjoy here.

Ah. The dungeon had been created in the crypts under the old church.

He was turning to follow the flickering flames of the lit torches threshold by threshold when a swirl of air warned him someone was rushing up on him out of the shadows. He lurched sideways, dodging and dashing for the threshold at the same time, but there'd been two of them and he was tackled to the ground by the second one.

Two of them, but not the Locke twins. Fairweather's men, in black uniforms, and for all Kit knew the same ones who had got the bag over his head back at the inn and then hit him hard enough to send him to oblivion. They smelled the same, of stale sweat and something heavy and sour.

One knelt atop him, crushing the air out of him. The other held a thin spiked rod, threaded on both ends, about as long as a nail and the thickness of one of Mrs Knight's knitting needles when she was knitting up a blanket. Kit knew from seeing similar spikes that it was iron infused with silver. The guards looked to Fairweather, who had glided out of the prison alcove.

At this point, it finally occurred to Kit that he might need to do the unthinkable and seek help. He tried to reach out with his Art, intending to open the manacles and the door holding the Myriad. But he was performing a delicate balancing act, using Christopher's fear for power without letting it overwhelm him, and the five seconds it took to wrestle it into use was a few seconds too long.

'You're right-handed, aren't you, Crispin?' Fairweather asked genially.

The guard hammered the spiked rod through the palm of Kit's right hand with a single sharp tap. He did not scream, but it was a close-run thing. The guard screwed on the rounded caps that would keep the iron from being pulled out of his flesh. The caps were fiddly; he cursed under his breath as he stripped off one black leather glove and squinted close to do the job, yanking without thought on Kit's tender flesh.

When the hitching of Kit's breath had smoothed out, he found Fairweather leaning over him, stroking his wild and sweaty hair, his guards impassively waiting.

"This is for your own good. If you insist on running, we have to put iron where you can't get it out.'

'I understand.' He had got the turmoil inside himself under control now but could not make his voice any louder than a rasping whisper.

'I regret the need to hurt you. I'll make the pain go away, Crispin.'

'I know.'

At a nod from Fairweather, the guards pulled Kit to his feet. He walked between them. Fairweather was just behind him. Kit could feel his hot breath on the back of his neck. They climbed the stone steps out of the crypt, entering the hall through a small side apse where a shrine to one of the obscurer saints once would have stood. There, they turned in the opposite direction from the double doors Kit had escaped out the previous evening, taking him through to the private spaces where the living quarters were.

Kit recognised the suite the guards delivered him to. While Fairweather dismissed his men, Kit walked through the small parlour and looked again at the tapestry on the bedroom wall. It depicted a scene from the life of a saint. Saint Crispin's life, the moment when he and his brother had been thrown into the river with millstones around their necks.

Suppressing a shudder, he forced his gaze away and hurried to look behind the tapestry. The secret escape tunnel had been bricked up, the mortar still fresh and pungent. It was no longer a threshold. His mind would not be forced to accept that it was still one behind the bricks, not with iron burning in his palm, and not without it either.

Kit would not, *would not*, give Fairweather the satisfaction of hearing him swear. He came out from behind the tapestry, face carefully neutral.

The deacon met him in the doorway. He was holding a cup of dark liquid. The sick-sweet smell of poppy syrup with its bitter undertones mixed with a gust of frankincense from Fairweather's robes. Kit swallowed bile.

'Show me your hand, sweet boy. I'll take care of you.'

Kit compliantly held out his throbbing hand.

The only way to get the iron rod out of his palm was to unscrew one of the delicate caps. Without help, that meant unscrewing one cap with the fingers of the non-dominant hand while keeping the other cap steady with one's teeth. It meant holding sensitive finger pads and lips to hot iron for as long as it took to achieve the slow and difficult task of undoing the small and fiddly cap. Most Artisans couldn't do it. And, of course, wearing silver-infused iron, they couldn't use their Art to do it either.

That was why Varley had come up with this method to hold the ones who were good at getting out of cages, before they were vanished to the mountain.

Kit could unlock an iron lock, even when he was wearing iron. He could probably open an iron door without touching it. He could even cross a threshold made of iron, if only for a very short distance.

But he could not, no matter how hard he'd tried, and he *had* tried, cross a threshold when he was carrying iron.

Fairweather stroked his thumb around the bar through Kit's palm. 'I'll make you feel good, Crispin,' he crooned. He raised Kit's hand to his soft mouth and kissed the pierced skin, tonguing the iron. Then he held out the cup. 'Drink, sweet boy. Drink deep.'

And Kit made a series of very rapid discoveries.

He discovered that he didn't overly much feel anger because it drained straight into the ocean of rage inside him.

He discovered the wall holding the ocean back, cracked by the copper knife and weakened every time Fairweather called him Crispin, was no longer capable of resisting the weight of it.

He discovered that the only reason he'd never been able to use anger to power his Art was because some part of him, likely the part he called Christopher, had been too afraid of what might happen if he did.

The part of him he might as well call Crispin wasn't afraid at all.

That part of him slapped the cup from Fairweather's hand so the thick dark liquid splattered the whitewashed wall. He whirled away and raised his hand to slam his palm against the wall.

Kit only just stopped himself in time. He'd seen a desperate orphan Artisan try this once; it was not sufficient force to drive the cap all the way through the palm, and yanking it the rest of the way out was not just agonising but liable to cause permanent and extensive damage to the hand, worth doing only if you were expecting to die if you didn't. Apparently Crispin had seen the technique but not paid attention to the result.

Crispin then tried to cross the threshold. Powered by rage so deep it was fathomless and far vaster even than the power granted by the standing stones, he managed to get from the door of the bedchamber to the door of the suite. Kit fell out of the threshold into the corridor, gagging, the iron lighting up the nerves in his whole hand and halfway up his arm before Christopher stirred and took it.

Wait, Crispin, let me open the caps, he thought, desperately trying to wrestle his Art under control.

Unscrew, not open, Crispin howled. Kit lunged upwards towards the doorway on the other side of the corridor. He barrelled into one of the black-clad guards. The man's ham-like hand wrapped around his upper arm and Kit darted his head down and bit him as hard as he could.

The guard, screaming a violent word, backhanded him to the ground, but that gave him the freedom to touch the next door, pushing himself a little towards it with his bare feet, and he was gone, spilling out a solid twenty feet down the corridor.

This time, he actually did vomit, hunched over on his knees as the guard, still swearing, ran towards him, pulling from his belt a truncheon that glowed on one end and started spitting sparks when he raised it.

Something clicked in Kit's head, and then he had scrambled up and was running, Crispin and Christopher working in concert, one powering their escape even through the iron, the other swallowing the growing agony of it. They made short traverses from doorway to doorway, no idea of direction, no idea of destination, no idea of any plan but getting away.

Eventually he had to stop running. He could not get enough air. He was moaning in terror and cursing in rage. Kit thought, *Christopher. Crispin. Five seconds. Five. Four. Three. Two. One. Stop.*

But this time the storm didn't stop. Kit slapped himself smartly, once on each cheek, and used the shock of it to push the terrified boy into his cage and the enraged boy behind his cracking wall, fighting him all the way.

Kit, whole in his mind again, looked around, taking stock.

He'd gone deeper into the mountain, of course, automatically following the path he had taken once before. That was his stupid sense of direction, screwing him over again. Ahead lay the vaults, but he certainly did not want to dead-end himself in there. Behind was a growing ruckus, shouts and clangs, guards gathering, he assumed. Ahead he could hear other guards begin to call out too in response.

Kit came to the corridor heading off perpendicular to the main artery that he had passed last time he'd come this way. This time he took it. It was dim, with only a few sconces of wax candles lit, but the way was clear enough, with doors every few feet. He hoped to find another hallway at right angles to this one, to take him back towards the old church. But there were no deviations.

He took a candle from a sconce and tried a door. It opened into a storage room, full of the holy, if not popish, paraphernalia of ritual: robes and chalices and arks and altar cloths and censors and brass crosiers and great iron candelabra, gleaming in the thin spill of light from the candle he held in a hand that shook.

'Body and blood, bread and wine,' he muttered. 'Transmutation Art.'

He glued the candle down to a table with wax and left-handedly opened a few cupboards, hoping for dusty bottles of sacramental wine so that he could power his Art without risking the confusing and insistent clamour inside him.

But his hasty search turned up nothing. He paused to try to focus his Art to open the caps off the iron rod and get it out of his right palm, but— *unscrew*, whispered Crispin, *not open*—it'd take just as long to twist his frantically flickering Art into a usable shape as it would to brave the iron and unscrew the cap manually.

Kit could see the skittering light of torches or lanterns growing in the corridor behind him. They had somehow guessed he had turned down this way, possibly because they'd met the guards coming from further in without encountering him. He went on, opening doors into a few more chambers as he went, to no greater avail.

Ahead he could sense the fresher air or reduced pressure that denoted a greater space, but no greater light; whatever was ahead was not a way out. There was one last door, which he opened, more out of thoroughness than any hope.

It was not a storeroom. It smelt like a barn that had not been cleaned for a long time.

He fetched another candle and raised it to see a long room lined with iron cages. The bars were inset with silver.

Most were empty, but three were occupied. Kit looked in and saw, first, the stark white face of the pain Artisan. In the cage beside him, the lightning Artisan, sitting hunched in the middle of their cage.

Kit catalogued a litany of odd facts.

The Bristol enforcers would have had their hands full escorting the Artisans who had attacked him in Lovelly to London.

And yet enforcers had been available to arrest the lightning Artisan at the Bristol city docks and the pain Artisan at Northfield.

Those enforcers wore black uniforms and carried glowing truncheons to subdue Artisans.

And yet when Kit had left London, enforcers had no such uniform and no such technology. But it appeared that Fairweather's guards did.

When the Bristol enforcers had been called on to retrieve these Artisans, it was Orphanage men, dressed in black and carrying those sparky truncheons, who had come for them instead.

In the third cage stood an unfamiliar girl. She wore a thin white robe just like his own, though filthy, while the other two were in ragged trousers and shirts, no coats, and no cloaks like they'd worn when they'd come after him.

'Who are you?' he asked them.

'You know,' said the pain Artisan. 'Don't you remember me, Christopher?'

At this, Kit came closer to the cage, not without a wary look over his shoulder. He did not have much time, but he did have some. He had thought the pain Artisan looked familiar and at being greeted by name, he stared at the prominent bones of his face until a vague memory surfaced.

'Michael?' he said.

Whispers in the dark between the Essex branch orphans said that Michael's Art had come on while he was strapped to the whipping frame, that he had used it to fight back. He'd been vanished to the mountain like the handful of other orphans who'd manifested Art while Kit was resident there.

'Varley *is* collecting an army of Artisans?' Kit said. He looked around at the other empty cages. 'I know Artisans are rare but I'm sure more of us were sent here, from the Essex branch alone.'

'Most die.' The lightning Artisan didn't look up. 'We're the strongest. We survived the training.'

Michael pressed closer to the bars, flinching away when his bare skin accidentally touched the iron. 'He breaks us so we serve him. Not many of us break in the right way.'

Kit nodded. Michael had certainly served the bishop when he'd lit Kit on fire with pain back at Northfield. They hadn't really been friends at the Orphanage. No one had really been friends at the Orphanage. It was only a small betrayal.

'There used to be more of us,' Michael went on, 'but then Varley found the copper knife. It drinks Art.'

'It drinks blood,' Kit said.

'It feeds on blood, but it drinks Art. Varley sacrificed us one by one, trying to take the devil from us. He wants to cure us.'

Kit wondered if it could be true that the knife had that power, or if that was just the artefact itself insidiously driving Varley to feed it by playing on his greatest fears and desires. It had whispered to Kit of safety, when he had held it.

'It killed us every time,' the lightning Artisan intoned.

'I'm next,' said the girl. She raised her hand and showed him a rainbow arching out of the palm of her hand.

'Oh,' he said. He'd been followed by rainbows since Bristol, and she had set them on him. 'That's a pretty weather Art.'

'It's a fairly useless one, except for marking targets,' she said. Like the other two, she spoke in the flat tones of the hopeless. 'That's why I'm next.'

She plucked at her filthy robe.

The lightning Artisan rose to their feet. 'Careful,' they said. 'You're wearing the sacrificial robe right now. He decided you were the least useful and put it on you.'

Kit tugged at the fabric. He stood before the rainbow Artisan's cage. 'Will you stop the rainbow from following me, please?'

'Will you let us out?' she said.

He started to back away again. He did have pity for them. He just didn't dare let them out, because they had obeyed Varley's order with every appearance of freedom back in Bristol and Northfield, and he couldn't trust that they wouldn't do so again. They were chained in their souls to the bishop's will.

'I don't think I can,' he admitted. 'You can't guarantee me you won't immediately do as Varley wants and kill me, even if you don't want to.'

'Not him.' The lightning Artisan stared at him with dead eyes, and then turned their back.

'Then my pretty rainbows will lead your enemies to you until the end of your days,' the girl said.

That gave Kit pause. She could be bluffing; many embedded Arts ran out after a time. On the other hand, hers had already lasted a few days. The end of his days would probably come before the end of her Art at that rate, so her threat was plausible enough.

'I stole the knife,' he pointed out. 'That's why he hasn't tried to cure you yet. That's why you're still alive.'

She shrugged, unmoved. 'Varley went away months ago. He's hiding.'

Kit bowed his apologies and backed away from the cages, back to the door. He leant out. The light back the way he had come was stronger and strengthening as the guards came closer. Their pursuit had been slowed by having to check every storeroom, but now he was truly out of time.

He turned back. 'Rainbows are light refraction.'

The Artisan looked at him blankly.

'If you refract light away from yourself, you'll be invisible.' There was that handy subscription library habit again. 'Bend the light away,' he added when her expression didn't change.

She showed no sign of understanding—what kind of education could any of them have had, locked away in the mountain and tortured into slavery—and he left them there and went on.

The hallway opened out into a cavern and ended at a cliff, a low iron railing marking it.

Kit stood on the edge of the cliff and looked around. He was on a sort of platform, half marbled, half bare rock. It held only an altar, dark-stained. The cavern was not huge; it was more an opening-up of the natural tunnel. But there was nowhere to climb to, up or down.

He looked over the edge again. Down at the floor below, there were dark patches and mounds, indistinct in the poor light, but he could guess what they were. This was a sacrificial ground; Varley might have thought it an apt place to try his cures but the knife had sought only sacrifice.

He hadn't fled. He'd been herded. He'd been herded to a sacrificial site.

Christopher panicked and Kit's mind went blank.

It may have only lasted a few minutes, but it had been long enough. Fairweather stepped out onto the platform, turning carefully to set a lantern, much more sensible than the flaming torches, onto a hook on the wall. Behind him, still in the shadows of the hallway, were a great many bodies. Kit had the feeling there would be guards at every threshold back along the way he had come.

Again, Kit counted five seconds down for Christopher. Again, it failed to calm the terrified adolescent boy, lost in fear for all those years, drowning now in Crispin's unchecked fury.

Kit didn't slap himself this time. He was thinking about Alex, gently holding him as he trembled in the alley after he'd fled from Fairweather in the square. No judgement. No false reassurance. Just patient comfort.

Christopher, Kit told himself. *I'm sorry I left you behind in the dark. I will never let him have you. We're going to get out of this but I need you to help me. Trust me.*

His breathing slowed. He felt the tentacles of Christopher's terror loosen. He turned his attention to Crispin, whose rage he would need, to cross the threshold with iron still piercing his palm.

Just a little, he told himself. *Please. Don't flood me. I won't let your head go under the water again, but I need you to help me. Trust me.*

He linked his hands in front of him, gave Fairweather his wide-eyed innocent look, and began to build an Artwork on the threshold just behind him.

The edge of the cliff, with its marble paving and its low iron railing, enough to make it manmade.

It hadn't worked in the summer pavilion back in Lovelly, when he tried to use the edge of the stage. But he'd been tired then, and over-extended on his Art, and rushed. Now he had Art sloshing through him thanks to Christopher's restrained fear, Crispin's checked rage.

He also had all the time in the world, because Fairweather liked, very much, to gloat.

'Oh, Crispin, why must you run from me?' Fairweather strolled closer. 'My sweet boy, don't be frightened. Varley's time is over. You'll be glad to hear that. All those times he made me beat you, and I never wanted to. You know that. You know I just wanted you to feel good.'

Kit watched him. He could feel the Artwork coagulating even around the hole made by the iron, the threshold trying to open, reaching out to find its other end, the other side of the wide gap in the tunnel, marked by another low railing. He could feel the iron fighting him, and Christopher taking the burn, and Crispin trampling all over everything with undisciplined mayhem. Kit, heedless in his extremity of the promises he had made, wrestled him into service.

'Varley took fright in the end,' Fairweather told him. 'Locked the knife away, killed the Artisan who did it for him, and ran away. He thinks someone's coming for him. Guilty conscience. All those dead Artisan children. I broke them to the traces and he threw them away on that cursed knife.'

Kit frowned, and then he understood. Varley had only ever been trying to cure the children. He'd been beating them, and murdering them, but he really had been trying to cure them too. *Not him*, the lightning Artisan had said when Kit had said they would do Varley's bidding if he let them out.

It was Fairweather who had broken the Orphanage Artisans to his will. Fairweather who had sponsored the commission on the knife, that had provoked Varley to set the assassination bounty on Kit from wherever he was hidden. And Fairweather who had deployed his secret army to intercept Kit when the first wave of assassins had failed.

Fairweather wanted Kit dead.

Fear and rage swirled around him. He tamped them down, tamped them down. They had put their trust in him and he was in control of them now. He built the Artwork.

He asked, 'Why do I need to die?'

'I never wanted to hurt you, sweet,' Fairweather said. 'But my path is with the cardinals. I must remove Varley to get there. He's standing in my way. And he's the only one who knows how you tempted me into sin and perversion in Essex.'

'It was your sin,' Kit said, as rage surged into a tidal wave. He smelt the sweet and bitter poppy syrup concoction.

He diverted the rage into the Artwork. It was going to have to stretch a long way and it was going to have to shape itself around iron, the iron in his hand and the iron in the railings at each edge, to do it. It was going to be the strongest Artwork he had ever made.

'I couldn't resist you.'

Shame was rising now, too, poking more holes into his Artwork, undermining it. Alex hadn't been able to resist him either. What sickness was in him that weakened strong men?

He heard Alex's low, fierce, warm voice. *He made his own choices and he put them on a scared boy.*

'It was your sin,' he repeated, stronger. 'Never mine.' He steadied; the Artwork steadied; his Art ran strong and true.

Fairweather shook his head, gently reproving. 'I can't have Varley trotting you out to discredit me. I knew he'd want to protect the knife more than he wanted to find you alive and take your testimony. The course of action is obvious. You understand, don't you, my sweet Crispin?'

'Yes,' Kit said. 'I understand.'

He quietly, quietly, reached out a tendril of his Art and unlocked three cages.

'I know how good you like to be for me,' Fairweather whispered, and reached a hand towards Kit's face. Kit went rigid, but only his eyes moved, watching those thick fingers curling to caress his cheek. 'One last time, Crispin, my beautiful boy.'

Kit smiled. 'I understand you're having a petty argument with a rival who knows your dirty secret and you've decided to murder me on the off-chance it occurs to him to use me against you.'

Fairweather's eyes widened in surprise and the encroaching hand closed to a fist.

Kit stepped backwards, toppling over the railing and off the cliff.

20

KIT REALISED HIS MISTAKE AS SOON as he'd made it.

If he went *in* a door, he came *out* a door. Presumably, then, if he stepped *off* an edge, he would step *on* to an edge on the other side of the threshold.

But he'd gone off the edge by toppling backwards and so now as he came out the other side, he was facing the wrong way and falling.

This was not a good situation for a man with a poor sense of balance and a poorer sense of direction.

His eyes closed and his legs kicked out, both without his volition. The iron in his palm burned white-hot. He felt the scrape of rock, a rush of air, a sense of dizzying space; he tilted, arms windmilling, no notion of which direction was safe to fall towards. His stomach lurched up as he began to drop, and then lurched down as he jerked to an abrupt halt in what decidedly felt like mid-air.

Someone pulled him to solid ground, his back scraping over the top of the railing on the far side of the crevasse before he thumped to the stone of the tunnel. Kit opened his eyes and looked up at an ashen Alexander Locke, standing slumped against the railing.

'Do you have impeccable timing or what?' he burst out.

Then he rolled onto his stomach and vomited bile. He was weak in every limb, at the very end of his strength. That had been a mighty Artwork. He wouldn't be crossing any more thresholds till he got the iron out of him and some food into him.

He sat back on his haunches, wiping his mouth with his shaking left hand, holding his right hand protectively to his chest. Alex was upright now, holding his shoulder, eyes winced half-shut. He must have had to grab Kit from his fall one-handed and the jerk of Kit's body weight had done something bad to his shoulder, maybe dislocated it. He looked down at Kit silently.

'Oh, no,' Kit breathed. 'Did I hurt you?'

'I'll get over it,' Alex said quietly.

Kit looked at him and then, distracted, looked across the cavern. He saw flickering torches and the white-clad figure of Fairweather, guards surrounding him. He'd been hoping to see the guards falling to lightning strikes, Fairweather writhing on the ground in agony. The Artisans were either escaping in the other direction or still hunched helplessly in their cages, too broken to run.

Fairweather wanted him dead.

'Can you make a pistol shot from here?' he asked.

Alex considered the distance and then shook his head. He rolled his shoulder and winced again.

Kit had already regretted the question. 'That's probably for the best, I suppose,' he admitted. 'How did you get here?'

Alex held down his left hand. Kit awkwardly slotted his own left hand into it and let Alex get him on his feet. 'Lulu and I broke in through that secret entrance.'

Kit's teeth clenched at that. The size of the two of them, the claustrophobia of that tunnel... He managed to say, calmly, 'That entrance was bricked up at my end.'

'It had side tunnels. Lulu was tracking you. You left a handkerchief behind. We tried to follow the side tunnels whenever they roughly led your way. We fell out into this main tunnel a few minutes ago and saw the lights.'

Kit looked past Alex and saw Lulu standing sentinel down a smaller rough-hewn tunnel. He nodded to her and she stared coldly back.

'Did you leave Edith behind again?' he asked, with a clutch of fear. It would be a logical move for Fairweather to go back to where his men had caught Kit the first time to take his friends as collateral. Kit turned towards the tunnel, still absently cradling his right hand to his chest. 'We can't let Fairweather take her.'

Lulu caught Kit's arm; he was hard-pressed to stop himself instinctively biting to get free. 'The knife?'

'Oh, you think I took it?' he said. That much was clear from her accusing tone. He felt his stomach drop in roiling disappointment. They had come after him to get the knife back, not to save him. Of course. 'I mean, I did, but—'

It hit him like a train under full steam.

He could tell the Locke twins that Reuben had taken the knife. He thought, despite their current suspicions of him, that they'd believe him, given their antipathy towards Reuben and Alex's newfound trust in Kit. He thought Alexander Locke was cockstruck enough, and certainly soft-hearted enough, to let Kit waltz him up and down the garden path a time or two.

But Reuben McAvey was Genevieve's husband and Genevieve was Ginnie, the cousin who had sheltered Lulu in London when her family had turned their back on her.

If Kit was in Lulu's place, and knew Reuben had taken the knife but didn't know Ginnie was still in Gallentry, he'd go like a shot for the McAveys' London home. Reuben wouldn't be there and Kit very much doubted that any possession he'd left there would be of enough significance to him to let Lulu track him. Kit would bet that he, like Kit, would be happy to abandon every last remnant of his life, down to and including his wife and unborn child.

But if Lulu was fast and lucky, she'd get hold of something he'd worn just before the Myriad had left London and that would be enough.

She and Alex would track Reuben down, and then Reuben would turn the air in their lungs to ice and kill them both in agonising, gasping, choking terror.

Or they would heed Kit's warning and show some caution for once in their benighted lives. They'd ambush Reuben and get the knife off him by any means necessary.

And that would be worse.

The knife screamed for blood and Lulu and her dreams of vengeance would feed it. But it wouldn't stop at Varley. Kit had felt the depth of its hunger for the few moments he had touched it. It would demand a tithe of heart's blood from every person who had ever crossed Lulu.

Both her brothers.

Edith Knight.

Kit himself.

Anyone she decided had known what was going to happen to her husband.

Perhaps not her cousin Ginnie, who had taken her in when her family had turned her out. But perhaps Genevieve of the Myriad, who had married Reuben with his contemptuously casual cruelty towards her.

Fletcher of the Myriad, for laughing at Reuben's casual cruelty.

The rest of the Myriad, for not speaking up loudly enough against that casual cruelty.

Every person who looked at her a little too long when they walked into a coaching inn or a tavern or a coffee house. Who looked too long at the broadness of her shoulders or the size of her hands or the strength in the lines of her androgynous face.

Every person who had shown horror with violent action or vicious words about unnatural habits or abominations against nature.

Every person who whispered behind their hands.

Every person who refused to meet her eye, refused to greet her or even to acknowledge her.

Kit had held the hungry copper knife and he knew, *knew*, to his very bones that it would find its perfect partner in angry, grieving Lucinda Llewellyn and it would drive her onwards until she had wreaked devastation upon all she loved and well beyond that small circle, or until Agency Artisans brought her down in mutual destruction, or both.

She could not be allowed to touch the knife, and therefore *they could not know* that Reuben had taken it. They could not even be given a chance to guess the truth.

They also could not know that the rest of the Myriad was imprisoned in the dungeon; if Reuben had left worn clothes behind, Genevieve would almost certainly insist on handing them over to Lulu to innocently track down her missing husband.

His only chance was to divert the Locke twins long enough that any items Reuben had worn had faded too much or already been laundered by the time Genevieve managed to connect with them to ask for Lulu's help.

Lulu had to be kept from that knife at any cost.

At *any* cost.

Kit said, 'Yes, I stole the knife.'

21

IT WAS AWKWARD TO CRAWL ALONG the low tunnels without the use of his right hand. Kit tucked it tight against the white robes and scrambled along as best he could, Lulu in front of him, Alex behind, both sharply professional with each other and ignoring him. Kit did not complain about the scrabble; after all, Alex was himself struggling with his injured shoulder.

In his thin and dirty white robe, it had been obvious Kit was not carrying the knife on him even in the dim light of the cavern. Lulu had asked him bluntly if it was back in the vault.

He had said no and when she'd started to demand more, Alex had said, 'Then let's get out, Lulu, and find out more then,' and they had gone.

By the time the three of them had crawled their way back out of the tunnels—Lulu led them astray twice which was not conducive to Kit keeping his claustrophobia under wraps—he was exhausted. He stood at the cave lip and looked down, and wondered how he was going to get to the ground.

Day had dawned while he'd been trapped with Fairweather. It was perhaps mid-morning on a fine, cold day. The wind played with his curls and he took a deep breath of fresh air. He saw that the rainbow still lingered above him, thin in the bright sunlight, and that more glinted in the moisture on the damp grey rocks beside them.

'Is that blood on your clothes?' Alex asked him.

The question was brusque, with no overt concern. Alex was holding his body stiff and keeping his tone neutral; the bounty hunter, the enforcer, doing a job. He had snapped into this mode as soon as Kit had admitted to stealing the knife. Kit supposed he should feel resentful that Alex had so quickly believed him. But then, they had both obviously already been thinking it.

Because he was a thief. That was all he ever was to them. To Alex. The pissant little thief, the wanton little bit.

But he could not resent getting exactly what he wanted, could he?

At Alex's question, he looked down at himself. The white robe was torn and dirty, but the scarlet marks of fresh blood daubed all over his front were now clearly visible in the daylight in a way they hadn't been in the darkness of the tunnels.

'My hand is bleeding a little,' he said. He flexed his remaining fingers, straightening them from their protective curl against his chest. 'It's fine.'

But Alex's eyes had been snared by the cap on the back of his hand, the smear of blood there, or the number of fingers. He turned Kit's wrist, carefully avoiding the scrapes left by the ropes, and found the cap on the palm, the entry wound still bleeding, the skin red and inflamed all about it. His fingers traced the gap where Kit's little finger had been and the grazes on his wrist.

He set a finger on the cap. 'Iron.'

'Enforcers haven't caught on to this trick yet?' Kit pulled his hand away.

It was throbbing, but when he pushed the pain towards Christopher, a habitual move, Christopher spat it back at him. Kit clutched his hand back to his chest, confused and a touch outraged.

Lulu turned from securing ropes and rolling them out down the rockface of the ridge. 'Leave it in,' she said. 'And don't feed him.'

She took to a rope, lowering herself hand over hand. Alex shook his head. He tied a rope around Kit's waist and then his own, and helped Kit climb down, Alex avoiding his right shoulder, Kit his right hand. He locked his right elbow around the rope instead and used his left hand and footholds to support himself.

It was hard and Kit slipped twice, saved from the fall by the rope between him and Alex. He was shaky on his feet by the time he made it to the ground, with more rope burns on his left palm, right elbow crook, and both calves where he'd wrapped the rope around his legs, the thin robe riding up. They were all covered in dust and scratches.

Alex leaned over him, not touching. 'Can you manage?' The question had more the tone of *We expect you to manage.*

'Yes, Mr Locke,' Kit whispered.

His body felt limp, and his Art lay quiescent, as did the parts of himself he had made the mistake of naming. The only effort he was exerting now was to present white blankness to Alex in lieu of real intentions, so that Alex would not have a chance of sensing his desire to keep Lulu from the knife. He didn't even dare try to push the pain of his hand onto Christopher again. He felt mutiny brewing there.

As Lulu led the way through the fields back to the town square, however, Kit tried to draw up enough Art to unscrew—*open, open, damn you*—the caps on the iron spike.

But as soon as he touched his Art, both Christopher and Crispin awakened and roiled and wrestled inside his head. He had made them promises he had almost immediately broken, and so now that the crisis was over, even compliant Christopher was fighting him and Crispin had all the world-ending wrath of a thwarted adolescent.

Really shouldn't have named them.

Kit was deeply embroiled in forcing them back into service to power his weakened Art when he was jolted back to awareness by a clip to the side of his head. He stumbled as he awkwardly raised his left hand to his throbbing right ear. Alex, behind, steadied him with one hand to his elbow.

'I asked you a question,' Lulu snarled at him, fist still raised.

'Please repeat it, Miss Lucinda,' he said.

'*Who did you give the knife to?*'

Kit kept giving her a hazy, distracted look while he weighed his options. He needed to keep the Locke twins away from Genevieve and the McAvey townhouse; he needed them to give up on retrieving the knife; he needed them to focus now only on taking Kit to the Agency in London, Alex's plan.

Which parts of the last few days to twist, which to deny, which to preserve? It would be easiest to hold close to the truth, and provide an account of Fairweather's plot while erasing Reuben's part in it. But that would likely send Lulu back into the Orphanage headquarters to hunt for the knife, and then they would unearth Genevieve and the hole in the fabric of the story that was Reuben would become prominent. He therefore needed his story to only incidentally feature the Orphanage.

'Answer!' Lulu raised her hand again, and Alex, who had been behind Kit, was suddenly next to him, catching his sister's arm.

'We need him in one piece,' he said. He was still talking in that dispassionate, professional way.

Kit realised he didn't have the time or the stamina to be delicate.

There was a certain amount of relief to be had in burning *everything* down. Crispin practically howled in his head in delight.

'The person who put out the commission on the knife, of course,' Kit said. 'Who do you think?'

The twins checked and he saw a heated glance pass between them.

'Give us a name,' Alex said.

'Commissions to commit crime are anonymous, Mr Locke,' Kit said. 'Obviously.'

He said this last with a contemptuous twist designed to play on Alex's sensitivity about being stupid. *Burn it down*, Crispin whispered. Alex frowned, but the cool mercantile persona stayed in place.

'It had to be one of Varley's rivals,' Lulu decided. She sped up, storming down the rough alleyway that led from the last field to the main square, heading for the front of the Orphanage headquarters.

Balls, balls, balls. 'Not from the way Deacon Fairweather was talking,' Kit said quickly. 'He's the Orphanage man who took custody of me, but he didn't get the knife. My employer was supposed to pay me but he sold me out to Fairweather and got away clear. Fairweather was happy enough with that outcome.'

'Good,' Lulu said. 'You little fuckweasel.'

They came out into the main square and Kit could see the carriage with the familiar Locke crest, with its crossed keys and its pair of leopards, readied with postilion and horses, all set to take them south.

Lulu swore and Alex said, 'Oh, Edith, why?' from behind Kit.

Edith Knight was on the steps of the old church. She was talking not to one of the young guards on duty at the doors, but to Deacon Fairweather, engaged in either an intense conversation or a low-voiced argument. They were surrounded by more black-clad guards.

'Him,' Alex said. 'He's Fairweather.'

'He came back,' Kit said. He let Alex have a real intention. 'Get Edith away from him, please.'

Two of the guards seized Edith. She looked tiny between them. Kit made an involuntary noise and Lulu and Alex shot forwards like cannon fire. Alex, sore shoulder and all, picked up the guards between them and Edith and tossed them down the stairs one by one, moving so fast that none could react in time to defend themselves. Lulu swung past him, punched one of the guards holding Edith and dragged the other off.

By this time, Kit had joined them on the steps. He grabbed Edith's hand and started tugging her out of range, dodging the skittled guards who'd been thrown down and were smart enough to not get back up in a hurry.

'Oh, Kitty!' Edith blurted. 'He sent those guards to impound the carriage. He said we were breaking town ordinances. I never heard of such a thing but I was trying to make sure he couldn't take our escape vehicle away.'

It was a move typical of Fairweather's sly and backhanded tactics. It seemed he'd recognised the Locke family crest painted on the carriage and had been moving against Kit's allies, who he'd known about even before Reuben had sold Kit, because, thanks to the rainbow Artisan, Kit had led the pain Artisan to Northfield, and then Fairweather's pet Artisans had reported back to him.

Kit abruptly regretted opening their cage doors.

'Take the Artisan,' Fairweather ordered.

The guards clustered around him moved forwards with some reluctance, because the Locke twins were standing between them and Kit. Lulu braced for the fight, leaning into it, but Alex stood tall, aloofly calm.

He held up his badge. 'I am the only one here authorised to arrest an Agency-registered Artisan.'

That enforcer badge was like some sort of Art. All the guards froze at the sight of its small and glinting shape in Alex's hand.

Kit met Fairweather's eyes. His men might have been taken aback by the sight of the badge, but Fairweather was terrified. His information had not been current. Alex had only been an enforcer for a week or so, and it obviously hadn't been something Reuben had thought to mention, if their conversations had even gone beyond the most superficial needed to swap the knife for Kit.

A sudden Agency presence in this remote Welsh town meant Fairweather's whole secret Artisan operation was in danger of being found out. He had been worried that Kit would give Varley ammunition against him within the Orphanage hierarchy, and not realised until now that he was also perfectly placed to arm the Agency in its mission to protect Artisans, even young and friendless orphaned Artisans.

Now he was going to have to kill not just Kit, but the Locke twins and Edith as well.

It was very unpleasant to realise how well he knew how Fairweather thought.

Kit almost called out, 'I haven't told them anything!' but the twins would assume he meant about the knife and that would send them storming back into the mountain for sure. Even the thought of Fairweather in a headlock while Lulu slapped him around for information wasn't enough to make Kit do that.

Just as easily as Kit had read the thought in the deacon's eyes, Alex read the intention. He pulled his pistol and pointed it at Fairweather. 'Not wise,' he said. *Give me an excuse*, his tone said. 'I'm on authorised business here.'

He meant arresting Kit, of course. Fairweather would take it differently.

Alex cocked the pistol, frowning, signalling Lulu to get back down the stairs.

'Take him,' Fairweather said in a low voice to his guards as he scuttled out of the way of the pistol's barrel.

They moved in a mass towards Alex, some of them pulling their glowing truncheons. Kit supposed they'd work just as well on normal people as on Artisans.

Alex lowered the pistol from trying to follow Fairweather to aiming at the guards, but he didn't fire. He was a wolf of a man but that made him strategic and willing to fight. It didn't make him aggressive and willing to pointlessly kill. There were too many, too close, for a man with a single pistol to fight them off even if he aimed true and fast every time, and so he chose to save his shot.

Instead, he tossed the pistol down to Lulu, said, 'Get them safe,' and threw himself at the guards, apparently on the theory that surprise was the best part of valour.

Momentarily advantaged by being a single target amid a sea of collegial blockages, he wrestled a truncheon off a guard and deployed it about himself with distinct intemperance, proving conclusively that the zap of the glowing end was effective against everyone, not just Artisans, especially if the truncheon was swung hard enough.

Lulu, without compunction, emptied Alex's pistol into the throng of guards, felling a few of them and gaining space enough to seize hold of Edith and Kit. She began to drag them away, cursing under her breath the entire time.

Kit watched as Alex lost the truncheon and threw a punch that jolted his sore shoulder. He staggered and caught himself, taking a strike from a truncheon on his forearm before hitting back. He wouldn't be on his feet for much longer. As Kit had the thought, guards got hold of Alex's arms and jumped on his back, driving him to his knees.

He shouted, 'Go!' at his sister even as she released her charges and ran back towards the fray.

Kit literally pulled himself together.

It had been disconcerting to have Christopher and Crispin thundering in his head like they were real, independent entities. Ironically enough, he had taken Christopher's compliance, unwilling or not, for granted. He'd always known his scared, lost orphan boy was part of himself. But Crispin's escape from behind the wall had changed the balance of power in his head, and Kit's broken promise to them had not helped him keep control.

Now, however, the feuding parts of his mind snapped into unity with a mutual cry of *Alex!* His roiling emotions vanished, and so did the pain. He was numb all over, in a way he now wondered how he had ever tolerated.

He found the remnants of the Art he'd been searching for.

He held up his damaged right hand, catching Fairweather's eye. He let him see that the iron was still in there, and then he clenched his hand into a fist and pushed out the Artwork.

The doors behind Fairweather flung open, slamming with an echoing crash against the walls. There was a ripple of sound through the hall and into the distance; Kit had opened every door he could reach to. That wasn't many, with his Art almost exhausted and the iron still in him, but the acoustics of the old church made it seem like a multitude.

The brawl had paused at the unexpected noise, and Lulu took the opportunity to lay about her with her boots and drag Alex out of the melee. The twins backed down the stairs, stalked by the few of the guards who weren't lying about and groaning.

'Go,' Alex said again, trying to step in front of Lulu. She was having none of it.

Fairweather looked unimpressed. Kit's Art, after all, was not particularly impressive, like a fireball or ice spears or lightning would have been.

He strolled to the edge of the steps to sneer down at Kit. 'And what did we just achieve, Crispin?' he called.

At which, Crispin pointed out that ribcages were technically manmade and able to be cracked opened.

Kit shushed him. 'I opened every door, deacon,' he called back. 'Front door, cell door'—a lie; he didn't dare let Genevieve out—'*cage* door.'

Fairweather's expression changed, and Kit smiled. Then a sort of swirl in the doorway to the church behind Fairweather caught his eye. He frowned at it; it was like hot air rising over the fields on a summer's day or like the last remnants of a—

'Get off the steps,' he shouted at Alex and Lulu. His tone was urgent enough, or his expression frantic enough, that they both leapt down on the instant.

Just in time. Lightning arced out of nowhere and hit the bright buckles of every one of the guards on the steps, scattering them like fallen leaves in an autumn breeze. The smell of ozone and roasted flesh filled the air.

Kit turned back to Fairweather in time to see his eyes go wide, his mouth wrench open wider. He shrieked in agony, falling to the ground and convulsing there. His finger clawed at the stone as he thrashed and screamed.

The pain Artisan was paying Fairweather back for everything he'd ever inflicted on any of them, and it was damnably satisfying. Kit watched with pleasure even as the Locke twins began to pull him and Edith in retreat across the square towards the carriage.

Then the shimmering air patches cleared and the rainbow Artisan stepped into view, as the invisibility lifted off Michael and the lightning Artisan as well. She held an ordinary carving knife that they must have stolen from the kitchens.

She plunged it unerringly into Fairweather's throat.

22

KIT GASPED; HE COULDN'T HELP IT. In his shock, his own hands came up to cover his throat and he bent over in pain as he hit his injured hand. That had not been what he had wanted. That had never been what he had wanted.

The rogue Artisans looked down and saw him, just as Alex murmured, 'But Bristol took them in, what are they doing here?'

The Artisans came bouncing down the stairs at them. Kit didn't know if they were aiming at him or if they'd heard Alex and been provoked. He straightened and stepped forwards, silently spreading his arms wide, signalling that the three people behind him were not to be touched.

He wasn't sure that was going to do any good. None of this was anything like he had wanted.

Ribcages, Crispin whispered again, and Kit shuddered.

'You were right about bending the light,' the rainbow Artisan said to him. She touched his arm and the rainbow above him vanished.

Then they were past him and heading across the square, the light refracting around them as they went, casting them back into invisibility.

Kit looked at his hands. They weren't clean, of course, not after the clamber through the tunnels. But they were clean of blood, which felt misleading, given Fairweather impaled at the top of the stairs and a lot of struck bodies strewn about and three rogue Artisans escaping southwards.

Lulu dashed past him; he thought she was going to Fairweather's aid, as pointless as that would be. She merely bent over him, eyed the torn-open throat, said, 'Not my knife,' and ran back down.

Alex got an arm around Kit's shoulder. 'Whitely?'

'Remember how you said I do a lot of things not on purpose?' Kit said dazedly.

Alex's arm tightened. Then he was urging Kit across the square, and Lulu was forcefully providing the same service to a shaking Edith.

At the very last moment, as Locke was boosting him into the carriage, Kit had a crisis of conscience. He couldn't leave a pregnant lady locked in a dank dungeon, even if that would help his cause no end.

With the permission of the two unruly residents in his head, he reached out a last small and precise Artwork and unlocked two sets of manacles. There. If Cecelia and Oliver couldn't get the other two free, it wouldn't be his failure. But it should take them long enough that Genevieve wouldn't come storming out of the doors throwing fireballs everywhere and demanding to know where Reuben was, giving away the game.

The carriage door closed behind them and the horses set off southwards on the main road out of town; Kit knelt on the floor where he had fallen in his hasty entrance and thought, *Safe, safe, safe.*

He had had a very long day and the sun wasn't even at its zenith yet. He closed his eyes and started to collapse against the upholstery. The pain came back as his two rioters withdrew their support.

Edith leaned down to hug him, reminding him that the day's dance was not over yet. 'That was horrible. Are you all right, Kitty, are you all right, oh, I'm so glad to see you.'

Before Kit could whisper anything in her ear—*Play along, play along, Edie*—Lulu had pulled her away.

Kit clambered onto the seat next to Alex and tucked his right arm into his armpit, mourning Christopher's obstinate refusal to eat the pain for him. He wasn't used to feeling anything beyond the occasional flash of discomfort anymore. He also wasn't used to feeling like he had actual people in his head.

'Right,' Alex said. 'We're headed for London, Lulu, and my plan. Is that what you want?'

'First thing,' Lulu said. 'Let's get that shoulder strapped up, Lexi. And I've got the laudanum Nurse left for me, too.'

'Let's deal with Kit's hand first,' Alex said.

'Yes, please, Mr Locke,' Kit said, darting a look at him from lowered lashes.

Lulu leant across from her side to shove him. 'Stop manipulating my brother.'

'My sincerest apologies,' Kit said. 'I didn't realise you held the patent on getting away with treating people badly by milking your tragic past for all its worth.'

It took a second or two, but then Lulu snarled in unabashed fury and made a grab for him. Alex's hand shot out and held her back, even as Edith put a careful hand on her shoulder. Edith looked concerned and highly confused.

'If you're counting on me being able to stop Lucy from beating the ever-living shit out of you, you're betting on the wrong Locke twin,' Alex informed him.

Notwithstanding, his intervention had called Lulu off, for now. Her eyes were narrow on Kit. 'Leave it in, Alexander.'

'You saw for yourself it barely slows him down, Lulu.'

'But it does slow him down, and that's what we need.'

Alex shook his head and gestured to Kit. Kit steadied his right wrist with his left hand and held his palm out with only the slightest tremble. He heard Edith give a little gasp and looked over to see she'd covered her mouth, tears in her eyes as she took in his torn and bloodied skin, the cruelty of the spike, his missing finger.

Alex slowly undid the cap on his palm, wincing every time his hand slipped and jostled the iron rod embedded in Kit's skin. Kit made not a sound, even when Alex drew the rod out and the tug of it against his raw flesh made spots dance before his eyes. Once it was out, he drew his hand back to the safety of his chest, hunching over it protectively despite himself.

But Alex took his wrist, wiped the blood away and used Mrs Knight's salve on the wound, before wadding a clean handkerchief against it and binding it up.

'You want laudanum?' he asked.

Kit flicked a look up at him, disturbed that Alex had seen he was in pain, disturbed that he was even in pain at all—damn Christopher for going on strike—and disturbed most of all that Alex was extending this kindness towards him after he'd flatly told the twins he'd stolen the knife.

'I do not,' he said.

Lulu then took her turn at playing nurse, ordering Alex to strip off his coat, waistcoat and shirt. Alex's gaze skittered to Edith. She sighed and rolled her eyes and turned to look out the window. He bared himself and Lulu used some long strips of cloth from her pack to position and hold his sore shoulder in a more comfortable position, moving with the efficiency of long practice. Alex dressed again and accepted the bottle of laudanum from her. He swallowed just a few drops, shuddering at the bitter taste.

Her nurturing job done, Lulu turned a hawk's focus back on Kit. 'Who commissioned you, Whitely? Where did they take the knife?' she demanded.

'How should I know?' Kit said, as unhelpfully as he possibly could. 'Never heard his name, never saw his face. Or her face, for all I know. And I wouldn't tell you anything even if I knew where he was or where he'd come from or where he's going. Which I don't.'

Lulu had produced a penknife, its small blade glinting wickedly. 'I see you lost a finger somewhere. Shall we even it up?'

'There's no point torturing him,' Alex pointed out casually as Edith gaped. 'You saw how he was, after the pain Artisan.'

'Yes, and I saw him flinching when you touched that wound on his hand.'

Kit, making his face blank, held out his uninjured left hand without a tremor, keeping eye contact with her. He'd thought he was going to have to see this through himself, but once again, the rebelling figments in his head snapped into service under threat and his pain vanished. Lulu could do as she liked, and Christopher would swallow it.

'What are you doing?' Edith was almost shrieking. She took Lulu's wrist and pulled, bringing the wavering blade away from Kit.

Lulu looked at her and then looked back at Kit meaningfully. He had not missed the significance of a few fresh bruises he could see on Edith; he also very much believed that Lulu was bluffing and even if she wasn't, Alex would never let her go through with deliberately hurting Edith. He shrugged, and so did Lulu. She made the knife disappear. The pain came back.

'What is going on?' Edith demanded. 'Kit was forced to steal that knife, he wasn't commissioned to do it. Why in the name of all the holy saints are you treating him like this?'

'Miss Knight needs to play catch-up,' Kit said.

'He, in fact, was commissioned, Edith,' Alex said, voice gentle.

Edith looked from face to face, as if waiting for them to laugh and let her in on the joke. 'No,' she said. 'He dropped the handkerchief on purpose so we could follow him.'

'I didn't. You saw what you wanted to see,' Kit told her.

She frowned. Her expression turned inward for a moment as she replayed the memory Kit was trying to twist. 'You did. You looked right at me and dropped it.'

'I looked at you to make sure you weren't going to wake up Miss Lucinda, and I dropped the handkerchief accidentally.'

'That is not what happened.' Her hands were fisting in her skirts and her face had gone red. 'Kitty, *that is not what happened.*'

'Christ's sake, Edith, think,' Lulu snapped. 'He's an escape artist, if someone threatened him, he'd just teleport off away from the threat.'

'He would have come to me and woken me up,' Alex said. 'He knows I'd have kept him safe.'

He would have turned your lungs to ice, Alex.

Lulu went on. 'No one could force him to do it, not unless they marched him into the room with a pistol between his shoulder blades and even then, it turns out the iron wouldn't have stopped him teleporting as he passed through the door.'

'They could have threatened—'

He could not have their thoughts turning in that direction. *Burn it down.* 'Your blind faith is what made you useful, Miss Knight.'

Her eyes went very wide and she stared at him with injury written all over her face.

'And the fire?' Alex asked slowly, his head cocked.

Kit shored up the walls blocking his intentions; Alex was plainly getting flames and he should only be seeing blizzard. Crispin, delighting in setting everything on fire, wanted to claim full responsibility for setting the fire that had almost killed Little Tommy, but Kit wrestled him down. He had to be thought callous and treacherous, but he didn't need to be thought evil. Edith wiped at her eyes and looked at him hopefully.

He sighed. 'No one lets a child burn to death if they can help it, but I won't deny it considerably advanced my aims in the village.'

'You sound so cold,' Edith whispered. Kit nodded, satisfied.

'Why did you help me control my talent better?' Alex asked, which was either a reference to the impromptu lesson or an oblique allusion to the fact he'd persuaded Alex to fuck him. Alex's tone was too calm to read it either way.

'That's obvious, Lexi,' Lulu said. 'He didn't want you reading his intentions.'

Kit nodded again. Thank God one of the three of them was working with him. 'You were getting too strong, it was turning into an Art. You would have been able to see through the false intentions I was feeding you. I had to—' He took a moment to gift Alex a meaningful look. '—take care of it.'

That was more than an oblique allusion. Alex flinched. 'But there can't be false intentions, only true ones.'

Burn it down. 'And who told you that bullshit, Mr Locke?'

Alex's head tipped back against the seat cushion. He sighed at the carriage roof. 'You did.'

'Well done, sweetie, you got there.'

Alex growled under his breath, but after a moment, he persisted. 'Why did you save me from the pain Artisan if you never ca— if you were never on our side?'

Kit hesitated for one moment; with Crispin at free rein in his head shouting at him to burn everything down, he was tempted to play the whole incident off as a performance between himself and Michael. But he wanted their thoughts away from the Orphanage and away from any hint of an Artisan who could have threatened Kit into stealing the knife.

And the incident could simultaneously have been unplanned but still useful to him, just like the Lovelly fire.

He said, 'To make you trust me.'

Lulu said, 'Yep. Can I take the finger yet?'

He dared glance at Alex and saw doubt written on his face. 'What about just then, with those rogue Artisans?'

This was *enraging*. Alex had been so quick to judge him when they'd first met and now Kit was telling him he had deliberately and unconscionably betrayed him and he was refusing it?

'You knew me for a pissant little thief within minutes of meeting me,' he said. 'Why are you so determined to think the best of me now?'

'Why are you so determined to make us think the worst of you?' Alex countered.

Kit looked out the window. *Burn it down.* 'Game's over,' he said. 'Can't be bothered playing it anymore.'

'Yeah, all right,' Alex said, and Kit heard him hit the seat between them with his fist.

He pressed on. 'The only reason you don't want to believe me is because you don't want to believe you were stupid enough to fall for my lies.'

'How's vengeance looking now, Alexander?' Lulu muttered.

'Still not as good as justice, Lucinda,' Alex said. 'At least it'll be simple to hand him over to the Agency now, instead of just plain cruel.'

And Kit took a breath and told himself he felt relieved.

Lulu hadn't seemed inclined to question him any further, once she had ascertained that he could not, or could not be made to, direct her towards the knife's current owner. But after a few moments of thick silence, she leaned forwards, snagging Kit's attention, her scowl now more puzzled than furious.

'When exactly did you take on the commission, Whitely?'

Kit stared at her with a large sense of betrayal. He was burning his life down and Edith and Alex had been reaching for buckets of water. Lulu was meant to be throwing firebombs, not towing in the engine with its hoses.

'When?' he repeated while he once again considered the best way to light it all on fire.

There had really only been three plausible opportunities for him to arrange his acceptance of the commission once his hiding place had been leaked—in Lovelly before he'd been captured, in Bristol after he'd escaped from the train, and in the middle of the night at Northfield. Both latter options relied too much on coincidence and connected too closely to the Orphanage, to the Artisans they'd seen escaping. They were rattling south at speed but all it would take was Lulu making the leap of faith that the knife was still in the mountain, put there by the rogue Artisans Kit had met with, and she'd turn them around. They'd run right into Genevieve; the road was too lonely for them to avoid each other.

Therefore, it had to be Lovelly.

'Try again, kitten,' Lulu said when he said as much. 'There's a reason we all arrived on the same train, and that's because that was the fastest possible time to get there once the news of your location leaked out from the Agency. No one beat us there.'

'I take it you are unacquainted with the new technology of the telegraph, Miss Lucinda.'

Alex said, 'I take it you don't realise that the train still goes faster than the telegraph outside the cities, Mr Whitely.' He had his head cocked.

Balls.

'If a telegraph message had come to Lovelly, everyone would have known it,' Edith pointed out.

Jesus, the pair of them. 'I meant an accomplice might have wired someone in Bristol about my location,' Kit said. That was weak, so he added, 'But I don't know why you all expect me to know my employer's itinerary.'

'If any strangers had come to Lovelly before you lot showed up, everyone would have known it,' Edith added helpfully, ignoring him.

Oh, for fuck's sake, Edith.

But he was having to fight off a smile as he shifted his tactics. This was getting to be almost entertaining, finding the delicate tipping point that would tumble them into properly hating him. The problem was, he could see an answering glint in Edith Knight, and Alex had sat up alertly like a hound on the scent, and even Lulu was looking thoughtful.

'Fine, there's no point hiding it anymore,' he said. 'Miss Knight, I didn't read the London papers religiously to make sure I wasn't in them. I read them because I have a collaborator in London who encodes new commissions into the personal advertisements for my consideration. My employer didn't contact me; I saw the commission and notified my London contact that I'd take it. I've done it dozens of times before. I've been fooling all of you. Because I'm a thief and a liar, and, as you well know, Mr Locke, a whore.'

He half-stood, swaying in the moving carriage, and presented them with a little bow before thumping back down and staring out the window so he only had to imagine the looks on their faces.

Then Alex said, 'You know what? I'll accept you were rooking me. But not Miss Knight. There's no possibility you've been rooking her.'

Alex was right; Edith Knight was the stickiest of all the sticking points in this story.

Burn it down, *Crispin.*

'Don't tax yourself, Mr Locke,' he said coldly. 'She was an easy target. Such blind faith—and negligent parents.'

Edith made a choked noise. 'How dare you?' she demanded. 'They treat you like a son, Kit.'

'If only they treated you like a daughter, for your sake,' Kit said. 'It would have made it harder to make you my victim. It's only lucky for you I tend to men.'

Edith Knight shot to her feet and backhanded him across the face.

Who knew it could be quite so bitter to get exactly what you wanted?

Lulu pushed the postilion as far as he would risk travelling with only the carriage lamps to guide him over the rough roads, and they finally stopped at a coaching inn a little after dark. They took a quick, silent meal, taking the expense of a private backroom given Kit's torn and filthy penitent robe and the stares their group had gotten walking in the door.

The others picked at their food but Kit mutinously refused to have a poor appetite. He would eat while they were still letting him eat. He was mopping gravy off his plate with a bit of bread under the cold gaze of Lulu when she suddenly threw her fork down and swore.

'What?' Alex asked. He had half-risen, perhaps to stop Lulu from lunging across the table and throttling Kit.

'The little fucker's right,' she said. 'I *am* using it to indulge in reprehensible behaviour.'

Alex wiped at his eyes in a *I'm too tired for this* type of gesture. 'What?' he repeated.

'My tragic past,' she said, with a roll of her eyes. She faced Edith. 'I'm sorry.' She was speaking flatly, looking more over Edith's shoulder than directly at her. 'I was angry but I had no right or cause to hurt you. It won't happen again.'

Kit saw Alex take and release a shuddering breath and slowly sit back down, shoulders released. Lulu's awkward but sincere apology to Edith had somehow relieved him more than it had the woman it was aimed at.

Edith raised her chin. Then she nodded once. 'We make mistakes. We make amends,' she said, with remarkable succinctness for her, and then added hopefully, 'We can all do that an'all, innit snugh?'

She was trying to look at all of them as she said this, and ended up looking pleadingly at Kit.

'You have to want to make amends to make amends,' he informed her as he insouciantly helped himself to a piece of chicken off Alex's barely touched plate. Her face fell.

When Alex shoved the plate away and stood, pulling Kit to his feet, Lulu stood too. 'Don't torture yourself, Lexi. Let me supervise him tonight.'

Alex's fingers tightened around Kit's arm. 'You can't,' he said. 'A woman alone in a man's room? You'd be ruined, baby sister.' Lulu smirked in amusement, but Edith gave a serious nod. 'Keep Miss Knight company.'

His hand stayed tight around Kit's elbow as they took the stairs. 'Stairs are thresholds, right?'

'How well you know me, Mr Locke.'

Alex snorted bitterly at that. 'If only, Mr Whitely.'

When they were in the room, Alex leaned on the locked door and let all his breath out in one long sigh. Kit kept his eyes down, waiting. Lulu hid her hurt and grief behind anger, and he expected the same from Alex. In fact, he expected worse, because he had pushed a kind man too far. He expected a reckoning, now they were alone.

But Alex wore his hurt openly, it seemed, and very quietly. 'How did you make it feel real, if it's not real?'

Crispin whispered, *Burn it down, burn it down, burn it to the fucking ground.*

Kit said, 'Practice,' and he smiled like an angel.

Alex made an incredulous choke of a noise. 'Ah.' He pushed Kit further into the room. 'Looking forwards to handing you over to the Agency.'

'I'm sure you are,' Kit said. 'You and your head start. *This isn't a transaction,*' he mocked savagely. 'Of course it sodding was, and a false one to boot. We'd be right here either way, as soon as I refused to do exactly your bidding.'

Alex put his big hand on Kit's chest and shoved. Kit stumbled back, caught himself, and said, 'Go ahead, I won't fight you.'

Alex shoved again and Kit fetched up against the bed. He shuddered and calmed himself and offered Alex his blankly compliant look. Alex, silent and grim, took his wrist and Kit shut his eyes.

And then Alex had pulled him over to the ewer and basin set on the table in the corner of the room. He took off the makeshift bandaging and washed the hole in Kit's hand, Kit shivering as he did it because he was still being so sodding gentle. He smeared the last of the salve on both sides, and over the stump, and bound the wounds up again.

Only then did he tie Kit to the headboard of the bed. He made sure the ropes were knotted tight around both wrists, but he was also careful not to jostle Kit's injuries. Kit kept his eyes shut. Christopher wailed in his head and Kit steadied him, reminding him they knew about knots now.

He stayed still as Alex readied himself for sleep, extinguished the candle, and lay down as far over on the other side of the bed as he could get. He patiently waited for Alex's breathing to slow and deepen.

Then Kit gathered his Art, his unwanted residents willing for once, and opened the knots.

He sat quietly on the edge of the bed, rubbing his wrists. He'd freed himself for Christopher's sake, but now he was considering if he should escape or not. He needed the Locke twins away from the knife, which meant keeping them away from Reuben, which meant keeping them away from Genevieve. At the moment, they were dead-set for London, which worked. He wasn't sure what they would do if he vanished. Without the justice plan to keep Alex focussed and appease Lulu a little, they might turn back for the mountain for clues about the knife. They might even deliberately seek out their cousin Ginnie, to enlist the help of the Myriad.

On balance, no. He was committed to his course.

'I knew it,' Alex said out of the darkness. He shifted over, one hand locking roughly into the back of Kit's robe. 'I fucking *knew* it.'

'I have no intention of escaping,' Kit said. 'You know that.'

'I don't know you at all. Were you ever even scared of your wrists being tied?'

Kit swallowed. *Burn it down.* 'No,' he said. 'I could always untie myself. Because I was rooking you right from the start.'

'I am done with your shit, Whitely.' Alex dragged Kit to where he had hung their coats. He searched his own pockets until he came up with the laudanum bottle. 'Take a good sip of this,' he said, holding it out. 'It'll put you right to sleep. No escaping then.'

Kit obediently took the small bottle in his uninjured hand. He smelled cinnamon and cloves and honey mixed into the tincture, and then a whiff of the same bitterness that underlaid the sickly-sweet poppy syrup that Fairweather used to dose him with after he'd beaten him.

In his head, Crispin howled in impotent rage at the idea of ever being so helpless again. 'No,' he said. *Never again.*

'Take the sip, or I'll hold you down and make you,' Alex said.

Kit threw the bottle across the room. 'Then make me.'

Alex, grip locked like iron around Kit's upper arm, towed him over to where the bottle had fallen. It was unbroken, having landed on the rug, and its stopper had stayed in place. Alex scooped it up with one hand even as he twisted Kit's arm and forced him down.

Fuelled by Crispin's rage, Kit thrashed and kicked and still found himself on the floor with Alex straddling him within seconds, body weight flattening him to the floor, knees holding his arms down. With quick efficient movements, the big man unstoppered the bottle and gripped Kit's jaw, fingers digging in to make him open his mouth. Kit tried to bite him and Alex squeezed harder, forcing him to stillness. Kit's chest was heaving with the effort; Alex barely had a hair out of place.

Kit met his professionally impassive gaze, own eyes burning. 'Don't.' He wouldn't insult either of them by begging.

It wasn't a betrayal. It wasn't.

Alex trickled a measure down Kit's throat, watched his eyes as he began to blink heavily, and then dosed him with more. When he finally levered himself off, Kit was drowsy and loose-limbed. Alex stoppered the bottle and lifted him, carrying him to the bed.

'Drugged Kit isn't as fun as drunk Kit, I don't think,' Kit told him as he laid him down. Alex rolled his shoulders as Kit stared up at him. 'Fairweather liked him well enough, s'pose.'

His words were slurring and slow. His tongue felt numb. He didn't think Alex understood him. Alex settled him under the blankets. He sat on the bed, back turned to Kit. Kit watched through heavy eyelids as his body slumped out of his ramrod-straight posture and he rubbed at his sore shoulder and then slowly tidied himself.

Locke the grimly professional bounty hunter had become Alex, who was merely miserable.

He lay beside Kit at last. He seemed tense despite his soothing grooming ritual and in direct proportion to how relaxed and loose Kit felt.

Kit cuddled into him. He remembered vaguely that Alex was angry with him, but he still smelt of sandalwood, his heart still beat steady under Kit's ear, and his strong arms still kept Kit safe as he tipped into deep and velvety darkness.

Alex

Kıᴛ sᴛᴏᴘᴘᴇᴅ ᴛᴀʟᴋɪɴɢ ᴏɴᴄᴇ Aʟᴇx ᴅʀᴜɢɢᴇᴅ him.

Alex had had to shake him awake in the morning, a first, and he almost fell over on the stairs, and did fall over in the yard of the inn, tripping on his own feet as he tried to climb into the carriage in the chill dawn. Even in the thin robe, he didn't shiver.

He looked small and bewildered and Alex wanted to hug him and he wanted to hit him and he hated everything about everything. Edith stared at Kit and then looked at Alex and didn't say anything, which made Alex feel worse.

Lulu merely looked satisfied, which made Alex want to hit *her*, which was when he bundled himself right into the corner of the carriage and paid extensive attention to the sheep in the fields they passed as the carriage rattled south.

He should be angry. He was angry. He should be much angrier. Kit had thoroughly, deliberately, and cruelly betrayed him. Kit had been so committed to the game he'd even held his cards steady while drunk off his arse, with his artful, manipulative *I think he probably loves you* so that Alex wouldn't even blink when he left their room, trailing intentions of sex while actually heading to his rendezvous with his employer.

But on the other hand, Alex had arrested him and strongarmed him into helping Lulu steal the knife in the first place. Kit had been under no obligation to treat him honourably. If the crafty lad had used every weapon at his disposal, then fair play to him.

If he'd been bloody convincing about it, then fair fucking play to him.

Meanwhile, Lulu's face settled into a thoughtful look that puzzled Alex with its familiarity until he realised it was, of course, the expression he saw in the mirror when he was doing some hard thinking of his own.

Kit didn't eat when they had breakfast at the second coaching inn. He didn't answer when Lulu tried to question him more about who might have put the commission out on the knife. He didn't eat when they had lunch just over the English border. He didn't respond when Edith tried to apologise for slapping him.

The laudanum shouldn't have affected him for so long. He was faking it to avoid more questions. He had to be.

He was acting a little more cognisant once they'd reached Northfield. Wetherby and Wellerman were delegated to watch over him while Alex and Lulu went to see Kingsford and Edith retreated to the library.

On the way to what would be an unpleasant interview with their disapproving older brother, Lulu stopped Alex. 'Did you see the look on Whitely's face when that deacon got hit by the pain Artisan?'

That was so far from what Alex had expected to hear—he thought she was going to demand they move on to the torture she'd already threatened once—that he blinked. He waited for more.

'That was justice,' she said. 'You see him when the deacon got the knife in the throat?'

Alex nodded. All the blood had drained from Kit's face; he'd looked as if he would flay the fox, throw up the contents of his stomach.

Then he'd fronted up to three rogue Artisans, blocking them from getting near Alex and Edith and Lulu like the fiercest of mother bears.

And then he had gleefully told them he'd been playing them and they meant nothing to him at all.

Yeah, all right.

'That was vengeance,' Lulu continued. 'Didn't look so pleasant.'

'What are you saying, Lucinda?' he asked.

'I'm saying, Alexander, don't make any decisions based on thinking I'm heartbroken that I didn't get my knife.' She held up a hand. 'Don't get me wrong, I could throttle the little weasel and if I have a chance to put a bullet in Varley, I'll take it. But I can live without the vengeance, if we get the justice.'

'Ah, what I'm hearing is that I was right and you were wrong,' Alex said, with a mammoth effort at his normal cheer.

'Don't get cocky, big brother,' Lulu said. 'Whitely still took you for one hell of a ride. That's not an easy thing to overlook.'

Alex nodded, chastened, and they went on into the study. Afterwards, Kingsford limped with Alex to the parlour, where the footmen reported Kit hadn't shifted a whisker from the settee where Alex had sat him down and ordered him not to move.

Kingsford said severely, 'I am very disappointed in you, Mr Whitely.'

Kit stirred, raised wide green eyes to Alex's brother and said his first words for the day. 'My apologies, Sir Kingsford.' He blinked slowly, frowned, and then whispered, 'Sorry, Kings.'

He ate dinner left-handed, a few helpings assiduously supplied by Wetherby, and went meekly to the guestroom with Alex. Alex gestured and he obediently held out his injured right hand for Alex to check. It was healing well. The Agency nurse would be pleased.

Then Alex took out the laudanum bottle, dread settling over him like a pall of smog. 'Will you make me force you again?'

'No,' Kit said. He held out his good hand for the bottle, but dropped it back to his side. His intentions, impossible to read, swirled behind their misting cover. 'Yes, I have to. Sorry, Alex.'

Alex put a hand over his face and then took Kit by the shoulders. Kit went from his usual cool and self-possessed self into a spitting and clawing wildcat on the instant. Alex wrestled him to the floor.

He despised himself. He'd despise himself more if he made Lulu or, worse, the footmen do it.

Kit lay under him, rigid and shaking, eyes alight with rage and hate. For an unpleasant moment, Alex found himself missing his unwilling compliance. Again, the smaller man refused to open his mouth and Alex had to grip his jaw to force his lips to part.

He had to give Kit more this time, for his body to go lax and his eyes to glaze over. That was par for the course; whether it was something about Kit's mind, body, or Art, he seemed to become quickly inured to outside influences. Witness how unconcerned he'd been, facing Fletcher and Cecelia's powers. Witness how he'd shaken off the effects of iron, an exceedingly rare ability among Artisans. Witness how he could now completely block Alex's reading of his intentions, whenever it suited him.

Or perhaps he could always do that.

Because he'd been playing Alex for the fool he was from the very start.

Alex sat staring down at Kit, splayed out under him with lax vulnerability now. There were bruises on his face from where Alex had had to grip him to force his mouth open the night before; Alex guessed they'd soon be overlaid with more.

His body was limp, his eyes were hazy, his lips were parted, his face was flushed. He looked almost as he'd looked when he spread under Alex and let him take him with passionate abandon, coldly scheming all the while.

He was laid open and vulnerable in exactly the way that Alex had so very much wanted to earn.

Alex wanted to kiss him, to bring him to pleasure, to take his face in his hands as he arched and gasped and demand, 'Is it real?'

He didn't know what would be worse, to hear Kit say, 'Yes, it's real,' and know he was lying, or hear him admit, 'No, it's not real,' and yet still not be convinced.

Because Kit was still hiding something, for sure, and Alex had no idea what it could be, after he'd announced all his other tricks with such cruel honesty.

Even with the higher dose, Kit stayed awake longer and his words were intelligible this time. 'Sorry,' he slurred again. 'He wanted to fight. He never wants to be helpless again.'

'Who, sweetheart?' Alex asked. *Are you fucking kidding me, Lexi*, said Lulu's voice in his head when the endearment slipped out.

Kit muttered something that sounded like 'Crispy,' before adding, 'We're doing a good job keeping you safe.'

Alex slid his hands under Kit and lifted him, feeling a twinge in his injured shoulder. 'Who are you keeping me safe from?'

Kit said dreamily, 'Treacherous snake.'

Ah. Yes. The treacherous snake who had destroyed Lulu's plans. The treacherous snake who had made Alex fall for him. The treacherous snake who had played him for an utter fool. The treacherous snake who had been defending himself the only way snakes knew how.

The treacherous snake who wrapped his arms around Alex's neck and murmured, 'Won't let him hurt you, Alex.'

You already did, sweetheart, Alex thought. He wanted to be angrier about it. He was just wounded, and it was worse because he felt like he had no right to be.

He laid Kit on the bed and tucked him in. He set Wellerman and Wetherby to take turns watching over him and slept alone for the first time since he'd arrested him.

He did not have as good a night's sleep as he'd hoped. Over and over, he relived the horrific moment he and Lulu had seen Kit's slight figure across the chasm inside the mountain, backing towards the railing, and he'd understood, with a quick clarity that was not usual for him, that Kit was about to cross one of his thresholds to their side.

Over and over, he dreamed the lightning dash across the tunnel floor to catch him, and over and over he missed him by a literal hairsbreadth, fingers brushing through his wild curls.

On the last try, he caught him at last, and then deliberately let him fall.

Alex woke. Outside the window, the sky was beginning to lighten. It was too early. He went to Kit's room, dismissed a sleepy Wetherby, and crawled into bed with his duplicitous, treacherous snake.

Kit murmured awake as Alex's arms came around him. 'Bad dreams,' he said thickly. 'Drowning. So angry. Better now you're here.'

'Now who's here?' Alex asked, wondering whose name he would get. Maybe the London confederate.

'Alex,' sighed Kit, the exact same desperate, needy way he'd said it in the alley when he'd clung to Alex as if his life depended on him. 'Alex. My love.'

Alex shut his eyes and refused to let his idiotic heart have its say. Kit was in a dazedly lucid state, and he had to take advantage. 'Did you take the knife, Kit?'

'Yes,' Kit said on an exhale.

'Where is it? Who did you give it to, sweetheart?'

Kit was silent. After a while, he whispered, 'Drowning. She'll drown. I won't let her.'

'Kit?'

But Kit nestled his face into the crook of Alex's shoulder, eyes slipping shut again, weight slumping against his chest.

Alex shook his head at himself and lay with Kit a warm lump in his arms, until he could bring himself to speak again. 'Time to wake up, Mr Whitely.'

He helped a languorous and dopey Kit into another set of clothes donated by Kingsford and made sure his hand was still healing cleanly, and then Wellerman drove them to Bristol with a picnic basket for the train. They caught the earliest London train, arriving three hours later into Paddington.

The low roar of London crashed upon them as they emerged from the arrivals hall. Alex touched his fingers between his eyes, his other hand holding on to Kit's elbow. The saving grace of London was that the sheer physical clamour of the carriages, omnibuses, carts, wagons, vans, works and improvements, bells, whistles, shouts and cries tended to do battle with the mental thrum of the inchoate intentions of the masses of people. It just about made it easier to ignore both.

Alex thought of a line Kit had read from *Little Dorrit*: *The crowd in the street jostling the crowd in his mind, and the two crowds making a confusion.* He rubbed his thumb over Kit's hand and imagined the dial Kit had so helpfully taught him to use. To stop Alex from reading his ill intentions.

Yeah, all right.

He and Lulu kept their two sprites safely between them in the press of pedestrians, street sellers and errand boys in their tiny top hats, made obscure by a fog, thankfully not as thick as it would get as winter set in. They reached the cabstand to hire a hansom. Given the general state of traffic-lock in the city, especially on a market morning followed by a half-day holiday, it would almost be quicker to walk, but Kit appeared in no state for it.

The cab ride was bumpy, and the noise of the city streets was too loud to comfortably converse. No one seemed much to want to talk anyway. The driver took them the long way around, an honest attempt to avoid the worst of the traffic. He had to be honest or risk a fine from the railway and his lucrative place at the station cabstand, even without considering the courage it would take to cheat Lulu.

They passed the British Museum, and Edith exclaimed, 'Smirke's Reading Room, I wish I could get a reader's ticket!'

But when she turned from the window to share her excitement with Kit, her smile faded and she curled up into her corner. Lulu took her hand and squeezed it. Edith squeezed back. They exchanged small, sombre smiles in mutual comfort.

Then Lulu started looking thoughtful again, which was as disconcerting as it ever was.

Kit stared into space vacantly, ignoring Alex, who was leaning forwards to hold his reddened wrist because he was very aware that the cab doors were thresholds and that the effects of the laudanum should have worn off by now.

For he knew, their flimflam artist was faking his vacant passivity as much as he'd faked everything Alex had thought they'd had between them. Alex was getting hardly a breath of an intention off him, just a kind of whiteness in the space where his Art normally visualised intentions, except for the occasional abstract flash that Alex could only translate as the desire for arson.

The Agency headquarters were just near the Foundling Hospital. Alex knocked, a prearranged signal that sent their driver circling back to pass the public baths down Coram Street, around the corner from the headquarters.

'Look,' Alex said. Edith Knight and Lulu looked silently but Kit's thousand-yard stare didn't alter, not even when Alex gently took his bruised face and turned it so he could see the façade of the bathhouse. 'Warm and cold baths. See, Mr Whitely?'

Then the cab was coming to a halt outside the headquarters. The Agency was housed in a tall red-brick building, modern in style and grim in outlook, purpose-built to both support Artisans and their endeavours, and imprison them when those endeavours did not suit the powers that were.

At some point, Alex saw, his grip around Kit's wrist had turned into holding his hand. He looked at their entwined fingers and then he covered his face with his other hand and screamed inside his head.

They had to do it. It had to be done. And who could argue that Kit Whitely did not deserve everything he had coming to him?

They all climbed out of the cab. Lulu looked longingly towards a coffee stall further along the row. Kit's head tipped back as he looked up at the grim façade. Alex felt a shift in the way he was holding himself, resignation sweeping through him.

Employees, mostly men, were streaming from the doors, ready for their afternoon off for All Saints' Day, a welcome break from their long hours. Many would go to spectate the same ceremonies the Orphanage hierarchy would be attending, to enjoy the pageantry of the upper echelons in their finery, street entertainment at its best. The Agency clerks and officers merged with the pedestrians on the pavement who were muttering as they parted around the four of them standing like rocks in the way.

Alex closed his eyes. Then he felt Lulu step close to him. She hugged him, which was unusual enough that he let go of Kit in surprise; the crowded pavement was not conducive to a swift escape, anyway. Edith took the opportunity to hug Kit and whisper encouragement in his ear.

'My brother,' Lulu said. 'I don't appreciate you nearly enough. I know what this is costing you, Lexi. We don't have to do it.'

It cost *her* to say that, he saw, but she said it, and she meant it. Kit was not forgiven. It was Alex she cared for.

'You said.' He was staring at her helplessly. 'You said you could give up on the knife, if you got justice.'

'I can give up on both, if it's what you need,' she said, and it was so simple and so brave.

He rubbed at his eyes tiredly. 'It's too late to do anything else.'

'I made the call, didn't I?' she said. She shook her head, slow and sad. 'I said you looked like I looked when I met Peter. Lexi, *he's your Peter.*'

'He's the thief who fucked us over,' Alex said flatly. 'And we need him.'

'We will find another way to get to Varley,' she said. 'If I can change my mind, you can change your mind too.'

Kit shivered and Alex saw him snap back into awareness. He shifted closer to him, hand reaching to take his sleeve, ready for him to push through the pedestrians squeezing past and make a last dash for freedom.

Instead, Kit smiled at Edith and patted her cheek. 'Hello, Edie. I'm sorry. I said some things I didn't mean. Make Lulu take you to the zoo to see that hippopotamus.'

Then he turned and looked the twins up and down, spat out, 'Grow a set, the pair of you,' and kicked open the doors of the Agency so he could storm inside.

Which left Alex in the rather odd position of chasing his own prisoner to the front desk, fumbling his badge out of his pocket and leaving Lulu and Edith gaping in surprise on the street behind them.

'You piece of shit enforcer,' Kit snarled at him when he snagged hold of him again.

Alex blinked. Kit, wielding his icy courtesy, was usually the equivalent of a stiletto through the ribs. That was a cudgel between the eyes that Alex was completely unprepared for.

The movement in the main hall ceased. Alex glanced around. He'd been disappointed upon his first visit to the Agency. It had reminded him of nothing more or less than the dingy administration office of his boarding school. The drearily dressed and bowler-hatted clerks and Agency officers staring at the commotion didn't much dispel the impression.

Kit kicked violently at Alex's shins and then lurched into him with every intention of biting him. Alex caught him and he jerked, thrashed and swore before flailing close enough to his ear to hiss, 'Control me.'

'Can anyone?' Alex said. He twisted Kit's arm behind his back and shoved him bodily into the desk.

'He's a feisty one,' remarked the registrar, catching both hands on his side of the desk as the whole thing rocked forwards. He rescued his inkstand before it tipped but missed the grab at his nib pen as it rolled off. He was the same man who had signed Alex in the week before when he'd taken his badge. Alex hadn't caught his name.

'My apologies, sir,' Kit murmured, instantly polite. 'Please allow me to retrieve that pen for you.'

'I've got it,' the registrar said congenially. He probably saw a great deal worse. He'd also probably seen people get stabbed with the steel nibs.

Alex eased up enough for Kit to straighten, but kept his arm hiked up behind his back so that any movement would wrench his shoulder. Kit leaned back into him, the heat of him apparent even through their layers of clothing. Alex could feel him trembling.

That had to be another play, though. Kit had never shown overt signs of fear except when he wanted to.

'Great Scott,' said the unflappable registrar, finally flapped when he straightened from fetching his pen and got a good look at Kit's face. 'You brought in Christopher Whitebrickleyhurst.'

Alex, hand still locked around Kit's elbow, agreed with this.

'There's been an arrest warrant out for him for at least seven years.'

Alex agreed with this too.

'You've been an enforcer for a week!'

Alex made his third mild noise of agreement, and the registrar finally snapped out of it. He unlocked the large safe by his desk and pulled out the big master ledger. 'Anything to add to his entry?'

It's not doors, it's thresholds. He defined for me exactly what a threshold is, because he trusted me and wanted me to trust him. Watch out for water and mirrors and edges. He can open thresholds and cross them and block them. He can make his own. He doesn't have to be touching a door to unlock it and he can open it too.

He's actually a very strong teleportation and telekinesis Artisan and not even iron can stop him.

'It's not doors,' Alex said. He cleared his throat. 'Not just doors, it's windows as well. And he's very good at locks.'

And that was all.

He glanced around, keeping it casual. Behind the registration desk was a grill, guarding access to the inner sanctum. Beyond the grill, the on-duty telepath sat on a tall stool, reading anyone passing by into the inner offices, where the full information for every known Artisan was kept secure. The stream of clerks was issuing from there.

'Oh, look at that,' the registrar said when he was done modifying Kit's Agency entry in the ledger. He tapped a line near the top of Kit's page. 'Happy birthday, Mr Whitebrickleyhurst.'

As if Alex hadn't been feeling shit enough already.

'Thank you, sir.'

'Maybe I'll bring you a piece of cake to the cells before I leave,' the registrar said, looking at him from over his glasses.

'Will it have a key baked into it?' Kit asked blandly.

'Oh, he's funny!'

'Yes, he thinks he's very funny,' Alex said, squeezing Kit's elbow and then easing off.

The registrar nodded to a nearby Agency officer to take custody of Kit.

As the officer moved forwards, Kit jerked his elbow back. But he'd let loose his intentions, so Alex swayed lightly out of the way and the blow only grazed his stomach. Kit then lunged forwards which such quick aggression that the officer skittered back again in alarm. Alex locked his arm tight around him, holding him still and harmless against his chest.

'Yeah, all right, I'll have my claim stamped before I hand him over, thank you,' Alex said.

The registrar waved at an empty desk in the corner. 'The claims officer already left.'

'Really?' Alex said, managing to sound deeply unimpressed. 'Skived off early, did he?'

'It's All Saints' Day! It's a half-day holiday, you know. I would have gone myself by now if you hadn't come in.'

The officer edged closer, caution writ large on his face. He had a pair of iron cuffs in his hands now.

'Oh, no,' Alex said, moving into the way. 'No, I'll take him through.'

'You're not allowed back there. The duty officer will take the paperwork and stamp your claim back in the cells and your bonus will be sent in the post.'

'The lad has escaped capture at least seventeen times,' Alex said. 'It was no small thing to get him this far. I'm not handing him over to have him walk out of here before my claim is properly registered.'

The registrar opened his mouth to keep arguing, and then happened to glance at Kit. Alex followed his gaze downwards; Kit, slumped indolently against Alex, was absolutely radiating innocence, the sweet, wide-eyed look that inevitably made people in authority assume he was planning mischief. Alex bit down an unwilling smile.

'Take him through,' the registrar said slowly, staring at Kit.

Alex nodded, clamped his hands about Kit's upper arms and walked him forwards, past the desk, to the grill. The telepath watched them come with some interest.

'You must be looking forwards to finishing this shit of a job and going for a drink,' Kit murmured. Then he shouted, 'You sodding wanker,' and slammed the back of his head up under Alex's chin—or would have, if he hadn't once again let his intention slip.

Alex evaded him easily, twisted his arm behind his back again, and marched him on.

A drink, he thought. *I am going to hand off this prisoner and go get a drink at the Cat and Owl. I am really looking forwards to getting that drink. I think I see a lot of whisky in my future.*

He didn't alter his steady pace as they passed under the eyes of the telepath Artisan, whose attention by rights should be on the criminal beside Alex; given the criminal was swearing and struggling and making quite the scene, it almost certainly was. But just in case, Alex thought longingly of finishing off a bad job and getting a drink. Then they were past and he felt his shoulders relax.

'Hoi!' The telepath Artisan's voice rang out behind them. 'Stop right there! You're hiding something.'

Alex froze. Kit slid out of his suddenly slackened hold and met his gaze. He was wearing Alex's finger marks in a chain of bruises around his jaw. They both turned back to face the telepath Artisan. Kit's intentions had gone to blankness again. He was smiling very slightly, the small smile he wore when he was doing something that pleased him greatly.

Alex could not have said if that look was meant to warn him to stay calm, or to gloat because he'd just thoroughly fucked Alex over. Again.

Kit was clever and observant, and it didn't matter that Alex and Lulu had carefully hidden the true plan from him. Knowing as much as he already did, as soon as he'd seen the telepath Artisan, as soon as he'd recognised that Alex wanted to go into the inner offices, Kit had held the power to ruin everything, burn the entire plan to the ground.

Indeed, it was Kit the telepath bore down on when she jumped off her stool. She was a tall woman with chestnut hair and she laid her long-fingered hand around the nape of Kit's neck without hesitation, staring into his eyes.

'I don't appreciate being touched without permission,' Kit said, twitching away from her fingers. The telepath gripped tighter.

'What are you hiding?' she whispered, frowning in concentration.

Kit held her bright blue eyes, unblinking, the tiny smile fixed on his face. He was plainly making a fight of it, even as they both stood unmoving. Sweat broke out on the telepath's brow. Her fingers were white-knuckled where they clasped tightly around Kit's nape. Alex didn't realise his hand on Kit's elbow was also gripping tighter and tighter until Kit flinched and tried to pull his arm away. His eye contact with the other Artisan broke.

'Got it,' said the telepath, and looked sharply at Alex.

Alex's heart plummeted to his feet. His hand was itching for his pretty French pepperbox revolver, his expensive gift to himself when they'd come home from the war. He hadn't recovered it after the fight in Gallentry. He'd fight their way out bare-knuckled if he had to.

'Good heavens, you did a number on the poor boy, didn't you? No wonder he was trying to hide it—so angry and humiliated, poor thing—and no wonder you're covered in guilt.'

'It was the only way to catch him,' Alex said, his voice sounding rusty.

'Move on so you can go get your drink.' She glanced at Kit again before smiling at Alex. 'Maybe I'll see you there, if you want to talk about it.'

Alex nodded, returning the smile, relaxed, comfortable, controlling his prisoner with a flex of his substantial muscles, flirting with someone pretty, the highlight of an otherwise grim day. He led Kit away, thinking how much he liked a chestnut shade of red on a woman. Behind them, the telepath Artisan made a satisfied noise.

They passed through the inner door and out of her sight, and therefore beyond her viable range. Alex looked down at Kit and saw he was still wearing the tiny smile that meant he was pleased with himself.

He was damned sure that Kit had just thoroughly snowed the Agency telepath.

'Kit—'

'It occurs to me,' Kit said brightly, 'that the telepath Artisans sit very close to the registrar, and they can no doubt read every single item that passes through his mind and the minds of registering Artisans. The Agency might want to look there for its security leaks.'

Alex paused, nonplussed. He looked back towards the red-headed Artisan.

'Not necessarily her,' Kit said. 'They no doubt have quite a few on shift. To the cells, Mr Locke.'

Alex, still glancing back, marched Kit onwards. The hallway opened up at a T-junction, a sign indicating cells to the left, offices to the right. Alex went left to the cells, and it was time to formally deliver Kit into Agency custody.

He knocked on the locked door of the small guardroom, looking through the barred window. A uniformed officer was there, expression dull and bored as he sat at a small table idly shuffling a deck of cards. He was alone, his intentions vague but full of resentment that he had his shift on the half-day holiday. He let them in, took Kit's paperwork, which would be added to Kit's full file stored in the inner offices, stamped Alex's claim, tossed him the keys and nodded down the corridor. He obviously expected no trouble.

Therefore, Alex was taken by surprise when he pushed Kit ahead of him to find a single large holding cell barred all about with silver-laced iron—and filled with Artisans who'd all made a concerted effort to murder Kit.

'Oh, hello, ladies and gentlemen,' Kit said. 'How was your journey from Lovelly?'

The two knife-throwing metalworking Artisans, sett-throwing stone-working Artisan, and rat-deploying pied piper Artisan scowled back, drawing together into a solid wall of anger on the other side of the bars. Alex could read their intentions easily enough.

Alex dragged Kit back to the guardroom. 'Pardon me. Where is the separate cell for the annoying prisoner that all the other prisoners want to shank?'

'Just the one holding cell,' the guard said indifferently. 'They're waiting for processing.'

'Then process them.'

The guard blinked. 'It's All Saints',' he said, like Alex was the unreasonable one here.

'Can he at least get a bath first?' Alex asked.

'It's *All Saints*'.'

Alex walked Kit back to the holding cell. He put the key into the lock. He stopped, his hand resting there. 'I can't do it.'

'You have to do it,' Kit told him. 'You're done with me but you're not done here. Are you?'

Kit was entirely correct. He had to do it. If he tried to walk out of here with Kit still in his custody, even the sulkily complacent guard was going to wake up. But his quelling grip on Kit had turned into an embrace. He realised he was towing Kit backwards just as the smaller man planted his feet to hold his ground.

'What are the rules, Alex?' Kit hissed, trying to push him off.

'My rule is I don't fuck over people I care about,' Alex said.

'I broke that rule.'

Alex smiled, because Kit had just accidentally given away that, actually, he did care. 'Well, it's not *your* rule, is it? But *I* don't fuck over people I care about.'

'One, it seems a little late given we're standing, and two, I broke the rule, so therefore three, you don't care about me, so four, the rule doesn't apply.'

'I care about you,' Alex said.

Once again came that abstract flash behind the mist hiding Kit's intentions that made Alex want to move candles and lanterns and matches and every sort of open flame well away from his reach.

'And that is what made you easy to fuck over, Mr Locke,' he said, his voice as icy as his thoughts were fiery. 'That, and the fact that you're really rather stupid.'

He crossed his arms, lifted his chin, and waited with defiant self-right-eousness for the result.

Kit, just as he had once accused Alex, went like an arrow for the weakness in others when he felt vulnerable, and that was one of Alex's weaknesses for sure. Alex duly felt a sharp flash of hurt and anger.

Then it turned in his head and he finally understood the shape of the game, if not the game itself.

Despite himself, he laughed. 'See, sweetheart, at this point, you're trying *far* too hard to alienate me. What's that quote from the Danish prince?'

'Oh my God, Alex, would you go ahead and hate me like you're supposed to?' Kit said in rising frustration, followed by a sulky, 'Queen Gertrude. "The lady doth protest too much, methinks".'

'I don't hate barely anyone,' Alex said, but did not add, *And I could never hate you.*

Shoving his hands into his curls, Kit scowled at him. Alex, watching him with morbid curiosity, could practically see him wondering what the devil he would have to do to get tossed into the cell.

Alex was quite interested himself. He wasn't sure if he'd get the stiletto or the cudgel next.

He got sweet Kit, who poked him and spoke in his normal tones, all fond exasperation. 'What are my rules, you soft-hearted idiot?'

'No pity,' Alex said, swallowing hard as he looked through the bars at the metalworking Artisans. The woman had her hand under her cloak. Alex wondered just how thoroughly they'd been searched for weapons, when the Agency relied so heavily on iron and silver to quell them.

'No pity,' Kit echoed triumphantly.

'No mercy.' The stoneworking Artisan was at the bars, giving Kit a look from head to toe that did not bode well.

'No mercy.'

'No help.' Alex sighed as he stared at the fourth Artisan, who must be the pied piper and looked a little like little Peter Llewellyn. He could probably reach untold numbers of rats from here, if he was strong enough to push past the iron.

'No help.' Kit was standing very straight. Behind him, the door unlocked itself and slid open. Iron couldn't stop him. 'And? Alex. *And?*'

'And you will always save yourself.'

And Alexander Locke shoved Kit into the cell with four murderously angry Artisan assassins and walked away.

23

K IT HAD SPENT A DAY AND a half in an opium haze negotiating with two figments of his own imagination. By the time he stood in front of the Agency headquarters and looked up the drab façade, he, Christopher and Crispin were mostly at agreement and integrated back into one mind. Control was ceded to Kit, as it bloody well should be, but he had now agreed to keep his promise and accept emotions he was well and truly not used to feeling.

He was having trouble standing because his knees were trembling. Habit and instinct begged him to push the fear down into oblivion. But if he wanted to express his Art properly, and not have it return to the chancy, hard-won thing it had been before—or even worse than that, now he had open rebellion in his head—then he had to let himself feel.

And what he felt right now was fear to the point of terror.

But he'd been inside the Agency before, when he registered himself, and so he knew about the telepath Artisan and he guessed Alex was going to have to get past the telepath to fulfil his plan. And Alex was not so good at guile. Therefore he indulged his more dramatic tendencies and made a bloody spectacle of himself, which was more fun than fearful.

Fear resurged quite drastically, however, when Alex locked the cell door behind him and strode off without a backwards look.

None of the assassins moved and then they did, the male metalworking Artisan lunging at Kit. Kit put a hand to the iron bars behind him, and suddenly he was standing on the other side of the bars, looking back through them at the four angry Artisans.

'How did you do that through iron?' said the pied piper Artisan. He was short and had dark Welsh colouring, though none of the accent. He was keeping well back from the bars.

'I go around the iron,' Kit said vaguely. He couldn't otherwise describe the way his Art was compensating for the holes iron put in his Artworks.

He waved a polite farewell and started back towards the guardroom, walking lightly along the far wall so he would get line of sight on the guard before the guard spotted him.

'Hey!' called the stoneworking Artisan, keeping her voice low. 'Hey, boy. There's guards out there.'

'There's one guard,' Kit said. *And quite a few thresholds.*

'You could still use help, though, right?'

Kit looked over his shoulder at her. She was the oldest of the four, grey-haired and a little on the gaunt side, like Artisans tended to be if they had trouble getting enough food to fuel their Art. She stood apart from the other three, and was running a finger over the iron bars thoughtfully. After a moment of that, though, she put the finger in her mouth, frowning.

'Not particularly,' he said. 'It's nice to have, I suppose.'

'Come on,' said the female metalworking Artisan. 'We won't hurt you, we promise. We just want out, too.'

'Hey!' shouted her partner. 'Hey, he's escaping!'

'Clifford!' she said, shoving him.

The guard came barrelling into the room in response to the yell. Kit backed up to the bars, looking innocent.

'Here, what're you playing at?' the guard bellowed at him, pulling a truncheon, not of the glowing sort.

Just as Kit put his hand on the cell door behind him so he could cross the threshold to the archway to the guardroom, the stoneworker threaded her hand through the bars to rest it on Kit's shoulder in casual camaraderie, effectively pinning him in place.

Without looking away from the nonplussed guard, now stalking forwards with his baton raised, Kit shifted his weight so that her wrist was pressed to the iron bar. He heard her hiss between her teeth, but she didn't relent.

'Fine!' Kit said, and opened the cell door.

The metalworking Artisans led the charge, working together in a way that reminded Kit of the Locke twins. Even without their pretty knives, they made a few complex moves around the guard that disarmed him and swept his legs out from under him. While he lay dazed, the pied piper tapped him between the eyes and hissed something that made him go limp.

'Compulsion?' Kit asked him. 'Aren't you an animal controller?'

'People are animals,' the pied piper said.

'No argument here,' Kit said.

The stoneworking Artisan, giving Kit a rude look as she rubbed her wrist, eased past him, followed by the pied piper. The metalworking Artisans, however, turned speculative looks on Kit. The male metalworker, in particular, looked like he might want some payback now he was free.

'I'll open every door between here and the way out,' Kit said quickly. 'Go on ahead.'

They exchanged glances before nodding. Kit followed them out of the guardroom, where the stoneworker was uselessly trying an Artwork to unlock the main door into the corridor. The metalworkers might have had more luck, if they had shaped their Art towards working on intricate metal locks instead of flinging metal knives.

Kit, holding back at the arch in case of double-crossing, opened the door for them as he had promised.

Then he took a breath and opened every door he could reach to. That was a lot of doors, when he was rested and fed and whole in mind. He felt them click-click-click in his own head in an expanding circle around him, rippling all the way out to the street.

There. If that didn't help Alex with whatever plan he was enacting, he couldn't be helped.

He leaned against the arch, disguising dizziness. It had possibly been a mistake to use so much Art to help the enforcer who had arrested him, persuaded him to trust him, and then drugged him and shoved him into a cell. He couldn't bring himself to think helping Alex was a mistake.

The other Artisans hurried out in a pack. They had a decent chance of escape, if they worked together. Kit did not trust them to do that and he did not trust them not to turn on him afterwards, so when they turned towards the front of the headquarters, he stopped and let them go on ahead.

He looked the other way, down the hallway towards the offices. He was in no doubt that Alex had headed that way. Indeed, a few more steps put him in sight of the heavy iron door that led in there, and it was sitting ajar. Kit had no way of telling whether that had been from his intervention, or if Alex had been fully prepared for breaking through a locked door.

He liked to think he had helped. He liked to think that beyond the door was a lot of locked rooms and cabinets that he had unlocked and that therefore Alex would find whatever it was he needed to find. Every part of him wanted to follow his line of sight and go through that heavy door and catch up with Alex.

He turned the other way.

As he went past the cells, where the guard still lay comatose, he heard a distant hubbub start up, shouts and screams and a few thumps and crashes which either boded well for the escaping Artisans, or boded ill. It probably aided Alex either way, at least.

He had to dodge a flood of rats scuttling to answer the pied piper's call; it was just as disgusting as last time, but it did tell him he was heading in the right direction—towards the kitchen and the alley it would surely let out on.

He finally found a set of stairs and went down into a large basement kitchen, quiet on the half-day holiday. The handful of kitchenhands left working watched him with dispassionate curiosity as he walked in. One disconsolate aproned boy was sat at the big central table, peeling his way through a mountain of potatoes. He looked up without interest as Kit went past him, out the back door and up the steps to the yard.

Kit came back down and in. 'Why is there no gate out of the yard?' he demanded. There was only a featureless painted brick wall on all sides.

'Security,' the kitchenhand said. 'People were trying to break in from the alleyway behind, so they bricked it up.'

'What if there's a fire?' Kit said. 'How are you meant to escape? You need a worker's union.'

'Is there about to be a fire?' a kitchenhand at the sink asked warily. 'Sir?'

Kit looked around. The kitchen, as one would expect in such a large, modern and well-funded building, was well fitted out, with polished cabinetry, gas cookstoves, icebox, and of course the big sinks with their indoor plumbing. In one corner, it had a water pump with a shiny handle.

'Find me a really big bowl,' he ordered. 'And you'll see something interesting.'

'I'd rather hold something interesting,' said the potato-peeling kitchenhand. Kit stared at him till he went red. 'I meant coins,' he mumbled.

'I'm sure you did.' Kit turned out his pockets. 'I don't have any. Find me the bowl anyway. Stick it to them for making you work today.'

The kitchenhand at the sink tipped out a tub holding dirty dishes and brought it over to Kit. 'Better hurry before Cook comes back. She's not happy about working today either but she'll take it out on you instead of helping you.'

Kit put the tub under the pump and filled it about halfway. He didn't want to waste the kitchenhands' interest by filling it all the way, and didn't need to anyway. He kicked off Sir Kingsford's expensive shoes—a few of the kitchenhands pounced and looked ready to fight over them—but otherwise was fully dressed as he stepped in.

'This is more mad than interesting so far,' the helpful kitchenhand pointed out.

Kit jiggled his legs and smiled. Hot and cold baths, Alex had said, and made him look. He pictured the building in his head. He'd only ever been inside one public baths before; they'd been plainly tiled and cramped and grimy. Those new ones down the street would surely be bigger and prettier. He couldn't imagine quite what they'd look like inside so he thought of the wet heat of the steam against his skin and the cave-like echo of the constant drip and slosh of water. He wove the Artwork together and released it; the threshold opened under him.

He dropped into it, just catching the gasps at the magic trick as he vanished.

He surfaced in the baths and flailed through the water, hair in his eyes, water in his lungs, echoes of his own name in his ears. He'd either missed the hot water baths, landing in one of the cold water ones, or the heating was turned off today because of the half-holiday. His teeth were chattering. That, even more than the bone-deep exhaustion, told him he'd used up his Art.

He should have taken off Kingsford's coat, at least. Of good wool, it was now sodden and heavy and weighing him down, threatening to drag him off his feet. Groping blindly, he found an edge and hooked his forearms over it.

A hand came down to touch his and he yelped and jerked away. He'd really thought the baths would be closed for the half-day holiday. He fell backwards into the water, at which point he discovered that swimming was not nearly as obvious as it looked. He sank like a stone.

Someone got him by the collar and pulled upwards.

'It's all right, Kit, it's all right, it's us,' someone further away was saying as he got his feet back under him and came up for air.

Kit shoved his wet hair out of his face and looked at an impossible face. '*Edith Knight?*'

'Alex told us where he hoped you'd be,' she said simply, holding out her hand.

Lulu was standing right behind her, stone-faced. Kit backed away but the hold on his coat was unrelenting. He looked and found Sir Kingsford Locke, cane discarded, kneeling at the tiled edge and leaning far out over the water with one hand locked tight on Kit's collar.

Sir Kingsford was braced, his face pained; Kit was in danger of pulling him in. Kit looked at him and he looked back and then he pursed his lips and whistled some awkward notes that Kit eventually recognised as *Whistle and I'll Come to You, My Lad*, that he'd teased Alex with, back in the baronet's study in Northfield.

'You really are the oddest duck,' Kit said.

'What is that common phrase my brother uses?'

'Pot, kettle?'

'Come along, Whitely,' Sir Kingsford said.

And Kit came along, out of the water and into some blankets. Lulu helped get him into Sir Kingsford's coach before vanishing, presumably to help Alex. Edith sat opposite Kit and Sir Kingsford and patted Kit's hand.

Kit curled up in a ball and put his head on the baronet's lap so he could sleep.

'Jesus Christ,' Sir Kingsford said, before clumsily patting him too.

24

KIT AND EDITH DID GO SEE Obaysch the hippopotamus at London Zoo, escorted by Sir Kingsford.

It was a strange creature, mud-coloured and something like an ill-proportioned hog. It slept like a lump and then rose and lumbered into the water, splashing them.

Edith was satisfied, but Kit was saddened, and his Art twitched within him with the desire to unlock cages.

Sir Kingsford tackled London much like his brother did, with a slight squint that spoke volumes as to how on the edge of tolerable he found it. The Locke twins made no reappearance, and so the baronet took Kit and Edith all the way home. Apparently, when his siblings asked his help, he gave it unstintingly.

When they arrived back in Lovelly, Sir Kingsford took a walk around the village and Edith's parents hauled her into their parlour and gave her a bollocking the likes of which the baronet could have taken notes on, for leaving the village so precipitously and without actually getting permission to go travelling alone with a man who had just been arrested.

Edith came out teary-eyed and morose. She flung her arms around Kit. 'They do care about me,' she sobbed, while Minnie nuzzled her.

'I *said* I said some things I didn't mean,' Kit said.

Edith glared. 'You know, you didn't have to take quite so much pleasure in acting the villain, Kitty.'

'I didn't!' Kit said, before smirking just a bit. 'When I burn something down, Eddie, I burn it to the ground.'

'Did you, though, luv?' Edith asked. 'Alex went out of his way to point out an escape route for you. And dug Sir Kingsford out of Northfield to help us home, too. That was planned before we ever got to London.'

Kit shrugged. 'Uncommon decency, I suppose,' he said, as nonchalantly as he could.

It touched on feelings he didn't want to face yet. After all, he had been in company with the man's brother for days. If Alex wanted to see him, he'd have seen him.

Kit celebrated his first Christmas with the Knights that year.

The Knights ate a lot of food, and drank a lot of nog, and apparently they put a lot of rum in the nog before they drank a lot of it, and so things got raucous. Meredith—who, to no one's surprise but everyone's scandalised delight, had broken her engagement to Young Tom and become engaged to Will—came and cried on Edith's shoulder.

This was to Edith's great annoyance because she was trying to read a letter Kit suspected was from Lulu.

Meanwhile, Young Tom got drunk enough to come and cry on Kit's shoulder, which Kit tolerated until Young Tom started planting sloppy kisses on his face and telling him he'd always thought he was very pretty. Kit was still unrepentantly petty enough to shunt him off to Will, who might, and who was roaring drunk himself, possibly also entirely due to Meredith, but for the opposite reason to Young Tom.

Either way, the ensuing scenes were enough to cause drama in Lovelly until the summer solstice.

Santa Claus indeed visited, leaving presents for all the Knight grandchildren, and for Edith, and for Kit, who found himself sitting in the wingback chair by the fire with a new scarf and a tin of biscuits, both quite plainly made by Mrs Knight, on his lap and tears in his eyes because he wasn't in disgrace with the Knights anymore.

Emotions were bullshit.

Visitors started coming back in time for the spring equinox; they would peak at the summer solstice. Both dates were celebrated at Knightstone Circle.

Strangers still made Kit nervous enough that he had got into the habit of casually keeping thresholds closed between him and them. Safe in his armchair in Edith's reading room, he had both the door from the main floor of the shop and the back door blocked.

Coat and boots off, he was bent over a music sheet, squinting slightly. It was a grey day and the reading room was dim even with the lamp lit. He lilted the words of the song quietly to himself; Christmas had also been when the Knights had discovered that Kit could sing—damn all that nog— and he'd been inveigled into the village choir for a performance in the summer pavilion.

He was trying to learn his part, because he was nervous about singing in front of people sober and also worried about letting his friends down, because emotions were bullshit.

He thought he might have to ask Edith for help with practising.

Well. Baby steps.

'Drop it,' Edith sang out, and Kit unblocked the threshold to let her bring her latest patron through.

Except the two sets of footsteps stopped in the middle of the room, and Edith said, 'Sorry, Kitty, he made a really good case,' and darted out again while Kit was still raising his head from the sheet.

'Edith Mary Rose Knight!' he shouted after her with true outrage, because the patron she had led into the reading room was Alexander Locke.

'Closing the store and getting lunch! I'll be a really long time!' she shouted back. 'Let's go, Lulu.'

'Good to see you, poppet,' he heard Lulu answer, just before the front door slammed.

Kit hopped up so he was balanced on the arms of his armchair in his stockinged feet, hand on the frame of the window, the convenient threshold located just behind his armchair and that was hardly a coincidence.

But he didn't yet make the crossing. He drank in the sight of Alex, tall and steady and smiling his wolf's smile. He looked good. He'd smell good. He'd feel good.

'Look at you,' Alex said fondly. 'You want to run so badly, don't you?'

'I still have two weeks' worth of preserved food stashed in the old chalk mines,' Kit said.

'Then I'll see you in two weeks.'

Alex sat in a chair by the table and flipped idly through the newspaper there, skipping past the articles about the British East India Company's troubles and pausing on the pages devoted to Artisans.

Reuben's death was reported there.

Also the trial of Bishop Varley, who had been delivered into custody by the Orphanage after incontrovertible evidence of what he had done to the orphans under his care was leaked from the Agency headquarters by an anonymous benefactor.

Also the sweeping reforms in the Agency designed to keep further leaks under control, not least of which was moving where the on-duty telepath sat.

But not the strange plague of pain attacks afflicting Orphanage hierarchy, because that hadn't been connected to the rogue Artisans yet.

Alex tapped on the newspaper absently. He probably wasn't reading past the headlines but he would know their contents well enough.

Kit folded his arms but the movement made him wobble so he slid down to stand on the seat of the armchair instead. 'Seems to me you should take the hint.'

'Seems to me you might want to see this.' Locke displayed an official-looking piece of paper. It had an awful lot of scrollwork and black edges.

'If that's a sodding arrest warrant, Mr Locke, I will have a sodding fit.'

'It's not, Kit. Come on.' He held it out.

'Why are you here, enforcer?'

'I handed in my badge. I turned out to be extremely corrupt.' Alex gave a *how about that* sort of shrug.

Kit rolled his eyes. 'Which of the very many commissions to catch me have you accepted, bounty hunter?'

Alex waved the black-edged paper. 'You really need to come and read this.'

Kit shook his head.

'That's not like you.' Alex set it down and aligned its bottom edge carefully with the table edge.

Kit huffed. 'It's easy to be brave when you don't feel fear,' he snapped. 'And now I do. And anger. Oh my God, do I feel anger.'

He plucked a book off the shelf on the other side of the armchair and threw it at Alex's head. Alex caught it.

'So. You. Can. Just. Fuck. Right. Off.' Kit punctuated each word with another book.

Alex, grinning, caught each one with ease and set them on the table in rapid succession; this was probably good, given Edith's reaction if she caught Kit treating her books like that.

'Why are you laughing?' Kit shouted, and threw another couple. He'd all but emptied the shelf.

'I'm not laughing at you,' Alex explained. 'It's just so good to see you getting furious about things you're entitled to be furious about, Kit.'

'Yes, well,' Kit said. He held the last book in his hands and turned it over. 'It turns out I have a really angry adolescent inside me and holy hellfire, does that boy likes to express his feelings.' He dropped the book back on the shelf. 'Tell me why you're here, Alex,' he said tiredly. 'I know I fucked you over but you handed me to the Agency. Doesn't that meet your definition of justice? Haven't I been punished enough?'

Those last words had just slipped out. He was too busy wincing at his own sentimentality to react as fast as he should have when Alex suddenly leapt at him. Kit recoiled, half-falling over the back of the armchair in a valiant but futile attempt to get his hand to the window. Alex barrelled into him, flattening him against the overstuffed cushion.

'This went downhill fast,' Kit remarked.

He shoved at Alex. Damn the man, he felt and smelt as good as Kit had known he would.

Alex sat up, half-straddling him, easing his weight off him but keeping his hands on his shoulders. His face was flushed in high flags along his cheekbones. 'Sorry. Sorry, Kit. I couldn't let that stand.'

'You're not letting *me* stand.' Again, he pushed, palms flat on Alex's chest.

This time Alex did not give an inch of ground. 'I am most certainly not here to punish you, sweetheart. I'm here to make amends.'

'For what?' Kit said, in genuine confusion. 'Off me, you arse.'

'For drugging you and throwing you into a cell full of assassins.' Alex was sounding patient. 'The first, more than the second, if I'm honest. Now go over there and look at that bloody piece of paper I spent months organising for you.'

He backed off, holding out his hand. Kit ignored it, awkwardly clambering off the chair and edging over to the table, keeping an ostentatiously distrustful eye on Alex, which Alex took with an annoyingly tolerant smile.

Kit quickly skimmed the black-edged paper. It was a death notice for Christopher Whitebrickleyhurst.

Kit got a strange feeling in his stomach, a moment of pure grief for poor, lost Christopher. In his head, Christopher stirred long enough to scoff at that. He took a breath, hand over his stomach, and another, and a third. It never really had been his name, he reminded himself.

Alex shifted his weight. 'Do I ignore this or can I hug you?'

Kit realised his eyes were burning because they were leaking silent tears. Because emotions were bullshit. 'You can stay the hell over there, Mr Locke.' He wiped his face.

'No one's coming for you anymore.' He gestured to the paper. 'It was the least we could have done for you.'

'The least you could have done was—' Nothing. The least they could have done was nothing. '—posted it to me so I never had to see you again.'

Alex gave a nod that was one-part hurt to three-parts accepting. 'Kingsford has business in the village anyway. I'm acting on his behalf.' He made a face that was disguising pride.

Kit looked up at that, but refused to ask.

'He's buying the Grange,' the big man said helpfully. 'Little taste of Somerset, a tribute to our mother.'

'You really do have a very nice older brother, Alexander,' Kit couldn't help but say.

'I *know*,' Alex said, with a roll of the eyes of his own, but he was smiling. 'It's positively disturbing how well you two get along.'

'Only for you.' Kit smoothed his hand over the newspaper, still lying open on the table beside the teetering pile of books. 'Varley's trial?'

'Slow. But the evidence is solid, the tide of public opinion is against him, and the judge prides himself on his reputation for both independence and severity. He'll hang.'

'Lulu is happy?'

'As she can be. She really did want to take his heart out herself, and it'd be better if the trial was for Peter's murder as well as the orphans' deaths. But she does quite enjoy sitting in the gallery and staring at him like his own personal angel of death. It's why he's sweating so much in the dock, which makes him look nicely guilty. And if he'd not found guilty. Well. She has her pistols in her reticule. And she has me to get her out of London.'

'Well.' Kit folded his hands together. 'Goodbye then, Mr Locke.'

'I'm not done, Mr Whitely.' Out of his coat pocket, Alex took a series of envelopes, laying them out like he was an extremely precise card dealer. He tapped them one by one as he spoke. 'This envelope has identification papers in the name of Kit Whitely, the sort of papers that would let you travel, if that's what you want. This one has your original birth records and everything else I could find about you and your parents. But in case you don't want to know everything, this envelope has just the name your parents gave you, and this one has just your parents' details.'

Kit put a finger on this envelope and pushed it, skewing it from the perfect alignment of the rest. He looked at Alex.

With a single finger of his own, Alex straightened the envelope back into its regimented row and answered the unasked question. 'They're dead, Kit. Judging by the dates, you were legitimately an orphan when you went into the Orphanage.'

Now there was a maelstrom of unfamiliar feelings. Emotions really were just absolute *bullshit*.

Alex collected him into his arms, and swiped under his eyes with a gentle thumb. 'All right, sweetheart?'

'Fine. I'm fine. Do I have brothers or sisters?'

'None recorded. But it seems to me you have an entire village of brothers and sisters, Kit,' Alex said gently, and then had to hug him again.

'Why did you do this?' Kit finally managed to ask. 'I betrayed you.'

'No, you didn't,' Alex said mildly. He lifted Kit's hand and kissed the stump where his little finger had been. 'This was frostbite, wasn't it?'

Kit stiffened, suddenly rigid under Alex's firm hands in a way he could not hide.

'It was Reuben, wasn't it?'

'I have no notion whatsoever as to what you might mean, Mr Locke. Let me go.'

'Just let me hold you for another minute, then I will.'

Kit grumblingly acquiesced, leaning into him. Alex nuzzled his face past his shirt collar and touched his mouth to the curve where Kit's neck became his shoulder.

Kit went limp against him. 'You don't have to let go,' he conceded.

'Good, because I wasn't planning to.'

Kit hummed his disapproval and Alex laughed against his skin. 'Come sit with me.'

Without waiting for an answer, he flopped into the armchair, bundling Kit into his lap.

'I am too big to sit—'

'Genevieve came to us,' Alex interrupted, instantly silencing him. He waited and Alex went on, 'I'm sure you can guess that she wanted help to find Reuben. We went to their home, and there was not a single item in it that Reuben had enough attachment to for Lulu to use to track him. Not even his wedding ring, which he'd left behind.'

Kit nodded. None of that came as a surprise.

Alex gestured towards the newspaper on the table. 'Lulu had to tell Ginnie he was dead. It seemed kinder than telling her the truth.'

'I understand that.' Kit wasn't sure it was the best course of action, but he understood the impulse to kindness.

'He disappeared on the same night the knife did. And then, once Lulu had touched his things and seen he had no attachments at all, it was obvious.' Kit waited for the accusation, but Alex went on, 'He wasn't your employer, though, was he? Did he threaten you?'

It was safe to talk about it now. He could tell Alex the truth, now.

He said nothing.

'He threatened *me*,' Alex said very softly, his mouth by Kit's ear.

And the words came out in a torrent. 'He said he'd turn your heart to ice. He said he'd turn you all into ice blocks and smash you. He said he'd make you breathe ice. He would have frozen your lungs, Alex. He would have frozen our blood in our veins.'

Alex was holding Kit tightly, rocking him a little. 'You kept us safe, sweetheart.'

Kit really was too big to be sitting in Alex's lap. Regardless, he squirmed about so he could throw his arms around Alex's neck, huddling into the comfort without hesitation or shame. The fear he had suppressed, that moment when he had realised he could protect himself, or Alex and the others, but not both, took him and he shuddered.

Alex ran a soothing hand over his back. 'I know it's not your natural tendency,' he murmured, 'but you could've confided in me, afterwards. I would have believed you. I trusted you.'

'I couldn't let Lulu have the knife,' Kit said. 'I couldn't risk that you pair would decide to go after Reuben. I touched that knife, Alex, and I couldn't let Lulu touch it. It would have eaten her alive.'

Cheek pressed against Kit's curls, Alex was silent for a long time. He might have been thinking about Lulu, or about the knife, or, as Kit sometimes did, where the hell Reuben had vanished to and what he intended to do with the knife he had been so desperate to get hold of.

'Drowning,' he said at last. 'You talked about drowning, in the poppy dreams. Is that what you meant? You were keeping Lulu from drowning?'

'In blood,' Kit said flatly.

'Jesus,' Alex whispered.

'You won't go after him, will you? Please say you won't.'

'We won't,' Alex said. 'It's for the Agency Artisans, if he resurfaces with intent. Or the Myriad. For now, it's better that he stays dead.' He shook his head. 'If he scared you as much as he did, he must have been— And what we did to you. What I did. I'm sorry, Kit.'

Kit shrugged, keeping his face buried in the crook of Alex's neck. Alex's hands slid up and down his back, up and down his back. Kit nestled in closer. 'You thought I deserved it.'

'Should have properly trusted you, like I told you I did,' Alex murmured. 'I should've known you'd not do a thing like that.'

Kit held back a laugh, since he had been and still was perfectly capable of doing a thing like that.

Just not to Alex. Or Edith. Or any of the other Lovely villagers or the other Lockes. Or… Well, all right.

'We knew Varley was an unregistered Artisan and we knew Agency agents collect information on unregistered Artisans. We knew they were holding evidence on Varley in their offices. We knew they were sitting on it.'

'All right.'

'I needed a famously hard-to-catch Artisan to justify why they should let me back there.'

'I guessed that.'

'I couldn't warn you, because of the telepath.'

'I know, Alex.'

'If you'd told me you have a secondary Art that lets you block telepathy—'

'I do not,' Kit said, offended. 'I just have a very disciplined mind that a telepath can't break.'

Alex sighed heavily against his skin. 'I wasn't expecting them to have their files locked away in rows and rows of unlabelled cabinets and I was standing there wondering how many I was going to have to break open when every single cabinet unlocked itself. Made the search a hell of a lot easier.'

Kit made a very satisfied hum.

'Though the buggers file by Art first rather than name, and you tell me what Art Varley has.'

'Filed under T for Telepathy,' Kit said promptly, 'subset A for Art-reading, sub-subset V for Varley.'

'That would have been very helpful when I was opening a hundred filing drawers looking for his name,' Alex said. 'Also: being able to read properly.'

He sobered, taking Kit's face in his hands so that Kit could not escape his sincerity. 'I arrested you and pressured you and shoved you into that cell. I took away your choices, which is the one thing you kept asking I not do.'

'You trusted me to take care of myself like I kept demanding you do.' Kit hesitated. 'The laudanum's a little harder to forgive.'

He felt Alex's nod, his acceptance; he let go of Kit, waiting for the guillotine to fall.

'I do forgive you, in case it's not obvious,' Kit added, since apparently it wasn't. Well. He was petty as hell; he probably didn't come across as the forgiving sort.

He heard the sound Alex made into his hair, and then he made another sound into Kit's mouth, since Kit had finally done what he'd wanted to do since the moment the man had walked into the room.

He broke off to say, 'Well, now, hold on there, Mr Locke. Aren't you reading my intentions?'

Alex's wolfish smile bloomed. 'I am not, Mr Whitely. I'm blocking them.

I've turned down the dial.' He kissed him lightly, eyes warm. 'Yet another reason I have to be grateful to you.'

'How will you thank me, baby?' Kit said, smiling wickedly and sliding his fingers into Alex's hair to pull his mouth back to his.

'Too much of the terrifying talking already, my little hedgehog?' Alex enquired just before he gave over. In fairly short order, he'd scooped Kit up off the chair and pressed him all the way onto the floor, never breaking the kiss.

'Get your clothes off, I want your skin,' Kit said into his mouth.

'Lock the door properly this time,' Alex countered as he sat up to strip off his necktie and coat.

'It's well and truly locked, baby,' Kit informed him, dealing with Alex's waistcoat—blue and green stripes reminiscent of a peacock's tail today—and shirt with nimble and impatient fingers, shifting his weight forwards to straddle him as he did so.

'Stop that.' Alex took his hips and rolled them over so that he was on top again. 'It's your turn. I'm giving you what you want, sweetheart. And you're going to take it. Anything you want, my love.'

He was gazing down at Kit with impossible fondness, maddening softness. Kit went still under him.

'Too much?' Alex asked again, not teasing him this time.

He eased back, so that Kit could have wriggled away if he needed to. Which was sweet. And annoying. And sweet.

'No,' he said. 'Just… Don't look at me like that, Alex. I'm not fragile. I'm stronger than I look.'

'Are you?' Alex said. 'Hadn't noticed.'

'Sarcasm is the hallmark of—'

'Don't you bloody start,' Alex growled in his ear, sending a lovely frisson down his spine. 'Kit, you're the strongest person I've ever met.'

Kit froze again. He was already flat to the rug with Alex propped up over him, and yet now he felt utterly flattened into the floor by the weight of more than the bigger man.

'Then stop looking at me like I'm fragile,' he managed to say.

'I'm not looking at you like you're fragile,' Alex said. 'I'm looking at you like you're precious. Because you are.'

He shut his eyes. His skin was not fair, and the room was dim, so maybe Alex wouldn't notice—

Brushing the backs of his fingers along Kit's cheeks, Alex murmured, 'Blushing. Goodness. That I lived to see the day.'

Kit could hear the smile in his voice, the smug git. 'Oh, shut up,' he said. 'Shut up and have me, already.'

'Can't do both,' Alex said cheerily, as his mouth followed his fingers along Kit's buttons. 'Which is it to be? May I have you, then?'

Kit hummed his distinct approval of the idea. Alex tugged his trousers and drawers down over his hips and made an approving hum of his own, before taking Kit in his mouth. Kit gasped and sunk his hands into Alex's hair.

Alex lifted his head, said, 'That's right, sweetheart, you mess me up,' and took him down to his root, throat rippling about him.

'This is going to be very quick,' Kit whimpered to the ceiling, in helpless thrall to the sensations, his fingers scrabbling against Alex's scalp.

Alex released him. He tightened his fingers around Kit's shaft. 'Nope. I'm making you work for it, my lad.'

He licked and sucked at just the tip and Kit moaned, his hips arching up of their own accord to try to bury himself back into Alex's warm mouth. He could hear Alex laughing quietly as he worked him to the very edge of release and yet not a single sodding inch further.

'Oh my God, you want me to die,' he wailed. Alex tormented him until he was writhing and cursing and pulling really quite hard on his hair, until he finally said, brokenly, 'Please, Alex, please.'

Alex paused. 'Won't this reduce your Art?'

'I don't need more Art,' Kit told him, meeting his eyes. 'I need you.'

'Fucking sweet-talker,' Alex murmured.

Setting one hand to span Kit's stomach and pin him in place, the big man took him fully in again and sucked, head bobbing up and down as his other hand caressed his balls and stroked up towards his hole. Kit's hands clenched; he cried out at a volume that made him glad the shop was shut and spent down Alex's throat.

Alex kissed and licked his way back up and devoured Kit's mouth. 'Beautiful,' he told him fervently. Then he moved to lay beside Kit, pulling him in tight.

'You and your cuddles,' Kit groused as he snuggled in and kissed Alex's bare chest. 'What now?'

'You take me to your room before we defile Edith's lending library further.'

'I meant,' Kit said, flicking his nipple lightly, 'what are the Locke twins planning to do now?'

'I believe Lulu is thinking of living at the Grange. At least for part of the year.'

Kit considered this from every angle before he said, 'The fuck?'

'Yeah,' Alex said. 'Technically she's overseeing renovations, but I think she'd like to know Miss Knight better.'

Kit hummed. 'She's been sending letters.'

'She likes to move slow,' Alex said. 'So do I. And then there was you.' Kit peeked up at him, but he was smiling. 'Also, she's rather interested in what Fisher Tom gets up to.'

'Oh,' Kit said. 'About as close to piracy as you can get, really.'

'Exactly. Fisher Tom doesn't seem quite so excited, but he'll come around.'

'And you?' Kit asked delicately. 'Joining the crew?'

'Well,' Alex said, drawing it out. 'We're not attached at the hip, are we? So I'm going to leave her to it. I'm thinking of travelling abroad again. Not India right now, of course, but we signed a treaty with Japan a few years ago. If it doesn't work out, China.'

Kit nodded, biting his lip. Emotions were bullshit. 'Sounds dangerous,' he said, though he knew nothing of either of those places and so was probably slandering them horribly.

'We'll keep each other safe.'

Kit frowned. 'But Miss Lulu's not—'

'I'm inviting you to come with me, *in case it's not obvious*,' Alex said. 'I didn't get you those bloody travel papers because I'm a nice person, you know.'

'Oh!' Kit said. 'Oh. Yes. I'd like that.' He shifted to look towards the side table by his armchair, where his music sheet lay abandoned. 'Can we wait a while, though?'

He heard the rumble of Alex's laughter where his ear was pressed against his chest. 'I'm not trying to take you from your family, Kit. We'll go when you're ready, we'll come back when you're ready.'

Kit chewed his lower lip. He was given to be selfish, sometimes. He wanted more than anything to be selfish right now. But he said, 'Alex, you spent an awfully long time following Lulu around because you felt like you'd failed her and had to atone. And now you perhaps feel like you've failed me?'

'No,' Alex said firmly. 'Well, yes, I did, but no. I just… I miss you like a limb, Kit, and I want to spend time with you and I want to know you better if you want to let me. I want to take you all the places you want to see in the world and I want to see sunsets in new skies with you. That's all.'

Oh, yes. That was all. Not much. 'Like a honeymoon, baby?'

Once again, Alex merely smiled and indulged Kit's deflection. 'Yes, like a honeymoon,' he said. 'Except we don't have to visit any relatives, so it's an enjoyable honeymoon. Come with me. Be with me, sweetheart.'

Kit turned his face into Alex's chest. 'I want to,' he whispered. 'But, Alex? You can't know what you're letting yourself in for. I'm on a long road. I'm not ever going to be easy for you.'

Alex laughed. 'Kit Whitely, you are the easiest choice I've ever made.'

Kit helplessly mumbled, 'I love you, Alex,' mostly hoping the man wouldn't hear him.

Trusting that he would.

'My God, you suck a man's cock and he gets soppy,' Alex said. While Kit was still sniggering, he slipped a soft, 'Love you, too, Kit,' straight past his defences, so that Kit just tweaked his nipple again instead of panicking completely.

Well played, Alexander Locke.

His hands slid over Kit's back, his warm strength feeding Kit's heat. 'Will you take me to your room?'

'Baby, I'll take you everywhere,' Kit said.

Alex smiled, a bright gleam amid the gloom. 'Yeah, all right.'

Bonus

Thanks for reading! Below is a bonus short story. If you just want to see Varley get his, you can treat this as an epilogue to the current story. But if you also want to see Reuben get his, you can treat this as a sneak peek of *The Use of Myriad Arts*, a follow-up story.

I T WAS THE SUMMER OF THE Great Stink, London further suffered the most oppressive heatwave imaginable, Parliament greatly regretted its riverside location, and Mrs Genevieve McAvey was attending a hanging.

She had come to Newgate to support her cousin, the widowed Lucinda Llewellyn, who in her turn was there to avidly watch the man who had murdered her husband swing.

The former Bishop Varley was sentenced to hang not for that murder, but for the murder of orphans. Since Lulu and her twin, Alexander Locke, had orchestrated the whole affair—uncovered the evidence, winkled Varley out of his hiding place, used bribes and other points of pressure to ensure a fair judge, that was to say a judge that would be fairer to their desired outcome than to the Church's at the trial—she was grimly satisfied with the outcome.

Genevieve saw the twins' distinctive uncovered heads, towering height, and broad shoulders ahead of her at the entrance to the Magpie and Stump. They had secured a prime viewing location upstairs, away from the heaving crowd she was currently forcing her way through with the magnificent bearing of a ship under full sail, ignoring the second glances her obvious situation engendered.

The sweat and stale perfume of the unwashed mass, the ordure squelching under her boots, the noxious smoke from the surrounding buildings: the once trying smells of London were a distinct relief from the fetid smell from the river that would smother the city as the day warmed into yet another sweltering nightmare.

'It's sickening how disgustingly happy that little shit makes you,' Lulu was saying as Genevieve approached her cousins.

'Supportive as ever, my darling baby sister,' Alex said amiably, looking off across the mob.

'I haven't strangled him in his sleep, how's that for supportive, Lexi?'

'It'll serve.' Alex turned and smiled at Genevieve. He could read intentions, a talent that fell only just shy of an Art, and must have sensed hers, as familiar to him as Lulu's, as she came up behind them, wholly centred on finding a seat as soon as possible. 'Hello, my dear. You're looking blooming.'

Genevieve narrowed her eyes at her sandy-haired, mellow-eyed cousin. What she was, in fact, was nine months gone with child, and dressed head to toe in black crepe, because she was gone with widowhood just about as long. She felt many things in the unnatural and ungodly heat and stink of London this summer—blooming was not one of them.

'Are you indulging yourself, Alex?' she asked as he took her arm to help her up the stairs to their rented room with a superlative, and no doubt superlatively expensive, view of the scaffold. Tall, broad, strong, her cousin was as affable as ever, a calm, comforting presence at her side. 'Lulu hasn't mentioned that in her letters.'

Her cousin replied in the affirmative, but in that tone that meant he was not encouraging further questions, which surprised her. She knew he preferred men and had never given him any indication that she condemned him for it, mostly because she didn't.

'How are your people?' he asked lightly, squiring her to her chair, so she was diverted into telling him that Miss Delacorte, Mr Oliver and Mr Fletcher were all quite well, thank you.

'And did you two pass a pleasant birthday last month?' she enquired in her turn.

'Exceedingly,' Alex said, sitting beside her. 'I received the best possible gift.'

He spoke with a smugness that either had to do with his current indulgence, or with the fact of his long overdue reconciliation with their elder brother, Sir Kingsford. On the one hand, it was a secretive sort of smugness, which lent itself to the former explanation, but on the other, she had sent her birthday congratulations via Sir Kingsford's country estate.

Once, the twins would have spent their birthday with her. She was, suddenly, too young again, trapped in her second Season, resenting the twins for their freedom, pitying them for their grief, and happy for them as they began to find their way—and yet, simultaneously in all this tumult, managing to feel sad for herself because she could not be a part of it.

A breakfast had been laid out, though none of them touched it; food tended to turn Genevieve's stomach this far along. Lulu, never one for dull social niceties such as enquiring after the health and wellbeing of old friends, sat and pulled from her ever-present pack an epitome of her secret vice, magazines and instructional manuals aimed at ladies. She'd consulted these heavily as a confused adolescent trying to replicate the pinnacle of womanhood, but these days found them merely a source of both comfort and amusement.

This one was called *The Arts of Beauty, or Secrets of a Lady's Toilet*. Because Lulu knew how much such books annoyed Genevieve, she made a show of reading from it with attentive regard, before giving up the game by snorting and quoting out loud, '"Those two heaving hills of snow"?'

They all chortled, like the utter children they were. 'Do tell,' Genevieve said.

'A countess recounts her methods for keeping the bosoms in order,' Lulu reported sagely.

'Unruly things,' Genevieve said.

They all laughed again. Despite her odd melancholy, it was a blessed relief to sink into frivolity with the twins again at last. Lulu had been lost in deadly rage since her husband's murder, Alex dragged along for the duration. Genevieve had not been able to support her as well as she had in their tumultuous adolescence.

Then Genevieve's own worry and grief had consumed her just as Lulu had begun to emerge from hers. It had been the twins' turn to fail to offer adequate support—they had gone coy and mysterious, and Alex had all but vanished.

But she didn't want her thoughts mired in darkness and recriminations today, no matter the setting.

'Have you seen the latest fashion plates, Lulu?' she asked, gamely reaching for lightness. 'Crinoline cages? Excessive this season, aren't they?'

'I don't know how I'm supposed to kick someone in the head wearing those,' said Lulu.

'Easier than in pounds of petticoats, surely.'

'Easiest in these.' Lulu kicked up an exemplary ankle, showing off her rather fancy Turkish trousers.

She regularly wore such pantaloons or bloomers in aid of her professional needs: she was technically an enquiry agent, along with Alex, though they mostly took bounties, mostly for Artisans. Alex had had a recent flirtation working directly for the Agency for the Benefit of Registered Artisans instead of merely taking contracts from it, but had not stuck with it. They'd been a team in that professional sense for as long as the McAveys, and that had been coming up towards fifteen years.

A wave of dizziness took Genevieve. She lost her thought, and found it again, rubbing absently at her stomach, the silken black crepe smooth under her hand. 'They make me feel *ancient*, these girls and their fashions.'

'Have you seen the ruffles this season?'

'Oh, God, the *ruffles*.'

Alex, thoroughly left out of this particular discussion as the two women literally talked past him, sighed extravagantly.

'Oh, as if you have a leg to stand on, waistcoat monkey,' Lulu said, rounding on him in mock outrage.

Her smile snapped off. The death-bell at St Sepulchre's had begun its slow and sonorous peal, tolling out the last moments of the condemned man's life.

Lulu's breathing seemed to stop. She rose to her feet as Bishop Varley was brought out the little door, where the dark gallows loomed. He was dirty and small against the mass of humanity jeering and shouting at him, hair grey, beard besmeared and knotted, back bent, hands tied before him. His lips were moving continuously; he was praying, Genevieve thought. He didn't look like a murderer. His feet stumbled across the uneven and dirty ground as two prison guards helpfully dragged him to the scaffold.

Lulu stood right at the window, as patiently intent as a lonely child awaiting the arrival of her favourite country cousins. If Genevieve hadn't come, she suspected Lulu would have bulled her way past the policemen at the barrier to stand directly under the beam.

But maybe not, for Alex had come, and he did not do well in crowds, and Lulu, for all her brusqueness, adored her brother. Lulu reached behind her, not looking around. Alex took Lulu's outstretched hand, their fingers interlocking.

Genevieve took his other hand, and felt him give her a comforting squeeze. It was not as if she wanted to watch a man dangle by the neck until he was dead, no matter what he had done, and especially when he just looked like a frightened and pitiful half-naked old man.

Lulu thrust her chin towards the executioner, a bulky man standing by the trapdoor. 'Slipped Jack Ketch a sovereign to botch it and use a short rope, make it really slow,' she told them, voice low. 'His assistants are keeping his friends back, if he had any left and they wanted to hang off his legs to hurry it along.'

'Oh, good,' Alex said, with a shake of the head. 'We're in for a show, then.'

'Fuck off, Lexi, I worked months for this moment.'

'I know, Lulu,' he said gently. He kissed the back of her hand. 'You go right ahead and enjoy every fucking second, baby sister.' He leaned for a better view, glancing around the excited throngs and murmuring something that sounded like, 'You too, sweetheart.'

His sister stared through the window, gaze fixed on the whey-faced and shaking excommunicate as the hangman tugged the merciful hood over his head. 'I know it's not a civilised desire,' she said. 'There's a reason I didn't invite Kings or Miss Knight to attend.'

'Would Sir Kingsford have come?' The oldest Locke cousin, half-brother to the twins, was notoriously reclusive, and gave his opinion on London frankly in his frequent letters to Genevieve.

'He would have come if I'd asked it,' Lulu said.

Alex squeezed Genevieve's hand again, pointedly. She started and then said, 'I could set him on fire, if you truly want him in paroxysms of agony?'

Genevieve was a weapons Artisan, and her Art was fire. Not that she usually directed it at people. Not even people who had murdered orphans and unassuming archaeologists.

Lulu snorted, seeing right through her. 'Thanks, Gin,' she said. 'I'll bear it in mind.'

On the scaffold, the hangman tightened the noose about Varley's neck. Genevieve could hear the howls and cheers of the crowd even through the closed window. The old man about to face divine judgement for his earthly crimes raised his bound hands and clutched them to his throat.

Lulu took out a ring, set with rubies. 'Journey safe to Hell, Varley.' She kissed the ring. 'I love you, Peter. This is for you.'

'He would've hated it,' Alex remarked to the air.

'Shut up, Alexander, he knew who he married.' She seethed silently before spitting out, 'Fine. I love you, Peter, and this is for me and the kitten.'

She pointed right at Varley, just as the executioner pulled back the bolt and the trapdoor dropped. She stood, motionless and fixated, through every moment of Varley's slow, thrashing, choking, tormented demise.

Genevieve turned her gaze from the scaffold, Alex's hand on her shoulder. She saw, above the jam-packed mass of joyous humanity, a very still figure, standing on the ledge of a barred window let into the thick wall of the prison, watching the death throes quietly.

Genevieve's attention snagged there. Such was the popularity of hangings, and this dispatch of a despised churchman in particular, that there were seats on the rooftops all round, but surely no mundane human could have reached that high vantage point. It had to be an Artisan, using his or her Art in quite the macabre way to obtain a safe, unobstructed, and priceless view.

And the figure, now squeamishly directing his gaze down to his feet with a frown, looked very much like a man Genevieve knew to be dead. Or at least, had been informed was dead, by the duplicitous pair sitting next to her. Just as they had informed her her own husband was dead, which she had recent reason to also now doubt.

The hanged man gave one last twitch and was still, dark-coated men moving in to cut the rope. Lulu raised her gaze and looked directly across the way at the Artisan who looked like Christopher Whitebrickleyhurst. They nodded to each other, once.

As a suspicion began to bloom in Genevieve's mind as to the identity of the little shit making Alex disgustingly happy, Lulu stepped back from the window and looked at the other Lockes.

'Well, then,' she said. 'Shall we go for ice-cream?'

By the Author

Thanks for reading. If you enjoyed this book, find more titles and bonus material at wendypalmer.au.

The Domain trilogy
Wild Imperative
Cursed Girls
Lost Child

Mosaic Virus duology
Bastard's Grace
Six Feet of Ridiculous
Mosaic Garden: Stories from Aspermonde

Artisans
The Uses of Illicit Art
The Use of Myriad Arts

Standalones
Fair Haven
Domesticated Magic

Milton Keynes UK
Ingram Content Group UK Ltd.
UKHW020957220724
445981UK00004B/282